INCUN

Also by Carol McKay

Ordinary Domestic: collected short stories
Creative Writing Prompts To Feed The Imagination
Second Chances: true stories of
living with Addison's Disease *(ed)*

with Eileen Munro
As I Lay Me Down To Sleep

Incunabulum

Carol McKay

Published in the UK by
The PotHole Press
Hamilton, UK
www.potholepress.co.uk

Typeset by The PotHole Press, Hamilton, UK
Cover design by Norma Martin

You can learn about Carol McKay by
visiting her website www.carolmckay.co.uk

ISBN (Print) 978-1-910033-08-1
ISBN (Kindle) 978-1-910033-09-8
ISBN (ePub) 978-1-910033-10-4

The PotHole Press

About the Author

Carol McKay's prize-winning short fiction and poetry have been published widely over the last two decades in anthologies and magazines such as *Gutter, Chapman, Mslexia* and *Wasafiri*. She co-wrote Eileen Munro's bestselling Scottish memoir *As I Lay Me Down To Sleep*, published by Mainstream in 2008, and was interviewed on BBC World Service about her ground-breaking ebook *Second Chances: True Stories of Living With Addison's Disease* in 2013. She won the Robert Louis Stevenson Fellowship in 2010 and was awarded a place on Magnetic North's Space/Time residency in 2018. Her story *In UK Now* reached the finals of the Dinesh Allirajah Prize for Short Fiction, run by Comma Press and the University of Central Lancashire, in 2019. Carol taught and mentored in creative writing through The Open University from 2004 till 2018. *Incunabulum* is her first novel.

Praise for Carol McKay's writing

'hallucinatory urban realism' - Suhayl Saadi
'tense and dramatic' - Jane Rogers
'uncompromising ... unsentimental' - Willy Maley
'warm but clear-eyed' - The Metro

And for *Ordinary Domestic*

'The author talks in the voices of the marginalized, the robbed, beaten and raped, the dispossessed. That she finds humanity not just in them but also in their persecutors is a measure of the power of her quiet, lethal understatement.'
David Manderson, author of *Lost Bodies*, Kennedy & Boyd, 2011, and *The Antihero's Journey*, Peter Lang, 2021.

'Carol McKay's skill is in the compassion she conveys for her characters regardless of their flaws or the chaos of their lives. ... She writes about the awkward topics (disability, adoption, incest, sexual violence) with such deceptive ease that it is our own discomfort and prejudices that we bump up against, not those of the author.'
Alison Napier, *Northwords Now* issue 21, Summer 2012.

a shprakh iz a dialekt mit an armey un flot
A language is a dialect with an army and navy
Max Weinreich (attrib)

Introduction

We thought it was another Sars outbreak. Or Mers. Covid-19 or swine flu. Some natural variation half a world away that only affected foreign people. We'd had so many false alarms.

I'd bought a studio flat in the outskirts: best I could afford on an Arts Grad's salary. I bought a double futon bed and covered it in a burgundy velvet throw. You could say I was optimistic, but the men at work were too dusty. Dusty old book jackets. And dust rubs off. I rubbed that velvet to dulled silk over the years, stretched out with a bottle of wine and my diaries filled with rants about climate catastrophe, nuclear submarine bases and sexual and emotional emptiness. Two dozen volumes I ran away and left there. Never went back. Maybe one day someone might gain something from them – even just firewood. They were burning with something, but it wasn't fear of what was actually to come.

There had been sarin, white powder, 9/11, Bali, on and on, Madrid, London, Glasgow Airport, Disneyland Paris. I was nearly there that week: four antiquarians from Incunabula up for antics after the Paris conference. Some antics we got up to: Polly with her cross-stitch and Dick and Willy rising to the cryptic crossword. I eyed a party of Dutch lads in tight tee-shirts and baggy pants standing by the hotel bar, the spring on my body-clock close to over-winding. 'See them?' I whispered to Polly. She secured her needle, wiped that white stuff she gets at the corners of her mouth, took a quick look and shuddered.

Why was I with these people? I imagined pushing in between the Dutch lads, simpering as I placed our next order. But Dicks and Willies are proprietorial: any sniff from an outsider and they come over Mister Masterful. Dick brought me an exotic cocktail with a stirrer in it. The closest thing to a phallus he could muster. And the Dutch boys? Saw two men, two women, no remainder. I didn't set them straight and bang went another opportunity.

Maybe Paris caused the first *frisson*, knowing how close we'd come to being caught in it. The way it happened at random: wondering where it would strike next. Maybe that's when my anxiety set in. Whatever caused it, I started stock piling then, stacking tins in the under-the-sink cupboard, fretting in case the bags of mung beans had holes in them and I'd open the door to a forest of primordial sprouts.

Amrit in the shop laughed at me. I was buying up every three-for-two offer: tins saturated with salt that he knew I never touched normally. I couldn't tell him I hoped I'd never need them.

Then the police intercepted a bomb plot in Hackney. Amrit's shop windows were smashed so often he kept the shutters down. But after the breakthrough in the Middle East, peace came like the sun from behind a cloud, and I remembered the way we felt when the Berlin Wall came down. *Jubilation sweeps the nation* was how the headlines put it. I was in the shop the day Amrit pulled his shutters up. Three old women started clapping and even a couple of teenagers stopped chewing long enough to cheer. I think Amrit felt he really belonged again. I put all my tins that were still within their sell-by date into a charity bag, hoping they'd go to Yemen, or Syria, or somewhere they weren't picky about too much salt in their diet.

They all died, of course – Amrit and the old ladies. And Polly, and Dick and Willy. Probably even the young Dutch lads. And maybe the Yemenis and Syrians too for all I knew. And Amrit's shop, and his neighbour's, and his neighbour's became my own limitless stock pile.

That was how it started. Finished? And we were left, not because we did anything exceptional, not because our skin was white rather than brown. Not because we were a certain religion or held a particular ideology. Not even because we were the biggest or the smallest, the thinnest or the fattest. You could

2

hardly say we were the best, the quickest witted, the fastest runners. We weren't all left-handed or asthmatic. We didn't all have an allergy to penicillin. We weren't all meat eaters or vegans. None of us had a clue why we'd been lucky enough to survive, or even if luck was the appropriate word.

The fact was that we did. By some fluke, we did. Peej and Wide Boy, Eric and Sara, Junkie and Brain, Basher, Limpet, Saleema and Salaam, not forgetting Bill and Grace and The Gaffer, and of course, me, with nothing better to do than start again.

And as I'd been the local history librarian it fell to me to record our story. History within history. There was all the time in the world to do it, The Gaffer assured me, and all the notebooks I could wish for, in stationery shops and warehouses, curling at the edges till they could be useful again.

Alice J MacAulay *BA (Hons), DipLib, MCILIP, FSA (Scot)*

Chapter One

I woke across the bed, with the quilt half over me and the daylight full up and I lay there for ages, examining my ceiling from this abnormal angle. I knew I'd gone to bed with a headache. The burst foil from the paracetamol and the water in the glass by the bedside reminded me. I'd been feverish. I touched my forehead, but the fever was gone. I wondered what time it was – it didn't occur to me to wonder what day – and straightened in the bed, kicking out the quilt to cover my stupid, ugly feet and because the heating didn't seem to have come on. But then, I was usually at work during the day, so the cold in itself didn't raise the alarm, since I only heated my flat when I was going to be in it. With the quilt in its place – that simple action taking most of my strength – I reached for my glasses so I could read the time, but my phone had run out of charge and there were no figures showing on the radio-alarm. I flicked the switch to listen to the morning news, but there was no sound. There was the kind of light through the window and the hush you associate with snow, and I believed it must have fallen, February snow, quiet during the night, and lying thick on power lines, sapping the city of strength. The time on my watch said eighteen minutes past twelve. I listened, but it was still ticking. I knew I should have phoned to tell Dick I couldn't come in – he insisted that we phone by half past nine – so I was vexed that he'd be vexed, but I felt as though I'd slept for a million years. Yet yesterday was so clear – the meeting about the new donations, the order to be dispatched to the bindery, Willy impervious to the cream from his fudge donut smeared on his chin. I put it down to a refreshing sleep, but my mouth was as curdled as Polly's and I reached out for the rest of the

4

water. There were specks of dust in it. And when I drank it, nonetheless, it tasted thick, as if it had lain in the glass for a couple of weeks.

When I woke again the light had changed and the room was even colder. My watch said four twenty-three and that surprised me, partly because it didn't feel like four hours had passed and partly because my heating should have switched on half an hour before. I listened for the sound of air and hot water in the radiators, but the house was silent. There was nothing from the radio when I clicked the switch, so the power must be out and that explained everything.

I sat on the edge of the bed and reached for my dressing gown. The air was colder than I'd known since I was very young and we only heated our living room. My feet found their way into my slippers, and I pulled myself up, feeling light and at the same time heavy. My stomach was concave. The ring on my middle finger, which had been snug, dangled on my knuckle. Gripping the chest of drawers, I crossed to the window. There was no snow. Nor were there any streetlights yet, and there was a curious emptiness to the black windows of the nearby houses. More curious still was my neighbour's car, immobile in the middle of the street. I couldn't hear any noise from its engine. It looked as if the passenger door on the side away from me was open, but in the semi-dark there was no sign of any of my neighbours.

I lay on the bed again and slept.

Next time I woke remembering a rash of blisters, more and more tiny bubbles that suppurated on my stomach, on the skin under my breasts, my cheeks and then my arms. I examined my arm when I held it out to try the radio. Still no sound. But there were no blisters either: if they'd been real and not dreamt they'd had long enough to heal.

Now my watch said eight thirty-six and I realised I had slept through till morning. I got out of bed, still wearing my dressing gown, and walked with difficulty to the window. The scene was just the same.

*

I was living in the tiniest little studio flat. That meant it was easy to make my way to the kitchen area. My fridge had gone off and the freezer was full of water. I took out some milk, but it was rancid. I was glad I'd a reserve of UHT. Tried to make some coffee but there wasn't any power so I couldn't, or cook the limp fish fingers or stick anything in the microwave. I cut the mould off some cheese then nibbled a few slices. The power cut seemed to be lasting. I thought about using the landline to order pizza, but it was too early for the shop to be open. I could save that for later, if they weren't rushed off their feet by people phoning in orders. Didn't know how they'd cook it, of course, but I assumed they'd find a way. Back-up generators like in the hospitals. It was nine o'clock now, so I dialled my work's number. Nobody answered. I guessed there were problems with public transport, or maybe work had declared a day off, given the difficulties the staff would face, travelling. My stomach was rumbling. I opened some sweet corn – no added salt or sugar – and ate it from the tin then tried to phone my mother, and that was strange, because she never went out so early in the morning.

I think that was the first time it occurred to me that things really weren't the way they were supposed to be.

*

I lay back down on the bed again and tried to keep track of time. In an hour or so I got up and forced myself to eat breakfast cereal with UHT milk. I felt a bit better after that, though I'd have killed for a cup of tea. I forced myself to wash in the freezing cold water and dress then took the decision to fold up my bed. The act of collapsing it exhausted me, and I ended up flopping down again, now it was a couch. My ankles looked so thin and I swear my skirt had a three-inch gap at the waist. How long had I gone without eating? In a way I was annoyed, because surely my mother might have phoned when she hadn't heard from me. Or my next-door neighbour. We weren't the closest friends, but I looked after her flat when she went to Ayanapa. You wouldn't call her tidy minded, but since all this happened, I've had the opportunity to investigate the way lots of people were living, and there wasn't an awful lot of minimalism. After a while I picked the phone up again. The anxiety had been building, somewhere at the back of my mind, about the length of the power-cut, the lack of response to the telephone calls, the amount of water my fridge had defrosted while the flat was so cold, and the way the family downstairs' car was still exposed like bone in the middle of the street.

I dialled my mum. It rang eighteen times. In my weekly duty calls she always picked up within five.

I dialled my work.

Eventually I dialled at random. Then it struck me. Damned anxiety! It was just my phone that wasn't working. Here I was, imagining everyone else in the world in trouble. I decided to go and knock at my neighbour's.

I slipped on my coat and shoes and unlocked my door. A puff of air came up the stairs with the change in pressure from my door opening. That was strange too, because usually our security entrance was firmly shut. I double-locked, and gripped the cold keys in my pocket.

I rapped at Laura's door, across from mine on the landing. She'd look on me as a complete and utter freak if I breathed a word of what I'd been imagining. Fortunately she wasn't in. By now I was unsteady, in spite of my corny breakfast. I held on to the wooden-topped banister and picked my way downstairs to try Marjory on the ground floor. She had young children; she only worked a couple of nights a week at a call centre, and anyway she'd left her car open in the street, so I was sure she couldn't be far, but she didn't answer when I rang her doorbell. I stood in the weak light of the communal hall, my fingertips braced for balance against the green wall. What else could I do? The only other flat was empty. I stepped outside for some air.

Marjory's dog was barking. He actually whined when he saw me. How long had he been barking there? I thought back. All the time I'd dipped in and out of sleep. Twenty-four hours? Forty-eight, was it? His legs were filthy: he'd been digging under the fence, as if digging an escape route.

'She's not that bad a mistress is she?' I asked him over the fence slats. His white fur was matted. I reached down to pet

7

him. 'Good boy, Bounder.'

He was a bounder. Bounded right at me. Clean up to waist height. I stepped back: I'd never seen him do that. I'd expect that from a Rottweiler, not a pint-sized Westie. He jumped again. This time his claws scrabbled against the top bar on the inside of the wooden fence till he fell awkwardly on his back. He jumped the right way up and barked again, wagging his tail at the same time.

I wondered if she'd just gone out, or gone away and left him. That wouldn't be fair. No wonder he jumped at me. I guessed he was hungry, but what could I do? I wasn't going to let him out. She'd quite a tongue on her, Marjory. I'd heard her caterwauling at her misdemeaning children. Wouldn't want to bring that wrath on my misdemeaning self.

'She'll be back in a minute,' I lied to him, keeping my fingers away. 'Go and wait in your kennel.'

I could have tried a few more doors, but I could hardly keep my knees locked. I'd sweat on my upper lip and my vision was going grey-black and starry, so I went in and leaned on the banister for a few seconds.

I had to sit or I would have fallen. The walls and floor swooned in and out as if there wasn't any substance to them. I lay down with the stairs pressing into my back. I thought I'd never make it upstairs again.

But of course I did. I lay on the couch too weak to try the radio. Hit my head against the hard frame of the arm and fell asleep.

When I woke up it was getting on for twelve. Tentatively I tried the radio, my laptop and the light switches. Still nothing. I picked the phone up to dial my mum, but now even the dialling tone had disappeared. The thing was fucked. And I never say that word. I threw the phone on the table.

I picked it up and replaced it properly. What was I going to do?

I needed to get strong again. Whatever it was that had ravaged me was on the way out. I knew that, because every time I woke I felt minimally better. I rummaged in the cupboards for something to eat and feasted on crackers with cheese and tuna mayonnaise. It was heavenly. Pity I didn't have tea, but bottled water was better for me. I drank two glasses to wash whatever I had out of my system.

Maybe lots of people had been hit by the same virus. It came on me in a flash, so if it was the same across the town, naturally all the services would have gone down, if people couldn't be roused from their beds for a couple of days. The health services would be struggling. My mother, retired from her role with the WRVS, would have been summoned back to roll up her sleeves at the tea-trolley. Probably, in a thousand households up and down these streets, people like me were reeling in post-influenza wobbliness, unable to hold themselves up long enough to go next door to ask what was happening.

I pulled my coat on and took my oversize umbrella to lean on. I was determined to knock on as many doors as it took to find the answer.

Out on the street for a couple of gulps of air, I was pleased to see the Westie had taken my advice. There was no barking and no sign of him digging at the fence. I went back in our hallway and tried Marjory's door again. Still nothing. In desperation I called through her letterbox. 'Marjory, your car's in the middle of the street. Is everything alright?'

There was only silence and a sweet and sour air stream through the letterbox brushes. I stepped outside and opened her garden gate, watching for the dog. I cupped my hands round my eyes and pressed against her window, steeling myself for I didn't know what sights, but her living room was in order. Well, apart from a mug and some chick-lit splayed covers up on the coffee table.

I closed her gate and leaned on it as another wave of tiredness swamped me. When was I going to be well? I sat on the porch step and looked at the street. No buses went by; I hadn't seen or heard a single car, other than the one waiting there for its driver. Where on earth was everyone?

I should have gone and investigated the car. If I'd been at full strength I would have. It had definitely been there

9

more than twenty-four hours. But deep inside, I was scared. Scared that everyone had been evacuated and hadn't told me; scared that something other-worldly had happened, and I wasn't important enough for them to want me. Scared of – I didn't know what. Even the dog, in his kennel or some hidey-hole in the bushes, had resumed his whining. I let my tears run without any intervention.

'Where is everyone?' I wailed out loud, but there weren't any answers. I looked at my watch; rested my head against the coarse bricks round the door. It was almost one. I thought about what I would normally do if I took a day off. Housework in the morning, a leisurely bath before lunch. I would do that now if the power was back on. I would make a bowl of soup and relax to the reassuring RP of the one o'clock news.

A seagull's yowl broke the silence. I watched the bird drop behind the abandoned Fiat, only to rise up again in a sweep of wings with something in its mouth. Roadkill, I thought. Some drunk's discarded pizza.

The Westie began to snarl. The bird squawked again and another arrived. It, too, dived. They mewled and the Westie growled somewhere. Sitting on the step, I caught a movement. Between the wheels of the car I saw the orange stalks of the gulls' legs, the grubby little white dog's paws, and something else entirely.

I struggled up, taking my weight on the golf umbrella, not willing to believe what my eyes were suggesting. I hesitated where Marjory's fence stopped then crossed the pavement, my eyes on the Fiat's metallic sheen. Closer. The umbrella point sank in the grass verge.

I leaned my weight on the umbrella and my fingertips on the body of the car. The rear passenger door was open. I could hear the dog crunch and lick. I rounded the bonnet.

'No!' I raised my umbrella. The gulls flapped up into the air around me. I focused on the dog and brought the brolly's point down, stabbing at the grubby white, hitting it with any strength I had, till it fled, yelping, its own blood mixing with the blood staining its mouth.

10

Chapter Two

When I saw Marjory's daughter on the ground that day I heard my voice thin and high, detaching itself from my body, just as my mind detached itself from the scene I was confronted with.

I looked at the dog's blood on the point of my umbrella, and how it smeared the yellow and blue panels that wound up to my hand and I threw the thing away.

The girl was on the ground. I couldn't bear to look at her. My ribcage bellowed outwards for a refill before squeezing each tight scream out through my throat. I ached with hysterics, but no one slapped my face to make me stop.

I moved to the other end of the car to make her disappear. I pressed both of my hands on the boot, my arms and legs shuddering as if I'd been strafed by a low flying aircraft, my bowels loose. My knees were ready to bend, but the gulls were on the rooftop. I saw the thick yellow horn of their beaks and the hunger in their eyes and knew if I let myself fall then, I would be their meal, all in good time. I moved my hands further up the bodywork, their sweatiness adhering to the paint like a fly on glass. Anyway, if I lay on the grey tar – the smooth tar, seducing me in my weakness – I would see the girl on the other side, between the wheels.

The horror besieged me. I imagined a rush hour of maggots, ants and centipedes following the current of blood under the car to colonise my feet and reconnoitre my legs. I sat on the boot and lifted them clear.

What about Marjory? The girl was three or four, not even at school; where had her mother gone?

My screaming had stopped. Was she on the ground too? I pressed my feet on the metal, my hand on the roof and inched myself closer. I could see the girl's trainer. Moving closer I saw the bloodied clothes and the red scraps of flesh on the leg, gnawed to the bone.

I retched. Perspiration blistered on my upper lip. I closed my eyes – opened them again – but there was only the girl.

I leaned on my back so I wouldn't see her. Looked at the sky. Grey-white clouds, same as usual. Breathed it. Bathed in it. Took time to recognise every sweep and fold in it.

I let my eyes lower to the house roofs, the upper windows: my windows, down again, right, Marjory's windows. I got up, off the car, and crossed towards the building keeping the obscenity at my back. Tried the handle of Marjory's front door and went in unchallenged. It smelled of foul pork and *April Blossom*.

Marjory was the pork. The phone was off the hook on the floor beside her. Burying my mouth and nose in my collar to block the smell, I glanced at her aquarium: the fish were floating belly up in cotton wool. I considered the stencilling on her wallpaper; her one wall accented mulberry; under my feet that noisy wooden flooring. There was a packet of cigarettes on the table beside the dirty cup. I lifted Marjory's lighter and flicked it to test it would work. Marjory's face was pasty and there were sores on it. I remembered my dream of a rash and looked at my arm, but my rash had disappeared. I was still weak and cold-sweaty. I felt light headed. Even thought my ears were buzzing till I saw a bluebottle fly up from the bottom of Marjory's trouser leg. Pinching her leggings between my thumb and finger, I stretched the edge and examined the neat white eggs satin stitched like embroidery. Let the fabric snap back.

I went into her bathroom. The blind flapped against the open window: I held it out so I could gulp in some fresh air then looked around. Two long, children's hairs coiled in a double S in her lemon bath. The radiator was a chrome railing with towels over it. There was white scum at the metal knuckles where it hadn't been cleaned properly, but she wouldn't have been expecting visitors. I lifted the bigger towel and brought it to the living room where I used it to cover Marjory's face and top half, uncomfortable in my deference, and short of breath. I left the house.

Back at my flat I locked the door behind me and pulled my heavy desk across it against I didn't know what enemy. I opened the fridge and took out the dwindling water bottle; drank, drank, drank till it was done then put the empty bottle back in the fridge. Then I poured myself a double double whisky.

The phone was still dead. I ripped the take-away menu into strips and fluttered them ticker-tape fashion over my face. Looked at my watch. It wasn't even two. I wanted to collapse into hopelessness, but where would that get me? The electricity might come on at any moment; by night, I could be drowsy in front of my fake-flame fire, toast-and-honeyed and frothy coffeed, wrapped up in a fleece and 'Sunshine on Leith', the police and emergency services' blue lights flashing behind my back behind my curtains. I would have given anything to hear that now.

I was worn out. But I climbed the step-stool in the kitchen and took down my candles; checked the emergency torch; laid it all by the couch with the lighter. Then I slipped off my shoes and curled up with the quilt burying me, and slept.

Chapter Three

I spent three days holed up, hoping for the power to go on, the phone to ring, my brother to knock on the door – or some rugged, thirty-something fireman with a flask of hot soup and a brace of muscles – but nothing happened. I slept a lot, fretted a lot, forced myself to eat a mash of uncooked vegetarian burger mix rehydrated with water from the former hot tank and stirred in to a small tin of beans in tomato sauce and other such haute cold cuisine. Discovered it wasn't so bad if I did like Jesus and transmogrified the water, though I only had four bottles of wine and frankly, drinking them and the last of the whisky was all that got me through, now I knew why the animals outside were howling.

After another few days I'd returned to full strength. I'd a cupboard full of pumpkin seeds and dried fruits, and they say there's a lot of iron in red wine anyway. I changed into my coarse blue jeans and that stripy fleece my mother had bought me by post from the Outdoor Store catalogue after I mentioned I'd joined the library's rambling group. Fetched my rucksack from its bag on the top shelf of my wardrobe. I unzipped my walking boots and waterproof from one of the vacuum-packed storage containers at the bottom of my fitted wardrobe then realised there was no electricity to suck the air back out of them. But what did it matter? Nothing mattered except that I had to go looking for someone. Anyone would do. A figure in authority, preferably, because obviously there would be, some kind of authority, waiting for me to make contact.

I packed my bag with two changes of underwear and a spare jumper, my long lavender nightie, a pack of sanitary towels just on the off-chance I might have another period, face cream, shampoo, my lipstick, hairbrush and toothbrush with an unopened tube of toothpaste, soft shoes in their own pink shoe-bag for changing out of my walking boots, a copy of *Number 9 Dream* because no matter how much I liked it, I could read it another three times and still find something new in it. A copy of *The Chrysalids*, because – well, because it made me feel acceptance about who I am. There was no electricity, so I couldn't charge my kindle or i-phone, so I dug out my old walkman with a few CDs then realised I didn't have any batteries. I took a handful of tissues that would do for my nose or instead of toilet paper, which was a considerable economy on space, paracetamol and my last individual carton of apple juice as a reserve against one of my headaches. Looking round my flat for inspiration reminded me to pack candles and Marjory's lighter. Thinking of Marjory made me think of towels, but I only had room for a small one, and then I thought of a bar of soap. I always kept a spare one in my soap box, so I slipped that in the rucksack pocket along with a facecloth, so I could wash. After all, there may not be showers in the authority's emergency shelters. I'd more or less accepted, now, that's where I'd be going.

My rucksack was crammed full and I didn't have any food in it. Or alcohol. I took out the soft shoes and said goodbye to David Mitchell's *Number 9 Dream*. Replaced it with the A to Z streetmap and my emergency sewing kit. Took out the lippie and hairbrush and gave myself a quick fix in the mirror. I looked awful. I hadn't been able to wash my hair for days during my recuperation, and the illness itself had made it oily. My skin was pale and possibly a little jaundiced, but the whites of my eyes weren't too bad and my gums looked pink. My teeth were unbearably yellow. Age, that was, not lack of brushing. I soothed myself with the reassuring thwick of the opening of the lipstick, and daubed colour on my mouth and cheeks. Smoothed it in and studied my reflection, aware, for once, I'd never convince anyone I was in my forties. I was alright if I concentrated on the disparate pieces – the thin nose, thinning lips, the elfin jaw-line, the tufted gingery hair, greenish eyes –

but if I stared too long in my eyes there were things I didn't want to see. Remember your education, I told myself. Clobbered my head de-tangling my hair and patted it into position. It was tidy. And anyway, it's the lipstick that makes people pay attention. Get the lipstick right and everything else falls into place.

I exchanged the hairbrush for a comb and put it and the lipstick in the rucksack's mobile phone pocket, with a pen and the slim notepad I keep for making shopping lists.

It was a little after ten o'clock. As part of my thought processes, my eyes strayed to the window. It was dry, with a little sun outside. I believed the house wasn't as cold as it had been which gave room for optimism. Spring couldn't be far off. I wondered how long it would take for bluebottle eggs to hatch in the strengthening sun, but I wouldn't be coming back to find out.

I rummaged in my cupboards for the last packs of raisins, nuts and seeds. I'd no room for tins, and anyway, they'd be heavy. Well, maybe a thin one of sardines. There really wasn't anywhere else to put it. Should I take out my shopping list? I cast a glance over at my journals. How diligently I'd filled those pages, pouring out all my embarrassing secrets. There were at least two. Two big ones. But what would I do if I'd nothing to read or write? And I still hadn't squeezed in my purse. It had everything – my money, my bank card, bookshop loyalty cards. Photographic proof of who I was. I checked inside. There was only forty-two pounds so maybe I should go to the bank. But maybe the Red Cross would give me anything I'd need. To tide me over.

I took out my nightie and deliberated over John Wyndham's *The Chrysalids*. I stuffed in my purse, another tin of sardines (they didn't need an opener) and my unopened jar of multi-vitamins. I snapped open the lid of the current one and swallowed two capsules with the curdy dregs of the UHT milk. The plastic stuck in my gullet and the only thing I had left to drink was a gritty inch left in the wine bottle. I drained it down, the heavy glass pushing back my lips and grinding against a tooth. But that wine felt good. Out came John Wyndham. I

16

opened the cutlery drawer and threw my bottle opener and a knife, fork and spoon into the bag. Fretted about the sharp knife. Compromised by replacing the ordinary table knife with a steak knife.

Was that everything?

I opened the cupboard door and lifted out my oldest photo album, careful not to further damage the brittle purple spine. It opened by itself at the usual place and I touched my fingertip to the tiny face. The tiny, tiny, pearly button face. I lifted the photo out and selected a few others. I put them in my purse then closed the album and put it back.

I took a final look around my flat with its peony pink walls and curtain swags. Fluffed up my cushions. It had been a pretty flat, if a lonely one, but it was time I moved on. I took the bag out of the kitchen bin and wiped round inside the bin with an anti-bacterial wipe. I'd put it in the wheelie outside on my way out, even if no-one ever came to remove it. If anyone came to my flat they'd know I'd been clean.

The last two apples in my bowl were a bit wrinkled but so was I. I put on my coat, hat and gloves, hitched the rucksack over my shoulders, and put the apples in my pockets to be eaten on the way.

Then, dragging the desk away from the door and into its exact place against the wall, its feet in the indents in the carpet, I bade farewell to my old ways and began my new life.

Chapter Four

You'd have thought the world was dozing. The cars were in their drives, the curtains were mostly shut and though the sun was up it was like a Sunday stroll after dawn. The only sound was a blackbird at the apex of a roof. It was too early to be mating and it was too early for any catkins, but I thought about that fly and wondered how many eggs were being laid in beds behind closed curtains as I walked. Change the subject. I didn't see any other dogs.

After half an hour I hadn't seen sign of any living thing but the birds. By now I was halfway into town. The residential streets of my estate were behind me. I passed the pub and the chip shop, still with their shutters down. The windows in the house above the shop were lifeless.

Fifty metres further down I came to Amrit's. If anyone was alive, I hoped they'd be here. A shop in a community was bound to be a rallying place. Amrit's shutters were closed but the one over his door was partially open. Initially I read that as a good sign, but something rattled the slats as I approached and made me jittery. I glanced behind but there was only the wind.

I'd been desperate for contact but now my insides were turning sour with doubt. Who'd raised the shutter? My voice was feeble, but I had to know. 'Hello?'

Three metres from the door, I was certain someone was watching me. 'Hello?' I called again.

A thump made me jump. Across the street a black and white cat pressed itself against the glass of a ground floor window. I could see the pink of its mouth as it mewed.

Amrit's door squeaked and I threw myself against some hedging. Thick, navy legs and white trainers appeared below the shutter then a curl of fingers.

'Who is it?'

The voice was female. But I had no voice to reply.

'Who is it?' Higher this time.

I watched the chubby fingers tug the shutter unevenly till it stuck.

'Who said 'hello' to me?'

A young voice, almost crying.

'Me,' I said, stepping from the hedge. 'I said it.'

She made a knees-out squat beneath the metal barrier. The wind teased wisps of her straw-coloured hair.

'Is there anybody else?' I asked her, spitting the words out. 'Have you seen anyone? Has anybody taken charge?'

All this while the girl straightened. The first thing I noticed was the chocolate at her mouth. The second, the shape of her face: the breadth; the slanting, trusting eyes.

She wiped her hand down the side of her duffle coat. 'Amrit doesn't mind if we eat his chocolate.'

I wriggled my right shoulder, trying to ease the burning sensation from the rubbing of my backpack strap. 'Is Amrit here?'

She waved behind her. 'He's sleeping behind his counter.' She moved her weight from one foot to the other, her thighs so thick coming down to her knees that she wasn't able to stand with her feet together. 'Everybody's sleeping. My mum's sleeping as well,' she said.

I kept a good couple of metres between us. 'And there's no one else?'

She shook her head.

My heart was still rowdy. I looked round the streets again but apart from the cat at the window it was deserted. And apart from us. I met her eyes. 'My name's Alice,' I told her, fidgeting with my gloves and preparing to shake her hand. 'What's yours?'

'Sara.' She held out a sweet wrapper. 'Do you want some?'

'No.' I pulled my hand back in and gripped it with my other one.

So now I had company. But she was ... I'm not good at

meeting people at the best of times. I registered ugliness in her stocky body and the bluntness of her face, which was quite despicable. Of me.

She looked around, one hand flat against her mouth holding in the chocolate. 'See the cat?' she said, drooling.

I followed her finger, 'Yes,' and put my bag down for a minute.

She used her mouth to eat and breathe and talk all at once. 'I like cats,' she said.

'Do you?' I wondered how I could get away from her.

'I've got a grey one. Smoky,' she said. 'But he's bad. I had to smack him.' She scrunched up her chocolate wrapper and pushed it into her pocket.

'Why?'

She walked over and sat on the boundary wall round the nearest garden. 'He was spitting. And he didn't want to stay in. So I smacked him. And then he ran away and I came out looking for him. But he's not here.' She looked straight at me suddenly. 'Why's everybody sleeping?'

I shrugged. I wasn't up to trying to explain. 'Did you say your mum's sleeping? At your house?'

'And my big brother.'

'Have you still been going back there?'

'Uh-huh.'

I sat down beside her. Her trainers were tatty. All the dots in the white upper were clogged like black pores. If I turned my head towards her I caught the smell of stale clothes and sweaty feet. I cleared my throat. I'd been eager for conversation, but we sat without speaking, just looking around. Usually there was white noise of gear changing, bus engines whining and squeals and chatter from the playground out of sight behind Amrit's shop. Even when this junction was quiet you could hear the noise of a train or the motorway in the distance, but now it was as if the silence of open moorland had descended on the town.

'I should be going,' I said, making an announcement so it sounded final. She put another square of chocolate in her mouth and didn't try to stop me.

20

I shivered: the cold from the wall was rising up through my coat and the backs of my trouser legs. I thought about Amrit, sleeping behind the counter, and bit my lip.

'Sara, have you seen anyone who isn't sleeping?'

She pulled out a bright yellow pack of chewy sweets and started working through them. 'Just you.' The eating noises reminded me of the Westie, but she must have recognised my expression because she closed her mouth.

I covered mine with my hand and concentrated. 'How long have you been going out? Since your mum fell asleep?'

Sara shrugged. 'I don't know.' Through a strip torn in the pack I could see a yellow sweet, then a green one and after that there was a red one. She burst it open and took the strawberry sweet, then offered me my choice of the two sour flavours. I chose the lemon one and she seemed pleased.

'Days and days?' I persisted.

She nodded and we chewed for a minute. Somewhere far away I thought I heard a dog barking. A couple of collared doves raced each other to land on the lamppost across the street. They started cooing and I wondered if it was Valentine's Day. 'And you really haven't seen or heard anyone?' Despite my fleece and my coat on top I was freezing. I wrapped my arms around myself.

'Well, I saw a man and a boy, but they were neds, so I hid in the garden.'

'Why?'

'My mum says neds are bad.' She looked around for any sign of them. 'That's who I thought it was when I heard you shouting.' She sniffed. 'I thought you were the neds that took Amrit's stuff.'

A man and a boy. 'Did they see you?'

'I hid in the garden.' She pointed into the thick hedge behind us. 'In there.'

'What else?'

'They smashed Amrit's glass because I heard it. And then they came out with all the stuff in the blue bags and the glass was clinking. They went away laughing.' Her eyes came out of

21

the story. 'I went in to see if Amrit was alright and he was sleeping, in at the back of behind his counter. I had to step over the broken bottles. He wouldn't wake up, but he didn't mind if I took the chocolate, because I told him my mum would give him the money.' She put her hot palm on me. 'Honest.'

'That's okay,' I said, and after only a moment's hesitation I squeezed her hand. It was pale and puffy, with dimples at the knuckles, but her fingers were grubby. 'Amrit won't mind.'

She pulled away and clasped both her hands in her lap.

I glanced sideways to look at her. I wanted somebody normal. I wanted someone who could look after *me* and tell *me* it was going to be alright. I didn't want her. By now the sun had disappeared in clouds and there was an icy wind rising.

'Why won't they wake up?' she asked me.

I pushed my collar up; held it up at my ears. Snapped, 'How do I know?'

She sniffed a couple of times.

'Oh look, don't cry,' I said and thought about touching her cheek. Her skin was soft and puckered, and she had long hairs curling from a mole on her chin. There was a dribble at her nose. 'Don't cry,' I repeated, but three drops fell from her eyes. I took my hankies out of my backpack, gave her one, and blew my own nose on another. My travel-packet wasn't going to last long at this rate.

'How many days have you been eating Amrit's chocolate?'

She shrugged.

I nodded to her bulging pockets. 'Is all that since the ned men broke in?'

'Yes.' She pulled them out to show me, spilling the wrappers over her lap and the pavement where the wind caught them and sent them twittering and rustling down the street. Sara got up and chased after them, spilling more and more each time she bent that stubby body to capture the ones that got away.

'Leave them,' I shouted, but she persisted in her plodding, so I gave up and let her do it. I picked up some of the ones nearest to me and told her to put what she'd gathered in the bin at the side of the road. I looked around again, wondering where the 'ned men' were and how long ago it had been. By the amount of wrappers, we were talking days.

'I'm going to see Amrit,' I called to her. 'Don't go away.'

She gave me a wave.

The padlock hadn't been burst. If anything it looked as if he'd been getting ready to lock it. Inside the shop was dark, with only thin slats of daylight through the strips of the metal shutter showing up the hulks of shelving and filching most of the colours. Smells more than made up for their absence. Rancid meat from the fridge unit was the strongest, but also withering oranges, the mustiness of cabbage, spilt gin – I picked them all out. As my eyes grew accustomed to the light level I noticed that the wall behind the counter was yellow pinboard and realised I could see it because the bottles had been cleared from the shelves. I went towards them, steeling myself for Amrit's body.

There were gritty footprints on the counter beside the penny sweets. I leaned to see where Amrit was sleeping and entered a pall of stench that almost asphyxiated me. I twisted away, gagging uncontrollably, and struggled through the door for air.

I dipped under the shutter and pulled it down behind me, to the ground. Then I hurried the three or four metres to where Sara was sitting, her tracksuit-clad knee waving to some internal song she was singing.

'Hello,' she said and gave me a beautiful smile. 'Did Amrit give you any chocolate?'

My knees shook and so did my bowels. I eased myself on to the wall beside her.

'We won't go to see Amrit any more.'

Soon the rain started. I tugged my waterproof from my bag and told her to pull up the hood of her duffle coat. I'd been heading into town towards the police station, but now I didn't know what to do. Sara had no-one. She had nothing. How could I walk away and leave her? I didn't know if I could bear to go to her house with its bodies, just to pack a bag for her. And what about my own family? Shouldn't I be going to find out about them? It was all too huge to think about.

We moved to the side of Amrit's building and leaned against

the roughcast wall, backs to the graffiti, watching the slanting rain. The streets were deserted. If only I'd learned how to drive we'd have been in town by now. If only. My life had been one big 'if only'. It would have made more sense if it was me who'd died, and I didn't know why I'd been left alive. I tried to make a plan. There was Sara and there was me. There were Sara's bad ned men – and bad may have been right, given they'd ransacked Amrit's drink. I was cold as it was, but the thought of them running about loose made me even colder. Yet surely they couldn't be that bad? At least with the quantity of booze they'd robbed they'd sleep for a while. Still, if there were four of us – God forbid, the implications of two such men and two such women – then presumably there would be others. Maybe even my mother. Some of my workmates. Where there was life there was hope, I reasoned. Or tried to. Maybe my brother, if DNA similarities played a part in it. He was a pen-pusher, but I imagined he was reasonably strong with a natural instinct to protect me, despite the decades when I'd browbeaten him, claiming I was his equal. Some equal. What I wouldn't give to have a decent man to shelter behind now. I thought about my brother's old smile. The way he used to grin when we were kids.

Sara tugged my cagoule and made me glance at her. 'I want to go home. It's cold.'

I looked at the chocolate smudging her mouth. She needed someone to look after her.

'I'm freezing,' she said, wrapping her arms around herself the way I had. 'I want to go home. I want to go home.'

'Okay.' I pincered the sleeve of her duffle coat. 'But we go home to say goodbye.'

Chapter Five

We packed a case that had wheels so transporting it would be easier. It was hard to be ruthless. Sara wanted to show me little treasures: her sunglasses and a salmon pink floral summer hat. I spent the last few minutes checking the kitchen cupboards, but there was nothing much left: a few oatcakes and an empty jar of Nutella, the inside smeared with the tracks of Sara's fingers. Sara, herself, was quiet when she came out of her mother's room. Her eyelashes were wet and we didn't speak.

By now the rain had stopped. I shouldered my rucksack which seemed even heavier than before. Sara's wheels whistled along the wet tarmac and left wavering parallel tracks that soon disappeared. My shoulders ached, and we still had over a mile to walk. Round the corner from Sara's I had to stop. I was a bit uncomfortable at the thought of wandering further into this part of town just on my own with Sara. It was rough enough at the best of times. Litter strewn all over the gardens. Broken down fences. The paper recycling bin beside us was bulging with greasy pizza boxes and plastic bags, and it wasn't the only one. And you didn't dare confront the people who lived here about it. They were hard. Pasty faced and unforgiving. It was a scary place. Anyway, I couldn't risk putting my back out, carrying this rucksack. I would have to take it easy.

'What's wrong?'

I told her my bag was heavy.

She put her head up, sniffing like a dog taking its bearings. 'My friend stays here,' she said. 'We'll ask if you can borrow her pram for your stuff.'

I hesitated but she sprang off, entered someone's garden and knocked their door.

25

'I don't know if this is a good idea,' I called out, conscious that I didn't have a clue who was alive or dead or just dead drunk. But she tried the handle of the door and walked inside.

My conscience told me I shouldn't let her go by herself, but my courage failed me. It was minutes before the door opened again and the hood of a full-size, coach-built, navy and cream shiny pram appeared in the opening.

'Here you are!' her voice sang out. 'Teresa doesn't mind if you take it.'

'My God, Sara,' I said, as she bumped it down the front steps.

Sara was ecstatic. She wheeled the pram down the path towards me, jaunty as its springing chassis. I met her at the gate, and as she bounced and turned it on to the street I could see that the navy rain cover was in place. Fastened right up to the hood, it covered the bottom three or four inches of the opening. Before I could react, Sara reached for my rucksack and with a one-handed heave swung it on top of the cover. 'It was in the back garden,' she said, grinning. 'Can I push it?'

'Wait!' I put my hand on her arm.

'What?' she said, her smile drooping.

'Did – '

'Teresa doesn't mind.'

'Is she sleeping too?'

Sara put on the foot brake and manoeuvred her case so that its handle was close to my side. 'It'll be fine.'

'What about the baby?'

Her eyes flicked to the navy cover.

Cautiously I unhooked the fastening at one side of the hood and put down the flap. I heard two intakes of breath.

'The baby!' Sara unfastened the rain cover all the way and reached in among a swaddle of blankets. It was lying on its side, facing away from me.

'Lou-Lou! Where's your big smiles?'

By its size, the baby could only have been two or three months. As soon as Sara lifted the stiff bundle to her neck I knew it must be dead, but Sara continued to croon to it. I could

26

hardly look. Why me? Why this? 'Don't you think you should take Lou-Lou back to her mum?'

'But her mum's sleeping.'

I turned my face away. I didn't want the pram. I didn't want any of this. 'Get her back to her mother!' I forced out, then turned away and threw up my breakfast in the gutter. When I straightened Sara was cradling the baby all the way back towards Teresa's house. I refastened the navy cover and let it go.

Sara took her time. I wished she'd hurry so we could get on our way. I was standing, useless, my rucksack against my shaking legs and her case upright beside me with its handle up. The pram I didn't want was a pram from another era. It was big, competent and empty. I knew I was going to give in to an awful grief if I didn't get out of there. I could feel the monstrous burden of it, a whale beaching in my chest.

'Hurry up, Sara,' I called to her. At last there was the sound of a door banging, but when I looked there was no movement from the baby's house.

'What...?'

The thought wasn't even formed properly when the wind brought the sound of voices. Rowdy and wild, I identified two of them like the gulls that had lunged at my neighbour's daughter. I couldn't gauge distance.

There was another bang and the roar of an engine. A foot against a pedal, revving.

'Sara!' I clasped my mouth in fear they'd hear me. Sara had called them neds. Already I'd endowed them with the vices of a crowd of football hooligans.

'Sara!' I grabbed my bag, stage whispering to her to come and help me. I slung it over one shoulder and it almost toppled me, the rising scales of the engine noise driving my own pace. 'Sara!' I tugged at the pram, but it wouldn't roll with the brake on. I abandoned it, clutched the handle of Sara's case, and blundered my way through the squealing gate back into Teresa's garden.

Still I was hissing for Sara. I let go of the case at the bottom of the steps, opened the door and pitched the rucksack in. As

I reached out for the handle I saw a blue car butt the street at the T-junction. Its window was down and I could see the passenger's baseball cap bobbing to the beat. I heaved the case in and slammed the door.

Sara was coming down the stairs. She saw me drop to my knees.

'What's wrong?'

I thought I'd die of fright.

She crouched beside me. A power drill of music eviscerated the street. 'Is it the ned men?' she whispered, still cradling the bundle.

I nodded. Would they stop at the pram?

The pounding reached our gate. I stretched up and fastened the door latch. The door was glazed in the upper half. I tugged Sara away from it. 'Why have you still got the baby?'

The music cut. Doors slammed and there was a muddle of words. All I could distinguish was the tone of them: one high and jubilant, one monosyllabic and deep. A single door slammed and I breathed again because I thought they were leaving. Then I recognised the creaking of Teresa's gate. There were footsteps on the path and I shrank into a ball.

Sara stood tall. She unlocked and opened the door. 'It's not the baby,' she said, unravelling the blankets. A doll fell and there was a clatter of metal.

'Sara!'

Sturdy navy legs rooted, she pointed a shotgun into the street.

'Leave us alone, ned men!'

I reached in slow motion, but she pulled the trigger. The entrance was filled with rupture and the smell of burning, and I watched her body hurled backwards into the hall.

Chapter Six

First I couldn't think. Then I thought the gun had back-fired and she was dead. Before I could get up and look, a dark shape flew in the door and then a second hurtled in and Sara screamed, but he ran up the stairs. I curled in a ball as small as I could till he went by. That was the shock. Who'd have expected the baby was a gun?

The young one came back down the stairs. 'What the fuck did you do that for?' he yelled at Sara. 'Fucking dimwit moron.'

She howled and huddled into the corner. I scurried over the floor and put my arms round her. The men went into one room after another. The older one was shouting commands. He seemed old – haggard, his eyes sunken – but he was a lot younger than me. He was gaunt, with his cheeks sucked in and an old jagged scar across his cheek. He looked straight at me. 'You two on your own?'

I swallowed and nodded.

'Top totty, man,' the young one said. 'Fucking luck we've got.'

Sara's wails were increasing.

'Shut the fuck up,' the boy said. 'Fucking dimwit.'

I felt myself swelling with rage. I blew up at him, exploding with all the pent-up fear I'd been carrying for the last three days. 'Leave her alone!' I yelled, my arms returning to wrap tightly around her. 'What's she ever done to you?'

'Ah, calm it!' he said and the older man sent him out to the car. 'Yakkity yak,' the boy said, turning round and miming my mouth with his hand. The one in charge just looked at us, hands on his hips and his brows low. Then he went into one of the other rooms.

Sara calmed down when the young one left, and after a while the older man came back to the hall and signalled me to the door. He grasped my elbow.

'This place isn't safe,' he said. 'Who knows who's out there? That's why we came for Micky's guns.'

'I've got a knife,' I told him.

'A knife?' He wrinkled his nose and cracked his chewing gum. 'Knives are messy. Rottweilers, madmen – there could be anything out there. You're better with a gun.'

I could smell him. Tried not to let him know it. Wood smoke and alcohol, maleness and grease.

He wagged his head towards Sara. 'She'll slow you down.'

A furtive check showed her rocking on the floor. Our silence was almost uncomfortable.

'Maybe you should leave her. Come with us.'

There was a proposition. One I hadn't had in such a long time. If I hadn't met her, I would have gone. They were rough, but they were men. I mean, they were human. But so was Sara.

'I feel responsible,' I said, the two of us looking towards her.

'Strangely enough,' he said, an embryonic grin stretching the spaces between his bristles, 'that's how I feel about The Wide Boy.'

'Did you not know him before?'

I withered at the sourness of the cigarette breath he exhaled towards me. He was still holding me by the elbow.

'Tried to avoid him,' he said. 'He's my daughter's boyfriend.' He sniffed. 'Was.' He turned his head away, glancing towards the car where the young man had turned on the radio.

He was only four or five inches taller than me. For a minute we stood together even though we'd nothing to say.

'He's wasting that battery,' he said at last, releasing my arm. 'Look.' He contorted himself to retrieve something from inside his jacket. 'Take this. If you're in trouble, give it a blast.'

I took the piece of metal. It had charged itself with his warmth.

'It's not going to travel miles, but you'll not get a signal on your mobile. If I'm around...' He bent and picked up two packs

30

of what I took to be shotgun cartridges from among the fallen baby blankets. 'I'm Peej, by the way.'

'Thanks,' I said, and meant it.

'You know, you don't just need to watch out for animals.' His eyes travelled up my body and down again, making me pull my stomach in. 'Don't assume everybody you meet is out to help you.' He nodded to Sara. 'Better to be like her. Everybody's going to be out for what they can get.'

As I watched him go I touched the warm barrel of his whistle to my lips and slipped its ribbon over my neck. The metal slithered inside my jumper and dropped with a heavy thump against my skin.

Chapter Seven

There was water in Teresa's tank so I told Sara to wash her face. I checked my watch out of habit. It was hours since I'd left my flat, but how far had I come? On Google Maps, a couple of miles. In terms of life experience, the circumference of the planet. Now I was hungry. While Sara was upstairs I rummaged in the kitchen cupboards. There was the usual dried stuff and an unopened pack of madeleines. I ate two quickly before Sara came down then we split them fifty-fifty. It was a real treat because they were still soft, full of preservatives. I looked at the sell-by date: we could go on enjoying packets of these for months.

There were plenty of tins in the cupboard, so we opened one of beans and one of meatballs in onion gravy and ate them cold. My conscience was relatively clear: according to the label, meat accounted for only twenty per cent. This house was a miracle – the kind of place to go in a nuclear attack. There were plastic-linked cans of fizzy drinks and multi-packs of sweets and crisps. Even better was the fact that the bodies were upstairs, so we could have the run of the ground floor without much risk of exposure. Strangers' houses smell musty anyway.

Outside it was beginning to get dark. The dogs had started howling, and I didn't think it would be safe to travel, so I locked the front door and told Sara to close the curtains. The living room had cold wooden floors, but there was a flokati rug at the fireside, and suede cushions and fake fur throws gave the illusion of warmth. There were scented candles everywhere and matches on a shelf as if Teresa had had foreknowledge of our situation, so we brought all the candles to a low table in the middle of the room and found they gave off a not unreasonable heat. It occurred to me I could light a fire, but though there was an elaborate marble and slate fireplace, it wasn't real. Early settlers lit fires in the middle of their huts, but if I tried that the whole house might ignite, so we contented ourselves with the candles. Their light was fairly cosy. Their fragrance helped disguise the other odour.

But what to do to pass the time? I looked for a book but there weren't any. Sara found a magazine and sat beside me, wrapping one of Teresa's fur throws over our shoulders. I read her the captions to the pictures. Pop stars and paparazzi. Celebrities and cellulite. I was vaguely uncomfortable, so close to another woman, and there was a curious smell whenever Sara moved: a scent of something more local than the candles. 'Peej' and 'The Wide Boy' had been smelly, and I was pretty certain I'd have a whiff about me myself after such a fright and so many days, but this one I didn't recognise from before. I assumed the nylon of her trousers was exuding heat. She probably hadn't changed in over a week.

It was a long night with little to do but think 'if only'. I'd wish I'd gone with the men then Sara would smile and I'd feel guilty. I yearned for my flat, but it was too late for that. I got up and looked out of the back window, but the whole area was dark. Even our tiny light might show for miles. I closed the curtain and hoped there was no one to see.

'What can we do?' Sara asked.

I found a pack of cards and we played 'snap'. Each time we snapped the candle containers trembled. She got so excited when she knew the last snap was coming that I let her win every time. I lost count of the number of games we played then at last she'd had enough and asked for something to drink. When I said yes, she went into the kitchen, 'being Mum'. It was cold when she had gone: the kind of cold that made the furnishings clammy. She came back with two frothing cans of fizzy drink, two packets of crisps and a twinkle in her eye.

'Party on!' she said, and slurped foam from a can.

It was when she bent to put the other on the table that I saw she was damp. 'Sara, did you spill something?' I asked.

There was a momentary silence before the wail began, low and then increasingly louder.

'Are you alright?' I asked, but that just seemed to make her worse. I put my hand gingerly on her broad behind.

She turned round, her mouth drawn back like a cartoon face, her saliva unswallowed. I couldn't take my eyes off it, stretching from top to bottom jaw and dribbling out.

'What is it?' I asked her.

'The ned men made me do it.'

I bent my head, resisting the temptation to plug my fingers in my ears, straightened up again and looked at her. She was stinking.

'Come here,' I said and pinched at the cloth. Urine had soaked to her knees and the dark blue of her tracksuit trousers had lost its shine and gone baggy. I rubbed the ickiness from my fingers. 'Why did you not say something?'

A wail was her answer.

What had I let myself in for? What did I know about learning difficulties? I should have gone with the men. I should have walked away and left her.

I looked back up at her. 'Swallow, Sara!' But all she could do was sob.

I took the cans and crisps from her hands and put them on the table. Her petite, upright grief occupied the whole room and I knew what she was really crying for. The candles flickered: the shadows they created on the pink walls were grey. The curtain folds fluctuated in relief like my world's known boundaries, and I didn't know what to do. I wished she'd shut up, but there was no sign of it. I patted her arm and unclenched my teeth to talk to her. 'There, there,' I ventured, rigid with distaste.

'I want my mum,' she said, garlands of mucus glimmering.

Who didn't?

'I want my mum.'

I held out a tissue, but she was too dim to use it. I wiped her eyes and got a clean one from my backpack for her nose.

'Stop crying,' I said, one hand gripping the back of her head while I squeezed slime from the front. 'You've cried enough.' I broke away and crossed the room to dart the tissues at the bin. She stood woebegone where I left her.

I'm not inhuman. I went back and wrapped my arms around her, stiff at first then surprised by how pleasant it was to be allowed to hold her. Her small body was plump: it was cushioned and soft. Smell rises, but smell's only one of your senses. My cheek responded to her hair in a way I used to know about. I relaxed in the familiarity of human touch.

Chapter Eight

Okay, so it wasn't fun having to go upstairs to rummage in a stranger's drawers. In the weeks that followed I became immune to it, but then it was worse than difficult. My torch light picked out Teresa and Micky thrown to opposite sides of their bed with the cover drawn up between them. I flicked my light to the floor while I struggled to control my breathing. The bed was in the middle of the room and there was little space for other furniture: I picked out an ottoman at the bottom of the bed; a cycling machine over by the curtains. I steered the imperfect circles of light over the headboard and saw them double in the glass doors of a wardrobe that ran along the length of the right-hand wall.

I'd found a bottle of perfume in the bathroom and soaked a towel with it which I tied at my nose so I could go in without being overcome by nausea. Confronted by the double mirrored wardrobe I was marooned between reality and its reflection and I wallowed in the blackness of grief and envy. I turned to the real corpse so I could see her better. Teresa's hair had fallen over her face. The torch picked out the very top of her burgundy satin nightdress with its fringing of creamy lace. Why did I never buy anything like that? One thin strap had slipped down across her arm.

Micky was turned away. The torch picked up the silver bracelet of his watch on the bedside cabinet beside his dud phone, his wallet and some change. I went round the bed to see his face. There was dense forestry down his chest and arms yet his shoulder and upper arm were smooth. I torch-lit the bed's topography, trying to imagine the lay-out of their legs, entwined, perhaps, feet crossing at the ankles, under the swirls of the duvet. In the centre, shaded from my view at first by the

36

quilt and the shadow of her father's shoulder, the baby spread its arms as if pushing its parents out of bed. Or asking to be lifted. That was hard.

I opened Micky's bedside cabinet and took out a box of condoms. There were four left. I shone the beam of light back on their faces: his turned towards me, hers facing the mirror. I wondered how many children they'd planned to have.

The torch gleamed on the glossy paper of a car magazine with a busty woman on the cover, holding a spanner. I closed the drawer, my breathing laboured in the damp towel but if I took it away the stench wrenched the stomach out of me. I put his wallet in my coat pocket, went back to the wardrobe and slid open the doors, starting at the noise they made like a thief.

I didn't care for Teresa's clothes, but took two pairs of stretchy slacks for Sara and toyed in the knicker drawer, wondering if any of it would fit. Her formed cup bras were too big for me, so I put them back. I fingered some pairs of pretty pants – checking as if she might be watching – but Sara'd packed a couple of pairs of her own. I closed the mirrored doors and took a blanket from the ottoman.

I filled the sink with water liberally doused with strawberry bubble bath that I hoped might compensate for the temperature. Sara steadied herself on the wall while I stripped the wet trousers, socks and pants down her legs and sponged her. She shivered, even though she held the fur throw round her shoulders, her whole body trembling with the cold. I've never been so intimate – her vast pink and purple thighs, the creases behind her knees, her private area with its tangle of crusty brown hair, the hard skin round her heels and her pretty toes. I straightened and passed her Teresa's thickest towel to rub the heat back into herself while I emptied the water swirling down the sink but she asked me to help her. I rubbed the backs of her legs and her buttocks then smoothed baby powder between my palms and into her creases. She nearly lost her balance pulling on her clean pants, so I held them while she eased each foot in turn into clean socks and trousers till she was almost snug. Then I sent her downstairs. I washed my own hands and face in water that must have been close to freezing in the pipes.

That night we put the seat cushions on the flokati and slept, curled together for warmth with our heads on suede pillows, my sleeping bag opened on top of us, Teresa's blanket and her two fake fur throws over that. We slept snugly till daylight drew its ragged perpendicular on the wall and turned up the dimmer switch in the room.

Chapter Nine

In the morning it was raining steadily. My mobile and Teresa's landline were still dead.

I wanted to track down authority, even though I knew we'd get soaked. It was the kind of day when you were glad if you could stay at home with the heating on, mug of soup in one hand and some treasure you'd found tucked on a side shelf in the other, Coppelia on the CD player or maybe Vaughan Williams.

In Teresa's house the damp penetrated our clothes from the moment of separation. We'd slept fully dressed so the only other layers we could put on were our coats, hats and scarves and that's what we did, the wool of our gloves hoarding minute digestive biscuit crumbs. I longed for a mug of milky coffee between my hands. Sara wasn't too pleased to get out of bed and into that rain.

'There'll be someone who can help us at the Police Station,' I assured her. 'And I'll buy you some chocolate.'

I pulled my cagoule on top of my coat and told Sara to put up her hood. It was even colder when I opened the outside door. The street hadn't changed but the pram cover had been left unhooked and the pram had filled with water. It took two attempts to upend it before we could load in my pack. Sara's squat hands gripped the coated handle and her stubby leg paddled for the foot brake then she was off at a healthy pace. The pram bounced along with her strides. I clicked the handle of her case upright and followed, my cagoule string pulled tight and the exposed skin on my face stinging in the wet. This arrangement was easier on my back, Sara was singing tunelessly and I found, in spite of everything, I was happy too, relatively speaking.

Lone blackbirds cut across us as we passed, signalling their peep-peep alarm. Sparrow-flight involved repeating three flaps then a dip across the gardens to argue in the bushes. Why had I never noticed these things? My breath puffed in front of me and my lungs were sponges saturated with damp. We didn't see anyone all the way to town. I felt, once or twice, the bump of Peej's whistle against my chest, but of the man himself there was no sign.

In town the bus station was deserted. Even the taxi rank had been abandoned and there were no more than half a dozen cars in the car park.

By now it was mid-morning. The shops should be busy, but the streets were empty. We crossed at the town's main junction without looking. We had stopped singing. Pigeons were the only living beings in the main square and they looked downtrodden by the rain. I saw our dreary reflection in the jeweller's window: we were a bedraggled pair. Sara put her hands on the glass, cooing at the trays of gold and platinum rings. It didn't even occur to me that we could take them. It was only much later that I thought about it, after the looters had been, but by then the things of real value weren't platinum or gold.

We turned the corner into the police station yard and I felt the dread. What if my optimism was wrong? Surely there'd be authority and it would be centred here? My hopes rose when we found the door unlocked but as soon as I passed into the vestibule I recognised the smell.

'Wait outside,' I said to Sara, the cumbersome pram providing an excuse.

I held my gloved hand over my nose and mouth and pushed open the glass door. The foyer was empty. Fresh posters on the turquoise walls advised locking cars and securing house windows. There were tidy piles of leaflets on the seasoned counter. I let the door go and took a step, the creak of the hinge the only sound.

'Hello?'

It echoed back.

I was conscious of my feet sticking on the vinyl. How many

Friday night brawlers dripped blood on it? I rested my free hand on the heavy wooden counter and called out louder, but I went unanswered.

'There must be somebody!'

Anguished, I looked over the counter, prepped for a repeat of Amrit, but the floor was clear. The half-glazed door beside the counter wouldn't open and there was nothing for me to use as a step; no foothold on the glossy frontage of the desk. I moved the leaflets, patting them into a tidy pile before reaching with two hands to the far end so I could slide across and swing my leg up, but I scraped my hip bones against the desk edge. I knelt up on the counter and rubbed them through my coat.

More important was the stench. My diaphragm was ready to invert again, but I forced myself to breathe through my mouth. I was becoming practised. I slipped down, pain spiking in my ankles, and entered a corridor of dark wood and frosted glass. The rooms on either side had desks, papers, filing cabinets and wall-charts but no people. I passed two bare rooms I assumed were used for interviews, but couldn't find the bodies that were guilty of the smell.

How could they all be dead? It surely wasn't possible.

I pushed open the door to the men's toilet and heard a scurry. Pale light from a high window yellowed the ageing ceramic wall tiles and accentuated their crazy paving cracks. The smell was strong here – stronger than the usual stink of men's pee – and I felt nausea in the hollow below my ribs. I whistled through my open mouth with every outward breath. The urinals were clear. I thought of Sara safe with only teeming rain in the yard.

'Hello?' I said, a girl's voice, scared. A scuffle and a ploop. The first cubicle revealed only the toilet bowl, discoloured below the water line and with its water level trembling. The second door stuck. Through the gap I recognised a uniform. Back in the first I climbed from the toilet to the cistern. I eased the top of my head up over the partition.

Risked breaking a leg as I threw myself down. I threw up twice with my body shuddering. Wiped my mouth with toilet paper and let it drop on the spill. There was a smear on my cagoule that was slimy on my fingers. I wiped it on a thick wad of quality paper towel and stumbled back into the corridor.

Downstairs there was a tramp in bed in one of the cells, but I assumed he was dead. In the staffroom further along the corridor a PC was stretched out on a line of red and blue square-cut PVC chairs. This was as far as I could go.

My hopes were gone. I sat in the staffroom far away from the cop and sobbed out my misery. I thought about Sara. She'd be soaked by now, but I didn't care. I took out Peej's whistle and blew it miserably though I knew he wouldn't hear. My crying stopped and I stared across the room.

Peej said the knife wouldn't be any good. The policeman was in full dress, with his truncheon and handcuffs at his broad leather belt. The only human parts exposed were his face and hands. His skin was a shiny browny grey with the tell-tale rash. If I didn't look at his skin I could pretend he was a dummy. I crossed the room and stood beside his boots. They stuck out like the hands of a clock but they were big and black with soles as thick as my wrist. There was chewing gum on the sole of his left boot. I concentrated on his laces and touched my way up his coarse, solid trouser leg till I reached his truncheon, but my hands couldn't work out how to release it without looking. My fingers fumbled disloyally. My lungs were squealing for breath.

I ran to the corridor for a gulp before trying again. I ignored his face with his blood sunk below his ears; ignored his feet. I focused on his massive leather belt, my lungs bursting, and jerked till the fastening came away. I thrust the truncheon in my front pocket but his rotten meat smell made me gag. An opaque window near the ceiling was the only source of ventilation. I dragged a table under it and climbed up. I tugged at the metal closure till it too came away and clean, rain-spotted air misted my face through the bars. I heard Sara's toneless singing and rejoiced. A fly buzzed past me. I closed my mouth and filled my lungs through my nose before jumping down. The fly persisted when I waved it away. I unfastened the handcuffs and CS spray from the policeman's belt, thought him a kind of blessing or goodbye and fled from the room.

42

Chapter Ten

Our town is separated from its neighbour by a river. One day, I'd assumed, we'd join in a sprawling urban conglomeration. Sara and I stopped on the bridge and my heart was as turbid as the water.

Sara and I walked two miles to the town centre, stopping only at a vandalised shop for sweets and because my back was aching. We sat for a while to rest on upturned crates, slaking our thirst with fizz. Sara didn't appear to have a care – fill her pockets with toffees and she was fine. Me, I knew that if this shop had been forced then someone was alive and that stirred up murky undercurrents of moods in me. Peej was unlikely to have made his way here when there were booze shops galore outside his front door. There must be someone else. Was that good, or bad? I persuaded myself it was good. That and the sugar buzz picked my spirits up. We used the toilet in the back shop before carrying on – not quite ready for peeing in open air.

The District Police Headquarters was deserted. I knew straight away. If they were active, I realised, there'd be jeeps on the street, cars in the car park. And there were none.

Still, I pushed the door open. I didn't go all the way to the bodies. Just yelled at the top of my voice and listened for an answer that didn't come. And if there was no authority here, where would there be?

At the top of the town the sun came out and the streets began to dry. Maybe spring wasn't that far off. I took off my cagoule and shook off the raindrops and as I did so the CS canister fell out and clattered on the tarmac. I picked it up and slipped it in the pocket of my coat.

Sara lowered her hood. 'Can we go for a burger?' she asked.

'I think the shop's shut.'

Immediately, Sara's mood dipped. What a strange girl she was. I tried to brighten her up by picking up some of the pop songs she'd been singing but how was I supposed to know the words? She sat down on a wet bench and peeled the sole from the heel of one grubby trainer with the toe of the other and my voice petered out.

'I'm hungry,' she said.

Vast shadows of clouds rolled out over the ground and away.

'What about your sweets?'

'I want a burger. And chips. I want a burger and chips with dip and coke. That's what I want: I want diet coke.'

'You've just had a drink. And we can't get burgers. I told you. The shop's shut.'

'Ice-cream.' Pathetically sullen.

I sat beside her and looked up and down the street for signs anyone had been there but it was deserted. The shop fronts were bright but newspaper leaves were mulching the monoblock under our bench. Over in a corner, by an area of raised planting, the wind was rattling an empty plastic lemonade bottle back and forward in noisy arcs.

'Ice-cream with sweets in it,' she said.

I clawed at my scalp with the nails of ten fingers then thrust out an empty hand.

'What is it?'

'It's what you asked for.' I glared, emotion clamping my mouth shut till the moment passed. Then I unwrapped an imaginary burger and nodded to her. 'Don't you want yours?'

She stared, blank, looking from my mouth to my hands then slowly mimed opening an invisible wrapper. A gleam came in her blue eyes. 'There's no dip.'

I shook my head. 'Here.'

She shuffled back on her seat and I leaned back too. For a few minutes we played, dipping our chips and biting them, looking around as if we were surrounded by clusters of ordinary shoppers.

'Hot,' she said, waving her podgy hand, with its rimmed

44

black nails, in front of her open mouth.

I had to smile. I finished my burger and mimed screwing the paper into a ball. 'That was nice,' I said. 'In fact, I think that was probably the best burger I've ever eaten. Not even fattening.' I tossed the paper into the bin. 'Bullseye!'

Sara took out her imaginary burger, put it on the seat beside her and screwed up the rest of the invisible paper bag. 'Bullseye!' She unravelled her burger and took a bite and her legs started swinging. 'What'll we do now?'

I sighed. What could we do now? I couldn't even think.

'Alice...'

'What?' I could hear the exasperation in my voice.

'What'll we do?'

'What do you want to do?'

'Go to the pictures.'

'Oh, Sara.' I felt my mouth crumple. 'It's shut. The cinema's shut.'

'Swimming baths.'

'Shut. It's all shut.'

'This town's rubbish.'

Wait. A pool brimming with blue water. 'Have you got a swimming costume?'

'In my drawer. It's red and yellow, but it's got a big splash of orange juice in the middle. Kid-on orange juice, I mean. My mum washed it.'

We weren't walking six miles home for that. I looked at the shops around me. Of course there was a sports shop. All I needed was something to throw. Me, a respecter of rules, and such a killjoy. But the thought of that clear blue water ... I looked at Sara. 'Do you dare me?'

The planted area was run down: it was easy to use the lid end of the lemonade bottle to dislodge a brick. It fell on the ground with a heavy thud.

'What are you doing?'

I heaved it in the direction of the window and yowled at the shattering glass. I think I was playing, just like with the burger. A quick check showed the street still deserted. I worked out another brick and smashed a hole big enough to let us through.

Sara shrieked with excitement. Inside, we chased each other back and forwards between tracksuits and trainers. Eventually we flopped on the ground. 'I can't believe I've just done that,' I said and let my head sink on the pillow of Sara's stomach. She groaned and slid away on the shiny floor, propelled by her rubber soles. 'No, I really can't!' I reached up for t-shirts from the stand and tucked them under my head instead. Sara slithered back and followed suit.

'I like being with you,' she said, a propos of nothing.

'Do you, Sara?' I felt a surge of pleasure and lay there, feeling the top of her head nudging mine. I don't think anyone had ever said that to me before. 'Well, I like being with you too.' It was hard to believe I'd just met her; I felt a kind of continuity of knowing her, my moods changing from one moment to the next just like hers. 'What else do you like?'

'Chocolate.'

'So that's what you're after!' I passed her our 'rations' and we lay together, happy enough for now. I knew what I liked. Defying everything I'd imagined and despite all the difficulties that had brought me here, I liked being with Sara. I even quite liked lying on the floor of that shop. I liked the purple balloon caught up in the rafters. I liked the way things grew darker towards the back of the shop. I liked the way the light from the windows glossed in patterns on the pale green vinyl. I liked –

I heard a noise over at the window. Keeping close to the floor, I twisted round so I could see. A man was cupping both hands against the glass and looking in.

Conscious of what Peej had said, I put my hand over Sara's chocolaty mouth and pointed. It wouldn't do any harm to be cautious. We drew ourselves in under the rail of t-shirts and watched him move to the hole.

'Anybody in?'

I willed Sara not to cry.

His foot crunched on the broken glass as he stepped through the window. 'Hello?' he said and stood with his hands in his pockets. My hand reached into mine. The man cleared his

46

throat and started humming.

Bastard, I thought. He knows we're trapped. I watched him from between two blue and white tee-shirts. He's got us trapped and he's enjoying it. I looked at Sara's face. Her slanting eyes were even wider. I could see the wavy lines thread through her pale blue irises.

'I know you're here,' he said. Coat hangers screeched as he pushed aside a stretch of jogging pants. 'I *will* find you.'

He worked his way down the right hand side of the shop. Sara and I started creeping up on the left.

We were nearly half-way there when the CS can fell again. It rattled and I knew he'd have looked so I didn't dare twitch. I watched it roll and knew he'd track back to us. I split the sleeve from a sweatshirt I was hiding behind. Then Sara caved.

'Get it!' she cried, half-standing.

He lunged, but I got there faster.

I sprayed in his face and we fled screaming. I thought I'd been fast round the bays of tracksuits; now I sprinted out of the shop. I tugged Sara's arm and dragged her with her stumpy legs kicking outwards in the first direction I could think of, which was the opposite way from the way we'd come. I didn't even care about our luggage.

I battered into a door and we rushed up a stairwell to cower at the window. The landing looked over the back yards rather than out to the front, but it was a sash window and it was open, so I could hear his roars, repeating, insistent, then more and more dispersed till they eventually stopped. Sara whimpered in against my chest, her arms encircling me so tightly I could feel my ribs cross and Peej's whistle dig into my skin.

'Let me breathe,' I whispered, prising her off, but the muscles in her arms were clenched the way a baby clenches a finger.

*

After half an hour we crept out and found the street deserted. Still, we played it cautious. We hugged the walls and shop windows, dashing, at the end, past the maw of the sports shop to the pram. Sara brought her case right up beside the pram handle.

47

'I don't think we'll bother with swimming costumes,' I told her.

My mouth was dry and my hands were shaking. I could smell the stink from my own armpits. I needed another drink, too. I needed a hard drink and fizz was a pathetically inadequate alternative. I reached in to the pram where I'd stored the half dozen bottles we'd liberated. And there was a note, woven into the webbing on the front of my rucksack.

'Look, Sara!'

I held it up to her.

'What is it?'

In very ragged writing it said, 'Whoever you are, I wouldn't have hurt you. If you want to get in touch, come to the outside of The Horsebrasses Bar. I haven't seen a soul for seventeen days. Not a living one. Eric.'

I raised the orangeade to my lips and gulped some then passed it to Sara.

'Well?'

She drank, gave me the bottle back and wiped away her moustache. 'Well what?'

'Do you want to?'

'My mum doesn't let me go to the pub.'

She was hilarious. 'What age are you, Sara?'

'Twenty-three.'

'He's only using it as a landmark.'

Mind you, the thought of a double scotch burning my insides boosted my courage. I re-read the note. He'd spelled everything correctly. 'I think we should take the risk,' I said and toyed with the weight of the CS spray, which was safely back in my pocket. 'He knows we're armed.'

Chapter Eleven

The Horsebrasses Bar was only a few streets away. It was a working man's pub, old fashioned and sited right on a busy corner.

I kept my hand in my pocket with the gas canister. I wouldn't take any chances. I thought about the knife I'd packed down the side of my rucksack, but as Peej said, knives would be messy.

We checked the building from across the street, but there wasn't any sign of him. The doors looked locked. 'Eric' hadn't said anything about when to meet, but I wouldn't stand around waiting for him forever.

Almost fifteen minutes had passed when I noticed a movement in the flat above the pub. A wiggle of a curtain. I hadn't thought he might be there, watching us. It made me feel uncomfortable, and I was about to release the brakes on the pram and move off when he appeared – red eyed still – from an unmarked door at the side. He nodded. 'You got my note.'

Sara linked her hand through my arm and I gripped the CS in my pocket all the tighter.

'Yes,' I called across then for a minute none of us said anything.

'Terrible, isn't it? This situation.'

'Awful.'

A pigeon landed in the road between us. It bobbed its funny walk and pecked at dirt before flying off.

'My name's Eric, by the way.'

'You said. In your note.'

'Of course.' He took his hands out of his pockets, folded them across his chest and tipped up the toes of his shoes. He didn't look the type to buy gear from a sports shop. His jacket was tailored and new looking; his shoes were polished.

'Where are you two from? Are you local?'

'Fairly.'

Sara was ready with her address but I dug her in the ribs.

'D'you want to tell me your names? Or something?'

I looked at Sara. 'I'm Alice. This is Sara.'

'Pleased to meet you.'

I'd say he was about fifty. No - fifty-five. He seemed respectable. Clean shaven. We could probably trust him, even though his hair looked unnaturally black for a man of his age.

'Look,' he said, stepping away from the wall. 'I've got the keys for this place – if you'd like a drink.'

A drink. I'd been living on wine for the week before I left my flat. In the last two days I hadn't had a swallow. My blood squealed at me to go across.

'I'm not allowed!' Sara's stage-whisper reached him before I could.

'Plenty of soft drinks,' Eric said. 'Whatever you fancy.'

From the corner of my eye I could see her glower.

'Cola? Irn Bru?'

Mine was 225cls of Pinot Noir or a double scotch. Or both. In two glasses. I could imagine the scorch of the antifreeze spreading down my chest. Oh yes. I relaxed my grip of the CS spray in my pocket, checked left and right and steered Sara across the road by the elbow.

He unlocked the pub doors and held them open while Sara pushed in the pram and I followed.

That scent seduced me. My eyes grew accustomed to the low light. It was an old style pub, its wood near black and upholstery scarlet. The windows were opaque with Art Nouveau etchings and tapering seagull droppings.

'What would you like?' Eric's hand lingered on my shoulder before slipping down my back, but I was half intoxicated in anticipation and my caution had been left on the kerb outside.

'Pinot Noir, if you've got it. And a cola for Sara.'

I settled in the corner of the first banquette while he chinked glasses behind the counter. For the first time in so long I felt alive again. In anticipation of alcohol. And this man, too, with no one to compete for him. I looked him over. His back wasn't broad but it was limber under his jacket. His hair was black and quite short but thick and I imagined its springy resistance if I were to touch it. Sara sat at my right. I rubbed the pile of the velour seat oblivious to the smuts on it and relished the pop of the wine cork, delicious odours ousting all others.

'This is nice, Sara. Isn't it?'

Eric brought a cola with a cocktail stirrer and straws and two flavours of crisps.

'Very nice,' she said, inching herself fully upright. I don't think her feet were touching the ground. Metaphorically, mine weren't either.

Eric sat on my left with one hand on the end of his thigh and one on the banquette close to my knee. There was a sharp crease ironed in his trousers and he was wearing a blue shirt and tie, which struck me as strange. I wondered if he'd put the tie on specially. Close up, he smelled of peppery aftershave. I'd a feeling he was making a pass at me and I admit, I was flattered.

'So,' he said, holding his glass up. We smiled. The wine was jugular red.

'Cheers.'

Oaky tannins mingled with the tang of Eric's hot proximity and both disseminated through the air towards me. In another life I might have had the vapours. Now, I was revelling in it. I felt good for thirty seconds, but my glass hadn't made it to my lips when I heard bikes. The growl of engines was unmistakeable, so loud it flustered me. I gulped two mouthfuls, turned to Eric and asked, 'Is that motorbikes?'

His brow wrinkled, moving the carpet of his thick black hair downwards. 'It's nothing,' he said. 'Don't worry about it.' His smile wasn't convincing.

'Is it?'

When he straightened and met my gaze his eye were still reddened from the CS spray and still squeezed up. He bobbed his head in answer.

'Do you know them? Will they come here?'

He opened his mouth but closed it again. Then shrugged and said, 'Don't worry about it.' He lifted his drink from the table, twisted the stem of the glass between his fingers and breathed heavily through his nose.

'What is it, Alice?' Sara said, wriggling forward, her breath stinking of smoky bacon. 'Is it the ned men?'

'Shhh,' I told her. I waited for Eric to say something. 'Are they coming here, Eric?' Outside, I could hear engines idling.

He frowned and shook his head. 'It's just some guys on bikes,' he said and put his glass back on the table. The roaring cut.

'Is it the ned men, Alice?' Sara said, slipping her hand through my arm.

I drained my glass. 'It's nothing, Sara.' I repeated, 'Eric?

He spread his hands, non-committal.

'Is it the ned men?' Sara's voice had a quiver in it.

Eric's eyebrow hairs were matted, higgledy-piggledy, because he'd rubbed them. His eyes were squeezed, but there was a light, now, as if reflecting an idea. Or maybe it was the light from the window behind me. He sat forward. 'Let's go upstairs.'

I could feel the wine spread through me like a blood transfusion. I looked at Sara. 'Sara, too?' I asked. 'I won't, without her.'

'Of course,' he said. 'Come on!' He tugged first Sara then me through a door behind the bar. He hauled in our pram and case while outside I could hear the clank of – I don't know – motorbike helmets being slung round handlebars? I hadn't a clue. He handed me the wine bottle and his glass while he locked the internal door. 'Go on!' he said. 'Upstairs!'

I still had my glass in my hand, but it was empty. We were crammed into the residential entrance hall. 'What about the pub doors?'

The clunking stopped. Through the adjoining door we could hear voices moving into the pub, and only men's voices. Sara was standing by a frosted pane of glass in what I assumed must be the door Eric had first appeared from.

'Move!' he hissed.

'Come here,' I called, smiling encouragement as the downy corners of Sara's mouth puckered. I didn't want her to dissolve again.

Eric took the wine bottle from me. 'Forget the doors. They knew they were open yesterday. Come upstairs!'

Sara's footsteps were loud, scraping each step but she couldn't help it. It was an echoing stone staircase, clammy with damp. Black mould spots were masking the window panes that looked out over the side of the property. I couldn't see anyone outside and couldn't see any of their bikes, except one, in the service lane between this and the neighbouring property. A sheet of yellowed newspaper had blown flat against the hub of its front wheel. 'Come on, Sara,' I said and pulled her, puffing, upstairs. 'We'll be out of the way up here.'

At the top was a plain brown door. Its single hardboard skin had been painted with brown gloss but damp had dulled the shine. Eric unlocked the door and pushed it open for us to go in then he double locked it behind us and put the keys in his trouser pocket.

I felt my cheeks heat. Could be the situation, but it was more likely the wine.

Through the floor came voices, raised in pleasure rather than anger.

'Why are the biker men shouting on you?' Sara asked Eric.

He paused as if to listen before putting the wine bottle on a central coffee table. 'Not me, Sara.'

I listened. 'E-rick. E-rick. It *is* your name they're calling.'

He pushed his black hair back with one hand and smiled broadly at me. 'Why would they be looking for me when they've the run of a pub? Refill, Sara?' He poured then put the bottle on the table in front of her.

'Another drink?' he asked me, taking the glasses from my fingers. 'Stop worrying.'

It certainly sounded like his name they were shouting, but I wasn't sure, now they'd stopped. Anyway, the wine was calling. I glanced behind me at his purple leather sofa, moved the newspapers off on to the floor and sat down. The newspapers were tabloids and they were over a month old. I hadn't thought of him as a tabloid reader. Cigarettes and a pair of balled socks were underneath.

He tossed the socks into a corner. 'Relax,' he said and perched on the arm of the sofa, still holding our empty glasses in one hand. He moved his other hand in an irregular pattern on my shoulder, making my stomach twitch.

'I'll protect you from these ned bike men,' he told Sara then he winked at me.

Should we be getting to know them instead? I didn't know. The noises from downstairs were gruff and didn't sound particularly welcoming. But what men's gathering ever did? I thought about Peej, but what good would a whistle do me here?

Eric poured us a large refill each that emptied the bottle. 'Crisps, Sara? There's some in the kitchen.'

I held my wine, untouched, on my lap in front of me. I watched his slim legs stretch out as he walked to the kitchen in the corner and I glanced at Sara. She blinked her pale eyelashes at me over the top of her cola, and I pressed my lips together in a hopeful smile.

I raised my glass towards my mouth and listened to the bike drivers downstairs. They sounded a rough lot, and I was happy to be out of the way of them. Eric seemed respectable, and I kind of felt safe with him. Safer than I would have felt with men who rode motorbikes. And he seemed to be interested in me. Okay, I was rusty with men, but the wine would make things easier. 'Eric seems nice, doesn't he?' I whispered, leaning in to Sara, who blushed and pretended not to.

'At last, we're having a party!' she said.

'But we'll not go downstairs. And we'll keep quiet so those men won't hear us.'

She nodded.

I looked around the flat, wondering how long the biking men would stay in the pub and wondering where we'd spend the night. There were two doors off the main living area, but one might be a cupboard.

'Do you like him?' Sara said, and nudged me.

54

Now I felt myself blushing. 'It's good to have company.'

I heard him come back from the kitchen. This time he squeezed on to the sofa between me and the arm he'd sat on. I was close enough now to see the pinpricks of black ready to push out through the skin on his chin and to feel myself drawn over towards his greater weight. I pulled to the side to resist, a little, hearing the leather squeak. But why should I resist? What morality police were there now, other than my conscience?

Eric was clean cut and wearing pressed trousers. He took off his tie and let it fall on the heap of newspapers I'd put on the floor at the side of the sofa. He loosened his top two shirt buttons. He'd supple looking shoulders and he was slim, and I could imagine his skin would be sallow and clothed with the dark hairs I could see at his throat and his shirt cuff. There was something rather animal about him, and I quite liked it.

I let my eyes examine his navy-trousered thighs and his sky blue shirt with its open collar. I smiled at him shyly then sipped from my glass. This was a new world. The old rules didn't apply any more. I could be whoever I wanted to be.

'All right, Sara?' he asked her, with an exaggerated second wink. He put his arm round me.

Sara sat tightly packed into the opposite end of the sofa. She smiled full beam at him and sipped from her cola.

'There's plenty of crisps there. Eat as much as you like, right?'

He wouldn't want her, with her slanting eyes and stubby body. No sooner had I thought it when I crumpled inside. Why would he want me? I was over 50. I'd fading ginger hair, I wasn't nicely dressed or even very fresh smelling. But he had slipped his arm round my shoulders.

'There's a pile of magazines on the bottom shelf.' He pointed to a cluttered unit. 'Lots of women's magazines and celebrity gossip.' More to me than her he said, 'You should find something over there to occupy you.'

He didn't break his dark eyes from mine till I did, putting my glass on the table to cover up embarrassment at my inexperience, and all too conscious that I couldn't control my breathing. One of those doors over there might be a bathroom. There might be water in the tank. There might even be perfume. I wished I'd given myself a proper wash at Teresa's last night. Well, it was too late now but I'd sort something out. I fingered my hair, teasing a knot out of it and tucking a wispy lock behind my ear. Eric's ear was reddy brown and had convolutions. There were black hairs there, too. But that was manly. His ear lobe was taut and ruddy. There was a vertical line of smooth skin between his ear and where his stubble began, dark dots on his cheeks and jaw line.

Okay, so I wasn't nineteen in a push-up bra and a mini-skirt. I was wearing shapeless denim jeans and clumsy trainers. It was a long time since I'd contemplated squeezing my feet into peep-toe stilettos. But he was a man and I was a woman. He said he hadn't seen a living person for seventeen days, so maybe he wouldn't be fussy.

Rumbles of conversation and boots came from downstairs. Eric was sandwiched beside me, his right hand resting half way over his thigh and mine. I leaned forward to pick up my drink for another hit of anaesthesia, and hoped he wouldn't smell me too much until I had a chance to clean up. I finished my wine and nursed the glass till he took it away from me and went into the kitchen for a refill.

I watched him go, my fingers knitting with anticipation. It had been a long time, but I was looking forward to it. Who could have dreamt that now, in spite of all this misery, my chance for a relationship had arrived?

Chapter Twelve

I woke up with a trapeze artiste swinging round and round on a pole inside my head and every time she completed a circuit I wanted to be sick. I opened my eyes. I was on Eric's purple sofa with his suit jacket thrown over me, stinking of cigarette smoke. I didn't know he smoked. My shoes and socks were off and there was my stupid foot with its frill of toes, sticking up for anyone to see it and nothing to hide it. I sat up too quickly to cover it, but got a flash of heat and cold with sweat bursting out on my upper lip and I had to roll back down again, clutching my foot and on the verge of fainting. I moaned and gasped and pulled myself up again by leaning on the sofa back. My mouth was thick with the kind of fat and grime that clog sinks and a line of it had crusted over on my chin. I rubbed at it and looked around me. There was a low level of grey light penetrating the greenish curtains at the window.

I couldn't remember anything that had happened. A tremor of panic fluttered through me.

I still had my jeans on and my heavy cable knit jumper. I couldn't see my socks anywhere but my limbs were cramped with cold, so I put Eric's jacket over my chest and shoulders to warm me. I desperately tried to work saliva into my mouth.

Where was everybody? I still had the trapeze artiste spinning round and pounding in my head and I had to let go of my toes so I could massage it.

Some things I could remember. Like the bike men arriving. And Eric inviting us up here. But where were Eric and Sara?

The glasses and empty crisp packets from last night were cluttering the coffee table, but the glasses were empty. I sat forward and tried pouring the dregs out of Eric's and Sara's into mine and my shuddering hands made the rims clink together, but the tiny drip that ran down Eric's to the cusp just levelled out around the rim and wouldn't drop, so I put my dehydrated mouth to it. It was bitter, but I had to have something to clean out the scum from my mouth. And a hair of the dog that bit me.

Where were they? I looked at my watch. 7.18 in the morning. Only just beginning to grow light. What time was it? March yet? February? I put the wine glasses down and realised my own glasses were on the table, too. I pressed the sides of my head in to stop the circus character then slotted the legs of my glasses over my ears. And there was Sara on the floor, her floppy hair poking out of a roll of quilt and blankets. At least I'd taken good care of her.

With a new clarity I remembered Eric's arm going round my shoulders and felt myself blushing. Where was he? And why did I do this thing that made me lose bits of my life?

My trousers were twisted to the right so I stood up, holding on to the arm of the sofa and fixed them. My insides were queasy. I felt as bad as I had when I woke up from the illness, and hoped I wasn't having a relapse. But I knew I wasn't. I'd lost track again and it didn't matter how many times it happened I drank too much again and again and hated myself for it.

Now I could see Sara I could also hear her gentle breathing, out through her plump, open mouth. Poor Sara, sleeping on the floor with her arm for a pillow. At least she was safe. As for me, I cursed my stupidity. This wasn't how I'd hoped to wake up in the morning. That wine drop was acid in my stomach now. I rubbed my thumbs over my temples and did a mental check. My tee-shirt was tucked in. My bra was out of place but only slightly. It was still fastened. I pulled at the cups and lifted each breast into place properly. Everything else about me seemed normal and that included the disappointment. What was going on? What had I done or not done? Where the hell was Eric?

More pressing than the need to know was the need to go, so, leaning on backs of chairs or the walls, I crossed the room and tried the two doors in turn. The first was a cupboard with a hot water cylinder in it. When I tapped it, it sounded empty. The second door led into an old-fashioned bathroom, long and thin and with a scummy green stain below the bath taps. There was brown water in the toilet, and it didn't smell too pleasant, but having no alternative I sat and peed and castigated myself for the amount of booze I must have drunk for it so have so effectively stolen the last twelve hours from me. I didn't even remember having been in that loo the night before.

There was a dull thud when I tried to flush and no water at either the sink or bath taps so I looked at myself in the mirror, at my downturned mouth and curd-grouted teeth then went into the kitchen for something to drink.

Sara was sleeping deeply. I squatted beside her and stroked her soft hair away from her mouth. Her lips were pouting, moist and youthful, and even in the grey of the morning I could make out the flush over her cheeks. She was swaddled in a red and yellow duvet with a turquoise and yellow one thrown over the top. No wonder she was cosy.

In the kitchen there was a pile of dirty clothes and of dirty dishes. The clothes were men's clothes, dark trousers, bright shirts, socks and underpants all heaped up in a corner. Three times what I'd wash for myself on a weekly basis. The lilac shirt on the top bore the fold marks from when it was in its original packaging. The bin was overflowing with cellophane wrappers. I opened the cupboards, looking for a clean mug, but there weren't any. Every mug in the flat was rimed with brown or what looked like dried tomato soup. I opened the fridge, but it was empty apart from a jar of pickle.

The tiny working space in the kitchen was crowded with bottles and dishes. Sara's cola bottle was the only one that had anything in it, so I unscrewed its top and drank deeply from it, washing the glue from my mouth. There'd be more in our pram downstairs for when Sara woke up, and more in the bar. I still wondered where Eric had gone, and the bikers, too. I still had this shocking headache and nowhere in that kitchen could I find any paracetamol but I knew I had some in my rucksack and presumably my rucksack was still in the entrance

59

hall downstairs, on the other side of the plain brown door. But when I went to it, the plain brown door was locked.

Panic set in. I hated being locked in. Always had. I'd never been one for small spaces: aeroplanes or inside cabins on overnight ferries. Lifts made me sick. Once I got shut in a van when we were moving stuff between two libraries and the wind blew the door –

'Alice?' Sara's voice. 'Alice, what's wrong?'

She was awake, sitting up in her bed of quilts and rubbing one eye and looking at me. I felt the batter, batter, of my heart up against my breastbone and quaking out through my ribs to the spaces under both arms, but when I heard Sara's voice I began to calm down again. I realised my hands were latched on to the door handle and I'd been tugging and shoving it, as if I thought I could break the lock from its recess.

'Sorry, Sara,' I told her, forcing myself not to look at the door, but, instead, to walk over to the sofa, past her, and sit down. The anxiety had increased the blood pressing and pulsing in my head and I almost had to lie down. 'The door's locked. That's all. And there's no sign of Eric.'

'Oh,' she said and lay back down, pulling the covers up over her cheeks, so that all I could see of her was her fine fair hair, spilling out of the nest of padding.

I suddenly realised she must have seen my bare feet, so I pulled them up and held them with the soles together, sitting on the sofa with my legs bent and my knees sticking out under my arms while I scanned the floor, unsuccessfully, for my socks and tried to remember what I'd done with them. I couldn't even see my shoes anywhere.

From under Sara's covers came the sound of snuffling.

Damn. She must have noticed them. 'You don't need to cry about it,' I said, angry she should be upset. They weren't that bad. I skirted the coffee table and crossed to the far corner of the room, over by the two doors, to where Eric had thrown the balled brown socks. I shook them out. They were crinkled into circles round the ankles and when I pulled them on they felt stiff under my soles, but they covered my secret and kept my feet warm.

60

'There,' I said. 'Sorted.' Hand on my breastbone I squatted by her 'bed' and shook her shoulder lightly. She squirmed half on to her stomach, clearly in a huff with me. 'Everything's fine,' I said. 'Eric'll be back in a minute.'

I stood up and sighed. Holding myself tense was exacerbating my headache, and it was freezing in the flat. Here I was, without even the clothes I'd packed into my rucksack. I'd lost everything. I sorted through some of the clothes that were in the pile on the kitchen floor and took some pullovers through to the living room, where I padded them around me on the sofa while I waited for Eric to come back.

Sara went back to sleep. I could tell by the way her head rolled and her fingers, clutching the edge of the quilt cover by her jaw line, softened and dipped. I tried to close my eyes again, but couldn't sleep. Light advanced in the room and I half sat and half lay, propped in the corner of the sofa where Sara had sat, and thought over what was happening. It was only eight days since I woke in my flat after the illness. Eight days. Maybe a Thursday. What was I supposed to do on a Thursday? Stock selection at Headquarters. Scanning the sports star biographies and misery lits for any worth preserving in our local history collection. How vacuous it all seemed, now; how rapturously ordinary. I still didn't know why things had come to this: why everything had been normal one day and the next, the world upended. I glanced at the door again. I hated being trapped.

A scuffle frightened me and I leapt with panic, but I heard heavy wing flaps on the other side of the window and realised it wasn't him.

I sank back into thinking over what had happened the previous evening. There were so many bottles in the kitchen, but I knew for a fact we hadn't emptied them. So what had we done? What had *he* done? And why had he locked the door to imprison me? The panic rose up again, bellowing my stomach out and in again as if I was going to be sick, so I had to press it, hold on to it, so I wouldn't lose control of it. I made myself move out of the sofa to wear off some of my energy. I needed a drink, so I went into the kitchen again, but the bottles were definitely

61

empty. I could try drinking the dregs, but there weren't enough of them to take away how awful I was feeling.

I tripped on the arm of one of the dirty shirts on the floor but managed to catch myself. Gripped the little ledge of sandy worktop that stuck out beyond the dirty dishes and leaned my weight on it for a minute. I was sick with my headache. In the wall-mounted cupboard there was a tin of rollmop herrings and a half-empty pack of ham stock cubes. Behind them was a bottle of balsamic vinegar, but just one swig of it made me gag so I hurried to the bathroom, banging my shin against the corner of the coffee table and making the glasses rock but Sara remained asleep.

I spat in the sink and stood, shivering. There was nothing to wash away the vomit. Nothing to wash away the diarrhoea provoked by the violence of the retching. I locked the bathroom door and cautiously stripped the trousers and pants from my legs, my whole body trembling. There was toilet paper so I cleaned myself up with that then stood there, staring at the soiling. There was nothing to suggest Eric had had sex with me, unless, maybe, he'd used a condom. It was hopeless: I couldn't remember. I looked in the bathroom bin but there was nothing. It could be lying in the bottom of the toilet, buried under days of urine and paper and faeces, or, maybe, as I did then with my soiled underwear, he'd dropped it out of the single little opening panel of the frosted window, out onto the ledge or into the back yard.

I pulled my trousers back on and fastened them. Above the sink, in the bathroom mirror, I looked at my reflection and saw a mad woman. A woman with reddened eyes and yellowed teeth, with a face that drooped like a deflating balloon and with lips pressed together in a thin, downturned line. I opened the bathroom cabinet and found a brown bottle of pills without a label. My head was killing me. Should I risk a couple?

'Alice?'

Him. I pushed the bottle into the cabinet and closed the door. I licked my lips, ran my fingers over and under my eyes to dry them and smoothed back my hair.

62

'You alright?' There was the sound of his knuckles, gently drumming on the door.

'I'll be right out.'

I tidied my tee-shirt, slapped some colour into my cheeks, checked the back of my trousers and unlocked the door.

Chapter Thirteen

He'd made me tea. I didn't know how he'd managed it, but he'd made me tea. There, on the coffee table, in the place of the clutter of dirty glasses and crisp wrappers, was a tray with a stainless steel tea-pot with real steam drifting from its spout, three mugs, a bowl of sugar and a jug of milk.

'Good morning!' he said. 'Sleep well?'

Once again, I felt his hand slither on my back, between my shoulder blades. He was freshly shaven and his black hair had been combed and gelled.

'Sit down!' he said, with his hand gently insisting, directing me towards the sofa.

'How did you manage it?' I asked, enjoying even the fragrance of the tea in the room. Hot tea. Hot, dry tea. My mouth was watering for it.

'Where there's a will...' He poured the coppery liquid into a mug. 'The milk's UHT – that's the only downside.'

As I nursed the hot cup in my hands I noticed Sara was awake again. She sat up and yawned.

'Morning, Sara,' Eric said, holding up a mug for her. 'Did you sleep well in there?'

'Yes,' she said, flushed with heat, or maybe a little shy. She was glancing up under her eyelashes at him. She scurried over to the sofa to sit beside me and reached out for the mug he'd poured her.

'The cup that cheers!' she said. 'My mum always says that.'

And that was it. Nothing more was mentioned. I drank two mugfuls and began to feel better. And yet, I was irritated. When I asked Eric why he'd locked us in, he said, 'So I knew you'd be safe.'

'But I needed my rucksack – my paracetamol.'

'Got a headache, have you?' He grinned. 'Yeah, well – we put away a fair bit last night.' Nodding towards the window, behind where I was sitting, he said, 'I brought it up while you were in the bathroom.'

While I retrieved my headache pills, he sat down in between Sara and my space on the sofa. When I squeezed in to my place, all too aware of the heat from his thigh and the fact that his hand was acting freely on my shoulder, I felt twitchy and pushed it down.

'Somebody's grumpy, this morning, Sara!' he teased.

I don't know why I was grumpy. Probably just the alcohol. But something didn't feel right. I hated not knowing what had happened. I hated the fact he'd locked us in. 'I can't believe you went away and imprisoned us. What if something had happened to you? What if those bikers were still here?'

Close up, he smelled of soap lather. He fixed his dark eyes on me, under those heavy eyebrows, a hint of a mischievous smile about him that reminded me of my brother. 'Imprisoned you?' He laughed. 'That's a bit strong. Especially when I told you I'd lock the door to keep you safe. You know – last night, when I asked you how you like your tea in the morning.'

I glared at him, feeling my own brows pushed down and scowling.

He half turned, resting his hand on my thigh. 'You don't remember?'

What a creep he was. I bumped my cup on the table and shoved his hand away. 'A cup of tea and we'll be going.'

*

Downstairs, the bikers had gone, leaving just their cigarette butts stubbed out on the carpet. Eric helped us to a few packs of nuts and crisps for breakfast then saw us on to the street. 'You're sure you don't want to stay?' he asked, arms folded and leaning his shoulder against the door frame. 'There's room enough for a menage a trois. Or we could move into one of the bigger houses?'

'No,' I said. 'I want to go into Glasgow. There must be

somebody taking charge.'

He blew out a long breath. 'Not a good idea.' He looked Sara up and down. 'Too many ned men.'

'I don't want to go to the ned men, Alice,' Sara said, on cue, dragging the pram handle closer towards me.

I frowned. 'Do you want to stay here then? Stay with Eric to look after you? Because I'm not.'

She met Eric's eyes then blushed and burrowed her gaze into my arm. I was wearing my own coat again now, retrieved from the pub window ledge and stinking of cigarette smoke and waccy baccy. But the fresh air would soon shift it.

Eric was rubbing his chin. 'Well, you know where to find me.' He looked over towards Hamilton, down the hill in the distance. 'I'll hang around here for a couple of weeks.'

I pulled up the handle of the case and fixed my coat collar. 'What about the bikers? Do they not worry you?' I asked him.

'Nah. I'll keep a low profile. They don't bother me and I'm handy for everything, here.' He indicated with his head. 'Minutes from the shops.'

'Where are we going, Alice?' Sara asked, keeping her eyes on me. 'Is it Glasgow? Is it to the ned men?'

Her chubby little face looked perplexed and worried. The blonde down on her cheeks made her so velvety that I wanted to cup her face but I resisted. 'Me, or Eric, Sara?'

Eric didn't say anything. I was glad when Sara moved closer beside me. 'We won't go to Glasgow. Not the ned part, anyway.'

That made her happier. We made our good-byes, then, Eric waving us off from the door. I didn't know where we'd go, but I automatically headed back towards Hamilton. The line of least resistance – downhill. A bee-line towards home.

Sara plugged in an iPod she told me Eric had given her. It still seemed to work. He'd attached some kind of mini-collapsing-solar panel to her backpack to charge it with, and we walked in silence. As we walked I thought over the night before and what little I could remember from it. Everything was clear up until I was sitting on Eric's sofa, with his hand on my shoulder. Then it went blank. I'd had blackouts before because of the drink. Of course I had. Waking up on the floor in a workmate's apartment. Being sick in a hedge in a suburban garden. Realising it was morning on my brother's spare bed. You messed up again, Alice, I told myself. Get over it.

I thought about the bike I'd seen in the lane at the side of Eric's pub, still with its newspaper page draped over its wheel that morning as we were coming downstairs.

And then I remembered Eric saying he hadn't seen a living soul for seventeen days. Well, that was a lie. He'd contradicted himself by telling me the bikers had been to the pub before. I stopped and Sara walked on, pushing the pram and singing the words of some song until she noticed I hadn't kept up and she dragged the pram back.

'What is it, Alice?' she asked, unwinding the headphone coil from her ear. 'Are we not going back to the wee shop?'

We'd almost reached it by now, the shop where we'd stopped on the way up yesterday.

'Do you trust Eric?' I asked her.

She looked taken aback and blushed. 'What do you mean?'

'Do you think he was telling the truth?'

She twitched her shoulders, stuffed into her thick duffle coat. Looked down at the pram then back up to me. There was an expression in her eyes – she looked like a pup I once had, before my dad died. My dad was stern and the pup was desperate to please. 'I don't know. I don't know him very well.'

I knew what she meant. I nodded and pressed my lips together, then drew a strand of hair from my mouth. 'Yeah. Well, let's keep walking,' I said, and she looked happier. She plugged her headphone in again and a part of me missed our communal singing.

Chapter Fourteen

We slept in garden centres, caravans and outhouses. We even spent a few nights in a motorway service station and another few in a road crew's portacabin. At least the site had a chemical toilet. Yes, there were bodies. I tied a scarf round my face to minimise exposure to the stench, and as much as I could I kept my eyes high so I didn't see. Most people who'd taken ill must have died in their beds, so the footfall in the garden centre and service station was reduced, yet there were still some sad souls who were caught there. We found them in the cafés and the toilets, curled or slumped, as if they'd been desperately crossing the country to be reunited with loved ones, to reach their own homes, that place we all feel we belong, but the sickness had beaten them.

Sara was sweet but I missed conversation – from silly, inconsequential chat on Facebook to discussions about current affairs and the latest library budget cuts or innovations. I missed, I suppose, Dick and Willy from Incunabula. And Polly with a new cross-stitch, and the way we'd plan an activity in support of our favourite charity. The Disasters Emergency Committee. Red Nose Day. Support for Palestine.

And then there were the dreams that troubled me. And the frights. The highs and lows of thinking I saw a living person. A few weeks after we'd left Eric that happened. It was late March or early April. The birds had started nesting, but there were no leaves on the trees. It was beginning to be less cold, though I was still swaddled in layers, unused to living life outdoors.

We'd dragged ourselves round a supermarket no-one had ransacked and had come out, pushing our fully stocked pram. The rain had stopped and it was close to nightfall. I felt safest in the half light, preferring to creep round the edges of outdoor spaces, close to shrubbery, rather than stride out across the open carpark. I heard a noise I didn't recognise and asked Sara if she'd noticed it.

'What?' she said, eyes innocent.

'That noise.'

'What?'

I tugged her earphone away. 'Did you hear that noise? I hissed at her. She teared up and I was furious again. I wanted this purgatory to end. I wanted my old life back, but most of all, I wanted someone new. Someone to take away the burden. My senses were scouring the area to locate where the sound was coming from. We were on a path that led from the supermarket to the train station. I drew Sara further into the bushes that fringed it. 'Listen!' I said.

We listened. A crow cawed. Sara's face lit up.

'No,' I snapped then listened again. 'There! A kind of rustling.' It sounded like someone was shaking a blanket, or maybe carrying one of those bag-for-life carriers that make crinkly sounds against your leg as you're walking. My eyes scanned the carpark, and along the path behind and ahead of me for activity. I felt euphoria that we might not be alone, but also dread it would be someone who'd be bad to us. Someone unprincipled, desperate – just out of jail, maybe, or whose mind had been twisted by the horror. Or just some ordinary man-demon, the kind all girls are schooled to fear and to protect themselves from. We took a few steps further along the path towards the train station and I fished Peej's whistle out from inside my layers of clothing, in readiness, only to realise the sound was some grey plastic sacking the wind was shepherding up and down the empty platform.

'Phew!' Sara said, but for me it was a massive anti-climax. I'd had enough of it. Taking out the whistle was the trigger and the turning point. Nowhere Sara and I had been had we found any officialdom. No-one had taken charge. And it had been six or seven weeks now. If there was a new power structure, or if the old one still existed, it must have been focused on London four hundred miles away and it could take decades to reach us. William the Conqueror had never made it. Even the Romans only hung about for a hundred years.

I pulled myself together. Apologised to Sara. I stood in front of her, facing her, and wiped tears from her cheeks with my thumbs. 'I'm sorry I was grumpy with you. I didn't mean to be.'

She cuddled me. 'That's alright, Alice. I still love you.'

That brought the biggest lump to my throat. I didn't deserve her. I wrapped my arms round her, too, and we clung together, till I drew away, my hands still on her shoulders. 'No, but really, I've been thinking over this. You and I have been wandering around – '

' – on our adventure!'

' – for far too long now, and not really getting anywhere. So this is what I'm thinking.'

She was so trusting. Those eyes. I could've done anything to her.

'What are our options? There's Eric.'

It was as if she was resisting the urge to smile. A little flush coloured her cheeks.

'But I don't really trust him.'

Sara's eyebrows raised.

'And anyway – I was a bit uncomfortable and scared about those bikers.'

There was never any hiding things with Sara. Every emotion was obvious crossing her face. It was clear she didn't fancy the bikers either.

'We know Peej and that boy he was with are still alive. I think we should go back to look for them.'

'The ned men?' Her bottom lip trembled.

I linked my arm through hers. 'Trust me. We could sneak back just now and spy on them. Like playing a game, yes?' I exaggerated all my facial expressions, trying to get her on side. 'We'll be able to find them because we know where to start, and they're probably not shy when it comes to making a noise the way we are. Know what I mean?'

She nodded.

'So we could go back there tonight.' I paused, braced for her to bawl in reaction. It didn't come. 'So, then, if they're nice to us, we could stay with them, and we wouldn't be alone.'

'But if they're not nice, you and me can go away again, on our own?'

'You and I will definitely be together.' Ouch. I'd said it. She returned a few teary blinks. And we turned the pram in the direction of Peej and Wide Boy's housing scheme.

*

Not scared of being seen?   Three hands pushing our pram full of provisions, Sara and I slowly climbed the ascending ground towards the peripheral housing estate where Teresa and Micky had lived, and where we'd met Peej and Wide Boy when they turned up to ransack Micky's illegal cache of guns and ammunition.

Half-way up the hill, I caught the first whiff of wood smoke, but couldn't see where it was coming from. We rested as the road levelled out, leaning on the pram handle, and sniffed the air. It was definitely wood smoke. It was spring, but it smelled like November. It was quite dark by now, and as we pushed off again and rounded the next corner, we spotted the amber fidget of flames between blocks of housing.

'Guy Fawkes Night!' Sara said.

They'd lit a bonfire, sparks shooting up into the night sky. Sara was so excited there was no containing her. No chance of seeing without being seen. She let the pram handle go and jiggled with excitement. We didn't even know for sure if it was Peej and Wide Boy. It could've been anybody. I told her that. Anybody alive, that is.

'But this is where they live!' she told me.   And then she squealed out loud for them, dragging me by my coat sleeve so I had to abandon the pram on the pavement and stumble behind her larger bulk up a path between two houses towards a field. 'This is where we always have our bonfires,' she told me.

'Hang on!' I gasped. Now I was the one hauling her by the coat sleeve. She pulled up, stiff, but they'd already heard us.

71

Let's just say the welcome was not so rapturous. Not at first, anyway. Emblazoned by the light of flames that were licking up past the entangled bones of broken furniture, Peej's face with its concave cheeks was terrifying. But the big two-handed gun he was holding out, aimed at us, was worse.

'It's us!' I said, and, when he didn't stand down, I lifted the whistle he'd given me and blew a shaky peep through it. 'Sara and Alice.'

Wide Boy materialised from the darkness. 'Aww it's Yakkity-Yak!' he said. He nudged Peej's arm, causing Peej to swing the gun away to the side, away from us and himself. 'Yakkity-Yak and Dimwit.'

'I am not Dimwit,' Sara said, indignant. 'She's Alice and I'm Sara!'

That was how we re-acquainted ourselves with the two most unlikely people in my social circle. It was one thing – in my early days in the libraries – doing 'outreach' at schools and during the summer holidays for boys like Wide Boy, or like the one I remember as Skliffy because of the noise he made, dragging his feet. Or the boy who constantly ran his palm up over the point of his nose. Or the one whose clothes hadn't seen soap suds in all the months since his mother bought them for 50p out of the charity shop. My life had changed so much since those days. I tried not to cry. One thing this catastrophe had taught me was humility. Here I was, trembling in my chest to be welcomed in to Peej and Wide Boy's company. Here I was, warmed from the outside and in by their fire and unquestioning hospitality. I sat on the camping seat Peej vacated for me, in front of that roaring fire, staring at my own layers of clothes whose mosaic of food stains and muck hadn't seen a soap sud for weeks, and felt each emotion flash over me just the way I'd seen it in Sara. I was so happy to be back here.

'You'll be wanting a drink, then,' Peej said, tucking his gun under an empty seat and picking up a bottle.

I felt the rush of blood in anticipation.

'Lee-Ann!' he shouted.

And then another person appeared out of the darkness. A

72

girl. A young woman. I stuttered when she was introduced to me. She was thin, grey and skinny. She was bleached blonde and had those stupid sculpted eyebrows. She stank of cigarettes and she was a mess. Even more than Sara and me. Lee-Ann was a junkie on cold turkey, sick for their gin and their cigarettes. And their attention.

'Hiya,' she said, and Sara smiled back at her. I kept my response to a minimum. She was young, but looked more thirty-nine than nineteen. That's drugs, for you. Smokes, and poor nutrition. And lack of vitamins. Peej seemed quite taken with her. She probably reminded him of his daughter.

Chapter Fifteen

I woke up on the grubbiest floor you could imagine. Cereal bowls furry with mould, drinks cans and empty bottles were scattered all over it. Someone was walking about and their feet were sticking to the tacky laminate. I could make her out in my peripheral vision. She lit up a cigarette and I remembered who it was. Lee-Ann.

'I'm just gonnie let a bit a light in,' she said. 'Gie the place some fresh air.'

I buried my face in the cushion serving as pillow. Dragging open the broken blind let the full sun shine in on the utter degradation of the human species. The part that was me, anyway. The sight and stench made me retch.

'Is this your place?' I asked her.

'Naw, this is – I don't know whose it is. Peej and the Boy's in the other rooms, but.'

I sat up, shielding my eyes but trying to see. 'Where's Sara?'

Junkie grinned. 'There she's!'

Sara was under the window, with what looked like curtains wrapped round her on top of her sleeping bag.

I leaned against an armchair. The seat itself was full of ripped-open mobile phone boxes. Someone had had a field day, out 'shopping'.

'Where are you from?' I asked her. I didn't want to use her name. Wide Boy had referred to her as Junkie, but not to her face.

'Ye don't waant tae know!' she laughed. And when she laughed, there was a flash of something familiar about her. Something about the eyes. Something –

Just then the door opened and Peej came in. His chin had

more stubble on it and his cheek-scar twitched when he grunted good mornings.

I was pleased to see him. He looked rough, and haggard, and God knows I'd have crossed the street to avoid him in the old days a few months ago, but he'd been respectful to me, and I felt I could trust him.

'So, doll,' he said, turning to me. 'This guy Eric.'

Apparently I'd told him about Eric and the bikers. I didn't remember doing it, but that's what happens. Anyway, Peej was curious. 'There's few enough of us as it is,' he said, when I was humming and hawing, so I gave in and we drove over. Peej would have driven over anyway, with my consent or without it.

There was no sign of bikers anywhere near The Horsebrasses Bar, but Eric must have heard our car, because I caught a glimpse of him at the upstairs window, curtain-twitching, a calculating look on his face while he examined Peej and Wide Boy, but then he brightened when Sara, Junkie and I got out. Next thing, he was downstairs, letting us in.

'We can maybe have a hair of the dog,' I said but Peej glared at me.

'You've had enough.'

So we went upstairs to that room where Sara and I had spent the night. Eric was clean cut and dapper because of helping himself to a perennial supply of new clothes. The flat was a bit whiffy, though.

Not for the first time, I felt I was on the fringes of a club I could never belong to. God, I hadn't noticed it as badly in decades. The men talked to each other. Disregarded me when I spoke. Didn't make any eye contact after the first few pleasantries. It was the same with Junkie and Sara. Though he was a bit of an ingratiating lech when he said hello to Junkie. He ran his hand down her back the way he had with me, but she, straight out, told him, 'Fuck off!' That raised a few eyebrows and for a millisecond I quite admired her.

Anyway, Peej suggested he come along with us. I wasn't keen. I found the memory of that night with him embarrassing, reinforced by the way he'd treated Junkie, and Sara seemed

75

flustered by it, too. But if there was one thing about Eric, he was affable. He and the men hit it off despite the obvious class differences, so it was decided. At least he had a bit of sophistication. I think maybe he had a wodge of resin, too, which might have had something to do with it.

But where would we go? The house Peej had been staying in was filthy. The flat above The Horsebrasses stank because of the choked toilet. Which is probably why Eric was ready to come away with us.

We made the decision to flit into the bowling club in Parkside. There weren't any bodies there. There was a kitchen, comfortable furniture – tables, chairs, soft seats. Right from the beginning we split into men and women. The men slept in the bar, the women in the function room. Peej stole a van and they broke into a furniture shop and got a half a dozen mattresses. I'd to tell them to go back for pillows and quilts.

'By the way, you look familiar,' I told Junkie when we were making up the beds. 'Did you use the local library?'

She clacked her chewing gum. 'Nuh.'

It must just be living in a small town that accounted for it. I'd have passed her in the street. Or maybe I'd seen her face in the crime column of the local newspaper. (Rolls on floor, laughing, as we used to say in social media.)

I tried really hard not to drink, but drink was one thing that was available. I told myself I needed the calories. In truth, I was full of aches and pains. My fingers and toes were white with cold and booze brought physical and emotional warmth to me. It also freed me from having to think. That sometimes meant I missed subtle signals.

'What dae you think a that guy Eric?' Junkie asked me one night when we were in our shared room and Sara was snuffling under her duvet. 'D'you no think he's a right creep?'

'Eric?'

'Aye.'

I wracked my brain. I had. But recently I hadn't. I'd been getting to know him and – to be honest – I'd liked the fact he was a cut above Peej and Wide Boy in education and manners.

And also, Eric didn't always have a go at me when he saw me start a new bottle. Also, let's face it, I'd have done anything not to agree with Junkie.

'He seems perfectly nice to me,' I told her.

She sighed and we went to sleep.

The clash came a couple of nights later. We were playing cards. I couldn't keep track because play kept changing direction, so I sat it out, settling myself on one of the long barseats against the wall, me and my bottle. I was vaguely aware of Eric moving into the space I'd been sitting in, beside Junkie. He was free with his hands – he always was, touchy-feely. Some people are like that. I was happy he wasn't like that with me. Knew better. Junkie was probably asking for it. She'd growled at him a couple of times but I zoned it out. I must have dozed off, but I woke up with a change of atmosphere. Peej's voice. Subdued. Insistent.

'The lassie told you to leave her alone.'

Eric raised his hands. 'No worries.'

I poured a drink. Peej went to the makeshift toilet.

'Och, piss off!' That was Junkie's voice.

Eric said something sotto voce. I couldn't make it out, but one arm was sprawled along the back of her chair and he was clearly far too close for her comfort. She shoved her seat back and he had to catch his balance, grinning. 'Come on,' he said. 'Just a bit of fun!' He reached for her breast – I saw that! And so did Peej.

Peej was mad. He set about Eric in a spasm of fury. He burst the skin above his right eye when he brought his head down on him. Peej's face was scarlet – there were lumps and bumps bulging on it. I'd never seen a man so overwound with anger. 'She fuckin tellt you to piss off!' he stuttered. 'So get tae!'

Sara came running and both of us were trembling. I knew Peej was dangerous. It made me question why I'd trusted him.

'Can we go, Alice?' Sara bawled between sobbing. 'I don't like him.'

'Ye'll stey where ye are!' Peej said, pointing one long arm at us. 'He's the one that's going.' He turned to Eric, who was

77

backed against the wall, head in his hand. 'Pack yer bag.'

The card deck was scattered all over the floor. Junkie and Wide Boy quietly worked together to pick them up. I needed a drink to steady my nerves.

Eric didn't take anything. He held himself upright and walked past Peej, out through the swing door. Through the window, we heard him start the ignition in one of the cars; we saw the sweep of the headlights and then he was gone.

Chapter Sixteen

That night, I woke in darkness to the sound of engine roars and Junkie shaking me to get up.

'Motorbikes!' she said.

She, Sara and I ran into the bar where the men slept. Peej and Wide Boy were already up. She was right. There were motorbikes out in the carpark.

'Fuck, Eric!' Peej said and thumped his hand on the wall. 'I knew I shouldnae trust the bastard.' He pulled Wide Boy by the sleeve, tucking him into the curtains. 'Watch for them. Tell me what you see.' I watched from behind the curtains, too.

Seven or eight bikes had turned into the car park and stood there, revving their engines. Peej rummaged in his kit for the shotgun he'd stolen from Micky's house. He tossed a hammer to Wide Boy. 'Come on.' The two men stepped out the front door, pretending they both had guns.

I couldn't hear what they were saying, but nobody moved. Sara's breath was steaming up the window and she wiped it. The biker leader glanced towards her and his body language changed. He adopted a pose. A kind of head-stag pose. Then Peej ratcheted the gun. I heard that. The man raised his head slightly, as if to say, 'Okay, okay, this is all just bravado,' then one by one they turned their bikes and left.

Except – then Eric came back. We were all just settling down again when we saw his single car headlights curve into the carpark again.

Peej wasn't happy, but Eric was persuasive. He said he'd driven out and the bikers had spotted him. But how stupid must he have been, turning tail and having the bikers shrieking and swooping straight towards us? What was he thinking? Did he really think a family car could outrun half a dozen motorbikes? That's what Peej said to me, anyway, after he'd calmed down a bit. Sara was funny, though, because she came over all concerned for Eric and insisted on helping him clean up his cuts and bruises.

I couldn't cope with all the tension. It dug up a lot of buried memories. That night I drank too much and took out my photos. I should've gone to see my brother, and my mother. We'd been through a lot together. But the gulf between her and me was just too huge to bridge, now. It was one thing making a routine weekly phone call. I could preserve my anger and my distance from her then. But now? Looking at her photo, now, I could see the resemblance. I couldn't imagine being so callous to a child as she was to me. I looked at the other little photo. The little farthing face.

'Are you alright, Alice?'

Junkie must have heard me snivelling.

'Of course I am,' I snapped and buried my photos in my backpack.

After I'd fallen asleep, someone ignited a Molotov cocktail and threw it through our window. The shouts woke me, and Sara's squeals. I came to with Junkie shaking my shoulder and I snapped at her again. I must have been really drunk. She helped Sara out of the window and tried to drag me after her, but I fought to go back. 'My bag! I need my bag!' I said, trying to peel her hands away from my arms. Peej got it; he burst into the room, saw what was going on and took control. Out on the grass, I clutched it and watched the smoke leach out of the windows and creep over the roof-tiles.

It didn't take long for the men to douse the flames, but it meant a sleepless night. And though there was no-one around we decided to move again quickly. We packed up the van with all the mattresses, bedding, clothes, tins – everything we owned. Everywhere we could think to go had bodies in it and by now – this was May and the days were getting warmer – by now you couldn't go into houses without breathing apparatus. Hospitals and hotels were out. Even the fire station.

We drove around trying to think of somewhere. Cones of

80

creamy flowers had opened in the chestnut trees. The hedgerows out of town were powdered with white. We passed two horses in a field yellow with buttercups and where it dipped, saw two swans brooding at the edge of a pool. Life went on. Without saying anything, Peej pulled over on to the hard shoulder. We got out and ate. I remember the cool damp of the grass on the underside of my knees, the all-pervasive scent of the mayflower, Sara and I looking for four leafed clover.

At one point, Sara rolled down the embankment. Next minute, we were all doing it. It made us forget we'd been arguing. For the first time since I was a child, I'd a sense of belonging. We napped in the sun for a while then piled back into the van. The encounter with the bikers had changed something. We were conscious of ourselves as a cohesive unit. Maybe the clarity of the air showed this was the moment, at the very least, to face what we had to face.

We let Peej drive us along the motorway. Several times he pulled over so we could see. The first time I got out. Up on the flyover, the streets beneath us were devoid of cars; the prison was austere, grey and unforgiving, its prisoners all doing life. The playgrounds round the tower blocks were barren as the day they were made, and over it all was the wind, which tugged locks of my hair like the ghost of the impish housing scheme kid I used to be and whistled in the fresh leaves.

Twice we saw body piles: a spaghetti bolognese of limbs, heads and clothing. We rolled up the windows and turned the other way. That was how we saw a single man carrying a guitar and walking with a border collie at his heels. Chis, he was called, and he came in the van with us.

Chapter Seventeen

That evening we returned to find our own place. Not the bowling club, but the town hall library. My library. There was no one there and it was big, with rooms over several storeys. I knew the staff room and kitchen would be comfortable. I don't know why I hadn't thought to go there sooner. Memories, perhaps. Too many memories.

We let the men hoist the mattresses, bevelling on their shoulders, and watched them carry them, stepping unevenly up the stairs. We women followed, made the beds and prepared the meal. I'd learned we could light a fire in a stainless steel sink and barbecue on the grill rack above it. Provided we kept the window open, and the kitchen door shut, the smoke wasn't overpowering and it didn't matter that it smeared the ceiling. There was water in the library, but I knew the old tank was contaminated from a story a janitor once told me about rats. There were sealed water butts in room-temperature 'coolers', and I'd left my coffee and powdered milk – and even my crossword, half done – in my locker. And an overdue book – a thriller – that Peej and the others enjoyed, the first of many, when I read it aloud. It was good to see their faces rapt in a work of fiction. But that first night we had Chis and his guitar for company, and we realised that in our rush to leave we hadn't brought any alcohol.

'I know where I can get some,' I said. I took Sara along the corridor to The Boss's office, lit by long sunset. The draught excluding seal round the door split when we entered. This room was always warmed by evening sun. Flecks of dust swirled upwards, agitated by our arrival. The Boss's seat gleamed tan leather: big, broad like his shoulders. Sara spinning in it was irreverent, but I didn't chide her. I touched the pressure point on his desk to release the drawer and took the key on the fob I'd given him. Sara was fascinated by his pens, his calculator, his coloured paperclips that she could link. I leaned over the chair back, my senses hoovering up any remnant of his scent.

Peej's hand stamped on the door handle. 'Did you find it?'

'In a minute.'

It was the third cupboard, lower drawer. It opened with the clink of bottles and we filled our arms with malt, brandy, cava. I put them on his desk so I could lock the drawer away.

'Why bother?' Peej asked.

'I like it to be tidy.'

He picked up the emerald frame on the desk, studied it and put it down. Opened his mouth as if he was going to say something then changed his mind. But maybe he read it on my face.

'Found a tin of chocolate biscuits, Sara. Chocolate fingers. You coming?'

The chair back braked against me as she jumped.

'You?'

I shook my head.

I waited till the click said the door was shut and put away the key. Sat in his chair. I slipped my fingertips along the smooth tanned armrests.

I wondered if he might still be alive. He and his wife. Maybe in some twelve bedroomed mansion in its own grounds out by Blanefield or Helensburgh. They smiled at me from the photograph. What a loving couple. I gripped it and peered at them for a long moment. Then I smashed the glass on the corner of his desk. I'd waited years to do it. I snatched the ballpoint from his desk set and scraped the pen across their faces. Christ, how I hated them.

Funny it hurt me so much after all those years. What's the loss of one baby, compared with the death of almost everyone on the planet? One baby. One tiny baby, born so many years ago. I confess I wondered if this would be the time to go and look for her. Then I told myself not to be so fucking stupid. So I went looking for a gallon of drink instead.

I woke up that first morning in the library, hungover and alone in a make-shift bed between home economics and romances.

*

'Alice! New people! Come and meet them!' Over the next months we made a good home in the library and though Chis moved on, we swelled our community with other strays. Bill and Grace came as well as the asylum seekers. They found us when Bill wandered in to borrow a book. Something to blank out time; something that didn't need technology.

I rested my hands on the banister on the way down through the library building to be introduced, held up because Sara had been sick and I'd been cleaning her up. Bill and Grace had straggled out of the city with their belongings in a shopping trolley and had met up with Basher and Limpet, on foot, following one of the country lanes sticking like spokes from the hub of the city. I don't know how they managed to strike up a conversation. Maybe they'd a lot in common: the women walking behind the men, both couples observing the same time-honoured power balance.

There were hand-shakes all round. Bill and Grace were frail elderly. We'd no idea how they'd survived. We drew them in to meet the rest of our gathering, and there was laughter and some confusion when we did the introductions. Grace seemed to think Wide Boy might have been her grandson, a role the teenage boy seemed to accept quite readily. I asked him if he was going to give them nicknames. 'Naw, naw,' he said, blushing. 'Bill and Grace'll do fine.' Maybe they were too old, too in love, too untouchable. They certainly became precious to us.

As for the asylum seekers – I'm ashamed to say I didn't quite catch their proper names. So I was quite happy when Basher accepted the name of Basher. We all just nodded when his wife told us her name. I got that it began with an L. Over the next few days, she clung to him like a Limpet, and that's how she became known. And grinning out from the back of her were the bright brown eyes of two children. The girl must have been about thirteen, I reckoned, and the boy a few years younger.

They looked fit and healthy enough.

'And what are your names?' I asked them. They were shy. The boy started playing with the door, pushing it back and forward in the door frame while Sara stared at him.

Basher said something none of us understood, except in the intonation. The boy sulked. There was a quick conversation between their mum and them, and then the older one, the girl, spoke in the local accent. 'I'm Saleema,' she said, smiling. It filled me with such hope to see children.

'And what about your brother?'

Basher called to the boy again. The child jumped and rushed over to his father, shutting the door with a slam that echoed all through the high main hall of the library.

'Uh-hu,' said Wide Boy. 'I think we all know what HIS nickname's gonnie be.'

*

In autumn we met up with Brain and The Gaffer. They'd formed a close relationship. We recognised that thing between them with the deep eye contact. Not sex: just survival. They came to us when we'd been arguing. Sara had been sick again and I was fed up having to help her change her bed. There were no washing machines, and the idea of hand-scrubbing vomit off other people's linen didn't have any of us signing up as volunteers. The hard reality of our new life was setting in and it made us argumentative. Some of us wanted to plant something to come up the following year, others couldn't see the point. The shops were stuffed with shelf after shelf of beans and potted noodles. Set against that, the fact that the last of the summer's heat had cooled and more than one of us had suggested moving south. Not to London, since the Thames could be running pus from all the bodies, but to France, maybe, or Spain. For some reason I was one of the ones who didn't want to go. Wide Boy did, and so did Junkie, but young people are always dreamers. Peej wasn't decided. Then Brain said he could cobble together some kind of car-battery-operated or environmentally friendly generator; The Gaffer corralled us into a vaguely democratic regularity, and before we knew it we were doing the conga together and heading into winter.

Chapter Eighteen

I resumed the work I'd been doing before the illness – transcribing sixteenth century court cases – only now I used an eighties typewriter I'd dug out of a heap in the basement. Sara kept herself busy, looking after Grace or the children, or spending time with Eric at the shops. He'd turned on the charm since the fight night, and – as far as I was aware – he hadn't renewed his pervy courtship of Lee-Ann. He was a model citizen.

I was more than happy to have him take Sara off my hands. I'd grown fond of her, no question, but she could be wearing. And I didn't drive, and she did love to go to the retail park. She came back, once, flaunting a little gold locket he'd given her. She made us all look at it, a glow in her eyes. So, she seemed happy enough, and for all of us, life settled into a comforting regularity. For some it was too comfortable: the women did the women's work and the men did the sitting around. The Gaffer, plump and pasty faced and reminding me too much of The Boss, seemed to sit for hours 'planning'. I watched his eyebrows rise with supercilious disdain if Peej, Basher or Wide Boy challenged his authority. I think he genuinely believed, even then, that he was designed for white collar work and they were designed for blue. Small wonder they didn't relish a return to civilisation.

These old buildings were cold. All the heat from the calor gas fires we'd found was sucked up into the glamorous ceilings; by November the walls were sweated with damp. I began to wish The Boss had had the whole place carpeted instead of going for the modern marble, beech and laminate look and I cursed the decision he'd made to rip out the ancient oil boiler in favour of nuclear generated electricity.

Brain was exempt from The Gaffer's supervision. He spent

his mornings sleeping and his afternoons experimenting with his generator. When we complained we weren't seeing results he rigged up a petrol driven one to raise the temperature a degree or two in the main library. But it was nonsensical: we had to open the windows to let the fumes out. When my fingers grew too numb to type I went looking for him to see if there was some way he could modify it.

'What are you doing?' I asked, catching sight of a faint blue glaze from the nearest computer screen. He was cycling on the spot, dark grey circles under his arms.

He swung his leg off the bike but pumped a pedal with one hand. With no self-consciousness he lifted the pale grey waistband of his sweatshirt to wipe sweat from his face, caught me evaluating him then ignored me and typed in commands one-handed at the keyboard.

I stepped closer, away from the door frame where I'd been hugging myself in Helen-who-used-to-work-here's heavy brown cardigan.

'Have a go at pedalling, will you?' he said.

I shrugged, but he'd looked away by then. Intrigued, I took hold of the other pedal and turned it. It reminded me of when my mother let me wind the handle of the wringer for the clothes. As I wound I had a flash of her leaning over the sink where she'd be washing, her crossed-over burgundy floral pinafore covering up her coarse woven skirt and knitted top. I thought a lot about my mother in those days and it wasn't all bad.

There'd be safety pins in the pinafore and kirbies. She'd straighten and open the kirby in her teeth, a drip rolling up her muscled forearm, her sleeves pushed up past the elbows. We only really had it easy for a generation, women. She'd stroke the hair out of my eyes and kirby it into place, then coil a short front lock of her own glossy brown hair and secure it with another pin. Then she'd feed the clothes through the rollers as I wrestled the handle through its mangling circle, the cloudy expelled water sluicing into the sink. In later life she was diagnosed with the repetitive strain injury tennis elbow: as if women like her had time for leisure like that. How hard would her life be, now? I chewed the inside of my cheek pretty much the way that guilt gnawed at my stomach. I knew I should go to see if she'd survived.

Brain's head was bent towards the screen. I didn't know how he used to wear his hair but it had grown in the couple of months since he'd arrived with us and needed kirbied. I didn't have any but I remember thinking how sweet his hair was with its blond and brown curls. It was greasy at the top – hygiene not being easy for any of us – and fell into ringlets, almost, knitting with the reddish brown young hairs on his chin. He must only have been in his mid twenties. Our future depended on men like him.

'Can you just do it the way I told you?' he scowled, pushing up the sleeve of his tracksuit to expose the same blond hairs and smooth skin up to his pointy elbow.

'I never learned how to go a bike,' I told him.

'It's not exactly going anywhere.'

The bike was a mangle of wires and metal clips with serrated, crocodile teeth and he'd rigged it, wheel-less, on a couple of wooden shelves. I climbed on and winced as the thin hard seat pressed against my bones.

With me pedalling he applied two hands to booting up and I finally realised the enormity of what he was doing. Imagine if he could make the computer work again and we could still log on to the Internet. Imagine if things were normal somewhere in the rest of the world and he could get in touch with them. No wonder The Gaffer had such faith in him.

'Harder.'

Now he was getting C:\ prompts and he typed codes into the screen. That was the limit of my understanding, but after eight months even I greeted the start-up beeps with a joy I didn't realise I could experience. My thighs were beginning to feel the strain but Brain was engrossed so I occupied my mind by glancing round the computer suite. Six workstations; 'new' leaflet dispensers stuffed with untidy leaflets; the empty water siphon. My legs were aching. Finally I said, 'I'm going in a cramp, Brain.'

His blond curls twitched but his fingers keyed in Go To 0650 or something. Too intent to be listening.

'I'll really need to stop,' I said.

He scratched his thumbnail down his back and said, 'I'll get someone.' I flinched when I felt his hand at the back of my waist as he passed behind me to the door. 'Keep at it or we'll be back where we started,' he told me. In the Perspex leaflet dispensers I saw his grey reflection bobbing up the stairs.

It really wasn't fair, making me do this. That's the arrogance of men. But I didn't want to let him down. My legs ran on the pedals; my eyes ran round the walls. The purple panelling was as good as last year when they'd installed it. I compelled my legs to work on completing one more and then one more up and down cycle. I always was good at endurance: that's how I'd made it in the old world. Now I was warm but the last symbol of MS-Dos code was flickering; my legs were heavy yet I wanted him to be pleased with me so I willed the power not to go out.

At last I heard feet in the marble hall behind me. I wondered who he'd managed to persuade. Their reflection seemed black on the leaflet dispensers. I groaned, 'At last! I thought you were never coming.'

'Are you that desperate?'

I flew off the bike at the unfamiliar voice but my legs wouldn't support me; I crashed my back against Brain's computer. Two strangers were standing in the doorway, one tapping his fingers against the door frame. 'My friends are coming back,' I said, trying to stand up on legs numb from pedalling.

'Your mate Eric, you mean? We'll not worry about him.' The speaker stepped towards me, his cheeks pulled up and exposing the yellow between the spaces of his teeth. Unruly ginger hair adhered to his scalp as if it had been wet and pressed to it and there was a pressure mark around his face that made the skin puffed and purplish. He lifted one side of Helen's Aran cardigan. I snatched it out of his hand but he picked it up again. 'She cannae wear that,' he said to his friend, 'if she wants to be a biker.'

'Get off!' I said and swatted him, but his hands repositioned themselves faster. I slapped his fists; I battered my hands against his shoulders. 'Get off me!' I said again but he dropped me to the floor and my weak legs couldn't do anything to prevent it.

The room shrank like one time I was stuck in a lift. I dug my nails into his armour. It was thick and black. I tore at his ears because only they were exposed and vulnerable. 'Get off!' I said, my words gasped, but I should've lain quiet.

His cheeks deformed under my fingers but his neck and jaw stayed strong. I pushed my fists into the warm folds under his chin, his whiskers wiry on the backs of my hands.

'She tickles!' he said and gripped my two wrists in one fist.

There were men's voices through the ceiling. And screaming. I thought about Sara. Saleema. The rape of the Sabine women. I even worried about Junkie.

I was too charged with fight or flight to feel it. I heard the toes of his boots squeak against the parquet. I saw leaflets dispense all around like confetti. Under the desktops I saw grey clumps of dried chewing-gum.

Then the first one pulled away and in the cold I felt the pain and drew my knees up but the other one split me again like a chicken, his lank hair drizzling oil on me. He breathed on me: catarrh and cigarettes. He sucked his drooling saliva at my ear and I cried for my mother.

Chapter Nineteen

They left when they heard shouting on the stairs and feet running. They didn't even ask if I was alright.

My hands shook as I drew up my trouser zip and fixed the little metal flap in place. I curled my ankles up to the side and drew Helen's cardigan around me, watching through the door as men ran downstairs towards the emergency exit, an eruption of them, black tar, howling and rollicking down the marble staircase with our men at their backs. A volley of hardback books flew over the banister and one of the new beech chairs splintered as it hit the white and black marble flooring, its lilac upholstered seat pad skidding between the intruders' feet.

My face was wet; I wiped it on the scratchy wool of Helen's cardigan. Poor Helen: Helen was such a livewire of a girl. I was glad I had her cardigan to comfort me. There were voices in the hall but they were our own, loud, panicked even, Wide Boy's high and girly and I thought he'd never live that down but he ran into the computer suite and barely took time to recognise me.

'Need to get a couple of they tables,' he yelled, his voice abrasive but familiar.

'Wide Boy,' I said, and cried with my face in the cardigan.

There was a pause as if maybe he looked at me. Probably wouldn't have half a clue how to deal with me. He just repeated, 'Need to get a couple of they tables. Barricade the door,' followed by the squeal-judder-shudder of furniture legs on the wooden floor and onto the hall's marble.

'Watch the computers.' Brain's voice.

I'd smashed into his live one.

'What happened?' he asked from the doorway. He was

nursing his upper arm. 'Did you fall on it?' He picked up a strip of jagged plastic. I must have smashed it. The bike and the computer had been knocked over and shattered. I'd let him down and I hadn't even noticed.

'I'm sorry,' I said, edging aside along the floor. There was blood on his sleeve. Not much, but he'd hurt it. He saw me look at it. 'Are you alright?' I asked him.

He peeled his fingers away. 'One of them hit me with a chain.' He pulled his sleeve up to show me. The chain had slit through the knit of the sweat shirt and left a ragged imprint in blue and red.

'There's a first aid box in the janitor's office.'

His attention had turned to the other computers. He was lifting them, awkwardly, in time for Wide Boy to push the heavy desks out of the room.

I finger-combed my tousled hair. 'Is everyone alright?'

He didn't answer, busy examining the damage I'd caused.

'Is everyone alright?' I repeated.

'Everybody's fine, Yakkity,' Wide Boy said, coming back in the door for another table. 'Just shaking.' He hesitated for a minute. 'Just like you.'

I nodded. My legs still felt like they could buckle under me but I rose to my feet, trying to act normal. The men were high and busy. I waited for Wide Boy to push-drag a table through the door.

'I'm sorry about your computer,' I told Brain.

'Yeah, yeah,' he said, his back still towards me.

I wanted the longest ever shower. To feel hot water washing it all away from me. I took two or three tight steps to the doorway, rested my hand on the curling grain where the second one had tapped at the door frame. I stared at Brain's golden curls and the spine of dampness down his sweatshirt and remembered what I'd been thinking minutes before. I felt sick. Then I said, 'I'll go and see the others.'

Chapter Twenty

They'd broken in through a basement window. The library had been built on a hill and the back basement windows used to be barred till some piece of modern regulation. Our men did their best to barricade them temporarily and we had a meeting that evening. The bikers had smashed up some of the library's paintings; they'd knocked over a couple of bookcases and pissed all over Basher's prayer mat and he was devastated but that was the only damage. I was the only one who'd been hurt but I didn't have any visible bruises. Limpet and Junkie were cuddling Salaam and Saleema; Sara and I sat side by side, not touching. I didn't tell her what had happened to me: she was already shaken. I didn't tell anyone. I wanted them to know but I couldn't tell anyone. I felt cold; I sat with my quilt round me. Not one of them looked at me and suspected there was something wrong. Not even Peej.

'Why did they do it?' I asked him as we gathered in the reference area to discuss it, but he just shrugged. Why did anybody do violent things?

Peej wasn't good at council meetings. Not just because of his speech impediment. The Gaffer tried to run them along the old lines; honourable gentleman, deferring respectfully. Peej was uncomfortable with all that and I was glad because I wasn't in the mood for it either. The Gaffer gave a speech; a politician's pep talk about hard times and how we had to band together and how this experience would make us more resilient.

I watched his puffy white skin and pumped up opinion of himself and my words stabbed out in the middle of his gibberish. 'But why did they do it? How is a big speech going to prevent them doing it again?'

The Gaffer stopped with his mouth open. Blinked a few times then raised his eyebrows. Eric made sympathetic cooing noises. I didn't trust him. Why did the bikers mention him? The old suspicions came back.

'Shut up!' I shouted at them. I knew I sounded petulant.

'Alice!' The Gaffer scolded.

'Well, I can't cope with it anymore,' I said, or something. Sara put her hand on my arm and when my throat cracked so that I couldn't speak she passed me the water bottle.

'It's been hard for us all,' The Gaffer said and clicked his pen a few times. 'So if we could move on to discussing how to secure the building.' Emotional outbursts didn't fit his meetings etiquette.

'Wait,' I said. The bottle glooped as I lowered it and around me everyone stopped talking.

The Gaffer sighed and licked his lips. 'What?'

'Ask Eric what he knows about it,' I said.

Eric looked blankly at me. Everyone turned their heads from him to me.

'Ask Eric.'

'Eric?' The Gaffer said.

He grinned, and ran a hand over his thick black hair. 'I don't know why she's picking on me.'

The Gaffer turned to me. 'Alice?'

I was sure they'd said his name. Hadn't they? Just before they'd raped me? I couldn't meet his eyes. I squeezed my hands in my lap and couldn't meet his eyes.

'Have you something to say about it?'

'What is it, doll?' Peej said, his voice softer than usual.

I risked a glance at him. 'I don't want to live here any longer.'

It was me who'd suggested coming here and in the five months till then life had been better. It was too dangerous, now.

'It was no big deal,' Brain said quietly. He blew on his wounded arm for dramatic effect. 'This place has everything. We just need to block up the downstairs windows.'

'Not really,' Junkie said. 'You don't have the problem of the ladies' toilets.'

95

He sneered. 'You can say goodbye to flushing toilets.'

'You don't seriously want to go, do you?' The Gaffer asked me. 'We've loads of space. Shops nearby. We've got everything we need.'

'Alice?' Peej said, when I didn't answer.

I pulled my quilt tighter around my shoulders. In another life the library had been my haven. My heaven. It had also been my place of greatest sorrow. And now the same extremes were repeating themselves. But did I really want to leave?

Sara kneeled up and put her arm round my back. 'If Alice's going, I'm going too,' she said.

That was almost too much. I couldn't keep the quiver from my voice. 'I don't want those men breaking in.'

Still excitable, Wide Boy said, 'But Yakkity, we can keep the bastards out!'

There was a rapping sound and we all looked at Basher, whose forehead was creased with concentration. He spoke to Saleema.

'Wait,' she said. 'He wants me to translate.' Apart from her small voice, there was no noise. Except The Gaffer's pen clicking. She slid back round to face the circle, her face tipping down as she began to speak. 'My dad thinks we should go and live nearer the country.'

The men on my side of the room strained to hear her. Peej said, 'Ask your old man what he really means.'

Over the top of the quilt, my eyes sought alliances while Saleema and her father spoke but mostly I met thin lips and closed faces. They all liked it here. They all felt safe upstairs, as if we were in some kind of castle. If I left, I would have to leave on my own with Sara.

The Gaffer was sitting close to me, on the other side of Sara. He stretched his pen out and tapped my quilt, making me jump. 'You don't seriously want to go, do you?' he said, quietly. His jowls folded on his collar. His eyebrows were in disorder and I could even see his nasal hairs. He'd made my heart thud just by tapping at me. He was big and coarse or at least I saw him that way and was repulsed by him. By all of them. I didn't know if

I answered him or if I just shook.

'My father thinks we should plant crops and look after the animals,' Saleema said. She had a dimple in one cheek when she bit her lips, shy about speaking in the men's company. She pulled her scarf closer round her neck and hair and her mother rested her hand on her back.

When I looked back at The Gaffer he was skimming through his notebook and muttering to Eric and Brain, seated on his other side. Grace asked Bill if we were missing Eastenders. Saleema's voice hesitated.

Peej leaned over and rapped Basher's tea tumbler on the floor. 'Let her speak.'

She pressed her lips together and swallowed. 'He thinks it would be a good place to go, out to the fields, where the brambles are. Where Peej takes us.' She was blushing.

'Dykend? Dykend? That's fucking crazy,' Wide Boy said.

'Saleema,' Peej said. He never found it hard to say her name. He mostly tripped up over Js, like his own name, Jamieson, which was why he always introduced himself as Peej. 'Tell your dad I'm with him.'

'What?' Wide Boy said and my hopes rose.

'But we fight to the last man first.'

There was a flurry like nausea round the gathering. I couldn't sit still. 'You don't mean it,' I said, while the words were still rumbling.

'Fuck, aye,' said Peej, his cheek ticking. 'Nobody's messing me around. We're here and this is where we're staying. They'll just have to get used to that.'

'Too right.' His echo.

'I don't want those men breaking in again,' I said, my eyes pleading directly to The Gaffer. But he didn't see. He was clicking his pen and his eyes were focused on the floor and it looked as if Peej had the upper hand that evening. I was assailed by loneliness. I sank my chin and mouth further into the quilt.

'Why don't we put it to a vote,' The Gaffer said, eventually. 'All those in favour of staying here in the library, raise your hand.' Immediately, he, Peej, Wide Boy, Brain, Eric and Junkie

97

lifted their hands into the air. Sara looked at me, her hand poised to lift but I frowned at her and shook my head the tiniest bit till she clasped her hand in her lap. She pushed her chin into the air, a satisfied smile on her face.

'Say it again?' Bill said and when The Gaffer repeated the proposal he shook his head. 'No, no,' he said, then grasped Grace's hand and raised it with his.

'Raise your hand to *stay* here, Bill!' I said and he stared at me then lowered his hand decisively.

'That's what I meant,' he said. And nodded.

'Basher?' Peej said.

Basher whispered with Limpet and Saleema then shook his head.

The Gaffer raised an eyebrow then set his jaw together while he looked at Peej. 'Split decision,' he said. 'We keep the status quo.' To the rest of us he said, 'Motion carried,' looked at his watch and scribbled in his notebook.

'We'll keep up the defence,' Peej said before The Gaffer had even finished, 'for the next few nights. If there's any more bother, Wide Boy and me'll go for more guns.' He was chiefly telling The Gaffer. 'I know where to get them.' His cheek ticked as he looked round the circle. 'If there's an escalation, we go out after them.'

The meeting broke up.

'Alice?' Peej said, catching me in the corridor. 'Are you alright?'

I couldn't bring myself to look at him. 'Yes,' I said. I went to move away but he gripped my upper arm. I tugged it back.

'What's this about Eric?'

'Let me go.' I broke away but paused at the door of the room I shared with Sara. 'Violence won't get us anywhere,' I told him, struggling to control my breathing. 'Violence only breeds more violence.'

He took his coiled belt out of his jacket pocket, threaded it through his trouser loops and fastened its heavy buckle. 'Sometimes you need to get tough if you want to live in peace.'

I shook my head, went into the room and closed the door.

Chapter Twenty-one

We waited in the library for three more days. Each night our men took it in turns to guard. Each night the bikers came back, making some attempt either to break in or otherwise harass us. The second night they did the petrol trick again and set fire to the tables blocking their original way in. The smoke percolated up through the building but Brain was on guard and had the foresight to douse it with a fire-extinguisher. I crept down the stairs with some of the others to see if he needed help. His eyes were wild but he was high on excitement.

'Why are they here again?' I asked Eric, while Peej was standing in the background.

'How would I know?' he said then completely cut me off by turning his back to me and entering into a conversation with Peej.

I heard them talk tactics; a decision was made to muscle some of our ancient filing cabinets to block the basement exit and window. A four drawer with a two drawer on top of it. They contained our 20 century ephemera – all our primary and secondary school handbooks; programmes and posters for events in the Council's halls and theatres; electioneering fliers and anti-war rally leaflets. All threatened. I pleaded but Peej wouldn't listen.

'Go to bed,' he said in a sweep from my toes to my face. 'You're just getting in the way.'

The bikers drank the night out in the car park. By morning they had gone but the bottles and cans they left clattered against the kerbs as the wind shook them.

The next day Peej and Wide Boy headed out with the shotgun brandished unashamedly in Peej's hand. They were gone for hours. I paced, those hours, two of my steps to every second. One hundred and twenty steps a minute. My library floor witnessed more footfalls than in a hundred years of borrowing.

They came back carrying two black holdalls. I saw the exultation on Wide Boy's face; Peej at least had the decency to keep his expressionless. He emptied the first bag on one of our heavy wooden tables, scarring it with the metal edge of rifles, hunting knives and bullets. As the contents of the second clunked to the table top I was sure I saw grenades.

'Have you all gone crazy?' I said. Since the previous day I'd cleaned myself up with a cloth and a bottle of water, had burned my clothes, and changed from the skin layer out, but I was still wearing Helen's cardigan. Now I folded my arms across myself, my fingers clinging to the seams. My stomach was sour and I pressed into it so I could speak. 'You're planning murder?' I said. 'When there's hardly anyone left?'

The Gaffer looked to Peej to reply.

'I'm not looking for trouble,' Peej said, eyes evaluating his haul. Then he raised his eyes to me before nodding towards the windows. 'I'm just protecting you from them out there.'

'Why are they here again?' I asked, but no one had any answers. The Gaffer was sitting on one of the tables, beside the one with the guns. 'What are they doing it for?' He folded his arms across his chest, kept his mouth firmly shut and looked to Peej.

I crossed to the windows while they familiarised themselves with their arsenal but I couldn't escape the jubilation in their voices or the shriks and clicks of the guns as the men served their initiation.

'Promise me this,' I called to them from the window, struggling to keep my voice under control. 'If they don't use guns on us, you won't use guns on them.'

Peej's sinewy hands manipulated a heavy grey gun. I thought he wasn't going to speak. His right hand jerked up and back, ratcheting the weapon.

'No promises, Yakkity.' His face was immobile and his stutter had disappeared. 'We need to keep a step ahead.'

I shook my head and turned to the window; thought about the anti-nuclear rallies I used to go to at Faslane and the pig-headedness of the opposition. How easily the whole thing kicked off.

'We're not the ones looking for trouble, Alice,' Brain said to my back. 'But I'm damned sure if they come for me I'm going to be ready.'

Chapter Twenty-two

I was playing snap with Sara, Salaam and Saleema upstairs when a bird struck the window. It bounced off and Salaam ran to see where it had fallen but it wasn't a bird. A second stone shattered the glass and shards feathered his head, shoulders and arms. I grabbed him away amid the screaming. More stones holed the glass and we huddled behind the paperback bookstands but they had too many gaps. Limpet teased at the fragments that had sliced into Salaam's face and arms. His short breaths exhaled in shrill screams, sore in my ears. Lines of bright red dribbled down his cheek.

The men had been posted in the basement and at the front door as soon as the bikers had returned but Eric and Wide Boy came running to investigate the screaming; Eric dragged us, bowed down, to the corridor that ran inside the front of the building while Wide Boy picked up one of the heaviest missiles, opened a window and lobbed it. He shouted through the windows at them, but there was too much of a cacophony to make out what he said.

I wanted out. I crouched in the darkening corridor, my insides convulsing; I wanted to run or I wanted a hole I could hide in. Saleema was trying to help her mother take care of her shuddering brother; Bill and Grace were brought to sit in the corridor with us and Junkie appeared with a thick length of wood and a candle.

Then there was a bang.

There were shouts and running. Someone began wailing. Men's voices boomed in the marble stairwell. I covered my mouth with my hand and discovered that my face was awash and that my lips wouldn't stop blubbering. The wailing went on and on. I wrapped my arms around my legs and rocked to obliterate it.

'What's the matter with her?' I heard Wide Boy say, far away, silhouetted against the stair window.

Wailing. Wailing.

'I don't know,' Junkie shouted, beside my ear. 'Got a fright or something.'

'She cracking up?'

'Shh,' Junkie said and I felt her arms pulling me tight against her. 'What's going on, Widey? What's Peejie doing?'

'He's fired the gun above their heads to scare them.'

Junkie's hand touched my cheek and I forced my face away from her.

'You're alright,' she said to me, wiping my face with her jumper sleeve. 'Calm down, Alice: you're alright. Peejie's taking care of it.'

*

The following morning I asked Peej to reconsider. Now the windows of the upper floors were being boarded up; the purple display panels had to be taken from the walls and nailed over the holes and broken glass. Only the topmost panes were left clear. A few more well-aimed stones would deal with those. Then where would we be? Prisoners in the dark, unable to see what was coming. He was three feet above me, standing on the table he'd used to give him height to board up the window. Peej was no giant: five foot eight, maybe, and thin, with no excess flesh on him, even though our diet then consisted of tinned and dried ready meals and biscuits. His sleeves were rolled up and as he turned to me, toying with the hammer, I could see the muscles in his wrist and arm stretch and clench with it.

'It's not me, Yakkity,' he said. 'They voted for the status quo and you know it.'

'But it wasn't a fair question,' I said, 'the way it was worded. You didn't get a majority agreement to stay.'

His eyebrows raised. 'And you did?'

'No, I didn't, but you know we'd have been equal if the other four had voted with Sara and me.'

103

He searched in his pocket for another couple of nails and put them in his mouth.

I carried on. 'You heard what Basher said about living in the country, and Bill and Grace.'

He wiped the nails out of his mouth again. 'You think Bill and Grace want to move again at their time of life? With all the stuff they've accumulated? We'd need a two tonne truck.'

Their room in the library was filling up with antiques Bill had raided from shops in the town, hurling them through the deserted streets in his shopping trolley.

I played my ace. 'Bill and Grace'll go where the homemakers go. You know that. Where Limpet and Saleema and Sara and I go.'

The tic on his cheek started twitching. He turned away and hammered three more nails into the purple panel then squatted with one hand on the table and jumped down.

'Excuse me.'

I stepped back and he moved over to where Wide Boy was struggling to manipulate the next panel. I watched them working; it took another five minutes but I didn't go away.

When he jumped down from the table this time I said to him, 'At least consider it seriously.'

From the door Saleema announced that lunch was ready.

'At least let's go and look at it.'

Chapter Twenty-three

After lunch a party of us went scouting to check what it would be like to live in the country. We went in the jeep with The Gaffer driving. I'd hardly left home since the summer – picking up that transcription work I'd been involved in before the illness – and on the few occasions when I did it never stopped surprising me how unchanged the town was. Houses, more houses; the factories standing idle; the gym: you could persuade yourself that people were alive behind those windows if it weren't for the deserted roads and the silence. And the jungle of grass.

When we reached the edge of town Peej jumped out and unwound the four lengths of barbed wire so we could drive on to the fields. Groups of us had been here sporadically to gather blackberries, mushrooms, and scavenge for any crops that might have self-seeded or that the farmer might have sown before he'd died, like the turnip field.

We knew a slope that faced south-east. South-west would probably have been better, but that was the way the land lay, looking over the river valley 600 feet down over the gentle rise that was the town of Hamilton. It had been one of our sunlit mornings: our days here usually start bright but you can guarantee it'll be overcast by lunch. That day, the sunlight had lasted. When we stood there that afternoon, me, Peej, The Gaffer, Basher and Junkie, the air was sparkling with freshness though there was the sharp bite of wind coming in from the east. Unusual, that, and it almost put me off, but I knew the predominant currents were from the west so this spot would be shielded from the wind and facing the sun. Good farming conditions, Basher assured us, the only one likely to have a clue.

We trudged over the rough ground. Autumn grass and docks

had grown thigh high and knitted. The three men walked faster, leaving me to follow with Junkie. She looked as pleased with my company as I was with hers. She walked with her arms folded and her permanent scowl. I still felt vulnerable so we didn't speak.

The edge of the wind cut like a blade. I stopped with my back to it while the men went off to examine something in some bushes. Even so, the tears rolled down my cheeks. The wind was to blame but I didn't really need an excuse. I was still feeling sorry for myself. I liked living in the library: I must have been a masochist to suggest this. Sure, I loved the country and had been happy to take an occasional turn foraging in the fields, but living here?

There was a farmhouse on top of the hill. 'Shouldn't we take a look up there?' I asked the men when they came over.

Peej followed my pointing finger. 'Too obvious.'

The Gaffer agreed. 'Any lights and activity up there would be seen for miles.' He put a pair of binoculars to his eyes. 'If they thought we were here, that's the first place they'd look.'

It was weird now he and Peej agreed on something.

'But you'd be better able to defend it,' Junkie said. 'Cause if they could see us we'd be able to see them.'

'D'you want to spend the rest of your life looking over your shoulder?'

I looked from him to her and thought I caught something of a quiver, but maybe that was the way it was when anyone spoke to Peej. You felt, with his speech impediment, that you were being let in to a special place, with the effort he had to make and the intimacy of the time spent in communication.

Junkie sniffed. 'My whole life's been spent looking over my shoulder.'

'So? Now's your chance to end it.'

I felt like I was missing something. 'What exactly is it you're suggesting?'

He turned his pale eyes to me, that watery blue like sunlight lightening up clear burn water, letting you see to the stones. 'A shaft I know about's worth a try.'

106

'A shaft?' My eyes met Junkie's. 'D'you mean a mine-shaft?'

But he wasn't answering. He and the other men brought rope from the car, secured it on the thickest trunks of the hawthorn bushes and took turns – all action heroes – at lowering themselves into this hole in the earth. I hadn't even noticed it was there. It was scary to think the ground opened up in the middle of the field like that. That it could open up and swallow you.

'That's what happened to that young man.' I said it to Junkie. 'Do you remember? A few years ago. Swallowed up when he was walking his dog.'

'Now Peejie wants us to live in it? Fucking right, man,' Junkie muttered. She found a perch on a boulder and sat with her parka hood up round her ears and her knees together, smoking. 'No fucking way.'

I went to sit beside her and she made room.

'What d'you think, Alice?'

If it was true, I couldn't believe it. I couldn't believe what they were doing. The place was desolate. The leaves on the trees had all but fallen. The sun was shining but I knew it could be bleak. Yet what kind of life now wouldn't be bleak? Hadn't I spent half a winter already, after the flu struck, miserable? The library was the only place that had given me any respite, but because of the bikers that too was coming to an end. Could we talk peace? Could I? After what they'd done? I still didn't understand why it was they were persecuting us. 'I don't know,' I told Junkie.

'Well I fucking do.'

'Do you think they're just doing this as a shock tactic?' I asked her. 'A trick on me, to jolt me out of my idea about leaving?'

She shrugged her shoulders and cracked her gum. Of course, she'd voted with them, I thought, so she could be in league with them.

Here at least you could see down the road was clear: no one would be able to sneak up on us that way – we'd hear the noise of their bikes from miles off, carried on the quiet air.

107

Peej and Basher had disappeared down the hole. The Gaffer was listening for them and waiting his turn to descend.

I pulled my coat tighter round me and picked a sticky willie bur off it. As much to persuade myself as her I said, 'They say it's warm underground. The miners used to strip off because it was so hot.'

Junkie didn't need to comment. The disdain in her eyes said it all.

There was no sign of Peej and Basher. The Gaffer, standing with his hands in his pockets, caught my eye. 'You'd rather have this than where we are now?'

I looked away, assuming the question was rhetorical.

'We could live anywhere,' Junkie said. 'Fucking Buckingham Palace.' She thought for a minute and scratched her scalp. 'Culzean Castle. I went there with the school when I was wee. Loudoun Castle country fucking park.'

There was a warm buzz where our thighs contacted. The Gaffer had turned away. 'Junkie,' I said, in a moment of weakness.

'What?'

I so wanted to confide in someone.

'What?'

Peej's head appeared in the tangle obscuring the shaft entrance. He grasped The Gaffer's hand and clambered out.

'Well?' The Gaffer said.

First he didn't say anything. He straightened up, pressed his hands on the back of his waist and stretched. 'It would be okay,' he said. Then he must have read our faces. 'As a last resort, right?' He took the strain on the rope while The Gaffer descended.

When it went slack he asked me if I wanted to go down but my thoughts were full of the news I'd wanted to confide in Junkie.

'Maybe. In a minute,' I answered.

'You, Lee-Ann?'

'Fucking right and I'll not.' She ground her cigarette out on the grass. 'You serious? You going to go down there?' she asked

108

me.

There was an orange tidemark round her face in the sharp daylight; a speckled line of dandruff from when she'd scratched her head was waxed in her hair. There was something comforting about her face when I was up this close to her. Probably just a Scottish thing. Something across the eyes.

'It's alright – I'll go with the majority,' I said, almost under my breath. 'Whether it means staying or moving.' I didn't know what I wanted, except to be safe and in company. I couldn't really face six wintry months wandering hopelessly no matter how much I loved Sara. I'd miss all the others.

We heard Basher's voice and Peej took the strain on the rope again while the two men climbed out.

'What d'you think, then?' Peej asked The Gaffer. From his facial expression, Basher was apparently a convert.

'It's sheltered,' he said and looked at me. 'Are you ready?'

I shrugged. I didn't have it in me to go rope climbing.

'You wanted this: I think you ought to look at it,' The Gaffer said.

'I don't think I wanted this,' I said, meaning the pit.

'Women and kids are going to have to live in it,' Peej added. 'On our say-so.' His eyes were clear to the bottom. 'I'll come down with you.' He blinked and his gaze moved to Junkie. 'Both of you.'

'That'll be fucking right.' She'd folded her arms again and stuck her boots out, legs crossed at the ankles.

'Alice?'

I looked from Peej to Junkie and the others. I still couldn't tell if they were scaremongering. I still didn't know what I wanted. And I knew I had a fear of being shut in so could I ever think it would be good to live down a pit?

'Ready?'

Peej would go down first. They explained how I should bear my weight, weaving one hand and arm round the rope like bindweed while walking my feet down the wall. Abseiling without a safety harness. My underarms were stinging with terror-sprung sweat and I could smell it through my clean clothes, which further upset me, but then they were rank themselves, the men, so they wouldn't notice. Besides, did it really matter? I was about to descend a black pit shaft with no idea of the drop and not a clue how I'd manage to climb back up and no time for even a thought about what kind of beasts and slime there'd be on the way down.

'Keep calm,' Peej was saying as he clambered in. 'I'll be right below you.' His eyes, bright in his gaunt face, winked. 'I'll soften your fall.'

From pit bottom we heard him call and the rope pulsed.

'On you go,' The Gaffer said briskly.

'How far is it?' I asked him.

'Not far. You'll be fine.' He looked away, over the hillside.

I curled the rope the way they'd shown me and glanced back at Junkie. She turned her head away from me. The Gaffer and Basher tried to hold the brambles back from springing in my face as I squatted beside the hole. The rounded edge was slippery with long grass and the hole looked black.

'I'm scared,' I said, searching The Gaffer's eyes, and Basher's, for Peej's calm. There was little in The Gaffer's.

'Go,' Basher said, moving my hands on the rope. 'Like this.' It was more words, I think, than he'd ever spoken to me.

I swung my legs in but couldn't think what came after. I sat anaesthetised by the smell of the soil, my feet in the void, lacking the skills.

'On you go,' The Gaffer said, his hand prodding my shoulder.

'I can't,' I said, trying to scramble back up to my feet. 'I don't know how to.'

Junkie laughed, a cynical peel. 'How the fuck d'you expect Bill and Grace to do it, well?'

'Come on,' The Gaffer said, his fingers and thumb firm on my shoulder.

My hands were fumbling. 'I just need to clean my glasses.' I let go of the rope and dug around in my pocket for a hankie.

'You can do it,' Peej's disembodied voice ascended to us. 'Alice – just hold the rope and dreep it.'

Dreep it. I remembered sitting on a gritty wall, tiny

compared with the height of it, and crying because I didn't know how to get down. And looking up to see the girls running back across the football pitch with my young brother, just fourteen months younger than me, and how he climbed it so he'd be able to demonstrate. So long ago and so alien. It was a world I thought was lost but it was still part of me.

I put my glasses back on and gripped the rope the way they'd told me. Trying to override my brain and act on pure instinct, I turned on to my stomach then let myself drop.

As I tumbled in I heard The Gaffer gasp.

There was a thump as the tree and the men caught my weight and I swallowed, the coarse coiled rope burning the back of my hand. Like a hanged man I dangled, scrambling around till I remembered to make my feet find the wall of the shaft and I could catch my breath again. I inched down, scared to let go of each secure handhold on the rope but knowing I had to let go or I'd be stuck till my arms gave out and I fell. If I moaned I didn't notice; if they shouted words of encouragement, I didn't hear them. I was only aware of the fibres of the twined rope gripped in my palm and my feet scrabbling against the slippery shaft walls. And spinning whenever I lost my foot holds.

Somewhere around me was the dribble of water. The top of the hole grew smaller and more distant till I couldn't make out the features of The Gaffer and Basher's faces against the bright full moon of the shaft opening. There was a damp earthy smell and knuckly root branches. My eyesight adjusted as the shaft grew deeper but it felt as if my shoulders were tearing; my arms being ripped out of their sockets. There was water and coal and mica gleaming. Nearer the bottom there were no more roots or glints but only darkness, till Peej's torch lit the rounded faces of protruding boulders and then his hands gripped my legs and hips and guided me down to safe footing.

'Alright?' he said, his hands on my arms.

There was relief and a certain mustiness. His breath was moist on my cheek.

'They won't pull the rope up, will they?'

'If they do I'll fucking batter them.'

He held the lit torch under his chin until I started to giggle. Heady stuff, adrenaline-fuelled.

'Will you hold my hand, Peej?'

He took it without speaking. His was dry and hot from the rope, just like mine.

He flashed the light round the small circle to show me, finishing at the entrance to the seam.

'It goes back for miles. I don't know how far.' The seam was only about chest height and he bent to go in.

I held back. 'It's not like that all the way is it?'

'No, no – it's fine. Look.'

He pulled me to a crouch and shone the light in. There was a slight rise to the ground and I'd a stupid thought about ramped access for wheelchair users but I shook it from my head.

We passed through the crouching bit. The earth was crumbly and slippery and would have to be swept. After three or four steps I was able to stand in the seam proper. Peej shone the torch on the ceiling above our heads and we could see the tool markings.

He shone the light on the floor and took a few steps. I followed him. He shone in a pattern of ceiling to ground, ceiling to ground then left and right so we didn't bump into anything. The sound was dulled as if I'd headphones over my ears. The ground was rough, but not as rough as I'd expected. There was no sign of wheel tracks or rails.

'The whole thing must've been hewed out and carried out on men's backs.'

'Aye. Real work that,' he said, swinging the light to follow the seam along the wall.

I touched the gritty surface under my fingers. 'I wonder when it dates from.'

He flicked the beam near my face, making me wince, then quickly pointed it away, fading out along the path. 'Not in our lifetime. Not even in my grandfather's, and he was a miner. But not in this shaft. I don't think he even knew about this shaft.'

I noticed he wasn't stuttering. Down here, alone with me, he was comfortable. But I didn't draw attention to it. Instead,

112

I put my second hand on his arm, hard inside his leather jacket.

'Do you think we could really live here,' I asked, 'or are you just using shock tactics?'

He lowered the torch to the floor between us. 'Eh?'

It was so quiet I could hear our separate breathing. Mine was quick, I admit it. I needed a man like Peej to protect me from what had happened.

'I wouldn't say we were wasting our time.' He was breathing through his nose now. He had a thin nose, thin lips. I knew what he was like without seeing him. 'Alice?'

I was inches from him. 'What?'

*

For God's sake. That wasn't how it happened. It was a missed opportunity to get that intimate. What he really said was, 'Want to walk along a bit? You can plan where to put your leather sofa and we can see how far back it goes.' Too vivid an imagination.

In the end we didn't go very far. The seam stretched on to where it began to look unstable. Grit and dust sprinkled on our hair and there were stones on the path. When Peej shone the torch on the ceiling we could see where they had come from, but this was a good twenty metres from the original shaft, and the rest looked solid enough.

Climbing out wasn't easy but it was motivating, knowing there was a chance I wasn't going to be buried. We'd still have to be desperate to want to live down there.

When I regained the surface Junkie was waiting for a verdict. 'Well?' she said.

I looked apologetically. 'It doesn't seem too bad. As a last resort.'

'Jesus Christ,' she said and turned. 'Youz are fucking mental. That's what youz are. Fucking mental!' She stalked off, pink boots bright in the fading grass, arms folded.

'Lee-Ann!' I called, but my voice doesn't carry far.

'Where's she off to?' Peej asked, gripping The Gaffer's hand for his final stages.

The Gaffer's brow wrinkled as his eyebrows lowered. 'Don't ask me,' he said.

We looked to Basher but he wasn't saying anything.

'Do you not think you should go after her?' I said.

The Gaffer was untying the rope and winding it round his shoulder; Basher and Peej were tidying the brambles and vegetation so no one would guess we'd been there. I looked to see how far she'd gone but I wouldn't have been able to catch her. And I was scared to be away from the men now. 'Peej?'

Peej stuttered when he spoke to me. 'You know what Junkie's like.'

He sucked bramble scratches on the back of his hand and watched her. 'You'll never force her to do something she doesn't want to do.'

I didn't like leaving her: I knew the dangers.

'I don't like leaving her,' I said.

Peej straightened. 'Junkie can take care of herself.' He took a cigarette packet out of his pocket and offered one to each of the others. 'We'll hang on a couple of minutes.' He lit up. The red ember ate at the cigarette end like the anxiety eating at my stomach. The stress I felt must have been obvious. He gripped my arm and walked me away from the others.

'Are you going to tell me what happened to you the other day?' He walked me till I'd fencing at my back and couldn't go any further.

'I'm just worried about Junkie.'

'Aye, well, I've told you. You don't need to worry about Junkie. Junkie's got a head on her shoulders.' He nodded, refusing to avert his eyes from me. 'What happened to you? Something did, didn't it? With the bikers. Wide Boy told me you were howling.'

I blinked up at him. After the darkness, the sunlight was dazzling.

'I'm not daft, you know,' he said, breathing smoke away from me, then turning straight back. 'Remember – I warned you everyone would be out for themselves.' And when I didn't answer he said, 'Well, something's made you change your mind about that place.'

But I didn't tell him, because Junkie was missing and it was

114

my fault.

Chapter Twenty-four

At the car, The Gaffer swung into the driver's seat. I got in the back with Basher; Peej wound back the barbed wire fencing while The Gaffer angled the jeep to go down the road. He moved off as Peej climbed into the front passenger seat, before he had closed the door, but Peej let it pass. There wasn't any sign of Junkie, even though we detoured round the neighbouring streets.

'She'll be offski,' Peej said. He stretched his arm out on the back of the seat and turned round to speak to us. The two leathers squeaked.

'What will we do?' I asked.

'What can we do?'

Basher was brooding through the window. The Gaffer caught sight of me in the rear-view mirror and shook his head.

'She'll probably keep out of things for a few hours,' Peej said. 'No way she'll stay away for long, though.' His fingers tapped the seat back till The Gaffer asked him to quit it. Then he sat facing front. We were a solemn lot. Usually we relished being in the car because we could play music, but no one made any moves to choose a CD. When we got back to the library Wide Boy and Eric took the jeep and the Maestro out to look for her but came back without a glimpse.

By now I was exhausted. I'd hardly slept since the assault in the computing room. Every time I felt myself drifting I reimagined it and woke up breathless. I took to lying facing the door and woke up after what sleep I'd had feeling as if my head was on a spike, my neck too stiff to turn.

As it grew dark on the third night we were all listening for the roars that meant the bikers were back. And Junkie was still missing. By now we'd reached the decision to leave the following day as soon as the bikers had decamped. If it came to it. As a last resort.

I pretended I was pleased to have passed the impasse. I spent the evening identifying what we'd need. I packed my holdall and helped Sara with hers. My main worry now was what would happen to the library if the bikers found they weren't barred from it. It would scar my conscience if I thought they'd ransack it. But I still hoped they'd see sense, turn and run. How could you understand men, though? I couldn't. I never had been able to, except maybe Dick and Willy but they weren't real men, shut away with the incunabula.

With these thoughts in my mind, and while the men finished their meal and changed guard, I took a torch and slipped away along the admin corridor. Our strong-room was at the end, along from The Boss's office.

It was almost dark. I opened The Boss's door and shut it behind me, pressing my back against it. Turned on the torch. I hadn't come in here since that first evening we'd got the booze. Had persuaded the others not to use it – well, there was too much clutter with his massive desk and chair and custom-built units. It seemed pompous now when we were getting by on so little. And he had been pompous – I glanced at the photo I'd damaged – I'd misread his manner as confidence when he was young.

I moved over towards the desk and pushed the pressure sensitive pad that released his tray, took the key for the unit behind me and unlocked the uppermost cabinet. It was where he kept the second of the strong room keys. It chinked in my pocket beside my own.

The corridor was still quiet when I left his office, though I could hear voices at the far end. Out of the window there was no sign yet of the bikers, and my thoughts took on the incantation of prayers as I turned the hope in my head that they'd have had a surfeit of this fun – whatever had provoked it – and that Peej's single gun shot would have frightened them off.

At the end of the corridor I pushed the two heavy keys into the door and forced first one then the other through its clunky circle, tugging up the weight of the handle as I'd learned to make the journey easier. The hinges creaked as the door opened into blackness as solid as down the pit we might shortly be leaving for.

I switched on the torch and closed the door behind me, remembering through long practice to remove the keys so I couldn't be locked inside.

There were no windows in this room and no escaping. The air was thick and dry. Paper dry. Against the walls, centuries old books from our special collections stood in glass-fronted, centuries-old, custom-built bookcases. I held the torch to the gleam of gold on their spines. Bibles, treatises, early architectural reference books; priceless illustrations of the flora and fauna on newly explored continents.

The darkness encased me as I moved further back. Here, brown leather bindings gave way to creamy vellum. I passed the black iron boxes I knew enclosed ribbon-wrapped bundles of family papers: wax sealed letters congratulating on births, or, black-edged, commiserating on deaths; bills and requests for payments; records of alms; pleas for support for young sons setting out as diplomats or missionaries to far away lands.

At the far end I rested my hand on the grey metal safe. For the first time I doubted what I was planning. The safe was four feet high and three feet wide. There was no money in it. But the bikers wouldn't know that. It would take explosives, surely, to burst into it – explosives that would devastate the treasures on the walls around me.

I tormented myself with the dilemma. Should I lock up the room, take both keys and hope they wouldn't get in, wouldn't even notice it? Or leave a note of the safe's combination so they could key it in and see for themselves the extent of the valuables our little town possessed?

I crouched by the dial and cricked it as smoothly as I could. Two tens to the right. Four twenties to the left. Five fifties to the right. Two thirties to the left then right to sixty.

I turned the massive handle upright and pulled. I didn't need to pause among the white clothed items to look. Reaching in to the bottom drawer, I took our most precious incunabulum out of the safe.

I shut the heavy door and spun the dial then quickly fluttered out of the room, pulling the door behind me and locking it with both keys. In the corridor it had grown even darker. From the staffroom harsh jangling suggested that Brain was trying to master the guitar but beyond that there was a rounder sound. The window confirmed that the bikers were reassembling. I returned the second strong-room key to its place in The Boss's room and for a few minutes I allowed myself the luxury of curving into his leather chair. It was cold but it was comfortable. In this room there were no sounds other than its creaking. I put the torch on the desk, shining into my lap and unwound the white cotton cloth. I didn't have any gloves and that troubled me. I scolded myself for not taking a few pairs – they'd been on top of the safe but I'd missed them in the weak torch-light and my excitement.

I drew the book out. Bound in white calf vellum, its skin was smoother than The Boss's chair. I let my fingertips enjoy it. I opened it at random and saw the 16 century blues and golds gleam in a brief glint of 21 century light. I traced with the tip of my finger the elaborate decoration painted on top of each woodcut and tongued the early printed Latin text. *O me miserum, orbis nunc confundus est. Our idyll has been overwhelmed by fate; how transient this life, this chronicle.* Folded it up again, checked the corridor was empty, and hurried to my room to hide the book at the bottom of my rucksack.

'Packs of cards,' I told Sara.

'Aw, well I'll not take mine then,' she said, rummaging at the bottom of her bag to find the ones she'd packed.

'Take them!' I said, overenthusiastically. 'Someone might want to play patience.'

Somewhere Junkie was playing solitaire. As the revs of the motorbikes and Brain's guitar lesson played on our nerves we women and children were driven to congregate in the upper room – our common room – which was now even gloomier because of the boarding over the windows.

The sun had gone down early, a combination of heavy cloud and the short November days. Sara lit the candles and placed them out of the children's reach around our circle. Limpet's children didn't stray far that night and I read some Roald Dahl to keep them engaged. Their laughter seemed curiously strained. On other floors of the building, I knew, Peej was mustering the men to take their places, to watch or to rest, according to when they might be needed. Brain's musical exertions had stopped.

I finished the story and Limpet put the children to bed. Normally The Gaffer let us have a bottle of beer but these nights none was issued because of the threat. I missed it: I could have done with it to steady me.

'What'll we do now?' Sara asked me, more irritating than a gaggle of six year olds.

'Maybe Grace would like tea,' I said. Tea-making was a speciality for Sara. It was a skill she could master, and serving it gave not only the recipient but Sara herself tremendous pleasure.

'Do you want some?'

I couldn't discipline my thoughts. 'No, thank you,' I said and went for a walk.

The stairwell was lit by lanterns. I felt exposed, visible through the stained glass windows, and stayed by the walls where I could. A wraith of cigarette smoke rose in the void. Downstairs, Peej was sitting on an Edwardian table, his elbows on his knees. I caught him flicking his cigarette ash on the marble floor before he heard my steps. Wide Boy and Basher sat on chairs at the opposite side of the table. Wide Boy was howking a stone from the deep tread of his trainers; Basher was whittling a piece of wood. Their evident good humour died when they saw me.

'Stay upstairs,' Peej said, slipping his feet to the floor and facing me.

'I don't know what to do with myself,' I told him. 'I'm worried about Junkie.'

'Junkie'll be fine.'

'Do you think she'll be trying to come back?'

He turned to Wide Boy. 'Go and find out how Eric's doing.'

120

Basher said he was going to check on his kids and Peej and I waited till their steps stopped echoing on the stairs.

'I told you not to worry about Junkie. She can handle herself.' He stubbed his cigarette out on a saucer packed with ends. He looked at my hands, worrying themselves. 'What's really your problem?'

The muscles at my mouth went into spasm. 'I'm nervous about what's going to happen.'

Peej's face started to tic. 'Not think we're all nervous?' He squeezed his hand on my shoulder. 'You'll be fine.'

I leant my cheek on his hand but he broke away and faced the table. He rifled for another cigarette, flicking two or three times before he got a light. 'I'm going to have a go at talking peace.'

'Are you? Do you think they'll want peace?' After all my talk about non-violence I didn't know if I could cope with being friends.

When he turned I saw he was smiling, one eyebrow raised. 'No, but I'll give it a try.'

Basher came quietly back, then Wide Boy.

'Eric says it's just the usual,' Wide Boy said. 'Sitting drinking. Lucky bastards.'

'You'll get a drink when it's finished.' Peej opened a holdall and took out a handgun. He checked it was loaded and tucked it in his waistband. 'Widey –go and get The Gaffer and Brain. Basher – you stay upstairs with Eric.' He handed Basher a gun and he went back upstairs without saying anything.

'I thought you were going to speak to them?'

Peej scowled, his cheeks tight in the poor light. 'Yak, I know what I'm going to do. Get back up to the others.'

I heard Grace ask about another tea as they assembled in the corridor above us.

'No,' I told Peej, firmly.

The Gaffer and Brain ran downstairs following Wide Boy. Brain was clearing his throat. Peej handed them weapons: it looked like it had all been arranged. I was a woman and Peej was just humouring me.

'I thought you were going to talk to them?'

They descended the stone stairs to the basement. The Gaffer was whistling; the white distempered walls amplified that and the slap of their shoes.

'When was all this decided?' I shouted, running down the half flight behind them. I clutched at the iron hand rail. 'You said if there was any escalation we'd go to the pit.'

Peej looked back between the ranks of his deputies. He raised his gun in salute. 'As a last resort, I said. As a very last resort.'

Chapter Twenty-five

At the foot of the stairs Peej and The Gaffer lit the lanterns. The old basement was lit up almost as ineffectively as it had been by the rows of naked dangling low energy bulbs whose silver light fizzled out within a metre radius. They left two of the lanterns on the tables close by the foot of the stair; the other two they took with them to the external wall.

Against that wall the grey, two drawer filing cabinet squatted on the green four drawer one, covering the old loading bay door. Jammed up against it was one of our massive wooden study tables, its varnish scored by the criss-cross hatching and graffiti of generations of disaffected students. Next to it an upright metal cupboard reinforced by columns of spongy cardboard book-filled boxes blocked the window through which the bikers had made their original entrance. Discarded to one side was the charred wood and metal frame of the study carrel we'd originally used to block it. Underfoot remained the crunch of poorly swept glass.

Wide Boy jumped on to the table and grabbed the top of the smaller cabinet. It squealed like something being slaughtered as he and Brain manoeuvred it briefly off its perch on to Brain's chest then hurriedly on to the long table.

'Watch my toes,' the Boy said.

Peej sniffed. I wondered if his cheek was still ticking. He cleared his throat and fastened the middle button of his leather jacket. He picked up his gun from the long table and put it back to front in his left pocket, half hidden by his arm, the handle in easy reach of his right hand. He sniffed again and ran his hand over his chin.

'Right.'

Brain and Wide Boy walked the big cabinet over the stone floor. It didn't spark.

The thick metal door was pocked with peaks of light and gullies of shade as if they'd taken a pickaxe to it. Whatever it was, it hadn't pierced through; the door was closed as firmly as ever.

Peej examined the door and snapped his fingers. 'Key.'

The Gaffer put them in his outstretched hand.

'Which one is it?'

A missile hit the back door and our men jumped. I could have told him which key but I was scared. I could hear the bikers outside, in session.

'Which one?'

'How would I know?' The Gaffer said. 'You'll need to try them.'

'Get that fucking light over here.'

Wide Boy held the lantern to the door handle and Peej tried three of the keys in succession. Outside, the graph of the bikers' noise dipped. We'd lost our element of surprise.

'Fuck this,' Peej said and looked for me. 'Get down here.'

I left the stairs. At close range his eyes were battened down; there was no clear light in them in this gloom. His brows shaded them too, accentuating his face's caverns.

'Here,' I said picking out the long silver one.

His hand briefly cupped mine as he took it. It was damp. 'Get back up the stair.'

I scampered, too afraid to be involved.

Peej touched his gun, breathed in and emptied his lungs through pursed lips. He gripped the round door handle and readied his left hand on the bar. 'Right.'

There was a roar when he pushed the door outwards. And drumming, faster and faster, metal beating on metal. I felt panic rise but needed to see what would happen.

Wind whopped the door to the wall. Peej took his stance in the doorway. Wide Boy handed him the lantern and he held it up in his left hand, his right hanging stiff at his side. Brain, The Gaffer and Wide Boy moved out of the bikers' line of sight. The roar subsided to the thrum of one lone drum.

'I want to speak to your gaffer.'

I couldn't see the bikers: only the downward slope of the car park illuminated faintly by the light from the lantern. I crept three steps down where I could see all of Peej and shivered in a chill swathe of air.

A gruff but educated voice called, 'I'm their leader.'

Peej left three beats. 'Tell him to quit that.'

The drum stopped. Below me, The Gaffer rubbed his forehead and breathed *Jesus*.

'I want you to leave us in peace.'

A laugh went round them.

'Wait.' The laughing died. 'Your point is...?'

'We've women and kids in here,' Peej said.

There was a high cheer. 'How many have you got?' the voice asked and my stomach tightened.

'We've *got* none,' he replied eventually. For the first time he stuttered.

The Gaffer whispered, 'He should've let me do it.' But I hadn't heard him volunteering.

'If youz want to j- j- – to belong to our group – put your weapons down.'

I tried to imagine Peej vetting the bikers, deciding who to grant refugee status to and who to send on his way. But he hadn't finished.

'If you don't want to, then fuck off and leave us alone.'

There were boos from the bikers.

The educated voice had a smile in it. 'What makes you think we'd want to j- j- belong to your group?'

Laughter.

'The offer stands.'

'Your offer?' More laughter. 'It didn't sound much of an offer to me. What about you, boys?'

The drum beat started again, a background pulse.

'Maybe we want what's ours. And the rest.'

There were handclaps, a few at first, and slow, in time to the drumbeat.

125

Peej shifted his footing. He lowered the lantern a fraction. 'You've had a taste of what we can do. But we've got more.'

Peej's right hand reached to his left hand pocket and The Gaffer breathed, 'He's going to do it!' Peej pulled his gun out and held it in his flexed arm.

The drumming stopped.

Peej straightened his arm, aiming at sky.

I slithered down another step. My hands clutched the iron railing. 'He's vulnerable,' I whispered. Wide Boy's eyes were bright dots when he looked at me.

Peej brought his arm down through to the horizontal.

Almost inaudible, the biker's voice. 'What if we've something of our own?'

I honestly heard the metal clicking. A bullet whizzed, invisible, thwicking into the metal door panel, making Peej jump back. He tossed the lantern on our floor and the paraffin ignited in a sheet of blue. He leaned out and grabbed the door by the safety bar. More hits tinged, high velocity. He clanged the door shut, scraped it the last inches and pumped the push bar till the door finally sealed.

Brain and Wide Boy beat the flames with rags but the rags ignited.

'They've got, like, meths in them!' I shouted. 'For cleaning book jackets.'

Wide Boy reached for the nearest fire extinguisher and squirted a jet of water, but it sluiced the flames towards me on the stairs.

'Not water!' Brain yelled, shielding his eyes.

There was plenty of illumination now. It showed The Gaffer motionless; I cowered from the flare then scurried back up three or four steps, sheltering my head from the heat and smoke.

Peej leaped past me. 'Get they cabinets back!' he shouted. 'And get your guns ready.'

'That one!' I pointed to the extinguisher at the top of the stairs.

He detached it and ran back down, his face contorted as he peered at the label. 'How d'you...?'

126

'Give me it.'

He handed it awkwardly, his gun in the same hand.

I took the plastic ring out, hoping the kids hadn't emptied it, and aimed a spurt of foam at the fire.

'The Gaffer – with me,' Peej shouted.

'Shite. Shite!' Wide Boy was saying.

'Hear the bullets?' Brain called. We could hear the zips as the two of them pushed and dragged the filing cabinets back. Upstairs there was screaming.

My eyes were stinging but the flames were losing. I watched the smoke billow down the length of the dark stacks to soil our share of the Scottish fiction reserve. No disaster plan could've been put in place if that had caught. There were no freezer shops we could rely on to discard fish fingers so we could conserve them. I rested the extinguisher on the bottom step against the rail and saw drops of blood on the step. But I wasn't bleeding. There were spots of it at the doorway.

'Did Peej get hit?'

Brain and Wide Boy wrestled the cabinet into place. They stopped and looked at me and at the smears under their feet.

I ran up the stairs following the blood.

Basher was with the women and kids in our top corridor. They were grasping each other, huddled together, but Peej wasn't with them. I ran into my room for the torch under my bed and ran out again.

'Where's Peej?'

'What's happen?' Basher asked.

I shone the torch over the floor and picked out the blood trail heading along the corridor. 'They've got guns,' I said, cautious of the kids. 'Brain and Wide Boy are barricading the basement again.'

'Are they alright?' Saleema asked. Her eyes were wide and black.

'They're fine,' I said. 'Everybody's fine.'

Except Peej, I thought. Except Junkie.

'Peej is –' Basher said, pointing along towards the room Peej shared.

I ran along, noticing that the drips were just as regular. At the end of the corridor I heard the two men's voices and called through the door so as not to alarm them.

'It's Alice.'

I pushed the door open. Peej and The Gaffer were loading up guns.

There was a small tear in the arm of Peej's jacket; blood slithered down his leather sleeve and smeared on his hand.

'You're hurt.'

He raised his eyes. He was mouth breathing. 'Can you use a gun, Yakkity?'

'No.'

He took the torch out of my hand and pushed the gun into it.

'No.'

'Alice.'

'Take it,' The Gaffer said.

'Take it and look after the kids.'

They passed me.

I don't agree with guns. I stood anchored by it. As they reached the door I said, 'Is it not time for the last resort?'

'Not yet,' Peej said, and hurried from the room.

Chapter Twenty-six

I didn't have anywhere to put the gun. No pockets or belt. But I didn't want to hold it and I didn't want to leave it lying around. It was heavy like a hammer, but other than knowing which end the bullets came from, I didn't have a clue how to use it. I hoped it wouldn't fire accidentally. I tucked my jumper into the waist of my trousers and dropped the gun inside it so as not to frighten the children. The metal was warm and heavy as it thumped on my chest. Heavier than a whistle.

When I stepped into the corridor Basher ran off after Peej and The Gaffer; Sara got up off the floor and cuddled me.

'Alice,' she said. 'I'm frightened.' Even in this gloom and with this fear, her eyes, upturned at the edges, showed her total trust in me.

'Are you packed?'

'Yes.'

'I'll get the rest to pack now. Keep Salaam and Saleema happy. Take them to our room.'

Her eyes dropped to the protruding shape of the gun she'd felt at my waist. I shook my head and mouthed, 'Don't say anything.'

We watched the children go then I told the adults everything. Up here, the smoke had formed clouds curling at the ceiling; voices too had reached them from the basement. I told them about the guns. I told them that Peej had been hit but that I didn't know how badly, other than that he was walking, as they'd seen, and was still in charge. If I'd held their attention when I read them thrillers it was nothing to the way I'd hooked them now.

'What can we do?' Bill asked, his arm rising from Grace's

shoulder.

'Pack,' I said. 'In case we have to leave in a hurry.' With the men away, and Junkie, and Sara and the children, there were only Bill and Grace and Limpet left.

Limpet would pack for Basher and the children; Bill and Grace would pack for themselves. I was already packed and so was Sara, so I packed for the men, taking the minimum they'd need. And I threw together a few things I thought Junkie might need.

There was gunfire from the upper floor of the library. Through the glass doors I saw the men had pulled down one of the purple panels and were shooting through the broken window. Shots were returned; in the dark I couldn't see the damage, either to the library or to these men I needed. I sat in the dark at one of the study carrels, my back to the action and my hands over my ears. I tried to remember how it had been with Dick and Willy, the flap they'd get into if a researcher used a pen instead of a pencil, and Polly sneaking a cross-stitch if the phone didn't ring while she was at the enquiry desk.

I didn't even notice Peej go past me and come back into the room again. I only noticed when his huge voice hollered through the broken window.

'Hold your fire!'

A few more shots.

'Hold your fire!'

The bikers' leader's voice responded, calling for calm.

Peej was standing with his back against the window buttress. He curled round to shout through the broken glass.

'Your last chance,' he said and there was silence. 'You've got two minutes to get on your bikes and get out.' He pointed to me. 'Start counting.' I could hear him gasping for breath.

Only Peej had been hurt. The bikers were bad shots and we had the protection of the building. The bikers, on the other hand, were in the open. But that didn't seem to worry them. A voice came from outside. 'Get out or what?'

Peej's hand rose to his jacket pocket. 'How long, Yakkity?'

Two hundred and thirty-three. I shook my head.

130

'What d'you do with these?' he asked.

Basher crouched and took the grenade from his hand.

'Aim at their bikes.'

I heard, rather than saw, Basher's arm movement. Outside, there was a clink as the grenade hit metal. Clatter and roll. A two second pause then shouting and the sounds of running feet.

Then boom and a succession of smaller blasts threw orange light and black silhouettes in the air. The building shook; glass became knives but none cut us.

We were caught in black cameo in the flames' light. Through the window we could hear a man crying; there were voices above the crackling fire. Then came the smell. Did I hate them so much I wanted that to happen? I pulled the gun from my clothes, brandished it in the air in front of Peej then bumped it on the table.

'Alice, go to the kids,' Peej said. 'Boff, check the boys downstairs. Nobody,' he repeated the word, 'Nobody open that door.'

As I left the room he was peering round to see what the scene was like. 'Jesus Fuck,' he said and turned back in.

Chapter Twenty-seven

None of us slept that night. Outside, charred and mangled and still smoking, were the remnants of the bikers' bikes. In the grey light, and from my brief, bleary glances, I couldn't see any body parts though there were more than a few charred stains.

Some of the bikes must have escaped because we heard them roar off. Later, we heard a car. Someone must've come back to collect the injured because the crying stopped. I spent the whole night awake, anger, fear and confusion corkscrewing through me till I wrapped my arm round Sara's plump warmth and fell asleep. Before the sun came up we gathered together for a war council.

Sara and the children were still sleeping. Our men, Limpet, Grace and I took our seats at the table in the staff room. We looked to Peej to give us direction but he was weary. His face was pasty; I wondered if he'd lost a lot of blood. His left arm was bandaged but the blood had seeped through and he was lighting one cigarette from the end of the last.

My energy had drained without bleeding. 'What now?'

He exhaled and stubbed his cigarette in the ashtray. 'We wait here.'

The Gaffer shook his head. 'No.' He looked round the other men. 'I mean, I was keen to stay, but not now. Look at the place.'

This staff room wasn't bad but my poor library was covered in glass; wooden book bay ends were ripped into; bullets had exploded through the pages of the crime fiction. Over it was a shroud of smoke, despite the enforced ventilation.

'It's still secure,' Peej said. 'And let's face it, they'll not be back.'

'You don't know that,' I said. 'They might come back with flame throwers.'

Eric scowled and scratched his leg. He'd lost the sharp crease in his trousers.

'Stranger things have happened.' My feet were cold and I rubbed them. 'They didn't use guns until Peej did. And now he's escalated it again.'

A snort made me look at Brain. 'It's hardly an arms race.'

'You just don't get it,' I said, on a sob as irrepressible as a hiccup. 'We're surrounded by dead people and now we find somebody living what do you do? Shoot them.' Crying was pathetic, but that was frustration. 'You think it all comes down to whose gun's biggest.'

'I gave them a chance,' Peej said, but I didn't look at him.

My eyes and nose were running and I went to my locker for a handkerchief. Inside was my favourite picture, of me sitting on the road at Faslane. I tore it off the sticky stuff and dropped it on the table. 'What was that all about?' I asked them. I was in my yellow cagoule and my green bobbled hat. My face looked fuller, like I was twenty years younger. Surely it wasn't that? I'd lost all track of time.

Peej turned it to him with his good hand. 'You're tired, Alice. You're not seeing sense.'

'What is it?' Limpet asked, about the photo.

'It's an anti-nuclear protest,' I said. 'At the nuclear weapons base forty miles from here.' I stretched between Grace and her and took back the photo. 'God alone knows who's in charge of them now.'

'They'll be safe,' Brain said. He looked at The Gaffer. 'The cores in these things shut down when there's a problem.'

'So comforting,' I quipped. 'How much better if we'd had the courage to disinvent them.'

'Can we move on?' Peej said. 'We're a hell of a way away from using nuclear weapons.'

'Let's hope the bikers are,' I said. 'Or the next biggest thing to grenades. Isn't that how it goes?' There was a territorial army base ten miles up the road. For all I knew, that was where Peej had gone for our guns.

'I think it's time we moved,' The Gaffer said.

'Someone with brains to take charge again.'

'Go to the pit.'

Our eyes turned to Basher.

'Nobody'll find us.'

Peej rubbed his eyes and sat forward. 'That's a desperate step, man. We're not that desperate.'

Basher prodded his forefinger on the table and leaned forward too. 'I didn't bring my kids to Scotland for this.' He jerked his tousled black head.

'I'm knackered,' Wide Boy said, crossing his arms on the table and putting his chin on them. 'Why don't we just sleep on it?'

The Gaffer shook his head and took off his glasses. He wiped the gunge from the corners of his eyes and cleaned his finger on his trousers. 'We need to move now,' he said. He polished his glasses on his sweatshirt. 'We can't risk being here if they come back.'

I was frightened about what they would do to my library, but it was put to the vote and that's how we decided.

'Last resort,' I said to Peej after the votes were counted.

'Hmm,' he said and closed his eyes.

Chapter Twenty-eight

For days we stood in the fields, morose and sodden. The November rain was constant. We wore layers of clothes one inside the other to keep out the weather, Christian Aid mismatched with Christian Dior. My legs were so plaster-cast in mud that I fretted about trench foot. Of the bikers, at least, there was no sign. We ruminated under the straggling trees in the rain, Sara and I, waiting for Peej to heal and worrying about Junkie.

The Gaffer and Basher and the others moved about around the shaft area, peeling back the spindly legs of wild roses. The Gaffer was over-bearing. With Peej down, he didn't have to vie with him for seniority. I could tell how this satisfied him from his body language: those supercilious eyebrows gave it away, as did his fists on his podgy hips, or the flick of his flabby finger as he directed operations, while Basher was the one to risk laceration from the thorns.

I was having none of it. But right then, I was having nothing to do with anything. In my bag, down at the bottom of the pit shaft, I had hidden a bottle of dry red wine that I was hoarding. It was my last defence. Knowing I had it there was comfort against this latest dark mood because I knew it could lose me an hour or two; could secure me another little smudge of oblivion. As the rain continued, swamping shoulders and hoods and soaking through my two coats and scarves, I obsessed more and more about it.

A Cotes du Bourg, its contents so rich they were almost black through the bottle green. A scroll of French on the cream label. The insides dark and thick to drink. I glanced at Sara, leaning against a damp trunk in the corner of the field where the hedgerows met, risking electrocution through her iPod, and wondered if I could find an excuse to foist her on Limpet. I craved the wine and I craved a corner of my own so I wouldn't need to share it. That's what I'd sunk to. I imagined the thwop of the cork being drawn and the glossy red flooding over my tongue and down my gullet.

'Alice,' The Gaffer called to me.

I considered ignoring him but it wasn't my nature. So I trudged over, wiping rain from my face with my sodden glove, too wet to feel it.

'We've been discussing making something more permanent,' he said, and described his concerns about the muddied opening, how slippy it was, how the men couldn't keep their footing when they lowered and raised Grace and the children in the flimsy improvised cradle they'd made from a tarpaulin.

I watched the rain drip from his nose and eyebrows.

'Well? What do you think?' He stuffed his hands into the pockets of his tightly fastened trench-coat. Behind him, Basher put up the collar of his brown tweed jacket and hunched his body forward.

'I think we should sit in the cars and wait till Peej is better.' I saw his shoulders sink. Nothing he said could have raised my spirits. Only alcohol could do that but I couldn't think how I could tell him. 'I'm sorry,' was all I could muster.

He shook his head and turned away.

The rain sapped everyone's energies. Even Peej, resting in the car while the windscreen wipers beat a rhythm or down in the dismal dark of the pit, had no enthusiasm. The other men made foraging trips – anywhere but the library – to bring bedding and mattresses and to ferry them down the shaft but Peej sat, dour and disheartened, and took no part in things. And nobody spoke much, as if speech had been robbed from us. As if using words would be to recognise how low we had sunk.

*

Two days later we were forced into the pit by a thunderstorm. One massive flash even reached into our hole, whiter than the lanterns and candles. We waited for the boom. One elephant, two elephants. The flash was so intense it must have been directly above us but we counted till we almost forgot about it. Then we heard a woman screaming. 'J – Jesus, that's J – Junkie!' Peej shouted and Wide Boy and Brain shinned up the rope to help her.

They sent her down in the cradle, squealing and shrieking and tugging at her skirt.

My insides were twisting. When she landed she was half-canned, shivering and dishevelled as if she'd been pulled from a river, her make-up and hair literally dripping. And in the middle of all that came more thunder, rumbling right through the ground and sending Wide Boy and Brain haring down the rope again. Or maybe they didn't want to miss a second of the spectacle that was Junkie.

She crawled through the tunnel, flesh falling from both ends of the damp tube she considered clothing. She climbed out, straightened up and wriggled everything into place.

'Fucking bastard.' Her eyes flared and flitted around her. 'Fucking amazing.' She saw me. 'Wild, man. D'd'you see that thunder?'

A scarlet bustiere. In November. No sign of a jacket. I asked her where her parka was but she said she'd lost it. Lost the heel of a shoe too. There was sick on her cling-film skirt and circles of purplish flesh in her tights. She was a tart; a hussy; Eric and The Gaffer tried to hide their smirks but I could see them.

Then she glimpsed Peej's bandage.

'Peejie!' she said, dropping into his lap. 'Come here till I kiss you better.'

'His arm!' I growled but neither was caring.

She pressed his face into her chest and Wide Boy chuckled. Peej cleared a bit of her away and said, 'It's fine, Alice.'

'It's fine, Alice,' she repeated, her bare arm out and waving towards me. 'Peej is fine. Peej and me's close, sure we are, darling?'

'Aye, doll,' he grinned. 'But you're a bit wet.'

No wonder I was annoyed at her. And him. First the gun fight and the arms race. Now this, in front of Sara and everyone.

'Where have you been?' Peej asked her.

'Did you see that thunder?'

'What were you doing out in it?'

She rubbed her nose. 'Had to get away from them, lover boy. While they were watching the thunder.'

'Who?'

'Eh?' She sniffed and looked around at our pit set up. Our bags and beds. Our early, unlit attempt at a fire.

'Who, doll?'

She turned back to him and tried to focus. A drip fell and glistened on the fleshy cushion pushed up by her bustiere. 'I'm wasted,' she said.

Maybe I'd misjudged her. Sara brought her a cup of warm chocolate, heated during the day and saved in a thermos. Brain threw a towel and Peej tousled her hair.

'I'm just pure fucking wasted.' She sniffed as he smoothed the mascara smears from her face, her eyes closing.

The men's eyes moved from her body to the floor. I went to my bed and came back with the spare blanket.

'Get away from who, doll?' Peej asked, tucking the blanket round her.

My ears were roaring with her silence.

'Nobody.'

She lay against Peej's chest swaddled in the blanket and we listened to the medley of water droplets falling from the boulders and roots that protruded into our pit shaft, plinking into the stainless steel pots we'd placed in the circle of ground.

In the darkened middle of the pit, Salaam moaned in his sleep.

'Isn't she wet?' I asked Peej.

'Sodden.'

He winced as he eased himself in his chair. She was leaning against his wounded arm. 'Give us a hand.'

Wide Boy and Brain hurried for the chance.

'Lay her on my bed for a couple of hours,' he said.

Should I have been nice to her? Be motherly towards her? 'You could put her in mine,' I offered.

138

'Mine's is just there, Yak. What's the sense in dragging her up to yours?'

I burst an indigestion tablet from its foil. What had she done to deserve that? Abandoned us, then come grovelling back, using her body to win the men over. A second time.

The only good thing to come of it was that The Gaffer let us have a drink to celebrate her safe return. Not the lager this time but the hard stuff. The water of life, the whisky, the aqua vitae, the uisge beatha. The only thing that could thaw the cold from me. Basher and Limpet didn't have any, but that was their business. It meant more for me of the only thing to stop my brain from churning.

There was another flash of light.

'Let's all get some sleep,' The Gaffer said.

And a little rumble.

We were cold anyway. With this rain we couldn't risk using Brain's new invention to run the electric fire. And at that time we didn't have any gas cylinders and only lit the charcoal when there was food to be cooked because though you might think the pit shaft an ideal chimney, the ceiling of the tunnel was lower than the ceiling of our living area; any smoke just hung about, fogging that top couple of feet. It was a bottle neck, that's what it was. I lay in bed and thought about the bottle in my backpack. But it wasn't a screw top.

When the candles went out our eyes strove against the blackness. I lay facing away from the back of the pit with its unknown depths, listening for any sounds from Junkie in Peej's bed and looking towards the entrance for every jagged electrical flash from the storm up on top.

It was a fierce thunderstorm. I've never lived through one like it.

And what had Junkie been up to? Over a week she was away from us; over a week she ran around the streets like a bitch on heat. Next day she still didn't want to tell us but Peej and The Gaffer made her. I was right behind them. A kangaroo court, or more correctly a vipers' nest one. And I made damn sure she didn't spend another night in Peej's bed.

139

'I was just pissed off.'

We were sitting on the men's beds, in the pit, the storm still pounding above us. No lightning now, just the rain coming in volleys down the pit shaft, or later, as we were still to find out, down Eric's wall in little rivulets, off to join some unseen underground stream.

'But where did you go, doll?' Peej asked. 'You'd Alice all worried.'

Strange to think.

She was dressed warmly now, head to toe in bottle green fleece. She brought her heels up on the bed frame and wrapped her arms round her calves. Sniffed. 'I just went for a walk.' She appealed round the circle. 'How could you think I'd fancy this place? Place for fucking losers.'

'But where did you go?' The Gaffer persisted. 'It's important that you tell us.'

She scowled. 'How?'

'"How"?' Limpet looked at me.

'She means 'why'.'

Salaam perched beside Junkie and tried to show her his game console. He'd been sleeping when she'd turned up and had only discovered her that morning when he woke.

Junkie put her legs down and wrapped her arm round his shoulders. Told him she'd missed him and said she'd play later.

'It's important,' The Gaffer said. 'You'd already visited this site. We need to know whose side you're on: that you're not going to lead our enemies here.'

As if I wasn't nervous enough. From here there could be no quick getaway. Our cars were parked outside a house in a street ten minutes walk away so as not to arouse suspicion. My biggest fear was someone cutting our rope and leaving us trapped. Might Junkie know that? I searched my brain to remember what she had and hadn't seen. There was no 100% Celtic or 100% Rangers for Junkie: she'd hoist the flag of whoever was winning.

'I wouldn't do that,' she said, the close walls of the pit amplifying her coarse guttural.

Peej gave a bemused laugh. 'Come on, Lee-Ann.'

140

She turned her head to him, as I did.

He leaned back against the pit wall. 'What would you not do for crack?'

We all turned to stare at her.

She picked fluff from her trouser leg then looked up defiantly. 'Right! Right. I'll tell you.'

*

For three days she'd wandered. Whenever she'd heard a car, she'd ducked. For food, she'd raided one of the small shops in the housing scheme, eating cold beans and curries straight from the tin. She claimed she was torn, really torn, between coming back to join us and striking out on her own. The houses, entire streets, she said, were stinking. And the dogs were fighting in packs. Two nights in a row she'd had to climb on to the roof of the garden shed she was squatting in, while a pack of six led by a mongrel with a coat of tangled fur barked and snarled at her. The third night she emptied a tin of gloss paint over his head and he howled off with his praetorian guard yelping after him. Twice, she told us, she approached the library. The first time she was still too angry. The second, she claimed, we didn't hear her shouting. She said she banged on the back door with the heel of her boot but tugged it back on and ran when she heard the bikers coming.

The next day she came again but we had gone. I didn't believe her because it was all too convenient. Though her pink suede boots did have pointed heels and the basement's metal door was full of indentations.

She said the bikes were scorched, black-charred carcases in the car park, but she could have regurgitated that from when we told her how it had happened. Or she could have abused the children's innocence, fishing for clues.

After we'd disappeared she took a walk up towards the hill but she claimed she couldn't see us. Of course, sometimes during daylight in that first couple of days the men were back and forward fetching and carrying – beds, bedding, climbing gear. And it was important that we women ventured down the pit to sweep out dross and rubble to make it habitable. Or as close

141

to that as possible. If she'd called on us, we hadn't heard her. Though, down that hole our ears felt swaddled in silence, only picking out the amplification of noises in the pit itself, the way an empty house used to whisper until its furniture was installed.

We did hear her screaming during the storm but then we were listening.

She'd thought the whole pit shaft idea was a ruse to scare us into wanting to stay in the library. She didn't think for a second we'd actually be living here. So she spent a couple of days scouring for us in some of the estates. She'd wandered into the bikers when they were at the height of their fury, watching their leader dying from his burns.

They went wild, she said, but she didn't go into details. Just screwed up her face. That was when I believed her. Peej put his hand on her knee and The Gaffer cleared his throat. She said she escaped when they were moving their precious bikes out of the thunderstorm.

Eric sneezed. 'Yeah, that was some storm, wasn't it?' He looked at me. 'Especially that mega-flash. For a minute I thought it was Faslane exploding.'

Brain gave a long derisory negative. He split the pack of cards he was shuffling. 'I told you – these things shut down at a whiff of trouble.' But the notion had been put there, that Faslane might have gone up when Junkie was out in the open. And if it had, there was nothing any of us could have done about it.

Brain said if it had been a nuclear blast all the trees would have been blown down, but forty miles away? I vaguely remembered, from my campaigning days, learning that a blast would leave this area looking normal. I hated not being able to Google it. That night I lay in bed and worried once more.

Chapter Twenty-nine

Next morning Peej declared himself much fitter and he certainly looked it, sitting up at our communal area with one muddy Timberland boot up on a box of lager tins and the other foot under his chair, his knee flopped out to the side. His face had – if anything – shrunk even thinner since I'd known him, till his skin was a taut covering of leather but that morning it was drawn up into wrinkles, because he was grinning. He even bade me good morning. So, with Peej feeling fitter and with Junkie returning safely, the whole company's mood lifted and since the rain had abated, we decided now was the time to build a secure entry system for the shaft.

The men stood round the top and inspected it. I'm only five feet two. I didn't know if they gave ground grudgingly or just didn't notice me but I had to squeeze myself in between The Gaffer and Basher's heavy arms so I could take part in the discussion. Basher said whatever we chose had to prevent any of the children slipping in. Peej said it should stop unexpected guests dropping in, too. Wide Boy wanted it to mean less work when it came to raising Grace from the shaft and Brain wanted to 'formalise the cradle by constructing a pulley in a wooden framework' over the top.

'Hmm,' The Gaffer said, elbows out, hands on hips once again, even though I was already cramped for space.

The thought occurred to me that he might be once again in competition with a newly vigorous Peej. As he gripped a handful of willow and leaned his bulk over the hole, one leg forward and his wellington toes slithering on the mud and grass, I almost wished the branch would break and plunge him over.

'Interesting idea,' he said, 'but a pulley system would require us to have visible winding gear.' As he said it, he caught my eye and it occurred to me that he might be trying to impress me. The idea repulsed me. Besides, I looked more Bride of Steptoe than Glamour Pussy. The only thing we had in common was education.

He straightened up and stretched one leg out as if to straddle the hole but it was obviously too wide. His stubby leg waggled above the void. 'Hmm?' he said again since no one had answered.

I looked at his fingers, twisting in the tree twigs, slippery and gnarled. 'What about a net?' I said.

He brought his leg back.

'Go on,' Peej said, pushing up his Beanie hat from his forehead.

'Some kind of rope,' I went on, 'secured round the edges like on curtain hooks.'

'Ha!' Brain said. 'Curtain hooks?' He exchanged a smirk with The Gaffer.

And The Gaffer's sneering upper lip angered me. How dare he? I knew that arrogant, officious type of old.

'Fancy a trip to Ikea or Harry Corby, Yakkity?' Wide Boy said and grinned at the others.

'The same colour as the undergrowth and invisible to the passer-by,' I said, an edge in my voice, 'but strong enough to catch anyone tripping in.'

Peej scratched at his chin and watched The Gaffer, waiting for his reaction.

He peered into the black hole. 'Wouldn't we be better with steps? Circling down?'

'Think you're Errol Fucking Flynn?' Peej stuttered and Wide Boy snorted.

The Gaffer released the twigs, letting the branches bounce up and shiver raindrops on us. Fastidiously he shrugged the water from his hair, combing through it with his fingers. 'Or what about the rungs they use in conning towers? We could knock in a batch of towel rails.'

I shook the water from my hat and wiped big drips from my glasses. 'I don't see how that would prevent someone falling.'

144

Right from the start we'd used a fixed and permanent single rope. It was our main vehicle for entry and our escape route. The first person out in the morning climbed up it with the cradle. We kept the cradle down the shaft overnight because it was safest and easiest. It was easier to conceal the end of a rope up top than a whole cradle. In those early days I lay awake wondering what would happen if someone found the rope and ran away with it. We'd be stuck down there for ever. Maybe mountaineering hand-hold things was a good idea, down one side so they wouldn't impede the cradle. I wasn't so sure about rungs, though. 'And wouldn't they need rawl plugs?'

Two wood pigeons launched themselves heavily off one of the big beech trees that lined the field edge and I considered them skewered for lunch. Then it occurred to me that we could drive spikes of wood into the shaft, leaving hand-holds sticking out that would be strong enough to take a man's weight. We could hammer them in; well, someone suspended in the cradle could. I risked humiliating myself again by describing this out loud. 'They'd be safer, more permanent, in case anything happened to the rope. We could even do it with iron spikes. Railing spikes. They could be pushed in, couldn't they?'

'That would work,' Brain said.

To my surprise, The Gaffer sucked at his bottom lip and slowly nodded. 'Alright.'

And as no one raised any objections, the men set to work after lunch, scouting for a railing they could dismantle. They found one on the local building site along with some thick netting.

So the wounded Peej joined The Gaffer to watch Basher, Eric and Brain taking the strain on the cradle while Wide Boy descended with the spears in his hands. It started drizzling again and the grass was slippery but despite that I went right up to the edge to look in. It seemed relatively easy to pierce the earth provided there weren't stones. If he struck something too solid, Wide Boy pulled the spear out and tried again. We weren't looking for a design award.

I pointed out that if any of us did fall in, the chances were we'd be badly lacerated and, without acknowledging that I'd spoken, Basher began to curve down the ends against some boulders.

'That'll be handy if we have to climb up,' I said to him, never one hundred percent certain how much he understood.

When Wide Boy'd finished and I grumbled at him for inserting all the skewers with the curves facing upwards, he smirked. 'Just giving you your curtain hooks, Yakkity. Anyway, they'll slash the bastards if they try to get us.'

Over the next few weeks the men shored up the muddy edge round the top of the shaft with decking. Home sweet home. Not that any of us expressed an opinion on whether we'd stay there long. That was something best left vague and unspoken.

Chapter Thirty

It was the monotony that gnawed at me, that winter; monotony of food and monotony of drizzly grey weather. We had six hours of daylight, the sun a dull lightbulb hidden by waddings of cloud and all I could think of was drink. Yet I didn't give in to it.

Monotony gnawed at Peej, too, perhaps more than the others. I watched him, down in the pit in the weak light from the camping lamps, and knew he was restless now he was physically better; could feel the same tension jerk and tug at my own body.

'Any chance of having wine tonight,' I asked The Gaffer, crossing and uncrossing my feet for the umpteenth time under my camp stool and trying to avoid the glace cherries in the tin of fruit I was eating. 'To make this more appetising?'

He ignored me because I think he was in a mood with us. The Errol Flynn jibe and my rejection at the pit head had clearly upset him and he'd followed that up by suggesting we prepare the fields for planting: a suggestion that had been met by all except Basher with stony resistance. Well, the ground was sodden and the weather was cold and we couldn't see any point in it; the shops were full anyway.

'What do you think?' I asked again. 'About having wine?'

He didn't answer. His forehead was wrinkled. I could make that out even through the dim light. His eyes were shadowed by his brow and his thick nose. 'I just feel we should make a start on it,' he said.

I guessed that meant no wine and felt the monotonous slump but he talked on.

'We all agreed a couple of months ago. Basher said it. It was his idea and we all agreed.' He leaned forward and put his tin on the pit floor, standing it upright between his feet with the spoon sticking up and the rough round tin top a ragged star in the lamp light.

'Mind when we used to get new potatoes?' Grace said suddenly. Her cheeks were round and red, which I knew though I couldn't see them. I could only see her eyes with her naked eyebrows pushed up into her forehead and her liquid eyes watery bright.

'Ayrshires, hen. Aye, I mind,' Bill said and gave her two pats to her thigh.

'Boiled in their skin and dripping with butter, a sprinkle of salt and coarse grained black pepper,' The Gaffer said. His face came alive with his smile. 'We could plant them.'

'I'm a bit more in the hunter-gatherer stage of evolution,' Peej said, out of the darkness, stretching his arms and legs in front of him till we heard his joints crack

'Mind our first sheep?' Wide Boy said. 'That was some laugh. You were roaring, Sara, and greeting.'

It was in the early days. We'd found the sheep in the field and had singled one out and slaughtered it, while Sara cried from the field edge.

'Well, you shouldn't have killed the wee sheep!' she scolded, at the memory.

I rubbed Sara's back then put my arm round her shoulders and gave her a squeeze. She really hadn't liked it, but it had been funny, the way she'd gone on about it. And it was funnier still when she'd relished the barbecued lamb two nights in a row.

'You scoffed it!' Peej said. 'And so did you, Alice.'

'That's my kind of vegetarian!' Wide Boy said and we all smiled.

Once the story had been told, we all fell silent. Then, out of nowhere, The Gaffer said in front of everyone, 'You should write these stories down, Alice. Give you something to do with your time. Keep your mind occupied.' And I wondered if he suspected more about my interest in wine than I thought.

That night Peej, at least, had some relief for his restlessness. He disappeared with Basher, up the rope, lithe as if they were born to it. I watched them go, knowing that, in the morning if we were lucky there'd be deer and if they hadn't been lucky they'd go underground to nap then rise when Limpet woke them and go out after rabbits. Or woodpigeons, careful to coppice them, not killing them all.

Chapter Thirty-one

We lost count of the days during the illness. That was our biggest loss: the certainty we had; the regulation. Brain set up a kind of sun dial so we would have an idea if we had reached and passed the solstice but even when the days began to lengthen, it was still so cold I couldn't do any writing. I took to wearing two coats – a size ten and size twelve – one inside the other and my hands were stiff inside doubled up gloves.

Every two or three days a few of us would leave the camp to forage for food, cutlery, blankets – all those normal things people do when they move to a new address. Only we didn't ask the post office to redirect our mail. We'd head out in small parties, one person driving, one with a gun, and maybe another two or three for shopping. I went occasionally, usually in the early evenings, in the dark, and usually only when the target was an out of town shopping centre. We chose the quietest car we could find – a sleek, black Audi – and conversation, especially in the first trips, was minimal.

Sara found herself a real fur in someone's wardrobe when we were scavenging and she said she was going to be a film star. She found a camera too, and wanted me to take her photograph, even though I told her it was digital. She couldn't understand, so I pretended. I told her we'd get the pictures back in about a week, by which time she would have forgotten.

She loved that coat: stroked it as if it was a living animal. I still couldn't bring myself to wear one, yet I didn't mind if she did. I realised I was making allowances, now, at very least for Sara. 'Not that you'll be able to fasten it if you put on any more weight,' I told her.

And then it was February. The fields were yellowed with age

the way old newsprint goes, with too much acid in its pages. A year before, when the aftermath hit me, I wondered if grass would ever grow again; cried when it did, and when the first purple crocus pushed through its leaves. That it would still do it, year after year, despite what had happened! The elation was overwhelming. I needed elation then, in those first days when I was alone, or alone with only Sara. We'd come a long way together, Sara and I, and although we were living in a damp pit that exacerbated my aches and pains, and though I was bored with the grey monotony and with winter, I knew my life wasn't all bleak.

Slowly, I began to recover from my experience with the bikers. My grazes and bruises had healed quickly and with no sign of the bikers, and the increasing comfort inside our pit home, my emotional state slowly returned to near normal. Making a start on writing the history kept my mind occupied when I wasn't in company and the bottle of red was still in my bag, should the need for it arise.

When the weather eased and the pit grew claustrophobic, we set up a couple of big tents and stayed outside more during day-time. The men got them from one of the outdoor stores along with camping gas and stoves. Initially, of course, we were nervous about the bikers, but the tents were green and if we erected them near the bushes they were fairly unrecognisable. We put up two of them – mostly just because numbers dictated that we needed two – and self-segregated into a men's tent and a women's. If a man went towards the tent with the women in it a flutter would go round the women occupants. And we could feel the hostility if a woman dared approach the men while they were in session.

For all that I was fond of Sara and the others, I missed having a space of my own. So, since The Gaffer had suggested that I write down our stories, I asked him if I could have a small tent for writing this notebook and he said yes. It was a big move for me. I went with him and Eric to the camping shop to choose it and chose my own folding furniture for it and my own lamp. I even chose a chocolate and ivory rug to cover the floor. On the way back in the car I thought about my old life: my old notebooks, and in particular the two secrets I'd written in them. My two secrets. No one here knew anything about either of them. I wriggled my toes in my boots; visualised the tiny face in the photograph. Even now, even with most of the world's population dead, I still wondered where she was. Not that I'd write about her in this new notebook. It would be all about this new community. A year was the longest time I'd ever gone without scribbling in one but it felt right, now, to take up my pen again. Anyway, if I had to listen to any more of Grace's twenty-four hour prattling I'd have jumped in the Calder.

Of course, it was too much to expect that I could keep the privilege of having a special tent to myself. One day I saw Junkie leave the stove where the women had been cooking. I could see from her face that she was hatching something and so I watched her as she walked towards me. She had high, broad cheekbones, her eyebrows waxed into tapering lines. Her silvery pink eye-shadow contrasted with the near orange of her make-up. A face like a hallowe'en cake, my mother would have said. I should have pitied Junkie because there weren't any new trends and she'd never have the nous to invent her own. She'd be trapped in that time-frame for ever. I watched her through my tent flap. She was wearing a new parka with her socks pulled up over the bottom of her trouser legs. Hands in pockets and jaw working, she made her way over to me. Bent her head through the flap.

'You busy?'

I put my pen down and rested my arms on the notebook. 'It can wait.'

She dropped the flap behind her and sat on my spare picnic chair.

'I wanted to ask you something.'

The light was green. I lifted my lamp on to the table and fiddled with the matches, trying to block out her chewing-of-the-cud.

'Well?'

She looked at her nails. They were square cut and she'd painted a band of white across the top.

'Alice, know how you've got this tent? Could I get a loan of it?'

I sat back. 'Why?'

'Och, you know what it's like – I need a bit of time on my own.'

I used the look I used to use in the library when unruly youngsters needed thrown out. 'But this is my tent, Lee-Ann. The Gaffer told me I could have it.'

'I know,' she said, wriggling. 'But d'you not think I could get a shot of it, like – when you're not here?' She picked up my pen and pressed the nib against the edge of the page till the two tines started to separate. 'I wouldn't get in your way nor nothing.'

The heavy gold she wore on every finger reflected my camping lamp. Because her mouth was open I could hear every chaw of her gum. More and more, that, and seeing her wilfully damage my best pen, began to irritate me.

'No!' I said. 'It's mine. The Gaffer said it was my place, to write our history. And give me that.' I yanked my Parker from her. 'I've work to do.'

'Peej said you'd let me.'

I paused, still pointing at the exit. Retracted my arm and sat back down. '*Peej* said?'

'Aye.'

I shuffled papers. 'What did Peej say?'

She took the chewing gum from her mouth and held it like a squashed bug away from her then leaned in close enough for me to see the unblended rim of her orange foundation. 'He said you wouldn't mind because you know what it's like to need a bit of privacy.'

Chapter Thirty-two

Round about this time, when we were sitting in the living area down in the pit one evening, my eyes lifted from a book I was trying to read using one of those little clip lights you can peg on to some of the pages. The book was boring but the author had been well respected and so I felt I owed it to him to see the book through. But my mind kept wandering. Sara was sitting next to me, as she usually did, playing a battery operated game, whose tinny little blips and jingles were audible even though they were plugged directly into her ears. I'd been reading about a minor character whose leggings clung to legs so long the main character was obliged to stand on four volumes of an encyclopaedia to be able to penetrate her. I closed my book over, concerned in case Sara might have been able to read the page I was at, and I looked at her.

What a pudding she was. Her hair was still blonde and wispy, as it had been a year ago when I'd met her but it was longer now. When she left it loose, its ends split on her shoulders, turning upwards in kinks. That evening she wore it tied back with a lacy scrunchie into a single pony tail. Her skin was soft in the light from the lanterns and I could see the fine blonde down that coated her cheeks. For the first time I took stock of the dewlap that padded what should have been the space between her chin and her chest. Since her head was angled downwards, while she followed the animation on her DS, her double chin rested fully on her chest so it was no surprise that she now breathed so noisily. She'd been quite plump when I'd met her but that evening I realised just how fat she had become. She was obese and the more I looked, the more I realised how her clothes were straining to hold her all in. The zip on the green top she was wearing had burst open at the ribbing round the waist and she had pinned it with what looked like one of Grace's costume brooches and across her bust (which covered her front and even seemed to have occupied all the space under her arms) the gape was bridged by a black and silver Anarchy badge. There was a gap below the waistband where her belly was protruding.

'Pull your top down, Sara,' I told her.

'What?' she said, struggling with her ear-plug.

'Fix your top. Your tummy's sticking out.'

She screwed up her face at me but tugged the bottom of her top and wriggled till she was covered again.

'You need new clothes again,' I said. 'Why didn't you say and we could have got you some?'

'Can we?' she said and enthusiasm replaced the irritation.

The January sales were permanently ending and the spring and summer ranges were permanently being introduced. 'Sure, why not?' I said. 'Well, we'll need to!' I asked aloud if any of the men would take us to the shops but Peej didn't seem to hear me.

'I'll take you,' Eric said. 'Do you want to go now?'

I couldn't backtrack because Sara had already bustled out of her seat. 'Any one else want to go?' I asked around the others but no one was interested; Peej was talking to Bill, Grace and Junkie. The others were in the middle of a card game. Limpet must have been putting the kids to bed.

'Will you be alright, just the three of you?' The Gaffer asked, looking up with a fan of red cards in his hand.

'Er – ' I said, holding my book in front of me. Eric was alright but it was the combination of him with Sara and me that felt uncomfortable. Slightly. No, a lot. Even after all these months I still cringed when I thought about the night Sara and I had spent at his flat above the Horsebrasses Bar. I still felt he'd something over me – something he remembered that I didn't. It didn't occur to me when we were in company but I still felt awkward with him on my own. I clutched my book, tugging at the clip-on light, willing The Gaffer – of all people – to see my discomfort and elect to come along but Eric said, 'It's fine

– you're in the middle of a hand!' so The Gaffer shrugged and said, 'Don't be long.' And that meant we'd no excuse. The idea of Eric smirking inwardly at the thought of being our guardian after what he must have done to me that night when I was out of my head on the couch made my stomach sink. But Sara was excited. As soon as I'd put the idea in her head she wasn't likely to let it go and she definitely did need new clothes. Seeing her standing it was evident just how rotund she'd grown even in the two or three months since we'd moved into the pit.

I couldn't even get away with sitting in the back of the car with Sara – Eric told me he needed me in the front as look-out. However, our trip was uneventful. Fortunately, once we got to the shopping centre, Eric was caught up with Sara's exuberance and I was able to browse through the aisles by myself, enjoying the colours of the clothes flaring red, green and turquoise in the circle from my torch. While the two of them giggled over at the sun hat and glasses area, I raided the oversize collection for elastic waisted jeans for her and tee-shirts that I could have wrapped round me doubled. When I went to rejoin them, she was holding her wrist up to him and he was holding the torch in his mouth, shining down on a silver bracelet with lots of dangly, diamante charms. When she saw me, she held up a red bikini for herself, the bracelet on her wrist tinkling and a shy little smile on her face as she looked from me to Eric. I didn't have the heart to tell her it wouldn't fit her. I took it from her but grabbed a huge one after her back was turned and we were ready to return to the car.

'I brought your purse,' she said when we neared the cash point. 'In case you needed it.' She fumbled in the back pocket of her jeans and brought it out. I'd completely forgotten it. It was about a year since the virus struck. A year since we'd started living together. Strange that she had thought we might need it now. As we sat in the car, Sara, chirpy, up at the front and me having the excuse of taking up the full back row with my armfuls of 'purchases', I opened the clip of my old purse and shone my torchlight into it. The light picked out the edges of my forefingers, engrained with dirt, looking just like the etched

156

coloured lines on the twenty pound note I spread, one-handedly, over my knee. There, too, was my chip and pin debit card, my library membership and my weekly ticket for the bus, dated 24 January. I switched off the torch. Outside the car windows the world was black but familiar. The past was a world away. I spent a full five minutes chinking and sniffing at my coins.

Chapter Thirty-three

Yesterday afternoon we were all out in the fields, having accepted what first Basher and then The Gaffer had impressed on us: that we had to face facts and learn how to dig. Junkie and Grace were the only two who escaped the induction, Grace because of her age and infirmity and Junkie because she complained of feeling poorly. When Peej told me I almost scoffed in his face but he furrowed his brows at me so I thought better of it. And when I saw her I realised she really wasn't very well. Her face was chalk-white instead of orange because she hadn't put her foundation on. It was strange seeing her like that, waif-like, like a little girl. I let her stay in my tent for the day – made it comfortable with pillows and such.

Anyway, we were in the fields. It was quite mild for the end of February: the birds were pairing off and we were making a start on some planting, or clearing. Limpet went back early with the children because she was on cooking duty but Grace had come along for the company and she sat at the field edge, singing. There was a delay while Basher and Brain rigged up some attempt at a ploughing mechanism and then Grace said, clear as Vera Lynn, 'Who's that young lad?'

Our heads turned to see a solitary figure strolling right up the middle of our road. Our men dropped their plough bits. We always carried binoculars – or, in my case, opera glasses – and The Gaffer trained his on the man.

'He's on his own,' he said, but you could never be sure. There were bushes up the sides of the road so anyone might have been hiding there, but I hadn't heard any bikes. Even so, I moved closer to the men and dragged Sara by the coat sleeve beside me.

The Gaffer looked around. 'Where's Peej?' There wasn't any sign of him. 'Peej!' he shouted.

'I haven't seen him since he took Junkie's lunch to her,' I said.

Wide Boy looked at the ground.

'What is it, Alice?' Sara asked me, her earnest face turned towards me. 'What's happening?'

'Forget it. Brain, Basher – come with me,' The Gaffer said. 'Eric, you stay with the women,' and they went to confront the stranger.

But then a collie sprang out of the bushes and I said, 'Oh look. It's Shep! It's Shep and Chis, Sara!' Chas for Charles, really, but Chis, because his cheek bones and nose were sharp and his eyes were stony. A face like a chisel, as Wide Boy put it, topped by soft sandy hair. 'God, it's ages since we've seen him!' It was lucky he was able to find us.

'Chis!' Sara said, her face alight with excitement. 'I love Shep and Chis!'

We all started walking towards him. We'd first met him last spring when Peej had driven us in to see Glasgow and he'd visited us a few times in the library but that was months ago. Anyway, by now the men were patting him on the back, the women – me included – were kissing him. His daft mutt jumped around, shepherding the children and everyone was exuberant. The Gaffer asked him if he'd seen any of the bikers. Chis said he kept out of their way and that made me grimace. We went back to the camp and of course we shared what we had to eat with him. Not that it was much: Peej had disappeared and Basher had been busy with the plough all day so we didn't have any fresh meat but Limpet had made a fresh batch of nan and we opened some tins of korma and stewing steak and made a feast of that. Because it was a special treat The Gaffer broke out the wine and later the malt and we sang to Chis's guitar. Sara had such a pop-star crush on him. She sat up close and he accompanied her favourite songs. I smiled in a fudgy amber happiness at her. She was way too fat to dance now so she just sat smiling into his eyes, star-struck like the collie at his feet.

I noticed Peej came back in time for dinner. 'Where's he been?' I asked the boy wonder.

'Dropping his effin trousers,' he said.

'All afternoon?'

Wide Boy didn't answer. I wondered if it was food poisoning, because the previous day we'd let Gracie do some cooking. Junkie had been sick, too, although she'd been funny off and on for a while. I hoped Sara and I wouldn't catch it.

It hit Junkie badly the night immediately after Chis's party. She brought up all her dinner. Self inflicted, probably, because of all the alcohol. I would have cleaned it up but I was in my bed. What a headache I had. It was nothing to do with the amount of wine and whisky I drank, though The Gaffer came over to me in the middle of the evening and told me I should be careful. Be careful? He should mind his own business. I told him that. I told him about my aches and pains that make it hard for me to climb up and down the rope sometimes and about lumpiness down my shin bones that I'd never noticed before and how my back and shoulders were stiff. He said it was psychological. Psychological! He said it might be because of this notebook: because I started reliving all the trauma of the first year of aftermath and he asked me how far I'd reached in writing the story. I told him I'd reached the bit about Junkie coming back in the storm (though that was a lie but I couldn't face telling him I'd got stuck when I had tried to write about the bikers). And he said, 'Well, maybe you're suffering from Post Traumatic Stress Disorder.' He said it would be making me worry about everything, like Faslane again, but I told him to mind his own bloody business. He thinks he knows everything. 'And that isn't helping,' he said, when I threw back the last of what was in my glass. If it was Post Traumatic Stress Disorder it would have more to do with the trouble I had with the bikers than any kind of possibility of Faslane blowing up.

Limpet cleaned it up eventually. That sour smell was turning my stomach and even poor Sara lay and groaned. The smell of sick was with me all night. Well, Limpet couldn't put it anywhere. Her husband wouldn't let her take it up to the top so she just had to store it down our far end, leaving the air with a sour reminder of Junkie's stomach troubles.

And Sara kept me awake with her tossing and turning. So fat she said she couldn't draw breath.

'No wonder,' I said to her, brutal because of the alcohol. I tugged at the chain of her locket. She'd worn it constantly since that day she and Eric had 'bought' it at the retail park, but if the chain was a bit short then, it was far too tight, now. 'Look at the size of you. You need to cut down what you're eating.'

She didn't look pleased but her breasts alone were enormous. I told her I was frightened I'd suffocate every time she turned over.

The groaning went on all night, long after all the party music and laughter had stopped. I hardly closed my eyes. She said she had tummy ache so she must have caught the same bug as Junkie. Basher and The Gaffer were right about one thing – it was time we introduced more greenery into our diet. The seedlings we'd tried to grow hydroponically when Brain rebuilt the cycling generator were straggly things, miserable to be living underground and didn't I know how that felt. Anyway, I dosed Sara up with vitamins and told her to drink lots of water. The local burn water's clear as glass. I know, because I've tried it. I filtered it through a pair of tights to keep out the bugs.

In the morning I gave Sara a double dose of laxatives. Just mild ones, to clear away any blockages. She didn't want to take them. Moaned and groaned, but I had no sympathy.

'Please, Alice,' she said. 'Please!' and grabbed hold of me as I stretched across to fix the covers over her properly.

'Sara!' I said. Her podgy little fingers were curled round my cardigan and even when I tugged it I couldn't break away.

'It's sore,' she griped. 'Don't leave me.'

'For God's sake,' I said, half shocked and half laughing. 'What are you like? So, you've got a sore tummy but what do you expect with the amount of crisps and sweets you got through at the party last night. I'm going to have to put you on a diet!'

She grizzled some more and said she didn't feel like coming up to the surface. So I let her stay in bed. I'm not that hard.

I told her I'd go down to see her at lunchtime but that I just wanted to write a little bit more in my notebook. Really, I just needed time on my own to get over my headache.

Alice's not going to be writing for a wile.
See Sara? No – I wo'nt write it.
Lee-Ann

Chapter Thirty-four

It was a weird day. Sullen and solemn – I think none of us had slept well, with the smell of Junkie's sick and Sara moaning. Not even the drinks at Chis's ceilidh had knocked us out.

When I came out of my tent that lunchtime after I'd napped, my headache was gone but I was experiencing that strange temporal dislocation when you sleep non-standard hours. Everyone had had lunch and no one thought to call me. They thought I was working.

The fire was almost out and I had to stir it and throw on more wood so I could boil the water. I decided I'd take a raspberry tea to Sara. We're still using the packets – dried tea lasts for ages – but eventually we'll have to dry brambles.

I moistened some couscous grains and left them to steam then stirred in olive oil and a generous squeeze of tomato with half a teaspoon of easy garlic, salt and coriander. Broke up a couple of young dandelion shoots small enough so she wouldn't notice.

The men were smoking in a group. Chis had moved on and The Gaffer was hassling the others to get back to work and I remember them laughing. Basher was to one side. Limpet was clearing the dishes.

They were frozen like a theatrical tableau, some Biblical epic, the hand of God coming. I had this disjointed feeling I was out of step. There were broad bands of black and blacker clouds in layers all the way down to the horizon and that dampness, stillness, swaddling.

'Sara still not well?' Grace asked me. She settled herself on the ground sheet close to the fire, adjusting the plaid blanket over her shoulders.

'This'll cheer her up,' I said, sealing the raspberry tea into a flask that would be easy to carry into the pit. And that was it. I put the flask and the boxed couscous into a bag and slung it over my shoulder. I wrinkled my nose at Grace and said, 'I'm not going to give her any more chocolate.'

'More for you and me!' she said and her worn face crinkled.

I didn't bother taking down the cradle. I was a lot nimbler by then, apart from my aches and pains, and I found it just as easy to climb down the rope once we'd tied some knots in it. I dropped the last couple of feet. The shaft was dank from the rain and the walls had grown a slimy green down some of the fissures.

'Only me, Sara,' I called out in the echo chamber of the shaft bottom. 'How are you doing?' It was rare any of us wanted to spend the day alone underground. She'd be frightened if she thought I was one of the men.

My feet splashed, fracturing the reflected sky. I bent to go through the lowest part of the tunnel into the solid darkness, feeling for the new stoop and pillars we'd installed at the beginning of winter when heavy rain had crazed the shale roof. I hadn't brought a torch but could see her light ahead of me reflected in Grace's gilt-framed mirror. I straightened up after the tight bit and picked my way between the men's beds and then the shadows and silhouettes of Bill and Grace's grave goods – her floral-shaded standard lamp, the mahogany coat stand that the damp was depriving of its sheen and a glass fronted display cabinet complete with treasures that tinkled when I squeezed past because only three of the feet made contact with the ground.

Sara hadn't responded.

'Still sleeping?' I asked her, projecting my voice apologetically through other people's space.

The pit was a seam that opened out reaching over eight feet at the near end. There was room for all our beds and baggage. The men were at the front to keep us safe. Basher and Limpet and their family came next then Bill and Grace. We'd managed to divide the place up with furniture and partitions. It wasn't perfect; it was a bit damp but it was warm as a womb compared with outside when everyone was in it. At the near end that we called our living area Brain had set up the bicycle and the hydroponic system that didn't work. And the old electric fire with its two bars that glowed and dimmed with the dwindling energy reserves of the legs of whoever was on duty.

'Sara?'

She didn't answer. The torch beside her still shone its arc on the wall. I put my hand on her shoulder and she was stiff.

Chapter Thirty-five

It was Peej I turned to when I discovered her and when I had screamed my way to the top of the shaft. I could replay him like some blockbuster movie. See him turning against that stratified sky, jettisoning his cigarette, slow motion body beginning its run. I regurgitated the bare facts like sick on the grass; he pushed me into the women and disappeared down the hole calling for Brain and Basher but none of the others to come after him. Brain resurfaced grey-faced and spoke with The Gaffer then went immediately down again. All the while Grace held my head tight against her chest, cooing, and the others crowded around me, their hands on my hair, not letting me see what they were planning, till I broke away, swearing and hysterical and ran to the edge of the field. The old fraying fence post scoured a layer from inside my palm as I cursed my ignorance and etched my guilt.

The Gaffer ordered Wide Boy and Eric to clear a space in the men's tent but Limpet started arguing and the action transferred to the women's. I saw the women go in and knew they'd be moving their belongings. They opened the tent flaps wide. I looked down the hill towards all the dead houses, my mind flat-lined. Turned back when the wind tugged a new silence to me, their words halted when Peej's dark head appeared from the shaft. I watched him clamber out then squat to help raise Sara's heavy, heavy body.

They'd wrapped her loosely in her quilt. In the dark they couldn't have seen how much blood there was or they'd surely have wrapped her in a second. One of the children started crying. My ears were cold without my hat. They stung as the wind scourged them, but not as much as my insides.

After they'd carried her to the women's tent – Limpet at the flap, telling them how to lay her, glancing towards me – Peej came down, checking for blood on his hands and clothes. I turned away. Early spring sun from a cloud gap spilled ink over half of the sky, blackening the tree lines. Lichen, drizzled on the bushes, became a filigree froth. Strange, the clarity of that memory. There was nothing Peej could say to me and he didn't bother trying. Didn't even touch me, though I could feel the pull between us. I sank to the ground and he hunkered beside me. It was hushed there, out of the wind.

'Did you know?'

I shook my head and opened my fingers in the new grass. At length he picked out a lock of my hair and rolled the tip of it between his finger and thumb. The rust of his leather jacket smudged in the corner of my eye but I couldn't look at him.

'Limpet and Lee-Ann'll take care of her,' he said and let go of my hair. His knee cracked when he stood up to go away.

We buried her later the same day. Further up the hill from our settlement, in a corner of the open field the buzzard flew over. What was the point in waiting? We'd all stopped work because of it, even the men, Basher weeping openly while the other men stayed boulder-faced. One of them did it. Must have done. But I didn't know who to blame.

When it was finished The Gaffer authorised a drink and gave me a bottle. I took it to the edge of the field and drank it. Later, Saleema brought me my dinner. She kissed me on the cheek and her hair on my face smelled of cinnamon. When it was late and they were going to bed Junkie came to see me. A short gold chain was spilling from her hand. A gold locket. 'I've sorted out some of Sara's things, Alice,' she said, squatting down beside me. 'Do you want to look through them?' But I didn't want her near, her of any of them. I didn't even answer her, just kept looking the other way.

'Well, I'll tuck them under the bed, for now, then,' she said and tried to stroke my hair but I shook her hand off. She stood up again. 'You can look through it when you feel up to it.'

I hated her when she walked away, her tight jeans and boots

stepping over the tussocks but I couldn't tell her that so I drank some more out of my bottle to make the hours pass.

Soon I'd drunk nearly all of it. Then I saw gold arcs, swinging from side to side, coming towards me out of the darkness. My hands slapped out against the light-streaked night as Peej lifted me over his shoulder and The Gaffer was there in the background, with his face closed down.

In the morning I woke up in Junkie's single bed. The one I'd shared with Sara had disappeared and there was a big space in its place.

Chapter Thirty-six

Sara had been pregnant and I didn't even guess it. Crazy, when I looked at Limpet at the funeral, seven months if she was a day. I saw the same shape, then, as Sara – the massive bust spreading horizontally over her abdomen. I didn't suspect it for a millisecond. I wrote her off as fat. Fat and mentally subnormal, just the way Wide Boy had, right at the beginning. What right had I to do that? I must have been blinkered: if anybody had known it should have been me.

And then, of course, I tormented myself about the father. It was at least the end of February. Possibly March. Just over a year after the disaster. Take away forty weeks would mean she'd conceived in May or June. I'd been responsible for her then. I'd been the one to look after her.

Thoughts and recriminations ran through my head. How could I let it happen? The day after we buried her I was rootless, blind to the usual routines. I was dimly aware of the others standing aside from me but I was absorbed with my guilt. Had she been hurt?

I went over my own experience with the two bikers. Twisted the paper hankie Junkie had given me that morning when she saw me drying my face on my sleeve. I walked to the field edge, twisting it and twisting it till the tissue disintegrated, leaving scraps and threads all over my gloved hands.

In June we were living in the library. The bikers didn't attack for another four or five months. That left Peej, Wide Boy, and Eric. It couldn't be The Gaffer or Brain – we didn't meet them, I was sure, till into the autumn. Bill was too old. And Basher?

A touch on my back made me spin. It was Salaam, sent by his mother to call me for lunch but how could I lunch with them when I didn't know who I could trust? At the camp, slightly uphill from where I was standing, I could see them gathered, men and women together.

Peej, Wide Boy, Eric, Basher, not Bill. June.

'No,' I said to Salaam and he ran off at speed and probably gratefully.

Peej, Wide Boy, Eric. Not The Gaffer or Brain. Not Basher or Bill.

Peej's voice reached me from the campsite. 'Something to eat?' He was holding a bowl in the air but I turned my back. I shrugged him off. I shrugged them all off, considering them all guilty. One of them could have prevented it, surely, but then, so could I? Should I?

I wished I'd told her about condoms but had assumed she was too dim to need them.

The air was still and so was I. It was almost spring-like but I felt only death.

'Come back to the tents, Alice.' The Gaffer stood behind me, not touching me.

My throat stretched tight but I couldn't make sounds. His gloved hand reached for my arm. 'No,' I said and staggered further off. From the side of my vision I saw him stand a while in the cold, his shoulders raised and his gloved hands shoved into his coat pockets. The white vapour of each breath he exhaled reminded me she wouldn't breathe again.

'Are you coming?'

I shook my head and he turned to go. 'I wish I'd already started writing the history in June,' I said and heard the catch in his breath before he walked away.

I lost part of my life when Sara died. Not just emotionally. I lost two months of time and my self-respect. That night down the pit I accused the men of abusing Sara but they all denied it. I challenged them, one after the other, the company stunned into silence at the accusations and the drama but one by one the men all denied it. Closed eyes, closed faces. I couldn't penetrate their armour. And with no way to test the DNA Sara's abuser's identity went with her into her grave.

171

'We'll never know, Alice. Let it rest,' The Gaffer said and with shaking hands he poured me another whisky.

And that's how my old curse came back: the heavy drinking. They meant well, giving me the booze, but they didn't know the real me, even if sometimes I thought The Gaffer suspected it. But if they did, if he did, he wouldn't have given me the daily bottle. It brought back the old ways. The reason I was overlooked for promotion. Why I was hidden away with the incunabula. Too much going on in my head and I needed the drink to subjugate it, anaesthetise it, throttle it with a garrotte and bury it.

They left me to drift, when I needed reeled in. I was a loose kite, needing someone to grab hold of my string. I was always a misfit. I kicked off my shoes and looked at my feet. I was even born a misfit. Day after day that spring, I sat at the edge of the field, spreading my toes in the grass, and watched the people I lived with in their ordered world, despising them for concealing Sara's murderer and despising myself.

*

Drink knocks you unconscious but only for a couple of hours. Then you need another one. I'd woken when it was beginning to get light. It got light early in late Spring, quite far north, while it was still the middle of the night. It even penetrated down our hole sufficiently for me to move without cracking my shins. Limpet had been awake. She said my name as I passed her. I grunted that I was going up to do the toilet. Everyone else was asleep. I took the keys from The Gaffer's discarded jacket's pocket and opened his drinks cabinet for my daily ration not even caring if the chink of the bottles disturbed him then I climbed up the knotted rope, cradling my bottle inside my jumper, my legs shaking but my hands strong. Outside was the same dead world I'd seen since Sara died. The metal lid twists and cricks then sings as it pirouettes on the bottle neck. The perfumed genie escapes. Suckered, you pursue, inhaling deep. You drink and he discharges the wretchedness from your throat, gut, shoulders, neck, consciousness.

There were flowers in the landscape. It was May again.

Fifteen months. It had to be May because the may was blooming on the trees. The hawthorn. It made my nose itch. When I lay down, at the edge of the field, I couldn't see the dead world; I couldn't see our tents go up in the early sunshine. I could only see the grass tips stretching for the sky, flat-bladed spears of green, translucent and veined in the euphoria of my whisky-fuelled eye-sight. By the fence posts, common mouse-ear flowerets shivered their tiny eight-pointed stars and on a coil of wind I thought I heard a baby's cry. I sat up, haunted by Sara's baby through the earth, and let another draught of whisky flood onto my tongue. I heard laughter. I shifted and sat against the fence post, watching the camp.

With Saleema supporting her, Limpet brought me her baby. Over the long grass she came, holding the baby in her arms, her emerald dress moving with the motion of her legs just as the surface of a burn moves with the current of the water. A gust slipped her hijab off and she pulled it up again to cover her black hair, smiling.

I pulled on my shoes.

The baby's skin was dewy with birth. Its eyelids had three lines and its eyes when they opened were an opaque midnight blue. I looked into Limpet's brown eyes and she readied to put the baby in my arms. I put the bottle down. He had hardly any weight or length, her baby, his arms and legs folded. I lifted him to my mouth and placed my upper lip against his forehead. Its sticky warmth provoked the sting in my breasts of a distant response.

Limpet looked weary. Saleema pulled my elbow and we went back to the camp.

173

Chapter Thirty-seven

While I'd been drinking, Junkie told everyone she too was pregnant. She wouldn't say whose it was; maybe she didn't even know. She didn't know when it was due. She looked six months when she stood without her jacket. Even in my muddled state I could make the calculation. If it was May and she was showing, she must have conceived at the end of last year so it could be any one of them. The poor baby had a better chance of being born infected with syphilis than a junkie like her mother.

And then there was better news. Peej had taken the 4x4 further out one night than he usually did. He was badger watching but he fell asleep in the car; didn't catch any badgers but when the sun came up he saw he was parked beside a field with only three sheep in it and when he looked closely he noticed they had heavy packets swinging between their back legs so he lassoed one with a rope and dragged it into the back of the car and put it to work straight away with some of our ladies. How Sara would have laughed at that. Laughed and blushed and covered her eyes with her hands. Peej and Basher went back in the car for the other two in case the first one's marble bag was empty. I'd no idea how long a sheep's gestational period was or whether the timing was right for love in the animal kingdom, just as it seemed to be in our world, but I hoped we'd have fresh lamb before the mint sauce went past its sell-by date.

At least, in my absence, the others got round to planting those potatoes. Since I went off the rails Basher had bashed about, insisting we had our food supply organised. So, not only were we now regulating meat production with him and Peej hunting and because of the sheep, but we were also in line to harvest our first, early summer crops. Good old Basher, and to a certain extent Eric and Wide Boy. I felt the beginnings of optimism. With The Gaffer's cooperation, I forced myself to drink only strong tea and water. I went through two days of alcoholic detox, supported by the closeness to Limpet and her new baby during the day, shaking out the poison's grip on my limbs. I woke from DTs and nightmares looking into Junkie's eyes.

As May went into June, the sunny weather ripened the green beans and broccoli they planted. The only snag was the caterpillars but suddenly I didn't give a damn about the environment. Not here, in our patch. If it came to a choice between the bugs or us, then I made my peace that it was the bugs who'd be dying. All of us were dying for a feast of green. In a few years, when we were more secure, we could go back to organic. That summer after Sara died, I had a hunger I couldn't satisfy for field fresh foods.

So many hungers. My misery was just beneath the surface. So while the young men chased Saleema and Salaam about the fields and there were picnics and laughter in the long, late evenings, I needed something to occupy me. Something other than drink to blank out time.

Nothing made up for the bond I'd had with Sara. Sara, who was a burden and a security blanket and my mission from that first afternoon outside Amrit's shop. It was a mission I had failed. It was a bond I didn't even see I had. I said to The Gaffer, in a rare moment of near understanding between us, that –

*

Wide Boy was training his binoculars on a kestrel fluttering in the sky when a stone flew straight towards it and only narrowly missed. He plummeted his binoculars. Coming through the grass, he saw two brown furred beasts that were too thick set to be foxes. He thought maybe they were deer. One of them reared up, took aim and fired a shot with a sling. He saw blue eyes in a grubby human face – two faces – before the stone clipped him on the shoulder. 'Hey!' Wide Boy shouted, running towards them and pulling off his binoculars.

175

Two girls stood up and ran away.

'Wait!'

Instinctively our men reached for their guns. Wide Boy had the edge on Eric and Brain. Soon, as the two girls were sprinting through the long grass up our hill away from us, Wide Boy was homing in on them, arm outstretched towards the bushiness that was Robina's hair.

'Got you!' he shouted.

I'd come out of the tent by now and had my opera glasses raised to my eyes. Robina fought like something wild. Wide Boy dropped his binocs and grabbed her upper arm in his other hand, twisting it behind her back. Then he pulled her head back with a fistful of that hair of hers but Robina ducked and jolted, throwing herself from side to side and up and down and kicking back at him with her feet. As if that wasn't enough, Robyn jumped on his back and dug her teeth into the flesh between his shoulder and his neck. I saw the bite she gave him. A bite like a wildcat.

Wide Boy yelled out with the pain. He leaned forward and dropped Robina. She spun round and jumped on him too, grabbing his head and pulling him even further down towards the ground, with her twin sister still worrying him with her teeth. I think if Brain hadn't reached them she'd have bitten the lump clean out and they'd have had him for dinner.

'Get them off!' Wide Boy squealed as first Brain then a panting Eric went running up the hill to help out. They grabbed one each then Wide Boy stood up again, rubbing his neck and looking at the blood on his fingers.

Those girls were hissing and spitting; legs jabbing out to the side. Eric and Brain forced them to crouch on the ground and lay their weight on them. The Gaffer hurried over with a length of rope and between the four of them they managed to subdue the two by knotting them into separate parcels that still had teeth and boots, if not claws.

'Bite this,' I'm sure I heard Wide Boy say, and he wrapped a length of cord round Robyn's head, tugging it like a bit between her teeth. I think it was Robyn. At that stage they were both dressed identically. The men brought them to the camp where we could have a look at them. The Gaffer and Eric guarded and interrogated them while Wide Boy and Brain took guns and went looking to see if there was anybody else.

We should have been glad to welcome them. Instead, we had mixed emotions. The men marched them to our camp fire and sat them on the ground sheet. Sitting, Robina heeled the fire and half burnt twigs and embers hissed on to the sheet, burning straight through to the grass beneath and leaving behind a thin pillar of plastic smoke. She shook her foot to clear smouldering ashes off her boot and each fragment fizzled on the mat which now had half a dozen irregular, brown edged holes and another half a dozen brown smudges.

'Tie her feet,' The Gaffer told Eric.

Eric grabbed her feet and pulled, tipping her bluntly on to her back. I felt for her elbow. He pushed till her knees bent, leaning his weight on her.

Watching it pained me. 'Eric,' I said.

Almost horizontal, he half turned his head to me. 'Doing what the man ordered.' He ravelled the rope round her ankles, tugging it tight till she moaned under him and I cringed. He tied it off and cut it with a tug of his knife while I fidgeted with the strap of my opera glasses.

The other was docile, learning from his treatment of her sister.

Limpet, Grace and I watched from the sidelines. Any comments – they're only children, or mind what you're doing; look at the colour of them; they've got the same blue eyes – were disregarded by the men, intent on securing them. I almost expected them to impale them on a spit for the fire.

I repeated, 'They're only children.'

The girls' eyes drifted over our clothes and faces; they lingered on Salaam, who pushed his way between the women to stand in front of his mother for a decent view. I supposed he was about the same age. No matter how much the girls' eyes investigated us, they returned with conspicuous regularity to their twin's.

Wide Boy and Brain came back and said they must have been alone. Wide Boy stood over them toying with his gun.

'You should stick them in Yakkity's tent,' he told The Gaffer. 'Make it like the prison.'

'They're only children,' I said. I'd sat down on a camp chair, keeping an eye on them and helping Limpet with Salami, who was girny and wanted lots of nursing.

'Aye, right,' Wide Boy said. 'More like wildcats.' He appealed to The Gaffer. 'Not think we should cage them?'

The Gaffer's mouth twitched. Indecisive.

'They're scared,' I said. 'Shut them in the tent and they won't know what's going to happen to them. Leave them here, let them see how normal our life is and maybe they'll come round a bit.'

The Gaffer patted Wide Boy's arm. 'We'll wait and see how they settle.'

I smiled to the ground. I checked the height of the sun and gave Salami back to his mother so Saleema and I could take our turn at cooking. We sat at the other end of the ground sheet from the girls and went about our business. I made sure we spoke loudly enough for the twins to hear us.

'Saleema – your dad should be home soon with his catch.' I glanced into the twins' blue eyes. 'Wonder what it'll be?'

'Maybe a deer.' Saleema smiled. 'Probably a couple of frogs and a toad.'

She'd pulled green beans from the field and we prepared them, setting up the camping gas stove. I brought barley to the boil and left it on a slow simmer, my stock pot almost filled to the brim with water. I added a whole packet of dried onion and six dessertspoonfuls of bouillon powder to give it flavour. The wind was wafting the steam away from me: I pretended not to notice the girls' minor head movements as they scented the food. I may not have been Masterchef, but I guessed it was the first cooked meal they'd had in a while.

Robyn's eyes were on me. 'Are you hungry?' I asked her. She turned away. 'You'll have your share.'

Both girls' wide eyes pulled towards each other.

'Maybe we'll even have fresh meat, once our other men come back.'

I stirred the pot while Saleema rinsed the vegetables with some of our collected rain water. Just then, we heard the low whistle that told us Basher and Peej were coming. Wide Boy put his finger and thumb in his mouth and whistled back and there was an air of expectancy in the camp. Not only was this one of our favourite times when we gathered in anticipation, but tonight we had the added surprise of guests.

Peej and Basher seemed massive when they entered the camp. Their boots, their thick clothes and heavy jackets bulked them out, even on an early summer's day like that one. On their shoulders they carried a coil of rope or a backpack for their shot; knives and smaller twine hung from the belts they'd fastened round their closed jackets. Sun had reddened Peej's face. It had been a windy day with more blue than the passing clouds had lead us to believe and it looked as if it had caught him out. Even Basher's skin colouring had darkened. I looked at them through the girls' eyes, seeing them for the first time and realising for the first time that we too were growing wild.

They walked without speaking up to the groundsheet and laid down their catch. Rabbits, tied by the feet in two pairs. Still soft, their heads bumped on the blue mat. I looked at the two girls then up at Peej.

'We've got visitors,' I told him.

'So I see.'

Basher's eyes swept the girls from bottom to top and back again. Their blue eyes stood out in the brown of their clothes and faces. 'They need a wash.'

'Aye,' Peej said. 'They might turn out to be human.' He took off the coil of rope and untied his belt. It swung to the grass by itself because of the weight. Then he sat on the mat and untied his shoe to knock a stone out of it.

The Gaffer recounted the story. Basher listened then went towards the men's tent, stopping to kiss his baby's cheek and look in Limpet's eyes.

'Should have seen the bite she gave me,' Wide Boy told Peej, pulling down the neck of his tee-shirt as he filled him in on the details The Gaffer had missed.

Saleema and I moved nearer the girls with the catch. By then, we were proficient at skinning and gutting. Since Sara's death I did it efficiently and without a conscience. I didn't even wince when I ran my knife up behind the neck separating the fur from the skin and crunching through the bone to sever the head from the body. The only thing I hadn't learned to do was clean the furs. With so many clothes unwanted in the shops we'd no need for learning how to prepare furs. Besides, it seemed just one step too far from civilisation.

For speed we cut the rabbits into joints and spiked them to roast above the flames. The carcasses we set aside in plastic tubs to be boiled for soup next day. Soon the smell of searing meat was teasing us. Oil and rabbit grease dripped into the flames and sizzled.

While we'd prepared the meat, Peej had smoked in silence, his two boots on the grass and his eyes on our movements. But we were used to that.

'You from here?' he said to the two girls. They stared, unresponsive. 'Should take they ropes off their heads,' Peej said to me.

I turned a piece of meat then licked the juices from my fingers. 'They bit Wide Boy. They've been a bit wild.'

'Aye, but they're kids.'

'I know.' I told him there'd been talk that we should 'imprison' them but that I wanted them to stay where they could see we were no threat.

Peej tossed his cigarette away and rose to his stockinged feet.

'They kicked the fire and burnt the mat,' Saleema said.

He glanced at it and stood over the girls, shaking his head slightly. 'Now that wasn't nice, dolls.' He squatted and I heard his knee crack. 'What happened to you two, then? Eh? On your own?' He reached over and sat one of the girls up, momentarily caressing her matted hair. She shrank into herself. He paused then sat the sister upright too. 'Let's get these ropes off you.' His hands were still bloodied with his kill. 'Put your head down.' He

180

leaned to see behind the thick scrub of Robina's hair to where Wide Boy's knot had tightened into the back of her neck, and loosened it.

I watched as he uncoiled the rope gently from the first twin's mouth. She licked her lips. Thick cord impressions were white and red on her cheeks. She didn't speak, just watched as Peej unbound her sister. I poured something to drink.

'Here,' I said, holding the cup towards the first one but wary of any sign of aggression. There was none. Just the flaring of her eyes and the eagerness to put her mouth to the cup. I didn't need words to know that. Bolder, I cupped the back of her head with one hand and held the orange juice to her lips.

Saleema poured a cup for the second and passed it to Peej.

'What's your name?' I asked.

The first twin checked with her sister.

'Robyn.'

'R- r- robin,' Peej said. 'That's how you're all fluttering.' He looked at her sister, pausing with her drink. 'She belongs in a tree.'

Saleema smiled and went back to stirring the pot.

'What about your sister?' I asked.

Peej took the cup away from her lips.

'I'm Robina,' she said.

'So youz *are* twins?'

'Aye,' they said in unison. And smiled.

'But I'm the eldest,' Robina said.

Identical twin sisters, speaking Peej, Wide Boy and Junkie's language. I wondered what nickname Wide Boy would give them.

*

It was decided at a council meeting that I should take over the youngsters' education. Partly, I think that was The Gaffer's idea to give me something else to occupy my mind with Sara gone, but now there were five it was time we started them at school and who else was there to teach them? Admittedly, Salami was still too young, but now I hardly had a minute to myself because I had to supervise four children every morning.   I hummed

181

and hawed when The Gaffer first suggested it, but really I was glad. It was such a responsible position to be in: since what we read would shape our society forever.

We went on a field trip to one of the local schools to get supplies. Eric volunteered to join in as parent-helper cum gun-toting outrider.

I was wary at first of going with Eric but he was sweet with the children and the trip was quite comfortable. There was no sign of the aggression he'd shown the twins on their arrival and the school itself was a treasure trove. I hadn't thought of it as a place we'd want to live in but it seemed the teachers had as choice staff accommodation as in the library. Only trouble was that some yobbos had vandalised it. Fancy that they'd still want to do that when there was hardly anybody left.

We trooped in to the shiny corridors and the children walked in single file behind me without being asked. So many habits survived from a time long vanished. Most of the things we needed were from the upper floors but I made a detour round the infant block so we could see the drawings on the walls. The kids chattered about the cotton wool tails on the spring bunny pictures excitedly but Eric and I fell silent.

Then I took them to the gym and we played an impromptu game of Dodgy ball. Some game the twins remembered. How super to have a large, bright, flat unmuddied hall to run in, echoing with laughter. I asked Eric if he remembered the sports shop where we had met and he grinned at the recollection. How Sara would have loved this.

After that we helped ourselves to soft drinks from the tuck shop – only four months past their sell-by date – then I gave the children permission to take bats, balls and hoops home with us. I left them to play with Eric in charge while I foraged for jotters, books, pens and pencils, worksheets et cetera. I didn't bother with black or white boards. Well, with only four of them I didn't see the need.

I was distracted for a moment at the school library. There'd been a delivery of new books. I noticed that their supplier didn't put the rubber ownership stamp on the bottom of page twenty-one the way ours did but all the other processing was the same. It might just have been something that had gone wrong with this consignment. I checked a few of the books on the shelves but they were the same. Strange when we were both a part of the same local authority. Showed just how easy it was for small changes to creep in and before you knew where you were you'd developed two completely different systems.

I made a mental note to go back and fetch some. There were brand new ones about individual European countries that hadn't lost that cracking sound when you opened the spine. They smelled sweet and delicious. The information in them would be useful to show the children how we used to live and help us retain our moral and democratic standards.

Squealing from the hall brought me back and when I got there Eric was playing chases with Robina. Well I thought it was Robina. If I'd had my way I'd have dressed her differently or cut her hair. She was a precocious girl, anyway. A bit of a flirt for a ten year old. Nothing like her sister.

Back in my tent, Robyn and Robina's resemblance set me to thinking. If ten year old twins could survive a year on their own, who else might there be? And then, if identical twins survived, presumably it was because they shared something in their genetic make-up.

I flexed my nipped and squished toes while I thought about it. It raised all sorts of possibilities and some uncomfortable issues I should have checked out.

Chapter Thirty-eight

When I wasn't teaching or writing the history I worked in the fields that summer. It was slave labour with no fat pay cheque every fourth Tuesday but it kept me from drinking and, more important, from thinking about Sara.

R and R were the bane of my life but I vowed to work them into shape eventually. They weren't demons but sixteen undisciplined months had taken their toll and who knew what they'd been like even before the aftermath. The last time I left them in the tent howls brought me running back to find Robina with her hand twisted in a chignon of Saleema's hair while Robyn was taking a pair of scissors to the hem of her chemise. Don't you worry, I said to Limpet, my arms folded on my chest and my foot outstretched. I'll soon have them remembering how to toe the line. Brain implied I was ratty because I was missing the drink but it wasn't that. Our emotions were enacted over a wider compass than they used to be, that was all. I'd grown a lot harder since Sara died.

*

Towards the end of July, the food was abundant and the weather was fine. Junkie was showing more and more which made me nervous but I was so busy with the school and the work in the fields and just trying to keep tabs on the twins that even though the days were long and the nights were short they still passed so quickly I was almost unaware of the void I was feeling about Sara. I say almost. If anything I suppose the arrival of the twins helped me to move on without her. No. I still missed her. I missed her like I'd never missed a single adult before. Except perhaps one, but I never really had him for long anyway.

We had to rearrange our far end of the pit. Now I was

sleeping across the passage from Junkie and physical closeness had led to a kind of manageable truce between us. Well, time had gone on and besides, she'd been good to me when I was coming down off the drink. When I got angry with her I still thought of her as a filthy tart but now she hardly went near the men. She spent her days in the women's tent where Grace was teaching her to knit and crochet. Every time I saw them there was creamy wool – not real wool, not wool from our own sheep since that would be too scratchy for a baby – billowing on to the ground around them in a scene of domestic harmony. In the evenings Grace taught the younger girls too, Saleema and the twins, though at first I thought they'd surely spear Saleema's eyes with the needles Grace gave them, and lick them as lollypops. But Grace had something that kept them knitting. Even Salaam wanted to join in and was peeved when his father ordered him out of the women's tent. Instead, Bill promised he'd show him how to tie fly-fishing knots. Whether he did or not I didn't find out, but I did see Wide Boy, one evening when I slipped out to go to the latrine, teaching him how to gamble with fivestones.

There was a scarlet sunset. Almost to the midpoint of the sky those tiny pillowed clouds glowed with a rubiness of their own and the base colour of the sky went from near white on the horizon through shades of blue to indigo, deepening in the east to almost black, where the night was chasing in. I was fidgety with what my dad used to call the drouth.

Peej was down by the fence on his own, leaning on one forearm on a post.

Since I couldn't have a drink I walked down to meet him, the sounds of the community quickly fading at my back till all I could hear was the swish of my feet through the grass.

His eyes flicked over his shoulder to see who it was but he didn't say anything. I slowed as I reached him, wanting to place my hand lightly on his jacket; screwed my feelings up tightly instead.

'Beautiful, isn't it?' I stepped forward and curled my fingers between the barbs of wire.

'Aye.'

'What are you looking at?'

He breathed out through his nose and scratched his cheek, grating through the coarse short bristles. 'This and that.'

The mountains to the north of Glasgow were lit by long, slanting sun. Dumgoyne, the remains of the old volcano, stood on its own: an outpost for the Campsie Fells. Much further north the tips of three peaks were visible. Between us and them was the city; despite its poisons, that night, gilded in yellow light, it looked cleansed.

'Golden,' I said.

'Eh?'

'The city. It looks golden. Untarnished.'

'Aye.' His eyes pondered it. 'Twenty-four carat.'

There was silence again. The clouds above our heads changed from red to purple and the brighter stars began to show.

'Have you ever been to those mountains?' I asked him, nodding to the three peaks.

He straightened; cleared his throat. 'Nah. Never was a traveller.'

'No?'

'Nah.'

More silence.

'What about you?'

I sighed and found myself unexpectedly blinking.

When I didn't answer he checked. 'You alright?'

'Yeah.'

'Still thinking about Sara?'

I shook my head and shoulders in a half no, half yes.

A flock of starlings did the flock of starlings thing, a hundred of them in the dying light, shimmering like a swatch of chiffon in an imperceptible breeze. Below, under the crooked branches of a beech, a column of midges mimicked camp fire smoke.

He returned to the view. 'I'm a city boy, me.' When I didn't reply he looked at me again. 'You sure you're alright?'

'Yeah, yeah,' I said. Then, 'Stupid, really.' I wished his eyes would go off me but they didn't. 'I lived up north for a while,

186

that's all. Long time ago. I – had relations there.'

Now he was really looking at me. 'Still waters run deep,' he said. 'You never told me that before.'

'No.' I took out a hankie and wiped my eyes and then my nose with it. 'It was a long time ago.' I hoped I sounded dismissive. I'd been thinking about it a lot, recently, but I certainly hadn't intended to talk about it.

'Right,' he said, putting his hands deep in his leather pockets.

The air was cooling. All the rosy and golden light had slid down the side of the sky and off the end of the world and the black was chasing it, gaining on it, creeping up to the midpoint.

Peej looked back to the tents. 'Time they were taking everything down.'

'Yeah,' I said. 'We'd better go.'

He held out his elbow for me to take it. When the grass was long it could catch me out. I was glad of his support and of him, physically, the tensile strength of his muscle and sinew under the polished leather.

In the women's tent, I heard the rustling of sweet wrappers and caught the knitting club with guilty expressions on their lamp lit faces, but I didn't mind.

'Bed time,' I told them and we all packed up.

Junkie and Grace had to be helped down in the cradle. They were both frail; both cherished: one for her memories; one for the hope she nurtured for our future. Me? I could never hope to achieve either. Free from aches and pains while we were living so much in the open air, I was able to scurry down the rope like a spider and settled the girls to sleep then got in under my covers, thinking about Sara and her baby; Limpet with her baby at the breast for a last feed before sleeping; Junkie and her baby, moving now inside her in the dark of the coal mine. In the darkness, I reached into my bag and took out my photo. With the covers over my head, I switched on my torch and studied the little farthing face of my baby, wondering where she might be. Wondering if the genetic profile that kept two twins alive without any adults could have kept my baby alive, so many years and so many miles away to the north.

Chapter Thirty-nine

'Ever thought of going up to find out if they're still there?'

We were in the MPV, Peej driving, me in the passenger seat, Robyn and Robina in the middle and Bill and Grace in the rear, off for a day trip to the coast at the kids' request. Well it *was* summer. We'd woken to fine summer holiday weather.

Peej's head jerked towards me then back to the windscreen. 'Your relations?'

The Moor was a narrow, twisty road that curled its way across a stretch of wasteland. Sheep in dragging fleeces grazed on marsh grass between the white ranks of Scotland's largest windfarm, its blades no longer turning.

I fidgeted with a bangle I'd taken to wearing. I found it on a visit to a voodoo shop. A crystal shop. It was turquoise. It was supposed to help me with my bones, my sore back and knees but I liked it for the colour and for the irregularity of its beads: greeny-blue knobbly bits on elastic. I took it off and put it on my other wrist.

'I haven't even been to see if my mum and my brother are still alive and they just stay at the other end of Glasgow,' I said and looked out of the side window. 'Not much chance of it really.'

Once, when Chis had come to the camp we'd sunk into the pits – metaphorically speaking at least – at some of the things he'd told us about the millions who'd died and then he'd taken up his guitar and started singing 'Ae fond kiss and then we sever' and some of us had listened and some of us had joined in; Grace with her sweet high waver, Bill an octave lower simultaneously mellow on the same old tune. There was a danger of becoming overly sentimental.

'Did they never get in touch with you?'

'No.'

He nodded. We knew what that meant. But then, other than going with Sara in the early days to ring the bell at my brother's flat, I'd never tried to contact them. And I was alive.

The car mounted a humpback bridge then turned a tight bend. There was a lifeless farm by the road and an overgrown garden. 'I went to check mines,' he said. Wouldn't believe it till I saw it with my own eyes.' We approached a major junction and he indicated left.

Ours was a three car convoy with Peej in the lead. In the wing mirror I noticed the other cars indicate though there was nothing else on the road to see. The main artery seemed to be largely clear of obstacles but Peej moved us into the middle lane. Occasionally there were a few cars parked at the sides – where drivers, presumably unable to make it home, had pulled over to die.

'Your daughter?' He'd told me she'd been linked with Wide Boy.

'Aye. And her mother.'

I looked at the dash. It might have been emotion but the speedometer was climbing.

'Are you in a hurry?'

Peej's eyes dipped to the dash.

'What speed, Peejie,' Robina asked.

'Just over eighty.'

'You going to do a ton?'

He checked in the rear view mirror.

'Do a ton,' Robyn said.

Peej's jaw line firmed. 'Ach, stuff it,' he said and I knew he was thinking about our previous conversation. His arms pushed out, horizontal towards the wheel.

'Ninety.'

Robyn and Robina's faces appeared in the hollow between the front seats.

'Get back in your seat belts!'

'Wait till we get round this bend,' Peej said, the speed dropping to sixty till the girls were secure. Then he picked it up.

189

'Seventy, seventy-five. Eighty, eighty-five. Alright?' He eyed the girls in the mirror.

'Aye!'

He flicked to me.

I was never greatly impressed by speed. I always preferred a cautious approach. I never much liked fairground rides or action films. You never knew when a machine could fail or when there might be human error. I was human, after all, and I'd made errors. No matter how clever and careful I might have wanted to be. But what did staying still achieve? 'Go for it,' I told him. 'A hundred or nothing.'

He took us to 120. Dead houses whistled by us. Abandoned cars and corpses passed faster than my eyes could focus. For a minute I was drunk on that blindness. But I was scared we'd come too fast on a three lane crash. We'd seen those; drivers too ill to prevent it. My hand gripped the door handle and the other pressed into the padding of my seat.

'Jesus!'

The twins were laughing but then the car began to rattle and Grace looked up to see what the squealing was about. The cars in our convoy were well back, The Gaffer first behind us, flashing a reprimand from the regulation speed.

Peej took his foot off the accelerator and gradually the needle drifted to a more sedate sixty.

I looked at my hands. 'So that's a white knuckle ride.'

'You alright?' Peej asked.

I nodded.

He checked the mirror again and I checked mine. The other cars rejoined us. The Gaffer could be seen to glower his disapproval but for once I couldn't give a damn. The girls went back to their headphones and I don't know what happened to Bill and Grace. I was enjoying this closeness to Peej.

Then, 'D'you want me to come with you?' he said. 'To check up on your family?'

I looked out of the side window again. 'My mother and brother?'

'Anybody.' He took his eyes away from the road for more

190

than a comfortable second. 'Anybody you feel you should have looked up before. Hard for a woman to do it on her own any more.'

'Look!' Robyn said.

Peej's eyes went front but the road was clear. The land had flattened. Between the buildings on our right flat water was shimmering.

'The sea!' Robina said.

Peej slowed down to thirty to take the turn-off towards the town and the girls wound their windows down. The air when it reached me was chill and sweet and salty all in one breath.

'I'd like that,' I said while they were distracted.

'Right,' he said, driving up to the beach to park. He creaked on the hand brake and we stretched our backs. 'Okay kids.'

They'd already opened their doors and were pulling off their shoes and socks.

'Not too far.'

I opened the door for Grace and watched the girls running down the empty sand, their summer clothes fluttering off like skins. I was still wearing my jacket but I had a secret underneath it: something that was a reminder of Sara. Grace unfolded herself and stood, tugging at the legs of her brown trousers and tidying her lilac fleece after the journey.

'Lovely day, pet,' she said, putting the handle of her bag over her shoulder. She fixed a straw sunhat on her head with a spangled pin. 'How do I look?'

'Beautiful,' I said and helped her round the back of the car to where Bill in his New York Yankees cap was waiting, elbow out.

'Ready, hen?' he said. 'A walk to the shore?'

The tide wasn't far out. The beach was twenty feet of loose sand and a band of solid wet brown earth. I watched the others' barefoot treads but didn't venture on to the beach. Car doors banged as the others arrived. Saleema kicked off her sandals and hitched up her voluminous trousers. She overtook me and gasped at the burn of the sand on her soles then at the iciness of the water. Salaam waded in in his trousers and Basher directed a jet of unintelligible sounds at him but even he headed to the water's edge to paddle little Salami's feet. The tiny baby winced and started to cry.

'Not too much, Basher,' Peej shouted, pulling off his socks. He shook his head at me. 'Stupid bastard thinks he's still in the Gulf.' He loped off to the water and scooped a careful handful to soak the back of Basher's shirt.

Basher convulsed as the water hit him. 'You bastard,' he said and handed Salami to Limpet. He and Peej sluiced water over the children.

The Gaffer walked towards me and we watched from the sidelines. 'You wouldn't catch me doing that,' he said, folding his arms and leaning against our MPV.

'Nor me!'

We watched in silence. We were right in the middle of the bay. An arc of sand stretched for a mile or more on either side of us, frilled mid-way with the brown tidemark of seaweed and a fringe of white. To my left, the land met the sea in the sudden bulge of green at the Heads of Ayr. To my right, from this distance, the traditional seaside town could still have been bustling. Close in there'd been no racks of holiday postcards and fluorescent yellow buckets and spades outside the few shops we'd passed; no shiny windmills spinning or sticky pink rock. Green, blue and orange triangles were strung on a cord between the lampposts but their radiance was certainly dimmed.

Ours was anything but.

Peej came up from the sea shaking water from his hands. His shirt was soaked; he started unbuttoning it. When he took it off I couldn't resist his thin white chest with its sparse hair covering; his ruddy neck and elbows; the hair sprigs under his arms and the sleek biceps and triceps that moved when he did, a pulley system that worked my insides too. 'Freezing,' he said to me, as if I hadn't guessed. 'You not going in the water, The Gaffer?'

The Gaffer kept his arms folded. 'Too much pollution.'

Peej looked down at the sea, perplexed for a minute. 'Crap?'

'Sewage. Did you never read about it?'

'That was years ago, man,' Peej said. 'Two at least. If anybody's shiting there now it'll be like one turd floating in an ocean. Excuse me,' he said to The Gaffer.

The Gaffer moved off the car.

Peej hung his shirt over the front door and reached in the back for the fishing rods.

'Well, maybe even from the bodies. Point is, you'll not catch me in it.'

'What the fuck d'd'you come for?'

The Gaffer put his hands on his hips. 'I was driving.'

'Playing the white man.'

Peej brought out the wicked in me and I couldn't stop smiling. I turned away but I think The Gaffer saw me. He didn't look too pleased and moved off.

'Up their own arses, some people,' Peej said. 'What about you? You not like the water?'

'Maybe later,' I said, pulling my jacket closer round me and trying not to look at his bare skin. I couldn't avoid it. Two chains jingled round his neck. Not those huge thick ones the neds wear – like Junkie. These were two thin gold chains: more tasteful, if you ask me, each with an unusually shaped pendant.

'What's on your chains?' I asked him, plucking up the courage. I was aware of the faint smell of his sweat with each tease of the sea-breezes. His nipples were small and hard with sea-water droplets on them. 'Can I see?' His hairs were curled and soft on the backs of my fingers as I lifted one of the pendants.

He covered them with his hand and turned away to his fishing rods.

'Stupid things my wife gave me.'

Two half 'I love you's. I remembered the type from the jeweller's.

'Listen,' he said. 'Tomorrow – naw, make it the day after 'cause I'll need to hunt tomorrow – we'll head up to your folk's place. While the weather's good.' He reached down to grip the handle of the bucket with his bait, knife and flies in it. 'Your mother and brother first, then maybe after that, moving on.'

'Yo Peejie!' Wide Boy and Brain were coming back after

193

reconnoitring the town. Brain was carrying a box of beers. Wide Boy had a couple of carrier bags, a grin on his face and a camera round his neck.

'Polaroid,' he said, putting the bags down and holding it up. 'Say cheese.'

Once again I thought about Sara. How she'd have laughed.

Peej straightened up and put his arm round me. I nestled under his bare wing, wishing that after all I wasn't wearing my jacket.

'Cheese!'

'Here. Wave it about for a couple of minutes till it comes through.' Wide Boy handed me the paper and went off to snap someone else.

Peej took his arm from round my neck. 'Basher!' He gesticulated with the fishing gear and Basher tapped Salaam's shoulder. The two of them walked bare foot up the sand towards us.

'There's a rod in there for Bill if he wants it,' Peej told me. 'We'll away and catch dinner.'

I was looking at the photo. Slowly the image was appearing. Not such very good focus, but a nice snap. Peej's body language was so open. One hand on his slim hip, the other round my shoulder. His head up, chest out, fully facing the camera. That sulky look men put on, never smiling for the camera. Me? I was caught huddled in to his underarm, a thin, drawn-looking middle-aged woman, my hair wispy and needing cut, my features indistinct. Looking frailer even than Grace. How could I expect him to fancy that?

'Let's see.' Peej pulled the edge with one finger. 'Not bad. We'll need to start a group photo album. Keep it with your writing.' His eyes held mine for a minute then travelled over my hair and down me. 'Why don't you take your jacket off? Get some sun about you.'

'Yeah,' I said, looking for a sheltered spot. I touched his arm. 'How long do you think you'll be?'

He exaggerated a critical look at my fingers. 'You going to miss me?'

I heard Basher snorting and I was glad The Gaffer wasn't there to witness my turn for humiliation. I swept my jacket off in front of them so they'd a good view of my skimpy scarlet bikini top. That raised their eyebrows if nothing else.

'We'll be as long as it takes, I guess.' Peej's eyes were travelling on my white skin. I prayed he wasn't thinking it was slack. 'Not too long, depending on if our luck's in.' I presumed he was talking about the fish.

When their backs were turned I slipped off my shoes to let my toes get some air. I was desperate to feel the touch of the warm sand. Maybe I could walk about like this and no one would notice. I wriggled my toes until they were buried, reaching the colder, damper layer. Then Limpet waved me over and I put my shoes on again.

Chapter Forty

The men caught mackerel and mullet and some eels and I didn't believe how good they could taste, cooked on a driftwood fire on the beach in the late afternoon. They held them up for photographs before we cooked them. Bill made us laugh, bragging his little tiddler was the biggest.

Earlier in the day Robyn, Robina and Saleema had gathered whelks and we'd scrubbed them with stones and rinsed and boiled them in salty water. We'd to use stones again after that to split them open, because we'd nothing to improvise as pins. It was years since I'd eaten whelks. Another part of my lost childhood. The Gaffer wouldn't touch them. Too much pollution he said but we weren't caring. They tasted good to us and nobody was sick. I tried to convince him everything had had long enough to filter out but he always thought that he knew best. He sat alone for much of the afternoon, by the sea wall, watching over us.

Wide Boy and Brain spent part of the afternoon on the beach, drinking beers. They passed the others out when we were round the campfire and Basher took one without a comment. I'd noticed he didn't have anything to say to Saleema when she'd uncovered her hair and rolled up her trouser legs. Even Limpet had stuck her ankles out, sitting up feeding Salami on the big boulders near the promenade. I thought we must be family now.

The only one who wasn't enjoying it so much seemed to be Junkie. In the late afternoon she lay down in the shade in our MPV with the hatch and the doors open for a breeze. I went to see if she needed a drink.

She didn't notice me creep up. I didn't want to frighten her so I called her name softly. Lee-Ann, of course, not Junkie. She didn't answer.

Her tee-shirt had ridden up over her stomach. Her belly looked tight enough to burst. She'd a brown line on it and a mole midway between the end of her tee shirt and the dropped waist of her grey towelling shorts.

I sat in the twins' middle seat and looked through the headrests. Such a pretty girl without all that make-up. A couple of hours in the sunlight had made her skin golden and sleep and rest had made it rosy. She'd slipped off her sandals and her toes were pretty and petite with pearly painted nails.

I was gazing at her when her eyelids opened.

'What?' she said.

I jumped, guilty, with nothing to feel guilty about. 'Hi,' I said. 'I just came to check you were okay. Did you want something to eat or drink or something?'

Her eyes closed again; she rubbed her palm over them and through her hair then sat up.

'Naw, I'm fine, Alice.' She looked through the window towards the others and yawned. 'What time is it?'

I checked my watch. None of us knew the time for real – Brain had tried to synchronise us with the summer solstice so we could confirm the dates and agree a time but it was guesswork. 'About twenty to six.'

She sighed. 'The kids are having a great time, aren't they? Wee Salaam's loving it.'

I followed her eyes. Salaam and the twins were burying Wide Boy. 'Maybe we should leave now,' I said and we both laughed.

'Are you sure you're okay?' I asked her.

'I'm fine,' she said. 'Just dead tired. I'll lie here for a bit.' She lay down again.

'Okay. Shout me if you need anything.' I looked at her when her eyes were shut. She couldn't have long to go. She was slim yet rounded: the pregnancy itself was the only weight she'd put on and unlike Sara, this pregnancy was plainly visible. I thought she looked close to nine months already. I said as much to Limpet and Grace when I rejoined them.

Limpet agreed.

Grace said, 'Aye, going to be a wee boy in the camp very soon.'

I thought she was getting mixed up with Salami.

'Naw, naw,' she said. 'She's carrying it all to the front. That's a boy, I'm telling you. That's how I told Peej to get me some blue wool.' Her eyes were pale and watery. 'For my knitting. I'm never wrong.' Her sunhat nodded.

Limpet and I smiled at each other.

'You never predicted what kind of baby Limpet was having.'

She leaned over to me and clutched my arm with skinny shiny fingers. 'That's because I couldnae see fur all that kafuffle she's aye wearing.'

Limpet met my eyes and a small smile pressed her lips together. She shook her head so I wouldn't make a fuss. She was old, Grace, and we both knew it; she had old views and her dementia was phasing out the politeness that regulated the rest of us.

We became aware of a sudden silence falling over the camp. When I looked up everything seemed to be normal. Peej and Basher had taken Salaam swimming as the afternoon sun raised the water temperature a degree and their three dark heads were visible, like seals. The Gaffer, Eric and Bill were half dozing and Saleema was sitting on a mat shielding her sleeping baby brother. The seagulls had argued over the fish heads and innards and had flown away.

Anaesthetised by beer and heat, Wide Boy and Brain were buried up to their necks in sand and sea-shells. Wide brimmed hats covered their faces. The only thing that told me which was which was the bottom half of Wide Boy's bare right leg showing above the ground beside his grubby trainers.

Limpet touched my arm and pointed. In their identical purple swimming costumes, Robyn and Robina were whispering together. Not a giggle or hoot did they make but covered the ground stealthily, signalling to each other and nodding and scenting to coordinate their position. With a metre and a half to go they lunged on Wide Boy's leg in a fury of growling.

Wide Boy burst out of the sand, shrieking and slapping at

them with his hat. 'Jaws fucking One and Two,' he said when they ran away. He checked to see who was watching and caught our eyes. 'Nearly crapped myself.'

The girls ran laughing into the water as Wide Boy and Brain swept the sand off their bodies. I picked up the camera from the heap on the mat and photographed them. Peej was in the background, standing knee deep in the sea in his shorts, hands on hips, lapped by sparkling water.

Peej was taking me travelling. I only had to wait till the day after next, then I was finally going to be able to talk about my secret.

Chapter Forty-one

I should have known Junkie would spoil it.

I was still teaching most mornings and though we felt too sluggish for an early start after our day on the beach, we'd brought back shells and stones and pressed flowers and they formed the basis of our lessons for the day. Eric drove me and the children to the school so we could use the library – classification number 577.699 biology of seashore life, 580.75 botany: collections & collecting. 594.1477 seashells. The school didn't seem to use full class numbers, abbreviating them instead to one or two decimal places. I tried explaining the numbers but the children's eyes glazed. I even told them that Melvil Dewey who invented the classification scheme wrote his introduction to it in non-standard English, spelling words phonetically, but they didn't show any interest in that either so I just found them lots of illustrations and information and we set about identifying, reading and copying into scrapbooks. It took us all morning but the kids were happy. I let them have a break half way through and we had juice and fresh nan then put our heads on the desks, snoozing in the sun over by the windows.

I kept imagining how it would be when I took Peej to find out about my family. That was the real reason I wanted the kids to put their heads down. Their constant chatter left me no time to dream. Peej and I in the car driving up through the highlands. The pent-up smell of his skin and his smoky breath; the creak of his leather jacket and the mustiness from his trousers. I skipped the bit about finding the remains of my mother. My brother. Concentrated instead on travelling with Peej.

Feet scuffling roused me. 'Stop that, Robina.' Side-ways grins they thought I couldn't see. 'Five more minutes,' I said, sounding like a child reluctant to get up.

Peej and I in the car. Something moody on the CD. 'Somewhere over the rainbow' by Eva Cassidy? Moody, but not sexy. 'If I loved you?' From Carousel. The good girl's always attracted to the bad boy. 'Summer loving' from 'Grease'? Peej with his sea-splashed chest and the hunter in his eyes.

A fart set the kids shrieking. I sighed and we got back to work but we were all fidgety. I took them out to the playground, Eric sweeping round it first with his gun just to check we were alone.

'Can we play rounders?' Robyn asked.

'Bags your team,' Robina said, grabbing her sister's arm before I had a chance to say no. 'Me and Robyn against Salaam and Saleema.'

'That's not enough. You two'll need to join in,' Robyn said.

I looked at Eric, putting my hand up to shade my eyes. He was still holding the rifle. 'What d'you think?'

He scanned around. 'I don't mind. Do you remember the rules?' He put the gun down in the middle of the playground.

I shrugged. I never was a team player. I let Robina organise us.

The Jaws were good at the game. Saleema was held up by her salwar kameez. Salaam quickly got the idea. Robina let fly a missile that he thwacked. He tossed the bat and ran, first base, second base – glanced sharp round for Eric's big legs braking at the bottom of the playground as he picked up the ball and tossed it back up to Robyn. She and Salaam raced for home base and Salaam just got pipped and stomped off, annoyed at overstretching himself.

'Oh, no,' I moaned melodramatically. 'Does that mean it's me?'

Robina zeroed one in at me. I misjudged the first one but they let me try again. This time I felt the bat shudder as I contacted it and the ball skidded fast along the ground.

'Run! Run!' Salaam shouted, jumping up and down.

I flung the bat, ran to first base and stopped. Saleema ran on to second but Eric let the ball slip through his fingers (cacophony of Twin Jaws snapping).

'Run! Run, Yakkity!' Salaam urged.

Saleema made it home and squealed in triumph but I got a stone in my shoe and squealed in pain.

'Ooh, that was sore,' I said and took my shoe off.

It was summer. I wasn't wearing socks.

'You've got funny toes,' Salaam said, coming up beside me.

'You ready?' Robina shouted and he ran back into the game.

I put my shoe on. Shit, shit, shit, I was thinking. That was a secret I wasn't planning on telling.

*

Peej had left before I got up; he and Basher. The plan was to catch something big that would last a day or two – no refrigeration meant everything we caught had to be disposed of in twenty-four hours. Fresh on a spit the first day, curried in a pot the next. That was the way it went. I supposed our boom and bust method was the historical norm and nature's own detox. A big catch this time would mean Peej could have time off to go away with me. If we moved straight on, Basher would be able to catch rabbits, wood pigeon, maybe some trout and if the worst came to the worst and it took us a long time there were the tins or the sheep. But our veg patch was blooming so I hoped they'd take advantage of that and not let it rot in the field. Limpet was a good cook. Even Junkie was sharing in the craft, learning from Gracie, Limpet and myself.

*

Eric pulled the car over to the side of the road at the point nearest the camp and let the kids spring out. We watched them race off to see what was cooking. I was starving. It must have been all that exercise – the real and the imaginary that I day-dreamed I was going to have with Peej. We were later than usual and high spirited. Eric and I chatted on the way from where we parked as if we were old friends and although part of me still felt wary about him, I supposed in a way we were close, because we'd lived in the same community for over a year and had been through so much together. I must have been in the mood to reminisce because I knew I was going to be reminiscing about my family. Anyway, we were almost at the camp itself when Eric gripped the rifle. 'Aye, aye,' he said.

'What is it?'

I looked towards the camp fire. There was hardly any activity. Old Bill was shepherding the kids towards the men's tent. Salaam was wriggling but Bill tugged him by the back of his collar.

Eric and I split without finishing our sentences: we could both hear noises from the women's tent. I ducked my head under the flap and caught a faint sweet smell I thought I recognised. Limpet was sitting cross-legged in the corner, red-eyed. Grace was sitting with Junkie's head at her chest. Junkie had her back to me, half-sitting, half-lying on Grace's lap.

'What's happened?'

'There, there,' Grace crooned.

I closed the tent flap behind me.

Limpet wiped her eyes and nose with her loose hijab. She met my gaze then shook her head and looked away.

I saw what she was looking at. There wasn't one bundle wrapped beside her on our rug. There were two.

I couldn't understand. We hadn't been gone that long. Why hadn't they come and told us?

'Has she had it?' I got on to my knees to see the arrival.

'No!'

Junkie growled and all my buoyancy dissipated. I shrank under the pressure of the atmosphere. The air was green and yellow, heavy with heat and sunlight and that coconut smell I knew I knew from somewhere.

'What's wrong?' I sat back on my heels. 'Somebody tell me.'

Junkie sat up and turned to me. Her face was flushed and she had red lines down the side that had been held so snugly against Grace.

'Alice,' she said. 'What am I going to do about it?'

'Sh, hen. Sh.' Grace's skin and bone arms with their pendulous flesh came up to hold her.

I looked at Limpet then at the two bundles. Salami's plump arms jerked as he woke. He cried out and Limpet lifted him. I saw the other bundle move.

I lowered my voice. 'Is everything alright?'

Limpet looked at me then latched him to her breast.

I moved on to all fours to crawl across the carpet.

'Leave it!' Junkie yelped. 'Don't touch it.'

I heard a whimper and put one hand on the bundle and one over my mouth. The smell was stronger here. I remembered now; I remembered the scent from the vernix. Junkie's baby mewed and I ached to lift it.

'Don't touch it,' Junkie said again.

She'd rejected it.

But it didn't matter, because I could look after it. I lifted the baby into my arms. There was hardly any weight in it. I turned it towards me and peeled its blanket from its face. 'No!' I gasped. My body convulsed and I bumped the bundle back on the ground.

*

Limpet fed Salami in silence. Junkie sobbed against Grace. I sat on my heels, rocking, and holding my fingers over my mouth. Salami sucked and gasped now and then from a summer cold. From time to time Junkie's baby whimpered and Limpet and I wiped tears. I didn't notice how much time passed. When Salami had been burped and changed, Limpet laid him back on the rug, leaving his blanket loose so he could kick.

'Will you look after him?' she asked me. 'I want to give the children something to eat.'

I nodded and she left, glancing to the back of Junkie's head and into Grace's opalescent eyes.

Salami jerked and jiggled. He couldn't roll or crawl yet but he kicked and wriggled, gurgling when he caught sight of us.

Junkie sat up and turned to face the middle of the tent. She looked past her own baby to Salami and sniffed. 'Your arms must be getting sore,' she said to Grace.

'No, no.'

She sniffed again. Salami cooed and jumped his legs. Milk dribbled from his mouth and I leaned forward to wipe it. He had huge brown eyes with lashes so long and curled they should have been a girl's. Normally I told him that.

He doubled his froggy kicks while I wiped and his exploring hand gripped the other baby's blanket. He pulled the cover from its face.

'No!' Junkie forced Salami's fingers apart and replaced the cover. She wasn't crying now. She sat back for a moment then lifted the baby and moved it out of Salami's reach. Her baby mewed and she pressed the heel of her hand against her right breast then her left.

'Does it sting?'

She looked at me, unaware of what she'd done.

I knew. I remembered.

'Are you going to feed it?'

'It's not an it, it's a boy,' she said.

I sighed, trying not to exhale too loudly. 'Are you going to feed him?'

Salami clucked and chuckled. We forced our eyes away from him to the other bundle.

Junkie put her forehead in her hand again and rubbed down past her eyes. 'I don't know what I'm going to do with it.'

'I'll need to go to the toilet, hen,' Grace said, patting Junkie.

'Will you be alright? Can you manage?' Grace was becoming stiffer; Junkie was taking on the role of her carer.

Grace reached for her stick and dug its point into the carpet. 'I'm fine, hen, once I get up!'

I helped her to her feet and held open the tent flap while she limped out. The sun was hot on the outside of the tent and I waved away a couple of flies. Disloyal, my eyes were drawn to the campfire where Limpet and Saleema were preparing the evening meal. I wished that Peej and Basher were back. Probably we'd make do with vegetables and nan. I'd had nothing much to eat since morning and it smelled as if Limpet had opened some tins of Tikka Masala to serve with the vegetables. I imagined the nan soaking up the sauces and my mouth watered. I pressed my hand against my stomach and ducked back into the tent again.

Junkie was sitting looking at her palms in her lap. Grime had worked its way into the lines. Her baby moved slightly and she rested her hand on it.

'When did you have him?' I spoke quietly; Salami had stilled and I didn't want to frighten him. I pulled the end of his blanket over him; he gave a last jiggle then his mouth pouted and he sucked in his dreams.

'It was quick. Just about lunchtime. The pains came all together.' She met my eyes. 'Was it the drugs? D'you think it was me? Did I do something wrong?'

I shrugged. I hadn't thought about it. I didn't know if we should blame anyone.

It whimpered again, sorer this time. She pulled away her hand and wrapped her arms round her knees instead.

'He'll be hungry.'

'I don't want to feed him.'

She'd had all the bottles ready and the tablets for sterilising but Limpet and I had tried to persuade her to breastfeed him. Well, the milk was almost past its sell-by date; besides, breast milk would pass on Junkie's immunities.

'Your breasts have got milk for it.'

She sniffed and wiped the water from her eyes. 'No way I'm giving my tit to that.'

'It's only disabled, Junkie. It's still your baby: it still has a right to – .'

'It's not disabled, Alice,' she shouted. 'It's a fucking deformity.'

I couldn't speak.

'And how's it mine?' she continued. 'That's what I want to know. How's it mine? How could it not have been Sara that had it?'

Salami gave a cry. I shooshed him.

'Or her.' She pointed to where Limpet had sat.

She stood suddenly. Stepped past me and unzipped the tent flap. It sounded like a rip, like something was rent. I watched her stagger towards the camp fire; saw the expressions on the others' faces with their mix of concern for her and concern that she'd come to seek comfort from them. Their relief when she walked past, wandering to the edge of the field. There was blood on her loose dress.

Limpet looked over at me but I shook my head. Grace was sitting with a bowl of curry. Limpet carried on serving.

I went back into the tent and pulled the zip down. Salami was sleeping. Junkie's baby moaned. I listened to hear if anyone was approaching but the world beyond the cloth walls was still.

I crouched and walked over to the bundle, knelt down and peeled away the first fold of the fabric.

The tent was taut like the skin of a drum but it pulsed with every little wind gust. I peeled back the second fold and looked at the body.

Junkie was right. There was no way we could feed this baby.

I heard Peej's signal.

I forced myself to stop staring at the creature and wrapped it back up.

My stomach rumbled. I unzipped the tent flap again and looked out. The men had caught some rabbits. I couldn't see anything else. They were dropping their catch on the ground sheet near the campfire and laying down their weapons. Clearly, they had sensed the mood in the camp just like Eric and I. Limpet was explaining and I wished I could hear what she was saying. I watched her talk, with a guarded look in her eyes and assumed she was veiling some of the meaning from the children who were still emptying their bowls. Basher shook his head slowly and put his hand on Peej's arm, like a gesture of commiseration.

I cleared my throat. Peej looked over to me but Limpet was still telling him something. He turned his head in the opposite direction, towards Lee-Ann. Then he nodded at something Limpet said and took off his jacket. I watched him walk over to Junkie with his long, tight strides. His white tee-shirt made the back of his neck and arms look all the more ruddy from the sun.

Saleema came towards me with a steaming bowl and a torn strip of nan. I licked my lips. I moved my head slightly to see Junkie wrap her arms round Peej's neck and hang from him. Peej's arms encircled her and they held like that till he loosened her and pulled his jacket over her shoulders, even though it was

207

summer.

'Here's your dinner,' Saleema said.

I put my hand out automatically, trying to see past her. I had to see what Peej was doing.

'Is Salami alright?'

I brought my attention back from Peej and Junkie. Saleema's about the same height as me now: a lovely looking girl with her hair almost completely black but with a touch of auburn and her skin in the summer the colour of the rosewood writing desk in my mother's front room.

'He's sleeping,' I said. 'Did your mum want you to lift him?'

'No. I just – wondered about him being with Junkie's baby.'

She was biting her lip. I wondered what age she was. Probably old enough to be a mother herself. What was I saying? She must have been fifteen or sixteen. I wondered how much she knew.

I stirred my meal then dipped the nan in it. 'Did your mother tell you?'

She nodded. 'The baby's not right.'

My turn to nod. I bit the bread, the water flooding my mouth to meet the sauce.

Her eyes flicked back to the campfire. 'How 'not right', Alice?'

I put the bowl down on the grass and took her by the elbow. 'Not right, Saleema. You don't want to know.' I pushed her gently back towards the camp.

'Saleema!' Her mother's voice.

Junkie and Peej were sitting on the ground, their lips not moving. He was holding her hands.

I looked at my meal. Turnip and potatoes bobbed in the red soup with chick peas and leaves. Spots of oil glistened on the surface. I waved a fly away and soaked sauce up with the greasy nan, playing with it, too hungry now to eat. Somewhere far away I heard a peewit call.

When I looked up again Peej was walking back to the camp fire. He spoke to Basher, taking him to one side. I wondered how good Basher's English really was. Basher was wearing his tweed jacket. It was almost as brown as his hand when he took something out of his pocket and offered it to Peej. Peej's whole body seemed to stutter when he looked at it. He paused anyway, the other man talking to him. Peej's head was down – I couldn't see his face. His arms were stiff by his sides and his hands were fists. Basher put his arm round Peej's back. I couldn't see his face either – just the black hair on the top of his head. Basher's head went from looking at what he held in his hand to Peej's face. I wanted to look in Peej's face too. I wanted to see the expression on his face when he was comforting Junkie.

Basher's hand held something out at waist height. They reminded me of a boxer and his trainer. Junkie was sitting where Peej had left her. A breeze trailed a lock of my hair into my soup and I removed it absently. I felt I was watching a movie with the sound on mute.

Peej looked up towards the tent and sniffed. He looked at Basher and back to where I was standing. The others watched from the campfire, or from where they were standing outside the men's tent, Brain and Wide Boy under Neanderthal brows; The Gaffer hiding behind folded arms. Only the children were animated. Salaam, Robyn and Robina were doing handstands. Peej's eyes moved towards them and Limpet chased them to the bottom of the field at the opposite end from Junkie. Peej took what Basher had extended to him and came towards me and the tent.

I zipped it quickly.

Chapter Forty-two

Peej stood six inches taller than me in his heavy boots.

'Move, Alice.'

I looked into his eyes but could only see his surface. His mouth was as sharp as the lines down either side. The folds on his forehead gleamed like waxed fruit.

'What are you going to do?' I asked, standing in front of the zip.

'J - Just move, Alice.'

I looked down the knotted muscles in his arms to the black thing in his fist.

'It's just a baby, Peej. A sick baby.'

He clenched my upper arm in his hand, squeezing hard, white knuckled. 'Move,' he said. 'I mean it.' I resisted. Then Basher called my name and I gave way.

Peej looked back to where Junkie was. She'd come half way to the fire and was standing with a hand at her mouth and Grace holding the other.

He unzipped the tent flap.

'Saabi!' Limpet said.

Peej knelt and went in.

'Alice! My Saabi!'

I crouched and put my bowl on the grass; wiped my fingers on my hip where the sauce had spilled over my thumb knuckle.

Peej lifted Salami and handed him to me. I held his mouth, still sleeping, hot against my neck and watched as Peej stared at the other bundle. It was a closed knife he was holding. Basher's sheep knife. He transferred it to his other hand.

'Have you seen him?'

A wasp buzzed at Salami's head then drew closer to my bowl.

I nodded.

He sat on his heels. There was dirt in the treads, soiling our blue carpet. He flicked the cover from the baby's face.

'Christ.'

'It's worse,' I said. I think I said.

He drew back the rest of the blanket and blew out.

'What are you going to do?' His head twitched but I couldn't see his face. 'Peej – don't hurt it.'

'Move back, Alice.'

The baby whimpered.

'I'll look after it,' I told him.

He held the knife in front of him. His hands were shaking. 'I will!'

He pulled out the blade and clicked it into place. I heard it clicking. Fists on his thighs he took a long breath through his nose. He looked to the side. Salami's blanket was there.

I checked Junkie. She was standing with Grace, her face pallid. I looked at Peej.

'I can look after it, Peej. For however long it takes.'

He closed the knife and slipped it into his pocket.

'Give it a chance.'

He twisted and hissed, 'How can you look after a kid like that? You're off your fucking head.'

He lifted Salami's blanket and wound it round and round his fists. In one motion he shook it out over the baby's face then put his hands on it, leaning his weight on the baby's face.

I cried out, squeezing Salami. Peej leaned on the little body as it writhed. My eyes searched for Junkie's. She crumpled beside Grace.

Only the roof of the tent was glowing as the sun began to slip behind the hill. Peej moved his hands and put his ear down to the body. Taut through his white tee-shirt, I saw the two strung muscles form their suspension bridge on either side of his spine. Salami sneezed at the nape of my neck. Peej straightened and tidied the blanket over Junkie's baby's face. He rose to his feet and this time I moved back willingly. He kept his eyes away, grimacing against the sunlight. Standing, he blew his nose through his fingers. I thought he stumbled as he walked to the fire. A shortage of blood to his head.

I walked towards Limpet and held out Salami. Down the hill, the field was disappearing into shadow. Only the children's heads gleamed in the slanting rays of the sun.

Basher clapped a hand on Peej's back but Peej walked on and stopped by Junkie. He ran both palms down over her hair then raised her chin and they looked at each other. Then he stooped to unfasten the spade from his discarded tool belt.

I couldn't help it. I honestly couldn't help it. Despite all the anguish over Junkie and her baby, I wondered where this left us for tomorrow.

Chapter Forty-three

How can you miss something that's never been? If you've never known your baby, how can you miss it? That evening, the children played as if nothing had happened. Wide Boy and Robyn carried on, dodging each other round the tents; Eric and The Gaffer's voices rumbled through the evening air as they played cards in the men's tent.

'Give your baby a cuddle,' I said to Junkie. 'Before you say goodbye.'

I'd wrapped the body up, tight, to make the disfigurement less visible. Wrapped it in a second layer of turquoise silk. When I'd tried to place it in her arms, Junkie had left her arms slack and turned away her head. The child lay where I'd left it on the carpet beside her. Outside, Peej was digging a grave. It wouldn't take long. In the women's tent, Grace, Limpet, Saleema and I held a wake with Junkie, for the time it took Peej to be ready.

'It'll do you good, a wee cuddle,' Grace said.

Stubborn, Junkie stared into a corner.

There was a stiff silence. I broke it. I said, 'You'll regret it if you don't.'

Peej stuttered through the tent wall. 'It's ready.'

She didn't move, except to fold her arms across her chest, tucking in her clenched fists.

Grace put her withered hand on Junkie's shoulder. 'Come on, hen.'

Limpet nodded to Saleema and they ducked through the flap.

I should have been next: I'd never really liked Junkie and she knew it. Any warmth she'd been shown had been shown by Grace, but she'd been there for me when I was self-destructive with drink after Sara. And I wanted to be there for her with this.

213

I understood about this. I knew what she was going through. Something of it. So I helped Grace up, pulling her slack free arm while she leaned on her stick.

'Come on, hen,' she said again to Junkie. 'Get it over with.'

'I'll bring her out.' I positioned myself between Grace and Junkie. Stooped, I edged Grace to the tent flap. When she was through – my hands pushing her rump and Peej on the receiving end as in some perversion of a birth – I stuck my head out. The women were standing around wrapped in their own arms and the men had begun to filter from their tent. It was growing dark and there wasn't much time.

'I'll bring her,' I told Peej.

He looked away. 'Hurry it,' he said and lit a cigarette, the red glow from the tip a point of light in the grey-black.

Inside the tent the air was yellow from the lantern. My shadow was bigger than me, moving over the walls as I crouched down next to Junkie. It would have been easier just to watch the giant deformation of the shadows, rather than bring myself to look at Junkie.

'Honestly, you will regret it if you don't.'

She met my eyes. She'd pulled on a soft blue jersey tracksuit jerkin and trousers. Baby blue. Her hair had been roughly finger-combed into a pony tail at the nape of her neck; sweat from labour and her tears had glued it at the roots into rats' tail locks of brown that contrasted with the dehydrated blonde of the rest and her gold hoops.

'How do you know?' she said, her voice flat.

I squeezed her arm. 'I just know.'

'But...' She lowered her eyes to the turquoise silk. 'I cannae.' She drew her knees up. Wrapped one arm round them and clutched her mouth with the other. Despite that, she let out one high sob.

'You can!' I said, voice identical.

Her eyes searched mine then she stared at the baby. She slid one hand under its shoulder and neck and brought it tightly up against her with her mouth against its head.

'Are you ready?' Through the tent cloth Peej's voice was low

214

and insistent. 'Time's getting on.'

We didn't like lights in the total darkness. They would make our camp a beacon for unwelcome guests.

'Wait a minute.' She twisted to me. 'I need to get something.'

She looked at the bundle as if she didn't know what to do with it, whether to put it down or take it with her.

'Peej,' she shouted and unzipped the flap then shrank away when she saw everyone standing around.

He put his head through. Didn't look at me.

'Can Wide Boy bring me my baby bag?'

He pulled his head away and zipped the flap again.

She was holding the baby like a real baby, her eyes not leaving it, her hands fussing with the folds of the turquoise cloth. Outside, the mumble of voices grew. Once or twice we heard the children laughing and I clucked my tongue.

'Don't worry about it,' she said. 'You can't stop kids being kids.'

The irony didn't hit her.

I straightened out a wrinkle in our rug and picked off blades of grass and Peej's dirt, transferring it to the edge. Wide Boy had to go all the way down the pit.

The zip went up and the mint and lemon baby bag was pushed in. Peej's voice stuttered, 'Hurry it, eh? It's time we were going under.'

'I just want to get something.'

She laid the baby gently on the floor at her other side as if it might hurt and took the bag on to her knee. 'I've got a wee thing in here,' she told me. 'It's just down – here it is.' She zipped up the bag and tossed it into a corner, eclipsing the light briefly. It was a brown knitted teddy, nine inches long, with black stitches for a nose, dark brown stitches for its eyes and big black stitches fanning out like lashes.

'A teddy?' I said. 'It's old.'

She held it out to show me and said straight-faced, 'My mammy gave me it.' It had a torn strip of red felt where there used to be a tongue. Somehow I knew that.

'It's – nice,' I said.

215

She lifted the baby and tucked the teddy inside its turquoise drape.

*

Later, at the top of the rope, I said to Peej, 'I'll understand if you don't want to go tomorrow.' His face was drawn. He was our hunter, our handyman, our foot soldier and tactician. As if that wasn't enough he'd become our executioner. Our mercy killer. There was light in the sky but hardly any at our eye level, especially with the brambles still in full leaf, but the torch he was holding, to help each descendant see their way to the shaft, reflected on his face, hollowing his eyes and cheeks and emptying them of softness.

Black bats shifted behind him as he handed me the rope. 'We'll go,' he said. 'We'll make an early start.'

Chapter Forty-four

We took the 4x4. Peej brought it over so we could pack it. I took the road map and some biscuits; Peej took his hunting belt and put two sleeping bags, ammunition and bottled water in the boot. His rifle he put on the floor near the back seat.

The mood in the camp was understandably sombre. Junkie had slept in the bed with Grace and wasn't up by the time we left. Leaving her like that was my only regret.

'We look after her,' Limpet said.

The sky was a steady grey by the time we were ready to leave. I'd looked forward to this, yet I felt heavy as I climbed in and clunked the door. I wound the window down. The Gaffer and Wide Boy had come to see us off and there was a smell of autumn in the air as we waved goodbye. Peej's face told me he hadn't slept. Hadn't slept, hadn't shaved. He concentrated on the road and I concentrated on not seeing.

He detoured to find petrol; the cars in the neighbouring streets had none left and we were having to go further afield to find some.

'This one,' Peej said. We drove straight into the crackly drive of a sandstone house and Peej broke into the garage. I watched him suck the tube like a straw and the diesel siphon into our bottle. He spat as the car in the garage emptied then saw me watching him through the windscreen. He looked away first, checking the diesel level. I sighed and looked out of the side window at the house. It was big; blonde blocks of stone, two storeys and a dormer. A limp 'for sale' sign was succumbing to the garden.

'Why don't we live in a house like that?' I asked him when he came back and switched the key in the ignition.

He didn't answer. Just gave me a look and reversed in a couple of turns so we could drive back out. Yellow roses were overgrown and spilling over; dock spikes were turning brown where lobelia should have been.

'Put on some music,' he said.

I'd forgotten to bring it. We stopped at the petrol station shop and he came back with more water, sweets, stew, noodles and some hum drum music.

'Thought it would do us for the trip,' he said but he didn't put it on.

Street after street of overgrown gardens. Junctions you could take in fourth gear.

I hated coming away from our camp. Maybe it would've been good to live in a big house again, but only if things could go back to the way they had been. I pulled my heels up on to the seat and circled my arms round my legs.

'Getting close?'

'Yes.'

I indicated the turning for my mother's street. Peej drove slowly all the way along it. There were speed bumps and peninsulas you had to weave round, giving way to oncoming traffic. It was a family friendly street she was living in. Which was ironic.

'Over there,' I said and pointed. 'The parking's there.'

My brother had been good to her. She had moved from the scheme I grew up in to a flat he'd bought her in a modern apartment block. Not a big building: four storeys high with private gardens. Her parking place was blocked by an iron bar contraption but Peej drove straight up to the door.

I was nervous as I got out of the car. Had to hold my stomach or my pulse would burst through it.

'You alright?' he asked me, taking the rifle from the back and pocketing a box of bullets.

'Yeah.' I gripped my bag. There were keys in it: there were also two surgical masks.

It didn't look as if there was anyone about. A ginger cat tracked through the overgrown lawn outside the house and a

218

flurry of birds went up. Papers and old leaves had silted up the entrance. I opened my bag for the keys.

'Is this the only way in?'

'Yeah.'

Peej looked round then booted the door in.

'You didn't need to do that!' I held the keys up to show him but he shrugged. 'Well don't kick in her front door,' I said, stepping over the debris at the entrance.

Peej had already walked in to the gloom, holding the rifle in that semi-automatic way, ready to use it if he had to. He looked at the names on the mailboxes.

'MacAuley,' I said. We had no need of surnames. It was more than enough having our personal names as well as the nicknames Wide Boy gave us. 'On the first floor.'

The pink stair echoed with our footsteps. The rifle butt clanged against the handrail and reverberated in the building blocks.

'They'll be chucking us out,' he said.

The geraniums on her landing window ledge had died. They should've been crimson. Instead, a spider had woven their blackened leaves into the curtain lace.

'This one,' I said, trying to isolate the front door key. I couldn't control my fingers.

'Give.'

'The gold one.'

I let him take it out of my hand and felt the grind of each notch as he pushed it home and gave a quarter turn.

Her draught excluder stuck and he shoved with his other hand, the rifle gripped under his elbow.

The door caught on the chain.

The house was silent like inside the closed coils of a shell. At least there wasn't a stench. I don't know how I'd have reacted if there had been a stench.

I put my face to the opening. 'Mum!' I shouted, then drew back.

The only smell I could smell was from being so close to Peej's jacket. He wore it day in day out: its animal smell had mixed with his own. The tiny bristles on his chin were grey; when he held his head down to look at me the skin under his chin went into narrow folds. His eyes were back.

'D'you want me to break it after all?'

'Please.' My breathing caught. I moved out of the way.

He stepped back then cracked his foot close to the handle. The door flew back, ricocheting off the inner wall. He caught it on the rebound.

'You wait and I'll check it.'

Suddenly I didn't want to go in. What was the point? Just to find her dead. And if she wasn't dead, wasn't there dead in her bed or in the living room, what would that settle? Then I'd need to go searching around the town, looking for her, or looking for her looking for whoever else she had gone off to look for. My brother or me.

Peej went in when I didn't answer. I stood on the landing, watching him, wondering what my mother would have thought of this ruffian prowling through her home. How are the mighty fallen, Mum. I was always a disappointment to you. How are the mighty fallen.

*

Peej stood in the gloom of the hall. I couldn't make out his expression. Then he closed my mother's living room door and told me to come in. I entered the hall, searching his eyes for clues to what he knew and I didn't. 'Are they your mother's rings?'

He held out her wedding and engagement rings. Worn thin at the palm almost to breaking point. Only two stones left out of the three, little chips of diamond that sparkled longer than she had.

I blinked; nodded my head and clutched them in my pocket.

He put his hand on my shoulder. 'She's in the living room. Sitting in her chair where she fell asleep.'

I felt the corners of my mouth pull down. 'Is she a mess?'

He whistled through his teeth. 'What a question.' Pulled me against him and clapped the back of my head with bony fingers. My face almost squeaked on the leather of his jacket.

220

'She is, isn't she?'

'Naw, naw,' he said. 'But there's no point in seeing her.' He pushed me to arms' length and wiped my tears away with rough thumbs. 'At least you know.'

I hung my head.

'Is there anything you want to take with you?'

I looked up. 'I need to see her.'

He scowled and his cheek started to twitch. 'D'you not believe me?'

I thought about Junkie. 'It's the only way I'll be sure.'

He blew out his sigh.

'Peejie...'

He looked around. 'Look – I'll cover her with a blanket. Then you can go in the room, right?'

'Right.'

I stood in the hall while he went into the bedroom. She had one of my early tapestries on her wall. A thing I'd done when I'd been at primary school. A kind of 'sewing by numbers' of a loch and mountains. She must have brought it with her from our other house.

Peej came back. 'There's nobody in the other rooms.' He paused, blanket in hand. 'Are you ready?'

I gripped my hands together in front of my waist. 'Yes.'

'Stay here a minute.'

He went into the living room. The door didn't fully close and I saw what he was doing reflected in the glass of the display units. My mother's grey hair was visible above the back of her chair. Her feet were sticking out. I briefly glimpsed her purple cardigan before the white blanket billowed over her.

'You can come in.'

There was a faint smell in the room and the sound of birds through the open window. But it was just as I remembered it; as if she might rouse from her chair surprised to see me. I stood in the doorway. I didn't want to move in: I just wanted to see.

Standing by her feet, Peej fidgeted. 'Is that you? Are we done?'

There was an envelope on the floor beside her chair. 'What's that?' I asked, pointing it out.

He picked it up. 'Must've blown off when I shook the blanket.' He turned it round and read it. '"Alice."'

I took a small step so I could reach it. Gripped it and held it to my stomach then my nose. My fingers trembled when I opened it.

I forgot all about Peej when I saw her looping writing. It was her: it was all her personality, the curving Ls, the sharp A of my name, but the writing was spidery.

Alice,

I tried to phone you. Bobby's gone. My boy's gone. I was going to come and see you, but I'm too weak.

I've looked out photos. Such a lovely baby.

I'm sorry, Alice. Things were so different then.

I couldn't read the rest. Tears plinked on the sheet of paper. I dabbed it against my jumper.

'Who's that, hen?'

I folded up the letter and put it in the envelope. He was holding a photo in a small frame. I pushed my glasses up my nose and winced with the realisation.

'Give me it,' I said, arm extended. 'Please.'

The three generations. Fancy her having framed it. I looked at the shape under the blanket, my breathing shallow and fast. 'I'll need to get out of here,' I said.

I turned out of the door, the letter and the photo in the frame tight together in my hand. I ran down the stairs and out to the car. Heard Peej take the steps two at a time behind me. I got in and slammed the door. Looked at the picture.

The fading brown and beige of the seventies. My platform soled boots that made my knees lift up off the chair. The black mascara round my eyes. My mum, not severe, for once, in this photo. The drape of pink crochet in my lap.

Peej opened the car door and slid in. 'I brought this,' he said, showing me the big framed collage he'd taken off my mother's wall. I pointed out my brother and my father.

He peered at the black and white one of me as a toddler. Looked at me closely. 'Aye,' he said. Then, 'What's that one?'

I flipped the frame up, hiding the photo against my stomach. 'Nothing,' I lied.

He didn't pursue it. 'Is that us?' he asked, tucking the big framed collage behind his seat.

I put the photo in the small frame into my bag. 'That's us,' I said, sweeping my hair off my face with two hands and reaching for my seat belt.

Chapter Forty-five

We drove north that same day. Thinking it best to avoid the city, we chose the M73 up past Stirling. Past the castle on its rock in the middle of that flat, flat landscape. Past the lighthouse of the Wallace Monument which I evaluated for penthouse potential.

As we ran out of motorway, Peej braked and pulled over just as the road dipped into a wooded slip. He stretched his shoulders and wriggled the crickles from his neck.

'I'm knackered, Alice.'

I liked it when he called me Alice. It was so much better than Yak.

'Are you?' I reached for a jelly sweet and offered him the pack.

He shrugged and squeezed his fingers in the corners of his eyes. 'I'll need to crash for ten minutes.'

I looked around as far as I could see with the bushes and the road on the right above us, tracing my finger on the yellow line on the map.

'Where does this road lead to?'

He took the map from my lap. I held my finger to show where we were and we leaned over it together. He smelled of cigarettes and Peejieness.

'We take this road by Callander.' He looked at the time on the dashboard then the luminosity in the sky. 'We could stop at Crianlarich for the night.'

The water in the bottle gurgled as he raised it to his mouth and drank, the craggy point of his Adam's apple swallowing it down. 'I mean, we should be able to do it in a couple of hours, but I didn't sleep much last night. I'll need ten minutes. You be alright?'

His cheek was twitching and his eyes were deep set and red.
'Of course.'

He pushed his seat back and made himself comfortable then
sat up again and twisted round for the rifle, putting it nose
down onto the floor between his legs. He squinted at me. 'Ten
minutes, right?'

I nodded.

He breathed in noisily through his nose, stretched his arms
rigid then relaxed. 'Don't get out the car.'

The packet crinkled when I reached for another sweet but
by now he was sound. I sucked three more, studying the map.
Loch Lubnaig, Loch Awe, the long high road to Oban and down
through the town. He was tired, so we wouldn't get there till
tomorrow. I could nurse all those memories through tomorrow's
drive.

Peej was snoring softly, his jaw loose and his mouth open.
His lips, his jaw bones, were thin. His nose was an irregular line
where the cartilage had been displaced. There was a half-inch
scar I hadn't noticed by the side of his eye.

I looked at my watch and took another sweet, exaggeratedly
careful not to disturb him. Outside the fields were vivid green.
The earth here must have been fertile. I pushed my glasses up
my nose and peered to make out the wording on two billboards.
'Doune Highland Games' one said. 'Coming soon, executive
villas, 4 and 5 bedroom detached.' I sighed and pulled down the
visor so I could look at myself in the vanity mirror.

I wasn't as bad as I thought. The day at the beach had given
me some colour and the fresh air was good for my skin. My neck
hadn't concertinaed yet, though it was a shame about my hair:
still tousy; still gingery. But not bad, I caught myself thinking.
Not bad for a mature woman. I glanced at Peej; he was still
sleeping. I looked at the butt of his rifle, his legs, the folds and
bumfles of his trouser zip and let out a sigh. I remembered the
way he'd comforted Junkie. Wondered if he'd have comforted
me that way. I looked at my watch then reached down to my bag
between my feet and took out the letter and the photograph.

*

225

Peej jumped in his sleep. 'What time is it?' His eyes were misty.

I looked at my watch. 'Six thirty.'

He put his hands into his lap and stretched. 'I told you to give me ten minutes.'

I wiped the condensation from my window. 'Will we get out and stretch our legs for a minute?'

'Aye, good idea. Might as well take it easy.' He turned the key in the ignition and reached for the water bottle. 'Pass us over the kettle.'

*

A dimmer-switch dusk closed in on us down the mountains. We reached Crianlarich just before night, prowling with our headlights off through its few streets for signs of hostile life before parking in the grounds of a railway hotel. Peej locked me in the car with the lights out while he checked it over. I was hidden in Scots pine and honeysuckle. I opened the window a crack. Buds and budding berries on honeysuckle twigs dandled on the car roof and bonnet and the wind in the high pine shivered a mournful sound. Grey in grey, Peej appeared round the building's corner, his gun in one hand and the red point of his cigarette in the other. We unpacked.

Apart from the overabundance of tartan on the hotel's walls and carpets, the stag heads and antlers and photographs of real or fictitious 'Grannie's Hieland Hames' the building was not unpleasant. By which I mean there were no body smells: if anyone had been living here then over the last eighteen months nature had done its work.

I paused in the foyer, my legs a combination of stiff and restless from the drive.

'No check in, doll.'

Peej stepped behind the counter and rummaged till he found a heavy torch.

'That'll do us,' he said, taking keys. 'Would madam like me to show her to her suite?'

Too heavy hearted for a holiday, I picked up my bag and we headed for the stairs but the gleam of his torch picked out the mirror of the bar gantry. The temptation was too much for both of us, so we detoured.

My instinct was still to act like a customer. Peej walked round the bar and slithered the torch beam over the malts.

'Glenfiddich? Highland Park?' he offered. It was pseudo-joviality. His voice was feigning brightness but his face was still dead. 'Hold that and shine it up there.' He passed me the torch and unscrewed the first bottle. 'Nice bouquet.'

Indeed. My nose came alive; water came to my mouth but I was supposed to have turned away from drink.

He looked under the bar and set up the first half dozen glasses. 'What d'you fancy?' Took another bottle off the shelf and examined the label. 'Highland Strathspey?' Two generous fingers he poured from each bottle and set them up in rows.

I breathed in the scent. The drinks were poured: it would be rude not to honour them. Anyway, we'd been through a lot these two days. I took a sip then swallowed the first gold. Savoured the coating on my lips. I could be lost again, but I couldn't resist. The fire spread through my stomach, burning away the last twenty-four hours' stresses just as doctors used to use maggots to cleanse away infection. I reached for my second.

'You like your whisky, doll, eh?' He raised his second glass. 'Cheers.'

'Slainte,' I said, and looked round, leaning my elbow behind me on the polished bar. The seats were upholstered in a different tartan from the blue and green carpet. There were more pictures on the wall – etchings of old highlanders in plain brown frames with wide white borders. Brass picture lamps with ribbons of red tartan tied round their necks were poised to shine down on them. On my left the low wall was topped with panoramic windows. Diners at the heavy wooden tables would have enjoyed a centrally heated view of the wild, forested hills and their fellow tourists.

'D'you think any real people lived here?' I asked, moving with my second drink and the torch towards the window and looking out.

'I think they're all dead.'

'No, I mean, in the old days. D'you think any of the people

227

who stayed here were real or were they tourists?'

'Ahya,' he said. He'd banged his knee in the gloom where I'd left him. 'Fuck sake, Yak, bring us over that light till I see what I'm doing.'

I sat at one of the tables but set the torch so he could see the step down from the bar. It illuminated him up to crotch-height. I wriggled my twitchy feet under the table. Peej brought our last two glasses and one of the bottles, then went back and returned with three or four packets of crisps. I peered at the sell-by date. It was well by. I burst them open.

'Just tourists doing what you're doing,' he picked up. 'A wee bit family history. A wee bit sight seeing. Bit of curiosity. Bit of trying to see where they belong.' He studied the menu. 'Beef in beer batter with chips?'

I swallowed the whisky I'd been holding in my mouth and raised my glass. 'Whisky.'

He dropped the menu and raised his. 'Slainte.'

'Cin cin,' I countered, unable to prevent a grin curling on my face.

He raised one eyebrow and upended his glass. I followed. He thought he'd got me with 'Skål' but I met him with 'Prost'.

'You're quite a woman,' he said and poured three more each. I felt lithe and sinewy with the drink. There'd always been a charge between us. Two days ago, at the beach – was it only two? – that charge had been amplified. Now he was across the table. I just had to make a move and he'd be mine.

He poured another round. 'Salud,' he said and I parried with 'Santé'. Where was my willpower to stay sober now? And my concern for Junkie? By the sixth my mind had gone slithery; he trounced me with 'Na zdorovye'.

'What?' I asked him, slurring now, my chin propped on my hand, my elbow on the table.

'Russian!'

'How d'you know Russian?'

'Ah,' he tapped the side of his nose. 'My old man was a commie.'

'A commie?' I drew back in mock indignation. 'Mine was an

alkie.'

'Aye? There's a surprise!' He sniffed; poured another round. When it dribbled on the table he said, 'Shite,' wiped it with his finger and licked it. 'Old times,' he said and held the bottle up. 'This is precious, you know. Nobody's making it.'

'You missed a bit.' A drip fell from the bottom of his glass. My tongue came out to lick it, same as his. But we were a foot apart. No spaghetti strand this: no risk of touching.

I put my drink to my lips, then remembered. 'Iechyd da!'

He sprayed me in Scotch mist. 'Yakky Da! I thought you were a fucking teuchter!'

I took the framed photo out of my bag and set it on the table.

Peej angled the torch at it.

'Poor Junkie,' I said, caressing the tiny image of my baby.

'Junkie?' He pushed his chair back, clattering it against the one behind him as he stood. He emptied the last generous measure of whisky into his glass but didn't offer me any. Downed it then picked up the empty bottle.

I sat back, confused and uneasy.

He weighed the empty bottle in his hand as if he didn't know what to do with it then leaned so close I thought he was going to glass me, but he hissed, 'Fuck Junkie.' He spun and sliced the bottle into the gantry, roaring as it flew and smashed, mirrors and single malts and everything.

I grabbed my photo and shrank in my seat, too fuddled to run. I thought about Amrit's shop and Sara, terrified of ned men.

He stared at it in the darkness till a last glass shard tinkled to the ground. 'Fuck it,' he said then slumped to the table. He balanced his chin on the heels of his hands. 'I don't want to talk about Junkie.' He sighed and inspected his empty glass. 'Fucking stupid thing to do,' he said. 'All that good whisky.' He turned his glass upside down on the table and nodded to the frame. 'Tell me about your picture.'

Chapter Forty-six

I'd just got used to wearing mini-skirts when the fashion changed. We were always slower up here, or maybe it was just me. I was a good girl then but I was eager to grow up. I left school and applied for my first job.

People talked about equal opportunities: mine was the first generation of working class girls who'd go far. My mother wanted me to go far. 'You'll have the opportunity,' she said. 'The opportunity my generation couldn't have.'

Before the interview I waited nervously in the marble hallway, reading the names of the men who'd fallen in the wars.

'Miss MacAulay?' he said and I whirled round. In those days he was a librarian: not the boss. He was straight out of Carnaby Street in his finely tailored suit. Midnight blue. High breasted, thin lapels. He jerked his head to flick a lock of dark hair. I saw his eyes explore me from my long straight hair to my American tan tights and, innocent as I was, I suspected I'd already passed the interview.

The job itself was alright. I supposed I'd probably go on to study; be a professional to fulfil my mother's dreams. But I was easily distracted. The other girls were fun; I discovered hot pants and Marc Bolan, disco lights and cider and babycham, Biba eyes and the curiosity of men.

In the mornings after he'd made up the daily work rota he'd join us at the shelves for book arranging.

I was working on a free standing bay. The other girls were at the science fiction. His heels clicked when he came to work the shelves beside me, making me nervous and excited at the same time. I finished my section and overlapped him, smoothing down my short skirt before tackling the top shelf. He was squatted, working on the lowest in his section. I tugged the top books tightly together, knowing it would quiver my skirt.

You get giddy if you stand up quickly, the blood slow to make it to your head. He should have leap-frogged to the section after me. But he pressed against me, his chest in his skinny, lemon shirt warming my back, his arms bracing themselves against the uprights, shadowing the line of my arms, the heat from the front of his legs hot on the backs of mine.

'You make me dizzy,' he said, breathing the words on my neck. He traced his fingers down the insides of my arms and sides to my waist. He must have been nearly twenty-five.

The two girls came round the corner of the bay and he let me go.

'Some people have better things to do than tidy shelves,' Lainey said.

He winked at me. We were in clear view of the counter where they had gone in readiness for the library opening.

I patted the books into place, all knowledge of the alphabet confounded. He stayed to finish his. Out of the corner of my eye I saw him push at the zip of his trousers. I'd had my sex education lessons. I knew exactly what was happening. I was exhilarated by the effect I had on him, but I was still in control.

At Hogmanay the library was deserted but we had to stay open till seven thirty. He told us we could bring in drinks and Lainey and I went out for Twizzlers and crisps and trifles to make it special. It was the end of the old year and I was ready for the new.

By seven o'clock I was on my fourth Moscow Mule. Beth and Lainey's boyfriends arrived and so did a couple of former staff members. We took turns manning the counter in case anyone came in but not even the tramp was there that evening. There was music up loud in the library staffroom and as I took my turn on the desk I could hear Lainey's strident voice singing *save all your kisses for me* above Brotherhood of Man's.

The staffroom door opened and he started walking towards me, sleek in his skinny black loons and velvet shirt. 'That girl knows how to party,' he said.

I was fumbling with the tickets, trying to count how many books had been borrowed. He leaned his forearms on the high counter and looked down at me, exuding – I don't know – confidence? Machismo? Whatever it was it had its effect on me; so did the vodka. I could hardly write the numbers in the issue book, the way my hands were shaking.

'Drink up,' he said, passing me my drink and I swallowed the last of it.

He left to lock the library doors then switched off the ceiling lights section by section. I stood at the desk waiting for him, the last light lit above my head. He half turned to look at me and hesitated, then he said my name and told me he needed me in the workroom. I followed him but he kept walking. There was a corridor off the workroom with toilets and the cleaner's cupboard. He pushed the cupboard door open. A metal bucket with a wet mop in it leaned against the pale green wall. He nodded me to go in.

He checked the corridor before he switched on the light and closed the door. He'd to shove it with the flat of his hand to shut it tight. Even then I could hear the beat and laughter from the party. He looked me up and down again and I met his eyes. I suppose I knew what we were doing there.

There were shelves of pine disinfectant and gold and red Brasso tins. One lone, unshaded light bulb hung from the ceiling.

'What about the girls?' I said when he put his arms under mine.

'One at a time,' he said, like a scene from a cheap romance. The mop pail scraped on the cement as he stepped in tighter.

He pushed his tongue into my mouth, smoothed his hands over my breasts and sides and down over my bottom. My knees were ready to collapse for him. My hands sculpted his body through his shirt's velvet pile. He slipped the elastic of my tights down.

I kissed his neck, unbuttoned his shirt and kissed his chest. I didn't know what else to do. He put my hand against his crotch and I rubbed it then he unfastened his belt.

His prick smelled different to anything I'd ever known. The

232

shaft was hot in my hand. The head glistened from a dark, crinkled nest. I wiped its stickiness on the emulsioned wall behind me.

He moaned and pushed himself into my pants. 'Take your tights off,' he said, trying to slide them down. 'Kick your shoes off.'

I almost froze but I collected myself. 'No,' I said. I stood on my tiptoes and felt him burst into me.

He gurgled as we rocked, my arms round his neck, my bottom lip on the rough and smooth near his ear. On the shelves, caustic soda and original Vim bleached my eyes till we rubbed the switch off. It went black and I was blind with it. The shock of my orgasm devoured me and I thrust my tongue into his mouth.

*

Peej picked up the photo and squeezed his eyes to see it better. 'I take it it was a bull's-eye then.'

I shuffled. 'Well, I was seeing him for a couple of months and then he got me transferred.'

'Handy that.'

'Yeah.' I looked at our reflection in the black window. Two saggy drunks. 'Soon as I told him I was pregnant.'

'Tough.'

I laughed. 'You said it.' I touched the edge of the picture frame, turning it so I could see. 'I would have so loved to keep her.'

'The kid?'

My eyes met his and I flicker-blinked. No eyelash-batting this time. 'But everybody told me I was too young.' I put my fingertip on the baby's head. 'She was so – ' I took off my glasses and laid them on the table. My life always looked better out of focus. 'So beautiful. But he didn't want her. My mum told me I should get rid of her. David Steele had made abortion legal years before but it was still hard in those days – the doctors here were more your Doctor Cameron with their old fashioned family values than your cutting edge Doctor Finlay.'

'You've lost me,' he said.

I forgot he was so much younger. 'On television.' I upturned

233

my empty glass in the air and awaited the drip. 'So getting two doctors to say my health was at risk was out of the question. Anyway, by the time I came clean about it to my mum I was over four months. I'd felt the baby kicking.'

Peej had slid his elbow down the table and was leaning on his hand. 'So you had it then. No shame in that.'

'Maybe not now.' I laughed, bitter at the memory. 'Then it was still an absolute no-no.' I sniffed and looked around, not seeing the furniture in the bar, but the old streets where I used to live; the women with their hair covered by scarves, the men with their coarse woollen ones tucked into the upturned necks of their grey coats. 'You couldn't stay at home.'

He sat up and lit another cigarette, directing the first out-breath of smoke away from me. 'So what did you do?'

*

My mother made me put in my resignation – sending it direct to HQ so it didn't go through his hands. He wasn't my supervisor now anyway because I'd been transferred to another branch. Then she made me write a letter. *Dear Mr MacNeill*, it started – that was the only way I ever thought of him. We did, back then; we always called the boss by his second name, and nine times out of ten it was a man. *Dear Mr MacNeill, I've already told you the details of a delicate issue.* It was foreign prose; she dictated it. *This matter needs to be resolved. If you do not meet me on … at … to discuss this so we can resolve it to my satisfaction, I shall be forced to take the matter higher. Yours sincerely, Alice MacAulay.* He came, of course, and my mother and I were waiting. She was supreme, my mother. She ground him under her thick set heel so hard even I winced. I still hoped he would marry me, but she knew what his type was like. She gave him a week.

I held my hand out when we left the café. The heavy glass door clanged behind us, the broken bolt of the lock indenting a deep groove in the door jam.

'Well?' my mother said to him.

Sweet wrappers and cigarette papers swirled about the blue and white mosaic on the floor of the doorway. An old man in a home-painted sandwich board warned that the end was nigh and a girl and boy with their hands inside the back waistband of each other's yellow loons slouched past us, in step, on the pavement.

'Next week,' he said, buttoning his car coat. He'd had his hair cut short. The big boss had retired and they were funnelling upwards for promotion. He took out his car keys, looked at my outstretched hand and said to my mother. 'I'll get it organised for next week.'

'You'd better.'

My outstretched hand was still waiting. My mother took it and turned me smartly down the street. I looked back and saw him looking back at me, but it wasn't wistfully.

*

Peej stubbed his cigarette in the ashtray. 'And?'

*

He got back to me. The last day of the following week. A telephone call. We'd only just had the phone installed. I was still nervous about using it, though working in the library had made it easier. As soon as my mother realised it was him she took the receiver away from me.

'Hello,' she said.

My heart had soared but now it tumbled.

'I see.' A pause. 'And you'll put that in writing?'

She put the receiver down. We were alone in the living room. Fortunately my father had died. My brother was still at school.

'It's settled,' she said. 'He's got relatives in some backwater. You'll go to her to have your baby. She's short of cash and not very bright so he'll pay for her to raise it.' Her tight fingers gripped my upper arm and she shook it. 'You're being given a second chance, Alice. You need to take it.'

'I don't want to live in some backwater,' I said.

'Well you shouldn't have got yourself into bother.'

She went over to the fire and rattled the coals with the poker. Ashes fell through the grate. Coals, half glowing red, half matt black with a waist band of white resettled themselves and she shook a few more lumps from the brass scuttle on top of them.

A spark shot at her and she swore. 'Time I was getting rid of this out-dated thing.'

'It takes two to get a girl in bother.'

She turned to me, sucking her burned knuckle. 'Aye, well he's doing his bit to put it right. Now it's your turn.'

I looked gloomily into the fire, now almost only showing black. A screen of thick smoke spirited up from it. 'What do I need to do?'

She moved to the window and held the curtain aside so she could watch for my brother. 'You've to pack all your stuff today and we'll meet him in the town at nine o'clock tomorrow.'

I chewed the inside of my cheek till it was sore. He'd be driving us. I tried to imagine a love nest in the country. If he was happy to pay for the baby, I could raise it. He could come to visit me. Scheme kids are always dreamers. But I'd read the Scottish ballads. I should have known these stories don't have happy endings.

She turned from the window. 'You know he's engaged to be married?'

My insides swirled as if I was going to be sick, but she hadn't finished.

'After the baby's born, you've to promise to have nothing more to do with him. Or it.'

There were teenage boys' voices in the street and a foot punted a ball.

'The baby'll be born round about September,' she said. She took a couple of steps into the room and bent towards me, her voice softening. 'He says you're clever. He's going to help you apply for university. Says the best library course is down in Wales.' She tried to push my long fringe out of my eyes but I shrugged her off. 'After the baby's born you can go straight down to Aberystwyth. Alice, you'll have a brand new start.'

We heard Bobby's key in the door and my mother jumped. She started to walk towards it, but issued a stern, 'Not a word,' warning.

Bobby pushed the door open and looked at us. He looped the strap of his school bag over the back of a chair and picked a banana out of the dish.

'Hi son,' she said brightly. 'I got a piece of news today.'

I watched her wipe her hands on her apron. That was her only sign of anxiety. 'My old auntie's not well up in the highlands. I've told them Alice and I'll go up to see her.' She looked at me. 'Alice's giving up her job to take care of her.' I can still see her joyless grin.

*

Peej sucked in saliva and straightened in his chair again. 'So that's who we're going to find.' I lifted the photo frame in two hands. 'My little girl.'

He stretched. 'She'll not be so wee now.'

You could see her dark hair. Her face was tiny. *A wee farthin' face* Mrs MacNeill called it. I kissed the photograph. 'She'll be forty in a couple of months. If she made it.'

Peej was quiet. Drink does that. Or maybe he was calculating. 'You're a good bit older than you look, Missus.'

I'd forgotten that. I had told all the others I was forty-odds. It should have been embarrassing, but he seemed relaxed and I was glowing with the whisky and the unburdening so I reached across the table and held his hand. For a long time I smiled into his eyes. 'Now you know all my guilty secrets.'

He didn't pull his hand away, but I think he winced.

Chapter Forty-seven

Daylight woke me. I'd grown so used to waking down the pit in the foetid black that daylight was painful. I moaned and put my head under the covers. My mouth was coated; my body, I realised, was not. My cold arms slithered on my warm sides. I sat up abruptly and took stock of where I was. In a hotel room. Carpet and open curtains in garish tartan red. Antique – surely – dressing table mirror in three parts reflecting a tousle-headed fifty-odd year old with chicken skins for breasts and grubby arms and neck. I felt rough alright. My head was pounding, my clothes were all over the floor, but there was no one else in the bed beside me.

I lay down again and put my fingers under the covers. Brought them to my nose. No smell of cum. Spunk. Jizz. Whatever people called it. Semen, even, if we were still using Greek and Latin. I didn't remember even going to bed last night. Yet another time. So where was Peej?

I tried to remember everything we'd done but my body did an Edvard Munch as if someone was trying to pull out my veins and synapses with crochet hooks. There was a boulder in my head when I tried to move it. I needed a drink.

I got up and tossed through my clothes pile for my pants. Couldn't find them. Slapped the overhang of the bedspread to see if they were caught underneath. Lost my balance and fell on my arse. Put one foot in one leg of my trousers and my toes came out the other end wearing a crown of pale blue knickers. By the time I'd whipped that lot off again – the chill air shrink-wrapping me with goosepimples – I realised I was going to have the skits and hallelujahed there was an en-suite that flushed. I opened the window and siphoned in the sweet smelling air. Life wasn't all bad. The cistern gave an empty clunk and the new loo water was as brown as the mucky sludge it had disposed of, albeit minus the stink.

I dressed and opened the door into the dark lobby. When had I last seen red flock wallpaper? The skirting board was painted in at least ten coats of thick cream and the cream above the picture rail right over the ceiling and down the other side gave the impression that I was on a ship. Or maybe that was the way my brain was reeling. Someone had got a job lot of highland etchings: one hung between every chocolate wooden door and behind one of them, I presumed, Peej was sleeping. I listened for four or five seconds for something I could identify as his snore but there wasn't a burr and I didn't have time to go hunting.

I walked on landlubber legs towards the emergency exit which I remembered led to the entrance. An old grandfather clock suggested it was twenty to three but he wasn't talking. Tocking. I needed a drink. My insides were squealing for it. I'd had a bottle in my bag but I'd left it at Dykend. I went past the reception almost politely nodding and stepped into the bar.

The invigorating smell of *uisge beath*. Eight steps it took me to reach it. Behind the bar the carpet was saturated in it and I cursed Peej for slinging that bottle. My hands shook and my shoes crunched on curls and spikes of glass. Strike! There wasn't a single, complete bottle left. Dregs of honeyed liquid glinted in scattered crescents. I shouldn't be drinking it, anyway.

There was a glass fronted cupboard with 'chilled' fruit juices. I took out a tomato and searched for a drawer for a bottle opener. Couldn't find one, tried the dunting technique my brother once showed me to tap the top off on a hard edge but only managed to chip the woodwork. Then I noticed an in-built bottle opener in the fittings and tipped the whole bottle down my throat.

But it wasn't what I needed. I spotted the coffee machine. One hand tried to still my wobble-board stomach while the other rummaged for a paper filter at the side of the machine. I found one and popped it in the plastic thing on a cleanish jug then carefully picked up the curls of bottle-bottoms and poured their precious cargo into the coffee filter. It wasn't just the hangover that was making my body quake. It was the prospect ahead of me of what I was likely to find. So engrossed must I have been that I didn't hear Peej step up for service.

'The master distiller at work,' he said.

I was happy I wasn't alone in looking rough. I turned round holding a bulb of brown liquid in a bottle neck. It too passed into the jug. 'Breakfast?' I asked and he coughed, 'Aye.'

He crossed over to last night's table and came back with my bag and our glasses. 'Might be today, eh?' he said, setting up the photo.

I rapped the last drops from the coffee filter and poured. 'A blend of my own,' I said and we raised our glasses. 'MacAulay's folly.'

*

We drove in silence all the way up to North Connell.   As we came out from Ben Cruachan and turned to skirt Loch Etive, the water calmly replicated the sky and the mountains and the whisky allowed me the brief euphoria of hope. The air was clean here. People could have survived in crofts and glens.

Connell itself had hardly changed, an affluent town with its solid stone buildings still glittering in the light tossed and fractured by sea and loch. We drove along the high main street. It still looked like the picture from the lid of a jigsaw puzzle but pushing between the cerise pink dianthus in its flower tubs and baskets were jagged green and purple thistle tufts. A wind blown birch seedling had established itself in the gutter above the betting shop.

We drove through the red iron girders of the bridge heading for North Connell, the joins in the structure parodying the rhythm of my pulse. Immediately on the other side Peej pulled up and got out, leaving the car door open. I thought he was going to be sick. He walked up to a neat old pub on the other side of the road and tried the handle. I assumed he must have a drouth. He glanced over at me once then walked out of sight around the back. I did think it strange that he didn't just put his foot on the door but my brain was straining. I'd washed down my one last paracetamol with the whisky but it wasn't having any effect. I was annoyed he was wasting time when we were so close.

He came back to the car. 'D'you not think that's a bit funny?'

'What?'

'No weeds.'

That was why it seemed neat. We'd got out of the way of seeing neat and that's why he'd spotted it.

'There's nobody in, but. Nobody answering.'

He perched on the car seat, one leg out of the car and reached for his rifle. He put down the visors to shade the windscreen and scoured the hills. 'They could be anywhere up there.' He put his binoculars to his eyes and moved over the deep irregular channels the burns had gouged down the hillsides. 'Wee bothies, barns – anywhere.' Look at where we had chosen to live.

He must have noticed something about me because he did a double take and put the binoculars down. 'You alright?' he asked. I could only nod. He swung his leg in and slammed the door. 'Better get on with it, then.' He took a drink then passed the water to me. 'How much further?'

'Just up the road.'

We moved off. My eyes ransacked the buildings. There were new bungalows, lots of them, built in the thirty-odd years since my few months here. I shouldn't have expected it to stay the same. There were gardens with yellow, blue and green plastic swings in them. Swinging wooden placards advertising PYO rasps. To the left the slow descent to the coast was broken by a rumbledethump of green hillocks that teased the tourist with sneak previews of the heights of Mull, alternating with triangles of the blackest sea.

'Nice country,' Peej said, making conversation.

Thirty years? Almost forty. Mrs MacNeill would be old.

'Left here,' I said. We turned off the road onto a track. 'It's at the end of this. About two hundred metres.' The house was hidden in bushes with only its roof slates visible.

He crept the car forward. 'Hold the gun as if you're going to use it,' he said.

241

It was such a big gun. I rested its nose on the dash.

'Where are we going, Yak?'

I pointed. 'Behind that scrub. You can see it.'

'Don't like this.' Peej's head tugged round to see behind him. The track was taking us into a dip. We slumped to a pot-holed halt and he engaged reverse.

'What's wrong?' I said above the high whine of the engine and the dunts as our wheels bumped along the pitted drive.

He backed out on to the road then drove up the hill another hundred metres to where it levelled out at the top of the incline and there was a screen of bushes.

'What is it?' I asked, annoyed he wouldn't say.

He pulled on the hand brake. 'Just not happy,' he said, looking beyond me. 'Stay here.'

He took the rifle and began forcing his way through the hedge.

'Wait for me,' I said, scrambling out of the car. 'You're not leaving me.' Not when I was this close.

He didn't look pleased but I faced him down.

'Watch that wire.' There was a low wire designed to trip up intruders who thought all they had to contend with was being lacerated by branches. I understood one of the advantages of leather: no matter how careful I was, the dense black twigs scored my skin or prodded like bony fingers. He held the worst of it off my face but I shrugged off his good deed. 'You only had to drive another fifty yards,' I sniped.

'Shut it!'

I felt wounded. Then I realised we were hunting.

We kept low, following the bushes along the dip in the hill where we were hidden from the house until the last minute. He kept the rifle ready; if we found anyone, I hoped he'd remember they could be my relations.

Through a bright tangle of sweet pea and clematis I could make out the black windows of the cottage. There were café curtains at two of the windows. A mountain bike was propped against the outer wall. It didn't look as if it'd been lying there eighteen months. I thought I could hear singing. We paused, listening, but only heard my stomach. Peej held his hand up for me to wait and he stepped out of cover to unhook the loop securing the fence. A wren's burr and whistle drew him. The bird hopped on to the washing line then flipped, its tail cocked. Peej waved me through and closed the fence.

It was tidier than I remembered. The flags had been swept. A half barrel of herbs flourished against the western wall. The windows were clean and had no spiders' webs. Peej ducked under the window and waved for me to follow. Round the corner the yard had been monoblocked in pink and yellow and the rusty iron post had gone, and the chain, and the dog. Instead, geraniums quivered in tubs. I swallowed.

Peej stood with his back to the wall, looking at the yard. I was still taking it in. The barn, I realised, had been fronted by a white panelled garage door. It was shiny: its opening was unencumbered by leaves. Peej crossed the yard to it and peered in through a small window, shading his eyes against the glass.

'Fucking Lamborghini.'

I prayed that The Boss wasn't living in it.

The storm door of the house was open revealing a multipaned glass door with a brass handle. Beyond it, I was sure now, I could hear music.

Peej met my eyes and I nodded. He adjusted the rifle, gripping it in one hand. He leaned on the brass door handle with his left and swung it open. We stepped into a modernised home of polished floors, scatter rugs and Ikea furnishings. The music I'd heard was Verdi. I waited in the lounge while Peej checked the rooms. There were flames in the grate and wood in the scuttle. I walked over to the dresser to look at framed photographs.

Peej came in as the music stopped in the middle of an aria. He picked up the CD player: it was one of those wind-up ones.

'They only play for half an hour, don't they?'

He noticed the fire. 'The house is empty.' He put the CD player down. 'They can't be far.' He saw me holding a photograph. 'D'you recognise anybody?'

I looked at the man and woman smiling with their arms

round each other and shook my head.

'Let's get back to the car,' he said and headed for the door.

'Shouldn't we leave them a note?'

'Advertise?'

'If they're close, don't you think we should find them?'

'You don't recognise them?'

'I don't think so.'

'Then, naw.' He gripped the gun again and went through the door.

'We could check the barn – the shed?'

I wanted to shout, to bring them running. 'They probably saw you with that gun and ran away. We could tell them it's alright.' I skipped to catch up with him. He was covering the ground faster on the way back. 'They might know something about the MacNeills. They might be able to tell me where she went.'

He ran and I ran after him. He pushed through the bushes to where the car was but this time he didn't wait for me. I couldn't see but I didn't hear it drive away; it was idling on the road where we'd left it. I tried to push my way backwards through the jaggy bush with my collar up and thought I was going to be trapped in it, like that medieval torture machine with spikes but another push and I made it. Tripped over the wire on to my back. When I got up I saw Peej holding the gun at shoulder height at the car window, but as I watched, he softened his grip and began to walk round behind the car to the other side. I saw why. Sitting in the driving seat was a man with his arms folded behind his head. He was playing the muzak Peej had 'bought' from the garage. The engine was running, but the driver's door was open. I walked round the front, rubbing the back of my head from my fall.

'Nice jeep,' he said in a southern English accent.

Peej didn't move.

'You can put your rifle down. I don't want it.'

Peej put his foot on the back door and leaned the gun into the man's face. The Englishman didn't blink: he looked down the barrel then straight at Peej. 'You'll make quite a mess if you use that at this range.'

Peej lowered the barrel and leaned his shoulder on the door. 'I ken fine what it'll do, pal.'

'Peej!' I said.

It was the man from the photograph. His voice was friendly but his eyes stayed fixed on Peej. 'Up from Glasgow?'

'Close enough. Closer than you.'

'Oh,' the man said, 'I've been here long enough to call it home.'

'Do you know Mrs MacNeill?' I asked.

'Mrs MacNeill?'

'Mrs MacNeill,' I said. 'She used to live here – forty years ago.'

He fiddled with his ear. He looked as if he might be military: clean shaven, clean booted, creased trousers. How had he managed that? 'I've only been here the last five.' He flashed his eyes sideways to me then returned them to Peej. 'Maybe old Murdostoun'll know.'

Peej dragged him out of the car by the collar, still digging the barrel of the gun under his chin. 'Who else lives here?'

'Call off your dog,' he said, eyes flicked to me again, but I let the seconds pass. 'Look,' he said eventually, 'There's a few of us hereabouts. Living in various cottages. Murdostoun lives in the pub you'll have passed in North Connell.'

Peej felt down English's sides for a weapon.

'You'll not find anything,' he said. 'We're quite civilised.' He spoke to me. 'I was just having coffee.'

'Turn.'

'In fact I've just opened a vacuum packed Arabica – we've a top class epicurean place in Oban.' He maintained the mannered bravado while Peej searched him, the nose of the gun pressed against the nape of his neck.

I think he heard my stomach rumble. 'Foie gras, too,' he said, 'if you'd like. With some French *toasts*.' He said it with an accent. 'We've even got butter.'

My eyes involuntarily strayed to Peej.

'We want to get talking to Murdostoun.'

'A coffee wouldn't hurt,' I said.

'What's this?' Peej slid a sheathed hunting knife from the back loops of English's trousers.

He half turned and smiled, keeping eye contact. 'You know, other than Murdostoun and a couple of others, you're the only people I've seen in eighteen months. You should let me – let us – welcome you.' He held his arms out away from his sides. 'I'm no threat to you. Honestly. Why should I be?'

I looked at him in his green and gold Barbour and Peej and I in our dilapidated George, grass stained, whisky drenched and coal blacked. And waving a gun. I knew who I felt was more intimidating.

Peej leaned in, switched off the ignition and pocketed the keys.

Chapter Forty-eight

After coffee and foie gras he took us down to meet Murdostoun. He rapped three long and three quick fire knocks, repeated it and smiled.

'It'll take him a couple of minutes.'

Peej was still edgy.

'He's an old man, Murdostoun,' he reassured him. 'No one's playing any tricks on you.'

What a grim, hard face Peej had on him. I hadn't noticed it for so long.

'Quite a view, isn't it?' English said. We looked at the firth. Well, I'll call it that. It was the sea loch opening.

'Is this what brought you here?' I asked him.

Peej tutted and moved a step off. I think he said, 'Naw, a fucking Lamborghini.' But we could all have Lamborghinis now if we wanted them.

'Yes,' he said. 'My ancestors were from the highlands. We'd passed this way on our honeymoon – my wife and I. Fell in love with the place. We spent half our honeymoon standing by that bridge, watching the ebb tide over the Falls of Lora.'

'Is this bastard answering or what?' Peej said.

The Englishman fiddled with his ear, still smiling. To me he said, 'Give him a minute. He's old.'

Just then we heard the bolts slide back. I counted three of them then one of the two black and white storm doors was pulled open and the man I took to be Murdostoun looked out.

The name hadn't meant a thing to me. I'd racked my brain for memories. Even his face didn't strike a chord, though his accent, when he spoke, was what I remembered.

'Visitors, Murdostoun,' English said and stepped in. The old man stepped back for me but he confronted Peej.

'He'll be alright, Murd. I've checked him out.'

He didn't give way. 'Glasgow, is it?'

Peej narrowed his eyes. 'Near enough.'

'What's your name, lad?'

My heart groaned as he stuttered over Jamieson. 'I call him Peej,' I said, once he'd finally got it out.

The old man gave way. 'Jameson's a fine name. But hereabouts we prefer a drop o' the Scotch.'

Moving slowly he slid the bolts again and made his way, leaning clunky knuckles on the wooden tables, back to the bar to set up four glasses. He filled them to a depth of two knobbled fingers with a Tobermory malt. I sniffed it when he passed it to me.

'The Ledaig,' he said.

The room was a bare one: none of the tourist aesthetics of tartan and antlers. This was a man's bar, kitted out in PVC bus seats and bentwood. 'A terrible business,' he said, clearly wanting to talk about the deaths.

First Arabica, then Tobermory peat smoke. My senses were stoked and trembling. I wasn't in the mood for making small talk.

'Mr Murdostoun,' I said. 'We've come for a reason.' I put my glass down and glanced at Peej who was sitting back from the rest of us where he could watch the door behind the bar. He made me feel vulnerable. I felt vulnerable enough as it was: turning the clock back had divested me of my maturity.

'Peej,' I said to make him look at me. He didn't say anything. English stretched his legs out. I went on, 'We've come for a reason, haven't we?'

Peej nodded almost imperceptibly. It was down to me.

'You'll be looking for somebody, I guess,' the old man anticipated. 'Not much other reason for passing this way.'

'That's right,' I said and leaned over the table, clasping my hands up under my throat. 'Do you remember Mrs MacNeill from the Shieling?'

He drank his whisky. 'Mary MacNeill,' he said. 'Mary

MacNeill from the Shieling.' He looked at me through undisciplined white eyebrows. In the light from the windows his eyes were the wateriest blue.

I began to reach into my bag for the photograph. 'Mr Murdostoun – do you remember I came here? One summer, years ago now –' I pulled it out ready to show him. He was only the second person I'd ever owned up to. My heart was pounding. Though that might have been the stimulants.

I passed him the frame and he looked at it, holding it at arm's length where the light from the window would hit it and it would come into focus.

'Aye, lass. And you'll be wondering what happened to her daughter.'

I swallowed hard.

'Well, it doesn't take much working out, Glasgow. But your search hits a dead end on both accounts.'

He rose and went back to the bar for a refill. Three slow knocks came to the door and Peej's hand reached for the rifle he'd lain across the table.

Mr Murdostoun pointed his finger. 'You'll not be needing that, boy. That's just the lads off the boat.'

English unlocked the door and two men brought the sea smell in with them and an old labrador that sniffed Peej's hand and crotch and slumped on the floor under his table. The men acknowledged each other guardedly and smiled shyly every time I looked at them. It crossed my mind to wonder if they'd any women in their community, but I didn't ask.

It didn't seem the right time to return to my questions. I put the photo face down on the table and listened to the men talk about catches and rabbits and moving from one car to another. They were eager to exchange news with Peej though he remained reticent. I revelled in the new company, my adrenaline firing me up now I was finally here. They hadn't experienced our bikers. That probably made a difference. I supposed, thinking about the Sheiling, that life could be quite good if you were English or any of these others. But then one of the fishermen – a man with a Polish or Lithuanian accent – asked Peej if he'd any spare women.

'No,' Peej said. End of story.

I felt a notch-up of aggression but English defused it.

'Murdostoun, you were going to tell our visitor about Mrs MacNeill.'

'Aye,' the old man said, remembering. 'Pass the boys that photograph; see if they have any mind of her.'

'I knew you when you came in,' the one who'd been introduced as Fraser said, hardly meeting my eyes. 'I mind you spent the summer then left your kiddie and went back to Glasgow.' He passed the frame to the other man. 'I was working with MacNeill's dairy herd while I was at the school,' he said. 'You were a good looking lass.' Yet he looked much older than me.

The other man shrugged, too recent an incomer to know me.

'Yon was bad blood anyhow,' Fraser went on. 'You'll mind, Murdo. Bad blood, come from bad blood. Not you, mind,' he said to me. 'No, but Mary MacNeill was never the one to bring up good kids.'

I breathed. 'What happened to the baby?'

Fraser's eyes met with the old man's before he said anything. He drained his glass and scratched the inside of one foot with the heel of the other. 'My sister was a teacher at the school: they couldn't control her. 'Margaret' she was: 'Margaret Mary' – looked like you.'

In my head she'd always been Heather. They'd made me put Margaret on the birth certificate.

'She ran away back to Glasgow.'

They passed back the photograph.

'So, lass,' Mr Murdostoun said, 'Didn't I tell you, a dead end on both counts. Mary MacNeill died of a stroke five, six years ago.' He shielded his mouth with his hand. 'Nephew sold the house to this English fellow. Still, he's not bad. Not bad to me, at any rate.'

The men talked sea currents and navigation charts and who would work their fleeces. Peej was sitting with his foot on a chair. I caught him catch me pinching my tear ducts as Murdo

250

poured me another half. Peej put his hand over his.

He took his foot off the chair and leaned over to me. 'D'you want to go home? The old fella's asked us to stay. Says they'll have a bit of a night of it.'

I was shattered. I was disappointed. I was hungover from yesterday and my nerves were stretched with the amount I'd drunk today already. But I'd hardly eaten a thing. I shrugged, indecisive. Fraser's buddy disappeared through the door behind the bar with his catch in the pail and the dog following him. Fraser sucked and blew on a mouth organ. A few minutes later we could smell the tang of salty fish frying. A robust young woman who turned out to be Murdostoun's grand-daughter came out of the bar door with plates of fish in batter with young potatoes and carrots and fresh greens all smothered in butter. She served Peej and me as visitors then English, I supposed from the body language, because he was her man, though she wasn't the one with her arms curled round him in the photograph.

I met Peej's eyes. We decided to stay till morning.

Despite my disappointments the evening was fairly pleasant. I was glad to have a woman to talk to, even though Tracy didn't know Margaret Mary or anyone except Mrs MacNeill. I relaxed when I saw Peej relax, stowing the gun at his feet once the whisky began to flow and he saw the locals putting them away twice as fast as he or I.

We spent the night in my old room at The Sheiling. Tracy used it as a sewing room. We had to clear reams of fabrics and spools of ribbon away to reveal the bed. There'd never been such colours – such frippery – while I was there and I wondered how it had been for Margaret Mary. This would have been her room too, but any trace of her had been obliterated by English's decorating.

Tracy assumed we'd be in one bed. I wouldn't have disabused her but Peej told her he'd sleep on the floor so she brought him some cushions and her spare quilt, blushing the colour of her fabrics.

'We could have shared,' I said, once Tracy had gone and we were alone with our candles.

251

He scratched down inside the back of his shirt neck. 'Nah,' he said, and left it at that.

Chapter Forty-nine

I felt quite empty on the way back in the car next morning. The mountains were picturesque but they were dying for the winter. A grey, short light wasn't enough to burst any more flowers into bloom. I watched a big brown bird manoeuvre on an air current, high up the side of a crag and wished I was with him. I wondered what the world would look like from up there. A desert land: all the people I cared about dead or disappeared.

Peej sneezed. Well, nearly all. My trail had gone cold and there was nothing left but to go back.

'Do you think we have to live down the pit, Peej?' I asked him, as I watched the curves of a grey cloud throw straight lines of rain over the slope of a hill.

The arm of his leather jacket creaked as he turned the steering column. 'You getting itchy feet?'

I remembered my restless legs in the hotel and my hopes of being alone with Peej, but that, too, had all gone wrong.

'We haven't seen the bikers for months. Maybe they've decided to leave us in peace.' I looked at his profile, with his sharp nose and his chin softened by a few days growth. 'Maybe we don't need to be living underground any more.'

He checked the dashboard clock. 'You've been seeing too much home decorating.'

It was true. Usually I steered clear of houses but in the last few days I'd been in my mother's, the hotel at Crianlarich, Murdostoun's bar and English's Sheiling. And there was that big sandstone house at the start of our journey where Peej had siphoned the diesel.

We were approaching a village.

'Maybe we'll talk about it to the others,' he said, and slowed to peer in the local shop window. He parked, reached for his gun and said, 'I need ciggies. Come on we'll get some stuff.'

We were wary, but it was deserted. He booted the back door in and we took what we wanted – pot noodles, bottled water, red salmon, mushy peas, batteries, magazines, postcards of a highland cow, paracetamol, sticking plasters, a See You Jimmy tammy and ginger wig, Platinum pens and bags of marshmallows – and drove the car further down the road and off to lunch at a picnic table on the shores of a loch. Iubhair or Dochart – I wasn't sure, from reading the map, which one it was; if it were the first I wouldn't even have a clue how to pronounce it. Walking along its gravelly banks I wondered if there were any Gaelic speakers left or whether we could rename it. I threw a stone in and called it Emptiness. Barrenness. Or Beautiful Rain for the shower of circlets that I could see pinpricking the surface over by the northern shore.

'Alice.' Peej's voice came to me and I turned and walked back to him. He was holding my photo frame in his hand.

'There's stuff in this.'

A corner of something had been sticking out and he'd started taking off the back of the frame. He handed it over to me, the frame with its loose glass, the three generations, the rough card back with its prop and in between – what? I sat at the picnic bench beside him and spread the papers out.

My mother had kept these. Close ups of my baby. Close ups of her in my arms; close ups of her in my mother's. My mother smiling at my baby. And in an envelope, a photo of a ruddy toddler in a tousy ponytail, one sock at her ankle and one pulled to her knee, the chained Alsatian in the background; one of a five year old on her first day at school; one of a dour thirteen year old with her brows down in a scowl. I looked at Peej.

'She kept these.' My hands shook as I held them. 'She was sent these and didn't even let me see them.'

Peej did what Peej does best: he didn't say anything. I pressed myself against the outside of his leathery sleeve, catching the teenager as a gust threatened to carry her, and I anchored her below the edge of the photo frame and studied her eyes.

'She's like you,' he said.

'But she's like him as well.'

I turned my face into him and he opened his arm out to let me cry against him, inside with his smell of smoky leather and the heat of his ribs.

After a while I broke away from him to tidy the photos. He picked one up and looked closely at it. It was one of the early ones, taken just after the birth when my mother came up to the Sheiling. The two-ply shawl she'd crocheted was spread out over the cream-coloured PVC couch and Margaret Mary lay in the centre of its intricate shells in her frilly pink dress.

'What's that?' Peej pointed his grubby finger at a little brown thing.

I took off my glasses and held the photo inches from my eyes. 'Och, that's her wee teddy,' I said.

I wanted to think of my baby, but instead I thought about Junkie. Only three days had passed though it seemed much longer. Now we were going back to face her. My escape from it was over: now there'd be the hard adjustment, and didn't I know how it felt to lose a baby.

In the jeep I asked him what he thought had happened to Junkie's baby, but he was unresponsive.

I remembered the night she came back from the bikers. It was something that had been troubling me since her baby was born. I clutched my hands in my lap. 'Do you think Eric was right when he said it was a nuclear explosion?'

'What?' He glanced quickly at me, his brows scowling. 'What are you talking about?'

'When Junkie came back, when we'd moved to the pit from the library.' I looked at him, almost wishing I hadn't started this. 'The night of that storm.' We'd been sheltered from it in our new pit but she'd borne the brunt of its full force. The timing was right. If she'd been in the early stages – in other words, if the bikers had got her, as time scales suggested – the radiation could have deformed it. But then the ground around us would be contaminated: our crops, our wild foods and even our animals. I thought about my aches and pains again.

Peej braked in the middle of the road.

'Nothing's going to satisfy you, Yakkity, is it? You can't leave things alone.' He leaned his arm on the back of his chair, twisting to look at me. 'Brain told you it was safe. He told you about the rods going in to shut it down but you're not going to be satisfied till you see it. Are you?'

I blinked. I hadn't expected anger.

He backed the car into the verge and drove forward, backed again and turned it in the direction we'd just come from.

'Have you forgotten something?'

He didn't speak. We drove back a mile or two then he turned off the road through private gates with an MPV in the driveway, jumped out and siphoned its fuel.

He was unpredictable. I waited, nervous, to see which direction he would go in when we rejoined the road. He turned left, heading back towards lochs Iubhair and Dochart.

In a quiet voice I asked him, 'Where are we going, Peejie?'

He flicked a look at me and picked up speed.

'Check that map. I think we can take the other road heading for Glasgow. Down by Loch Lomond and then cut across at Tarbet.'

I studied the map. It would take us down the road to the Gareloch and Faslane. If there had been a nuclear explosion it would be devastated and that would explain what had happened to Junkie's baby. If not, then it must have been deformed because she'd done drugs or because it had been the bikers or for no good reason other than nature's devilment.

But why did I care?

The scenery closed in, brooding and beautiful. Inside the car we were quiet. Yet there was something that was eating at me to ask him.

I put on a CD of service station Vivaldi. 'Peej,' I said, remembering how they'd sat together, hand in hand, oblivious to everyone. How she'd spent the first night underground sleeping in Peej's bed. 'Were you the baby's father?'

He took his eyes off the road and stared at me. The corners of his mouth puckered but he didn't say anything. His hands were clenched on the steering wheel as the car accelerated towards a corner with the mountains closing in.

'Watch!' I said.

He looked away, the brakes pushing me against my seat belt as he slowed to take the bend. As soon as we were round it he growled, 'Fuck knows who the father was. Junkie was a mess. She'd have shagged any bastard for a dose of blow.'

I left it, my heart thumping. I concentrated on the violin music, flipping through my photos again as he drove us to Faslane.

Chapter Fifty

When we got there Faslane's trees were as lush by the edge of the road as when I'd last seen them; if the leaves were beginning to curl it was only at the first touch of autumn. The dry stane dyke by the roadside was still smothered in fronds of bracken and slippery with moss.

Peej drove us straight towards the North Gate, with the manner of a man who'd never experienced any challenge there. I looked up to the tops of the massive fences coifed with their coils of razor wire and remembered two young men in kilts shinning up the lampposts to display their meaty thighs and their banner proclaiming a nuclear free zone.

It was curious without the tomfoolery and singing, the painted faces and costumes and the ranks of yellow jacketed policemen shoulder to shoulder, fellow participants in the sport.

'They say the seepage of radiation actually boosts the growth – accelerates it – which is why it's so green at nuclear sites,' I told Peej.

'And that's bad?'

We had stopped, nosing the gates. Peej looked out of his side window. 'Looks fine to me.'

We got out and stared in through the wire.

'Fucking prison camp though, isn't it?' he said, putting his fingers through the meshing and rattling it. He shouted, but nobody came. The security box was empty; the mesh railing twanged until it stopped. There didn't seem to be any birdsong but that didn't mean the birds had died of radiation: since moving to the pit I'd learned there was always a time of day when we didn't hear birds. Sometimes nature was really quiet without even an Eastenders' dog-barking moment or a lone seagull crying.

We separated. I pulled at the bracken fronds and sniffed the fragments, troubled over his reaction to my question about Junkie. The fresh air did me good yet I was also troubled over how fresh the air could really be. It was incomprehensible that there could be nuclear weapons within metres of us; that there could be Trident subs in the sleek grey water we'd driven beside. I scanned the loch for metal fins breaking the surface. The loch itself was submarine dour. So were the clouds. The road was damp and there was more rain in the air. My fingers were stiffening with cold. I pushed them into my pockets: the weather was definitely changing.

Peej called to me. 'You ready?'

It was another part of my life I needed to let go. The danger might still be here, just as it had been for decades, nuclear subs ready to fire their warheads on the virtual squeezing of a radio-controlled trigger.

'I suppose so.' At least I didn't have to worry that it had already happened.

Back in the car, Peej slowed as we drove by the peace camp. Time had made its brashly painted caravans only a little less gaudy. It was a harlequin; a pre-school TV programme presented by anti-globalisation anarchists. Dog-eared banner tatters had been swamped into the greenery by a year and a half of unmediated rain.

'Did you live here?' Peej asked.

'Hell, no.' I laughed. 'Without sewerage or central heating? You must be joking.' I waited for him to turn towards me and smiled. 'I was too much of a crapper for that level of commitment. Didn't mind coming up for the day, but I wouldn't change my life for it.' I looked away, back at the multi-coloured caravans. The order in my life had been far too precious then. Now look at me.

We settled in to the long drive towards Glasgow. Somewhere in these lifeless houses, I thought, I might have a grown-up daughter. A middle-aged daughter. I wouldn't know where to begin to search for her. Was I going to have to give *her* up? I

259

glanced at Peej's profile: all these dreams I'd had. It had been a trip of mixed results and conflicting emotions.

'Do you think Chis might know about Margaret Mary?'

He shrugged and kept driving. I wondered if he was thinking about Junkie waiting for us back at Dykend.

*

We were tired when we got home. I'd seen Peej slowly close down with every half hour behind the wheel. Maybe it had been a bad idea to drive through Glasgow but it was the quickest way and anyway, I didn't feel so bad now I knew the bodies in the houses were past the worst of the putrefaction. In fact it gave me hope that we could find somewhere to live. I didn't want to spend another winter underground. I wanted a nice life like the one at the Sheiling. Wasn't life ironic. Yet our return did feel like a home coming. Robyn and Robina cuddled me: I lifted my arms and they slotted right in. Limpet's children were full of smiles and Limpet herself was at the fire, she and Saleema preparing nan, slapping the dough from hand to hand.

The children's voices brought the men from the tent. The Gaffer clapped me to his chest, which was leaner than I remembered and his arm muscles were firmer. Basher held my shoulders and nodded, a soft expression on his face. We gave out all the gifts we'd brought – saving the See You Jimmy hat and ginger wig for Salaam. Wide Boy said he should be MacSalaam now: he was a true member of the clan. They were excited to hear about the survivors at North Connell; almost as delighted at the gift they'd given us of butter.

I asked Old Bill how Grace was and he told me she was taking care of Junkie. I cast my eyes briefly in Peej's direction. He was sitting on a stool with his elbows on his knees, concentrating on something dreadfully interesting between his feet on the campfire mat. His cigarette smoke trickled round the fingers of his right hand. I gathered up the nerve to go into the women's tent on my own.

Junkie was lying on her side facing Grace who was still knitting. I wondered if they'd held that position since we left.

'Hiya,' I said, crouching beside Junkie and laying my hand

260

on her arm. 'How are you doing?'

Her face was blotchy and her eyes were red-rimmed. Grace started singing. An old Helen Shapiro song from the era when Grace had been fully alive.

I clapped Junkie's hair. What could I say? I understand? I lost my baby and I've just lost her again? I sat in the tent feeling jinxed. First me, then Sara, then Junkie. The women in this camp didn't have much luck with babies. Or men. Other than Limpet and she was the only one of child-bearing age in a stable relationship.

It looked like she or Saleema had cleaned the carpet. Thank God for good old family values. As for the rest of us – the eighteen months after the illness had socially dismantled us, though some of us didn't need global catastrophes to make calamitous disasters of our lives.

I patted Junkie, smiled at Grace and left the tent. Maybe it was time we came out of the Stone Age and rebuilt some kind of normality. I went into my own little tent, that was just the way I had left it, and wrote some of this down.

Chapter Fifty-one

That evening I mooted that we should move into one of the big houses, but I was outvoted. Basher was happy where he was. He listened eagerly to Peej's account of the oats grown by our northern neighbours and added them to his plan for over-wintering crops. Brain, it transpired, had been working on some modifications to his generator that involved car engines but with a hose pipe exhaust so the fumes wouldn't suffocate us. It meant we could have heat and light and even music without having to cycle the Tour de France to get it. Bill and Grace outvoted me too; they said they were too old to uproot again. And then The Gaffer raised the perennial bogeyman of the bikers.

I looked to Eric but he was quiet. The few days away made me see everyone with keener eyes. Even Wide Boy had matured. Maybe he was sad about Junkie. A couple of days before she'd given birth he'd been chasing one of the twins round the tents and I had grumbled at him; now he was sombre and it occurred to me that he might have had a soft spot for Junkie. He and Peej had been with her since the beginning and she was only a year or two older than him. For all I knew he could be the father of her baby. Someone was. Someone'd got Lee-Ann pregnant just the same as someone had got Sara pregnant. That night I lay in my own bed down the pit, listening to the grunts and groans of men on their backs. Legitimately, if you believed in that sort of thing, Basher was the only one who should be sexually active. I pulled the covers away from my ears and tried to identify any noises he was making. Prurient, and voyeuristic, but we didn't have any telly.

Bill was easy – he snored the highest; Wide Boy just breathed loudly. Down at the far end, unseen through the sludge of blackness, two men were strong and indistinguishable with the same halting rhythm and to my right Robina's snuffly nose caused even her to give out occasional snorts. But there were no noises of ecstasy. No sex. And Junkie, if she was crying, was weeping without sound.

What a turmoil of thoughts I was having, stimulated, no doubt, by the turmoil of my life in the last four days. I thought about Fraser and his friend at North Connell, looking to Peej for spare women as if he might be able to supply them like car parts or cauliflowers. And the bikers, womenless, drinking and fighting themselves to extinction. At this rate, those who'd survived would be founding no dynasties.

I turned on my side, fidgety without a drink to help me sleep. What we needed was a couple of men and plenty of young women like breeding cattle. I took stock of our fertile ones: without Sara we were reduced to Limpet and Junkie, and she wasn't exactly pure quality livestock. Soon, at least, we'd have Saleema and then Robyn and Robina. Good job we'd found them, though a bit of a drawback that their gene pool was the same. It went round and round in my head what would be most appropriate: stable relationships or mass promiscuity: loving, protective husbands or different rides on the carousel. Maybe the men would like it, but would it be fair to force our girls to have sex with each of them? I didn't fancy it. Peej, of course, no question; Basher – I'd a certain curiosity. Eric – our history made me nervous. Brain – young, slim and vigorous – without a shadow of a doubt. Wide Boy? Once he stopped picking his nose. Who else was there. The Gaffer?

He was a pompous prick but since he was losing his yuppy-fat he might not be too bad in a lie-back-and-get-it-over-with scenario. Though I didn't know what I was worrying about: I'd never be in the rota because I was too old. I was well past my sell-by date. No matter how much I deluded myself.

My genes were dying out just as surely as if I'd died in the illness, unless Margaret Mary was alive and fit to have kids. I sighed and rolled on my back and pulled my covers over my head again then stretched my legs out for a bit of the DIY we've all been reduced to.

It must have been the rush of blood to the head that did it.

Chis, I thought. I hadn't thought about anybody having sex with Chis.

And bizarrely, the way these things go, I only had to wait a few weeks before I spotted the figures of Chis and his dog strolling up our hill.

Chapter Fifty-two

It had been months since we had seen him and it felt so good to see him again. Chis was a jester from his turquoise jumper to his floppy sandy hair and his lop-sided smile. It didn't matter how down we were, he brought news, music and jokes that made us think the management had declared a holiday.

He even jigged when he walked. I was coming out of my tent when I caught sight of him swinging the guitar case on to his shoulder and jiggling up over the broken fencing to cross our field.

'Chis!' I shouted to anyone who was listening. 'Chis's coming!'

Robyn and Robina had never met him. They looked down sneering noses as he threw himself on one knee and asked Saleema to marry him. He hobbled forward on his knees, kissing her hand as she backed off, flustered but flattered and throwing her scarf over her face and head.

'Leave her alone!' Salaam scolded, trying to drag Chis's arms away. Chis got him on the grass, giggling.

'Robyn, Robina,' I called. 'Come and meet Chis! We'll have no more classes today.'

That raised a cheer. Before long everybody came in from the fields to welcome him.

I was bursting with questions but there were so many people wanting to talk to him and he of course had been walking so he was thirsty and tired and needed fed. And so did his dog. Shep sprawled at our campfire with his chin on his front legs letting the kids pet his smooth black head. We kept a couple of cans of dog food for him, but he was always well fed in lumps of rabbit or deer. No wonder his coat was so shiny.

Chis told us he'd been visiting over Edinburgh way. Livingston and Bathgate were stone dead. He'd stopped with a small group in Ratho, who'd begun grazing sheep on the airport fields and they took him up to Armadale where they'd made some connections. Good mix, he said, men and women, young and old and already a couple of healthy babies. I looked at Junkie when he said that, because we hadn't broken the news to him. Anyway, the Armadale people told him there had been trouble in Falkirk and the new seat of power was in Camelon.

'Have you had any more sightings of your bikers?' he asked Peej. Limpet presented him with a hunk of nan stuffed with rabbit and he stopped talking to lick the juices from his fingers.

'Nothing for a good few months,' Peej said. 'But we've been keeping a low profile.' Peej didn't stutter much in regular company. He was relaxed with Chis; more talkative than at any time since we'd come back from North Connell.

'Did you notice the strips where we've been working the land?' The Gaffer asked him.

'Eh?' Chis rubbed the grease on the side of his trouser leg and swallowed half a bottle of cider.

'We've been planting over on the field.' The Gaffer pointed. 'I'm just a bit concerned it'll be obvious so we've been sewing it in strips just wide enough to reach from either side hoping the growth around it'll hide it from down the hill.'

'Aye, I never saw it.' Chis looked around our faces as he reached for another nan. 'Good chuck,' he said to Limpet and she smiled.

'We've been travelling ourselves,' Peej said, nodding at me. 'Yak and me went up north – to Connell; found a wee clan up there. Not many women though – just the one. In fact, they're looking for spare lassies.'

'Aren't we all?' Chis said.

Peej grinned suddenly, the tight skin on his face creasing into lines around his mouth and eyes.

Eric said, 'I hope you didn't say they could have any of ours.'

Bill was at my elbow ready to pour a refill – a Zinfandel, to go with the meat. He started to laugh but stopped because he realised Eric was being serious. I caught Wide Boy winking towards Robyn and Robina, but Robyn dumped her food and turned away. I thought about querying it but I didn't want to miss out on wine or my chance to enter the conversation.

I took a big glug. 'Chis, do you ever hear anything about any Glasgow groups?'

Only Peej knew what I was thinking. He had his hand on Salaam's hip as the boy climbed in between the adults' legs to play with the dog. 'Is it not time you kids were going to your beds?'

Chis scraped a fibre of meat from his teeth. 'I've only had contact with one. They went to live in Pollok Park, in the big house – plenty of room, you know,' he nodded to Peej and Basher, 'away from the bodies and with plenty of farming. It's got its own sheep and Highland cattle. There was even a kids' zoo with a couple of dozen chickens. Hens and a cock. Ready-made production system, know?'

'That was a good idea. Pity we didn't have anywhere like that,' I said, talking to Peej. 'Eggs would be wonderful, and chicken.'

'Aye, the folk up by Armadale have got some and all, and cows, so they've worked out how to milk them, but I went into a hen house once – about two weeks after the illness – and there was nothing but fluff and feathers. In this big hangar. They'd all died with nobody feeding them. What a stench it was, man. Ammonia. What a waste.' Chis looked to Basher. 'Can you not get milk from your sheep?'

The conversation was ranging away from where I wanted it to go. The men were talking and I didn't have the strength of voice to interrupt them. And it looked as if Peej had forgotten what I wanted to ask Chis. Limpet told the children to say their goodnights then she and Saleema started to clear away the dinner things and I should really have got up and helped them. It was beginning to darken; time was getting on and now we were heading for October we didn't have much daylight after about six. Then Robina tugged at the back of my sleeve.

'Robyn's not feeling well,' she said. 'She wants you to go

down with her.'

I was still waiting for my opportunity. 'What's wrong with her?' I know I sounded impatient.

'She's just gone all sick and shivery. She wants to go down to her bed but she wants you to come as well before the men go down.'

She hadn't been right since I'd come back. I thought about Wide Boy winking at her. 'Has Wide Boy upset her?'

'Wide Boy? No.'

The men laughed. I'd missed what it was they were talking about. I looked round and Chis, Peej and Basher's faces were animated, lit by the fire. Beside me, Wide Boy was laughing too.

I put my hand on his sleeve. 'Did you do something to upset Robyn?'

The smile disappeared. 'Nuh.'

Chis called, 'Ah! What you been up to?'

'Oh come on,' The Gaffer said, 'I think he'd prefer something with a bit of meat on its bones!'

I turned back to Robina. Robyn was standing back from the camp fire. I couldn't think what could be wrong with her. The food tasted fine. I got up and put my hand on her forehead but she didn't have a temperature. She was trembling, but then it was cold away from the fire. I still wanted to ask my questions.

'Look,' I said. 'I'll take you down but I need to come back up to speak to Chis again.'

'No!' Robyn squirmed and clutched my arm to her stomach with both hands. 'Please, Alice!'

The men would sit there for no more than half an hour or so. Chis had said he was tired; if there was any singing and music it would be tomorrow.

'Behave yourself,' I said, pulling my arm away. 'You've got your sister with you, and Salaam and Saleema. Just go down with them for now.'

She sobbed but it didn't melt me. I could see the mucus glinting at her nose and I told her to wipe it.

'I'll come with you, babe,' Junkie said and took her hand.

The twins went with her to where Eric stood at the top of the shaft to help them. I went back to join the circle and waited for my chance to ask the question.

The men were still talking. I held off for a lull in the conversation. It came when a tipsy Bill asked for someone to walk him to our latrine area and Wide Boy and Brain went for support. I felt a bit exposed then, with just me and Grace on one side, Peej, Basher, Chis and The Gaffer on the other. Eric was fiddling with the cradle, waiting for Limpet to come back up after settling the baby.

'Chis,' I said as he took another deep swallow of his cider. 'That Glasgow group you were talking about. Do you know if any of the women were called Margaret Mary?'

He broke off from his bottle and studied the ground. 'Margaret Mary?' He shook his head. 'Doesn't sound familiar. Margaret Mary. I think I'd have remembered a name like that.'

I kept my hopes in a tight grip.

'I don't think so. There's a Jillian and an Emma. I remember that.' He winked at Peej and the fire burnished his eyebrow. 'And an Angela. There's a couple of others, but I can't mind a Margaret Mary.'

'Or just Margaret then, or Maggie? Peggy? Late thirties.' I was becoming desperate. 'Early forties? She maybe talked with a highland accent.'

'No, definitely not.' He pressed his lips together. 'Wait.'

I sat forward.

'Did you say May? There was a lassie called May Leung. No, but she was Chinese. Sorry.' He turned to Peej. 'Have you got another one of they ciders?'

Later I spoke to Peej when we were breaking up the camp for the night. He'd had a few; he wrapped his arms round me and kissed my forehead with his thin wet lips. I felt his knee in between my knees and I felt a surge of hope. If only, if only. If only Peej and I could always be this close. I didn't know where I was with him and at times like these it churned me up with frustration, waiting for the firmness of a real kiss. But he clearly wasn't even thinking about it.

He held me out. 'You just going to let it be, doll? This Margaret Mary business.'

'I don't know,' I said, squinting up at him. 'I mean, she might be using another name. Or she might belong to a different group.'

'Or she might just be gone.'

But she might just as easily not be.

'I think it's time you let her go.'

I put my face against his jacket, placated by the feel of the stubble on his chin teasing the hair on the top of my head and his arms around me. I wound mine around his waist and squeezed him. 'I don't know what I'd do without you Peej.'

'Ha!' he said and skelped me. 'Bed!' he said and passed me the rope.

Chapter Fifty-three

Maybe Peej was right. I lay, restless, guessing from Junkie's sniffs that she was crying herself to sleep and I vowed to stop grieving for a daughter lost forty years ago. I vowed to throw myself into the community. Peej too had lost his family. Maybe that was why he wouldn't commit to me. If he loved me, time would out him. *I* would out him. Meanwhile, I would work on it. And if he didn't love me I would still work for my community. I was a mother who didn't have any children and there were children here who didn't have any mother. It was settled.

The next day I asked Chis to play his guitar for the children and we turned it into a music lesson. He knew songs from Bob Dylan to Concerto de Aranjuez and Baa-baa Black Sheep to Jessie J. It was a good day.

That night we had a party. We took the opportunity to tidy the pit to make enough room. After a quick lunch Eric took Wide Boy, Brain and Salaam down to the fruit trees of the Clyde Valley and when they came back we had a big session making puddings. You have to be inventive when you've no eggs or milk, but it's not so bad if you can get hold of a vegan cookbook. And there's so much free food – rowan and elder berries, brambles and beech nuts for the taking. And for method we've got Grace. She might not have much short-term memory but ask her the quantities for fruit crumble and she's a celebrity chef.

Basher slaughtered a sheep and we roasted it on a spit. The smoke it sent up and our laughter must have broadcast an advert to anybody in the neighbourhood but I knew that Peej and Basher would be wearing their guns. And Eric was out somewhere, our self-styled roving look-out. Brain and Wide Boy had been down in the pit most of the late afternoon sorting out some kind of lighting system with Brain's contraption.

I showed Robyn how to make Homity Pies. She hung around between Junkie and me the whole day till I wondered if she was frightened of Chis. It's the most docile I've seen her, but when she was taking a pie over to Limpet to try it Junkie said it was probably her age. That made me look at her more closely. They'd told me they were ten when we found them but already I'd noticed their busts developing. Lack of good nutrition might have put their growth on hold. Now Robyn looked twelve or thirteen.

There was a smir of rain but it wasn't going to spoil things. Only as it settled in with the dark did we collapse the tents and start heading down the pit.

Brain had rigged up disco lights and a sound system. Circles of red, purple and pink were circulating on white sheets that he, Saleema and Wide Boy had pinned up. They'd even made a rudimentary dance floor.

Basher and Limpet sent the hot food down in a bucket and The Gaffer passed round glasses of Champagne.

'What are we celebrating?' Grace asked. She looked at Junkie. 'Is it you, hen? Is it your wee baby?'

Bill grabbed her and kissed her on the dance floor and said, 'Naw, it's for you, pet. That's fifty-four year since you asked me to marry you.'

'Och, you!' she said, and drained her champagne so she could get into a dance hold. 'Is it the first waltz?'

'Hold on,' Chis said. He reached for his guitar and sang and played 'The Anniversary Waltz' and I had to blink repeatedly. Junkie too, but that would be for a different reason.

The food was fantastic. So was the drink. I think we needed to blow our fuses after the upset we'd been through over Junkie.

Apart from Gracie putting her foot in it, Junkie was bearing up well. From time to time I watched her. She'd been quieter in the five weeks since the birth but I was worried that tonight she'd put away an excess of Bacardi Breezers. Peej was watching her too. He must have had the same premonitions.

Chis stopped playing after the first waltz and let Brain show

272

off his prowess as an MC. The kids danced to his mixes; I noted that Robyn seemed to be feeling better. I had two glasses of champagne in quick succession and felt puggled: combination of the exertion over the baking in the autumnal air then the cocoon of music, food and bubbles. I didn't really feel like talking to anyone. Well, Chis, maybe, but he was busy with the young ones – Brain between plays and Wide Boy. I didn't know what age Chis would be; like stone, he was ageless. I watched him there, that sideways smile.

'Is this you checking out the talent?' The Gaffer put a chair beside me and sat down. 'You're grinning away, looking at him.'

I took stock of myself and rearranged myself tidily.

The Gaffer's elbow hung off the back of the chair, loosened by the wine he'd been drinking. He was half turned in to me, half watching the kids dancing. 'They're loving it, aren't they?'

I could feel him studying me for a minute.

He asked, 'Do you still want us to leave?'

Eric reached over with a champagne bottle and topped up our glasses. Tiny volcanic sparkles pinpricked my hand. I held up the glass so I could see the purples and pinks of the disco lights through the ascending streams of golden bubbles. 'It's like the nursery rhyme,' I told him. '"When it's good it's very, very good, but when it's bad it's horrid."' I shrugged. 'I mean – if it could always be like this it wouldn't be so bad. But I like my comforts. And the sun shining through the windows.'

He gripped my knee and shook it. 'You'd get bored with heaven, Alice.'

Off he went to speak to someone else. I looked down at my knee as if I could see his infra-red handprint. He was right, of course. I was surprised he knew. But he'd been the one to suggest I write the notebooks.

And then Eric yelled, 'Chis for a song.'

Wide Boy and Brain disappeared while Chis reached for his guitar and a stool. The disco lights roved over his body. 'Captain Scarlet and the Mysterons,' he said and some of us laughed. All these extinct cultural references. The pink and purple spots died and a white spot focused on him instead.

273

'How do you plead?' Brain's voice said, somewhere behind me.

I'm telling you that because of what came later. Then it just seemed funny, but maybe you needed to have drunk a bottle of bubbly. Anyway before too long he had us captive. Junkie filled the youngsters' hands with fizz cans and sweetie rations; they settled themselves directly beneath him, listening to 'Puff, the magic dragon.' For the first time in ages I thought about Sara.

Peej sat in the chair beside me while Chis was singing. He crossed his legs and put his arm along the back of my chair making a blip of excitement beat at my waist again. I wished I knew where I was with him. I glanced to the side but he wasn't even looking at me: just at the kids ogling Chis. He'd a stupid half smile on his face. That scar and the raised eyebrow.

'Are you enjoying it?' I asked, leaning in to whisper to him.

'Och, aye. Change is as good as a rest.'

People began clapping. Peej sat forward in his chair, hearty with applause. Chis acknowledged him and played the first bars of an Oasis song. Peej whistled and stomped his feet on our earth floor.

After half a dozen songs Brain put some CDs on – hits of the nineties, hits of the noughties – and urged us all up on the dance floor. Just as well we didn't all get up, since there wasn't enough room, but I did have a couple of dances. The Gaffer asked me up. I danced with him but thought about Peej sitting where I'd left him. He'd be watching me flirt with his arch enemy. But when I looked he was sitting beside Junkie, his arm along the back of her chair the way he had with me and the two of them murmuring close in to each other. I tried to believe he was only showing concern for her but really I was contorted with jealousy.

So when the dance finished I dropped The Gaffer and hurried over to Peej.

'You dancing?' I asked him.

'Naw, just these fucking crabs making me itchy,' he said but he got up with nothing but a sideways glance at Junkie. I smiled to her, serenely.

It was a Bruce Springsteen song. Even a fifty-odd year old

can look and feel good after a few drinks when that kind of music's playing. And it's fairly dark. Just me and Peej on the dance floor, making love without the inconvenient exchange of bodily fluids.

This was going to be my moment – I'd made my mind up – but I noticed Chis insinuate his way over to where Peej had been sitting. He turned in towards Junkie and stretched his arm out along the backs of the chairs behind her. His fingers began kneading her shoulder. She knocked back a Bacardi Breezer and added the empty to the clinking collection at her feet. I'd been thinking about the way Sara had idolised him.

I didn't want Peej to notice Chis moving in on Junkie but that was for a different reason. I kept his back to them. I made him stay up with me for the next one but then he insisted. 'That's it, doll.' And pushed me off the dance floor. I saw him look over towards Junkie but then he headed for the shaft bottom for a call of nature.

I sat on my own and emptied my drink. Then I looked for another one. I'd had too much but I could pay for it in the morning. Anyway, what else did I have? I looked around me. Everybody was dancing, or laughing, or caught up in some kind of conversation. Even Chis and Junkie. And then something else occurred to me. I remembered how he left, so quickly, the day we'd buried Sara.

Peej came back and I asked him to get me a drink but he went to have a word with Basher. I wracked my brain. The champagne was making it difficult to interrogate my memory but I struggled to do it. Then Peej came over with two glasses of something that smelled like G and T and a dish of Limpet's savoury spiced garbanzos. Maybe this was my moment. He hadn't looked towards Junkie once.

'Stupid bastard's been trying the malt.' he said into my ear, above the cacophony of Wide Boy, Brain and the two Jaws shrieking and dancing.

I looked at Basher. 'Basher?'

'Basher,' he nodded.

'Does he not know it's alcoholic?'

He grinned. 'Allah'll forgive him in the morning.'

'Chis,' Basher called. He crashed between two chairs, ploughing a furrow to him. 'You must play now. For me. We'll show these Scottish bastards how to dance.'

Chis left Junkie, whose eyes flicked like a lizard's tongue to Peej and me.

'A man's dance,' Basher said. He dragged Peej by the arm on to the dance floor while the others cheered.

'Don't know if I'm ready for this,' Peej said.

Chis played something Moorish and Basher clapped his arms above his head, leading a line of Peej, Wide Boy, Brain and Salaam. As usual, I didn't know where Eric had got to. Back on look-out, maybe. Limpet and Saleema sat between Junkie and me, giggling and glancing up at me to share the joke. I tried, but my smile was stiff; I couldn't make it reach my eyes.

The dance only lasted a couple of minutes before Grace shouted at Chis to sing some proper songs. Basher didn't seem to be offended. The men left the dance floor all arms round each others' shoulders. Saleema gave up her seat to her dad then she and Brain disappeared behind me into the dark. Peej sat heavily beside me, tossing a handful of chick peas into his mouth.

The younger kids clustered round Chis and they sang the songs he'd taught them in the morning. The whole scene looked so innocent. I waited a minute, looked at the oily curl of Peej's ear then said, 'They make me think about Sara.'

'Aye?'

I picked one of Junkie's long hairs from his sweatshirt and very deliberately discarded it on the ground. 'Don't you remember how she used to idolise Chis? As if he was a pop star.' I looked back to Robyn and Robina. 'Maybe that's what was wrong with Robyn last night: you know what pop stars try to get away with.'

His brows lowered for a minute, even the raised one. 'She looks happy enough now.'

'I've been sitting here trying to remember the dates of his visits. Do you remember?' I had to keep my voice from warbling. 'The first time we saw him was just before we moved into the

276

library. Must have been late May or early June last year.'

Out of the corner of my eye I saw Peej's ankles crossing.

'Nine months,' I went on, 'before Sara died.'

When Robina stroked Chis's calf Peej's arms folded. I dared to check out his face. His eyebrows were down, and yes, there was the tell-tale tic. When Chis stopped playing, Peej didn't applaud.

I sucked down the last of my gin and tonic. I shouldn't have; I'd already had far too many.

Peej reached to the floor for his and knocked it down his throat in one.

'That's it. I'm gasping for a drink,' Chis announced, and this time Wide Boy appeared on his own to put on the CDs. Chis took a beer from the crate and opened it. He tipped half of it into his mouth then we watched him focus on Lee-Ann.

'I mean,' I said. 'How well do we really know him?' I hooked my arm over the back of my chair and leaned my breast on Peej's upper arm, looking beyond him as Chis settled into the seat beside Junkie. 'Junkie, now,' I said. 'I mean, is it even six weeks?' Peej's head twitched towards Lee-Ann but he checked the impulse.

Anyway, Limpet and Basher would have blocked his view. Limpet seemed agitated. She turned to me. 'Did you see where Saleema went, Alice?'

I shook my head.

When she and Basher stood up to go to look for her I had an unimpeded view of Chis's hand on Junkie's short skirt. 'Maybe Chis used to be in the navy,' I whispered in Peej's ear. 'With a different girl in every port.'

Peej lunged towards him. His roar nearly caused a roof collapse. He threw Chis half way across our dance floor and it took Eric, Wide Boy and even The Gaffer to drag him off.

By then Robyn, Robina and even Salaam were screaming, Shep was barking and blood was dribbling from a dazed Chis's nose and mouth.

I did it because I felt I owed it to Sara.

But also because of the drink.

Yet it was more than that. I looked along at Junkie. Maybe my plan had backfired, though. For the first time in five weeks her eyes were smiling.

Chapter Fifty-four

My aches and pains set in again the day after Peej threw Chis around on our dance floor, the pink, purple and white lights marauding over the bloody mess.

'What the fuck came over you?' The Gaffer shouted over the music, the last couple of words embarrassingly loud when the music cut.

Eric and Wide Boy still gripped Peej's elbows. In the moving white circle of the disco lights I saw his forehead was pasty. Unable to do anything else he worked up saliva and spat.

'Ask him.'

Chis was half on the floor, half against the beer boxes stacked against the wall. I heard them clink and wondered how many he had broken. One of his legs was bent at the knee and the other was extended. It looked as though he'd spilled a beer on his crotch.

'Keep him away from me,' Chis said, lip swollen, words thick.

Peej feinted, Chis winced; Eric and Wide Boy held Peej firm.

'You keep away from the girls,' Peej yelled, louder than the dog's barking. Old Bill was holding Shep back. I had Robyn and Robina tucked in under my wings. Robyn was trembling. I squeezed both of them.

'Fuck off.' Peej shrugged to set himself free. 'I'll not go for him.'

'You sure, mate?' Wide Boy said.

They checked with The Gaffer then let Peej go. He feinted again and Chis whimpered, but Peej didn't follow through. He turned to look at Junkie. When I turned too I noticed Saleema and Brain sliding back into the company out of the darkness. They separated, Brain slinking round the side wall towards the front, Saleema soundlessly reappearing behind her parents, whose quest Peej's violence had brought to a quick halt.

Peej pointed at Chis and challenged The Gaffer, 'Ask him who got Sara pregnant.'

I saw the change on Chis's expression and heard the others draw breath.

After a minute, The Gaffer started righting chairs. 'You,' he nodded at Peej. 'Go outside and calm down.'

Peej pushed his hands into his jacket pockets for his cigarettes and bent to where we stowed our tents. I followed him.

'There's somebody's tooth.' Salaam said and held up a bloodied fang.

'Give it to Peej,' The Gaffer said. 'He can wear it round his neck.'

Salaam took a step but Basher's long arm intercepted him.

I shrugged the girls off and went through the low tunnel. 'Don't go,' I said to Peej at the pit shaft bottom. 'It makes you look like the bad one.'

'Story of my life,' he said. 'But don't worry. He'll pay for it in the morning.'

*

We gave Chis a fair trial: The Gaffer insisted but with the victim lost and no forensic evidence it came down to trusting somebody's word. We sat round our camp fire up top with the light autumn wind flapping the tents and loosening the leaves on the bushes around us.   It was Peej's word against Chis's. Peej said Chis must've taken advantage of Sara and Chis said he was innocent. He did look quite innocent with his sandy hair flopping over his eyes. His shoulders were tense and he was shaking. His face was swollen at the mouth where Peej had knocked his tooth out and his eyes were still reddened. Even his voice suggested he was innocent, switching between anger and despair with not a hint of deceit or of his usual good humour. Yet he tried to pin the blame on Peej, saying he must be covering up to protect himself. But which of us could believe Peej could have done that to Sara? Peej, whom I remembered that first time I'd met him.

Peej, Sara's ned man, of whom she'd been terrified. In reality, he'd been protective of us; of both of us. I couldn't believe him capable of child abuse. He'd so missed his daughter, after all, that he'd adopted her boyfriend, Wide Boy, just as I'd adopted Sara. And Peej had shown nothing but kindness to Robina and Robyn. It had to be an outsider who'd hurt Sara. I chewed the inside of my cheek. It surely had to be Chis.

The Gaffer called me to give my suspicions. I looked round the faces and could see people make their mental calculations. Everyone knew how she'd worshipped him. The timings for his visit seemed to fit. And look how important to us Peej was. I sat down again to find my hand nuzzled by the sleek black head of Chis's dog, Shep.

The Gaffer looked at his notebook and cleared his throat. Then he raised his eyes to Peej and clicked his pen. 'All those who believe that Chis is guilty of abusing Sara leading ultimately to her death, raise your hand.'

Taking confidence from one another we held our hands up. Basher. Limpet. The Gaffer. Bill and Grace. Junkie. Eric and Wide Boy. Me.

'All those who think it was Peej.'

We met each others' eyes all round our circle.

'It's a lie!' Chis said. 'I'd never touch her. It's not true!'

The Gaffer wrote the numbers in his book then cleared his throat again. 'I'm ashamed of you, Chis. Not only did you take advantage of Sara, whom we all know was a child in a woman's body, but you abused our hospitality. You abused our trust.'

'Fuck the lot of you,' Chis said and struggled to control his breath. There was silence while we stared at him. 'Fuck the lot of you.'

Shep barked and ran from his place beside me to lick Chis's face. Chis put his arms around him. 'It's not true and you're going to find out the hard way.' He wiped his face as he stood.

'Enough,' The Gaffer said. 'Now, get out of here and don't come back.'

Chapter Fifty-five

Next day as the class worked on a piece of writing I'd given them, they sang the songs Chis had taught them. A little bit mournfully. But I had no regrets since it was Chis who'd abused Sara. As they sang, part of my mind revisited the previous months one more time. I thought about Sara, and felt relief that we'd found her some kind of justice.

It was as if our community was checking a series of tick boxes. Births, tick, deaths, tick. Truth, justice and the way, tick. What we hadn't had yet was a marriage, though it looked as if Saleema had got herself a boyfriend. I wondered how Basher and Limpet would feel about that.

Robina was mumbling to herself. This close together, five of us in my little tent, there wasn't much opportunity *not* to hear her. She was driving black furrows through what she had written.

'Have you got a problem?' I asked her, grumpily hung over and full of aches and pains.

She rested her head on her hand, shoulder squashed up against her sister. 'How d'you spell "haud"?'

'"Hod"?' I repeated.

'Aye.'

I put my pen down and tucked my hands under my armpits. The walls of the tent were billowing and wintry showers would occasionally slash against them. Half submerged in reminiscence I was pretty surprised that Robina was writing her story about the building trade.

'A builder's hod?'

Her face screwed up. 'A what?'

'A builder's hod,' I repeated.

'Anybody's haud. Like "haud a wean's haun". Or "haud on." "Haud yer horses." How'd'ye spell it?'

'Oh! You mean "hold",' I corrected. 'You say, "hold on" and "hold your horses".'

'Naw,' she sneered. 'Nobody says that. Holed. That's stupid.'

I couldn't be bothered with her; felt a knot of annoyance tighten in my midriff. 'I'm not in the mood for this, Robina. Look it up in a dictionary,' I said. 'It'll say H-O-L-D.'

She put her pencil to the paper but then dropped it and slouched back in her seat. 'I'm not writing that. Nobody says that. Stupid. You're needing a new dictionary.' She looked from Robyn to Salaam and Saleema. 'How'd'you spell "haud"?'

'Wait a minute!' I said, before any of the others could answer. 'I gave you the proper spelling.'

'Naw you never.'

I felt my heart beat quickening. I would never have made it as a proper teacher. 'Robina,' I said, trying to keep my voice steady. 'The word is "hold". H-O-L-D. Any other way of spelling it is just ...slang.'

'So hold your wheesht!' Robyn laughed at her.

But Robina didn't. 'Peejie and Widey say "haud". So do Bill an' Grace. And me and Robyn.'

I could see Salaam and Saleema smiling behind their hands and keeping their heads down. Robina was now swinging on the back two legs of her chair with Robyn grinning openly at her.

How did I ever think I could be a teacher? Or a mother? 'The correct form of the word you're looking for,' I said, straining for dignity, 'is "hold".'

'Who says?' she said, and swung in silence for a minute till I wished she would topple.

Who says? Who says?

*

December and January came and went and I spent them in agony. It was all I could do to get up in the morning and I even had to ask for a lift in the cradle because I couldn't face the rope. My back, my knees, my hips were all stiff and swollen and I sat

283

with my two coats on and the Russian fur hat Basher had found me from some men's shop and my neck and chin were lagged by my new tartan scarf that grew more and more saturated with moisture each time I breathed out. The Gaffer told me it was because of the dampness: he wiped his hand down the inside of my tent to show me and his fingertips came away wet. He was unusually kind, bringing me cups of steaming soup, but I still worried it might have been because of Faslane, even though Peej ridiculed me for not believing the power of my own eyes. Then I thought maybe it was something in the burn water I'd been drinking. The nitrogen from the fields, maybe. Or just my nerves.   I tried to hold lessons for the children through the first half of November. History. Sums. Our days were short: our lessons even shorter. Our fingers cramped on the pencils in our fingerless gloves. Only little Salami's fingers were warm, tucked up against his mother when she'd bring him to visit me. The time my mother came to visit me she called my baby her little pie. Gracie called Salami a little sausage.

It was round about then that I stopped giving lessons in the tent. There were too many complaints about the cold. It wasn't really anything to do with Robina being bolshie or the spelling of 'haud'. Even though it did make me think for a minute. About Melvil Dewey and his campaign for phonetical spelling. About Esperanto. Language blending and developing.

Anyway, I agreed to teach for a quick half hour down the pit at night. The rest of the time I told them to read. I held out in the tent for another few weeks, needing my own space. Peej popped his head in sometimes, just for a second, just, presumably, to be sociable.

I mentioned that I was worried about a nuclear winter but he shook his head at me.

'The worst's already happened, Yakkity,' he said, scrunching down in front of my desk and squeezing my sticky-out fingers on my double-gloved hand. 'It's not going to get any worse than it is now.'

But my joints had been stiff and sore all winter, making me feel old. I couldn't even face writing in the journal. Anyway, there wasn't very much in the way of news.

Until Junkie told me she was pregnant again. She told me when we were waiting to go up the rope in the morning, though I'd guessed because she'd been sick again. I must have been walking around the campsite blindfold. Clearly things had gone further with Chis at the beginning of October than any of us realised.

Chapter Fifty-six

By February my tent had been packed up and stowed out of the way for ages and I was going stir-crazy. We'd been snowed in our hole for almost three days. They always said if the ice cap melted all that cold water would divert the stream of warm sea flowing up from the Caribbean that keeps Scotland's west coast mild. How unfair, I told The Gaffer when he was cycling, trying to coax heat from the electric fire, if they were right and now they were dead it was us, the survivors, who'd have to face an ice-age struggle. 'Och, Alice,' he said, on a long exhale. His knees went up and down another few rotations then he added, 'stop worrying about everything.'

I was so grumpy. Robyn had slept in my bed half the night. She'd had another nightmare: woke up wet and it was too hard to change her sheets in the pitch dark. It was easier to pull the damp clothes off her legs – remembering Sara – or up over her head while she shuddered and sobbed in an agony of pre-teen self-consciousness, 'Don't let them see me.' Easier to do that and let her slip in beside me, her ice-cube feet freezing my calves and thighs. 'Don't let him get me,' she said, pulling my arm over her and imprisoning it at her waist until she fell asleep. Nightmares, even though Chis was long gone.

We were eating in the pit too. But the food was bad: reliant on tins. For weeks, the hunting had been poor. Even scrawny foxes were running over the fields, hunting in daytime. Eric came back from one of his trips down the Clyde Valley brandishing an evil looking iron trap he'd found in the people's history museum. He put it on the table and demonstrated how to trigger its jaws with those rusted, biting teeth and I said I'd rather go back to being vegetarian. Basher and Peej swore they'd try to avoid using it but we all knew things were looking bleak. The men were already using snares. Last week they came back with a badger which had tangled itself in the wire, winding it tighter and tighter round its neck till it cut into its skin, slowly strangling it to death. The blood had matted its fur yet Limpet and I stripped it and cooked it and nobody asked any questions about whether or not it was ethical.

The fresh food from the trees and bushes was finished. The rosehips Grace showed us to boil with sugar to make into syrup only stayed fresh for a couple of weeks; the haws from the hawthorn and the flowering cherries made the crudest of jams.

What I would have given for a fresh, sweet orange, the skin stinging between my fingers; tiny swollen gourds of juice swelling each segment and bursting into my mouth. Or a lemon – the sourness curling the sides of my tongue. We'd sunk to eating lime juice from a plastic bottle, dripped into sugar on a spoon, taken to avoid scurvy. We'd run out of cartons of pure orange juice and cranberry. It was already two years since the illness; even the tins' use-by dates were being overtaken. Only Bill and Eric's elderberry wine held any promise, blooping away through the day and night, though it would take about a year for it to ferment, according to the book they found in the bookshop. At least the whisky was aging nicely.

Snowed in, Grace started to irritate us with her singing, and we even fell out over the choice of music Brain played on the battery CD.

'Read us a story,' Eric said the second night, but I wasn't in the mood. 'Go on – just a couple a chapters.'

I brooded. Disturbed sleep, no fresh air, no privacy. We all brooded. The inactivity was getting to the men.

'Och, read a couple a fucking chapters, Yakkity,' Wide Boy said. His voice had taken on a man's bitter edge; the outsize chunk he'd bitten from Eve's apple rocked as if his voice was trying to dislodge it from his throat.

I gave in, reached over to the book pile at the side of my bed for an old-fashioned adventure and walked past Bill and Grace's chinking display cabinet to the front of the pit, where we'd cleared that communal space. Robyn scurried at my back.

'Sit here,' Eric said, making place beside him, but there was only room for one. 'You want to sit on the floor, babe?' He took the pillow from his bed – yellowed where he'd dribbled – shook it and put it on the floor between our feet.

She was stiff legged, stiff armed; holding herself rigid against the damp.

'Not like sitting on the floor any more?' Eric said.

'Thinks she's getting too big,' old Bill chuckled.

'Leave her alone,' Wide Boy's low voice came back. His brows were down: that nedish way, and there were red rings under his eyes. 'She doesn't need to if she doesn't want to.'

I looked around the company to see if anyone else could read signals that were oblivious to me. Junkie broke the silence.

'Come over to me, pal,' she said, moving her chair to make a little room. 'Go'n get your stool and a cushion.'

'I'll need to go to the bucket again,' she said and darted to the back of the shaft. When she came back she cuddled closer to Junkie.

I sat beside Eric, cleared my throat, and read. 'The fogs were still dripping in from the Atlantic when Merewyn met the stranger' – Anya Seton's *Avalon*, my copy almost brown with age and handling – and soon everyone was silent. While I read, I could feel them all settling. My voice rose above them, weaving between them. Junkie was playing with a lock of Robyn's hair. Bill had his eyes closed. Peej listened with his head down, eyes on his feet, stuck out away ahead of him. Beside me was Eric's noisy breathing as he became absorbed in the story. I could conduct their emotions with the rise and fall of my words.

After I read to them, The Gaffer permitted us all a couple of tots and we started to tell our stories.

'I was born in the mountains, close by where a thin stream of water trickled and its banks were green. My first memories are of watching the women working, preparing nan for garbanzo stews; my brothers and sisters with dusty feet and kohl-blackened eyes. Building miniature fortresses with stones. My sister lifting me to balance on one hip, shielding me from the sun or the wind with her hijab. And the men, their beards and clothes white-dusted, filling the village. One hoisting me by a single arm to ride on his shoulders.'

'I was born in a single end up a wooden close at the back of the pictures. Ma mammy used to take us out to the back to hang up her washing and I mind ay a big dug sniffing me. Ma faither wisnae there much – I kennt later he was cried away to the war with conscription. The rid fire skinkling in the grate: the wee iron ring ma mammy would swing oot so she could heat a pot a soup. She didnae keep well, ma mammy. Ma brither coughing; coughing and coughing – funny, the things ye mind – and the neebours saying *that boy needs to see the doctor*, and ma mammy's voice *A cannae afford it*. Her warm shouder in the set-in bed, turnt away and shuddering; my mither greeting without a sound. And the bonnie horse with his black plume, stoppt at our close mouth.'

'I was born into a fairly middle class family. My father was a clerk so he went to work wearing a collar and tie, and a suit. We were one of the first families in our street to have a car and a television. Got that for the coronation. 1953, that would make it. Not that I remember that: one of my older brothers told me. I was the generation that got the chance to make something of themselves. Stayed on at school and became an administrator in local government. But I always wanted to help other people: that's why I went into local politics.'

'I was – born into a fairly – working class family. Aw fuck this. – We'll be here all night. Somebody else. – Wide Boy.'

'I was born – what're we doin'? Earliest memories? Fuck me. Right – I was born up by Park Street. Eh – I mind fireworks in the middle of the night, flashes and crackles. In fact, one of ma mates got scarred with a banger. And I mind selling fags roon the back ay the factories with ma brother. Aye, I mind that. And trying to get *his* daughter.'

'Aye, ya wee bastard!'

'Go on, Peej. Try again.'

'Sure yez can – wait for it? Aye? Right, well I mind prowling through they bushes up top looking for frogs and taddies. Falling into a patch of brambles trying to catch them and licking the blood fae ma knee when it got all scraped. I mind beggin' ma mammy for a dug or a hamster and – one day funnin the cat next door'd caught a wee moose. It was hauf deed but I kept it in a big empty beetroot-jar and fed it on dandelion heeds and leaves and handfulls of nuts and raisins I knocked fae the pick'n'mix doon at – Woolworths. I mind of Woolworths! That'll do it.'

'I'm sure I remember being held up against my mother's shoulder, my mouth on her neck. I remember the boy next door creeping up behind me and kissing my hair – he was only five or six. He blushed to the follicles in later years if I dared mention it. I remember when the money changed to decimal. I remember money! I remember when the biggest treat was my dad winning at the dog-track and bringing home a big brown poke full of special sweeties. Fry's Five Boys and Peppermint Cream. Mmm. Munchies and Mintola.' [No point in telling them the bad stuff.]

'I remember the man downstairs calling me into his house so he could give my mother some lettuce. And what he did when he closed the door.'

'Eric!'

'Only kidding.'

'Really?'

'I'll tell yez something. I mind growing up in a children's hame. Ten ay us to a pair of house parents. Getting hame to ma own ma whenever she said she was gonnie be clean. A house full of fucking needles; shite on the floor fae a daft dug that never got took out. Ma ma's man swallowing beer on the settee with his shoes aff and telling me to chainge the telly. Chainge it yer fucking self, I says to him and he says, Magrit, d'ye hear her fucking sweerin'? Clattering me and giving me a black eye and ma ma just watching him. And then coming in to see me later. She'd a soft voice, ma mammy. A wee singsong voice, and she'd be clapping ma heed as if I was the fucking dug.'

'A remember the long journey.'

'Do ye, Salaam? So do I.'

'I mind ay everybdy dying. Gonnie come to the bucket with

290

me, Robina?'

'Does anybody remember the Atari?'

Last night I woke up in the black, aware of someone moving about.

At night the men use a bucket at the bottom of the pit shaft; the women come to the back of the pit to use the bucket there. In the middle, Bill and Grace have a stainless steel pot with a lid that they keep at the bottom of their bed.

I tried to identify the movements. It didn't sound like Robyn or Robina: they only had to step out of bed to reach the back of the shaft, which was handy, considering Robyn had this chill in her bladder. But this was coming from the other end.

I wondered if it was Saleema. She and Limpet had to walk past Bill and Grace's beds to reach where the women slept. I'll remind you – shaft bottom, living space, men's beds, Basher protecting Limpet and their family, Bill and Grace, women's beds, pit back. To enhance our privacy, our beds are interlocking like the teeth of a zip, with our heads against the outer walls and our feet in the middle: to get to the back you have to climb over them or weave between them. Junkie's bed comes after Bill and Grace, then there's mine, then Robina's, then Robyn's.

I heard the chink as someone rocked Grace's display cabinet. I listened to the sound of breathing, noisy nose breathing, and knew straight away it wasn't Limpet or Saleema, or even Grace. I vaguely recognised that breathing.

When no one made a sound, the movement started again.

I'd a fleeting thought about Sara and Junkie becoming pregnant. Then a hand gripped the rail at the bottom of my bed and I remembered when I was reading and who that breathing belonged to. I curled up, but I should have stayed still as stone.

'Cramp in my foot,' he said and turned back towards the men's beds. I rolled on to my other side to watch him go.

Chapter Fifty-seven

On the fourth morning I shinned up the knots in the rope and gulped snow-filled air like a submariner whose ship had been sucked under the Arctic ice and was finally released.

Even though it was only daybreak, I'd been in the dark so long my eyes stung with the light. The snow glittered like tinsel, each distinct snow flake catching the low sun and relaunching it. Despite the anguish it was god-almightily beautiful. My gloves and trouser legs were soaked through from the saturated rope and from scrambling over the pit edge. When the wet weather had made the opening treacherously muddy our men had built wooden decking round it, with wooden wall supports going four feet down inside the neck of the shaft and a proper ledge down there that we could secure our safety net on. Now it was all hidden under a foot of deep soft snow. It clung to me as I climbed out so I stood quickly and brushed it off before it could penetrate and make my bones ache even more then I squatted again, hiding in the bushes and conserving heat.

The world's sound had been switched off. And it was bitterly cold. Any March warmth was still days away, with the sun unenthusiastic at the horizon. There wasn't a single blemish on the snowfall around the pit and I was reluctant to create the first.

I'd waited till I was sure Robyn was asleep. I needed this distance to be able to think.

No one else was up. No one, I was sure, had heard me slip past their bed and pull on my boots. I'd paused between the men's beds and listened to their regular breathing. My torch, shining down, had given me enough light to make out their rough shapes. Basher had been on his back, Wide Boy was on his stomach and Brain and Eric faced in opposite directions. Peej was half on his front, half on his side. I risked directing the torchlight over his body. His bare arm was thrown on to the pillow; his watch glinted when it caught my light. In the next bed, The Gaffer was sleeping on his back with his arms folded under his head.

The long bramble shoots around me were blackened with moisture and white-iced with snow. Only when you looked closely could you see the hooks they used to grapple over each other.

I looked downhill over the snow. The whole foetid conurbation had disappeared, buried in it. A bark of snow fell from a twig on the periphery of my vision. I didn't know if I should bury this.

I stood to let the blood circulate in my legs, lifted my feet in turn and shook them then crouched again.

Now the sun had burned off the clouds clinging to it at the horizon; it was radiating girders of light and heat in gold and peach. I told myself that spring wouldn't be far away. What was it Peej had said? The worst had already happened.

By the time I decided to go back into the pit snow-melt was dripping from the grass overhanging the shaft entrance, but my heart was still frozen.

*

When I launched myself down the rope I heard a scuffle at the bottom and realised the drips I could hear might not just be from melting snow. 'It's only me,' I called down the shaft.

'Oh – Jesus – fucking – Christ!'

I dropped beside Peej.

'Have you any idea how upsetting that is?' he said.

'Sorry.'

He waited.

I waited.

'So, are ye just gonnie stand there?'

'It's beginning to melt outside,' I told him.

'Good. I'll go out and have a look at it.'

Neither of us moved.

'Once I've had ma pee.'

'Right,' I said, and left him to it.

Brain and Wide Boy were still sleeping. The Gaffer was wet shaving and looked embarrassed as I passed as if I'd caught him in an act of extreme intimacy. Eric was sitting on the edge of his bed rubbing his eyes and brows. He inspected me over his fingers.

I called out softly as I made my way through the other beds. Living so closely we've developed strategies to protect our privacy. I'd thought, till then, that they'd worked.

'The snow's melting,' I said to Junkie, seeing her awake. 'We should be able to get out soon.'

'Good,' she said. Then, 'I think I can feel ma baby moving.'

I'd a pang of jealousy when she said that; I always did, when women I worked with spoke about their babies. I'd still no great love for Junkie, but even if I thought she was a tart, I wouldn't wish that misery on her again.

'That's good,' I said, and sat on the edge of my bed.

Her voice was quiet. 'I think it's got more life about it than the other one.'

I nodded. 'Good.' I meant it that time.

Robyn was still asleep in my bed. She'd spread out, relaxed, asleep, in a way I hadn't seen her when she was awake. Not recently. When I thought about it: not in months.

'She have another nightmare?' Junkie asked me.

'Yeah.'

'She wet the bed?'

I nodded. I'd wait until they were up and out before I stripped it. 'The thing is, we've almost run out of sheets.'

*

By the following day the snow had cleared away as completely as if it had never been. New grass was shooting through the yellow, suffocated turf. We managed to put the tents up again and light a fire. The grass was swampy, but I took the kids out on to the road and did some races to get the blood moving. Robyn was quiet, compared with her identical twin. Well, she didn't compare. They were very different now, one lively, exuberant to be out of the pit, the other introverted; one putting gel and baubles in her hair, the other leaving hers to flop lank and dull over her face. Part of me – the disturbed-sleep wearied part – was annoyed because I thought she was a teenager who should pull herself together. Part of me was beginning to have uncomfortable suspicions and was concerned. She disappeared into the women's tent between Grace and Limpet as soon as I let her.

Wide Boy saw her. 'What d'ye think's wrong with Robyn?' he asked, seeking me out as I was putting her sheets into the wheel barrow I used as a wash tub.

He'd grown tall – nearly six feet, I'd guess – and though he was lanky the work Peej and The Gaffer had him do was thickening his legs and his neck and shoulders.

'What?' I asked. One of the sheets had made me hesitate. I tilted it in the bright daylight. There was a black hair, thick as a wire, on it, which I pulled off and let fall, but it wasn't that.

'Is there something the matter with Robyn?'

I looked way up at him. Eventually I said, 'I think she'll be alright,' but I wasn't convincing. I bundled the sheet back into its bin bag.

'Look,' he said, scratching the top of his head so it sounded like wood. 'A know there's something wrong with her. She's been getting worse and worse since you and Peej went up to North Connell.'

The stock pot of snow melt I was heating on the gas stove fizzed and I turned to it, watching the bubbles form up the sides. After a time I shrugged.

'If ye know something, I want ye to tell me.'

I looked back to where some of the others were gathering at the cooking fire for the porridge Junkie was serving.

'I've just got suspicions,' I told him.

'What about?'

How could I tell him? I didn't have anything concrete. I shook my head.

'Yakkity!'

The surface of the water trembled. 'Help me with this.'

He lifted the pot over to the barrow where four days of Robyn's sheets were waiting – all except the one I'd kept aside – with the soap powder turning blue against their yellow stains. He poured it in, the cascade drumming on the metal; a puff of white steam rose into the air.

I stirred the brew with a length of wood and said, 'I'll let it steep.' I balanced the baby safety gate over the top and took the pot from Wide Boy to put the next lot on to boil. 'Aren't you going for your breakfast?'

'Somebody's been at her, haven't they?'

I wiped my nose on my sleeve, shocked that Wide Boy might actually know. 'Maybe she's just moody.'

'That's crap and you know it.' He moved my hand away from my face. 'Who is it?'

I saw The Gaffer look up from the camp fire. 'Leave it,' I said. I didn't want him to make a fuss or the others would notice. 'Let me deal with it.'

Wide Boy's brows were down and his eyes were hard but they were deep blue and the lashes were long and flicked and I realised that – give or take a spot peeking between the individual curling beard hairs on his cheeks – he was strong, confident and good looking. I thought about the low-life loser that had been my original impression of him. If he'd stayed in the scheme, he'd be a drug addict and a criminal. This life had been the making of him. But that was immaterial now.

'Who is it?' he said.

Out of the corner of my eye I saw The Gaffer rise from and approach us. 'I know who,' I said. I felt a panic bubbling through me at the admission and I tried to control it. 'I think I know. But I'm not telling you; I don't want you to mess everything up.'

'Is everything alright?' The Gaffer asked. He was jutting his chin up but he kept his mouth open after he said it and I could hear his breath forced through it.

'Oh, piss off,' I said, scowling at them both, now. 'Just get out of my way and leave me to get on with this!'

I did regret it after I'd said it.

296

'I want to talk,' Basher said that evening. 'Please come around.'
We were down the pit again: it was evening, and cold, and no
matter how cosy a camp fire might seem, our underground living
space was cosier by far when the rain had sleet in it.

Brain had been taking a turn on the cycling generator,
providing our light and some heat. The Gaffer lit the lanterns
so he could dismount and we gathered expectantly at the living
area. Basher stood with his fingers fidgeting inside the cuffs of
his brown jacket; he buttoned and then undid the front again
and cleared his throat. His eyes were so black in our dim lantern
light and under his floppy hair that they almost held no light.

As the others took their seats I glanced at Saleema. Her
mother was holding her hand.

Basher cleared his throat.

'I want to make an announcement,' he said. 'About Saleema.'
My eyes flashed to Brain.

'Here at Dykend we've had burths and deaths,' Basher said.
'And difficult days. Am I right?'

There were nods and mumbles, but Basher talking was
something rare for most of us, certainly Basher hogging the floor
with a speech, so we were eager to hear what he had to say.

'We've all buried our faimlies. And now it's Spring. A new
year. Soon we'll be planting again.' He paused. 'So we should
celebrate with a wedding.'

Grace had to have his words explained to her, but she
understood the 'wedding' for herself.

'I know I'm the luckiest man here. Because, though ma wife
and I lost three kids to the illness, we kept each other and also
two other children and now we have wee Saadi.'

'Salami,' Wide Boy called out.

Basher grinned but disregarded him. 'And now ma oldest
lassie is a good age for to get married.'

Saleema's head was down. I looked at Brain again.

'And I have asked The Gaffer here, Mr Francis Hutchison,
who is a very good man, hard-working and respectable, and he
has just this afternoon said that he will be happy to mairry ma

daughter.'

There was some kind of time shift in the shock I felt, as if I'd just been transported here, which would explain why the event was incomprehensible. The two men's faces were bright with self-congratulation; poor Saleema, when she raised hers, had clearly spent many of the past hours crying.

The rest of us had our mouths open. Brain alone seemed to have known this was coming. He looked as miserable as Saleema. I met Peej's eyes and he shrugged as if to say, 'What ye expect me to do about it?'

Saleema and *The Gaffer*? I was surrounded by people who were beginning to offer their congratulations. I didn't know if it was because of what was going on with Robyn, or irritation because of my sleeplessness, or whether it was because the last thing I wanted was for someone to be happy, but for whatever reason, I stood up and shouted, 'Hold on a minute!'

I couldn't prevent myself. I just couldn't. I ignored Basher and directed my invective at The Gaffer. 'You're not really going to try and get away with this, are you?' The Gaffer, for his part, had the decency to look uncomfortable. 'I can't believe you can do this. She's a *girl*, for God's sake.'

His mouth opened but I didn't give him time to fill it. 'She's breaking her heart.' I appealed round the gathering. I paused briefly at Brain but something made me keep schtoom about him.

'And look at you,' I said. 'You're what? Fifty? And you expect a young girl of what – fifteen – to actually marry you?'

He blinked.   'In Basher's culture they arrange their marriages. If he thinks I'd provide a secure fut-'

'In Basher's culture?' I said. 'In *Basher's* culture?'

The Gaffer's eyes went from side to side like a spy doll with a switch at its back. 'Yes.'

'Isn't that convenient?' I made expansive sweeps around me. 'But where is Basher's culture?' When I looked at Basher his face was even darker. 'I'm sorry, Basher. I respect your rights as an individual, but surely we're forging a brand new culture, here and now.'

298

'I have to take care of my daughter,' he said, his eyes almost invisible under his lowered brows.

I looked at the women in the group and thought how far western women had come, up until about two years ago when disaster slapped us right back down. And I thought about polygamy, and the bikers, and the fishermen at North Connell who asked Peej if he had any spare women. And I saw all the freedoms ebbing away but I wouldn't let them go without a fight. 'I think we should sound the death knell – right now – for forced marriages.'

I sat down. All I could hear was the elderberry wine gurgling. Basher must have been doing a translation. The Gaffer caught his breath and stepped back up to the precipice.

'I'm shocked, Alice,' he said, running his hand through his hair as if he had gel on it. 'I'm shocked at you of all people. You used to work for the Council. What about multi-culturalism? What about respecting the rights and wishes of others?'

'Exactly!'

Hesitation.

I went on. 'What about respecting the rights and wishes of *everybody*?'

Limpet spoke up. 'Saleema wants to make a good marriage, Alice.'

'It is my right,' Basher said quietly, 'and responsibility, to make good arrangements fur the safety of my daughter.'

'Basher,' I said. 'I respect that you feel a strong need to protect your daughter. God, the way things are now I can fully understand and endorse that. But *The Gaffer*!' I pointed at him, standing with his arms folded. 'Surely her consent has to come into it? Her volition? Basher, she doesn't want to marry *The Gaffer*.'

Like a flock of birds who change direction in flight, the company's eyes revolved towards The Gaffer.

'But there's one decent, hard-working young man here that maybe she *would* like to marry.' How could he not see that? I pointed in the opposite direction. 'She probably *wants* to marry Brain.

The whole flock of us turned to consider Brain.

Chapter Fifty-eight

In a way it was a good diversion. Later, while the others played cards in clusters or pairs or read privately, I moved towards the back of the pit where Robyn's mattress was propped up against the tunnel wall to air. Wide Boy followed me, at my elbow.

'I'll give ye a hand with that,' he said and Peej's head went up.

'Aye, me too.'

'I can manage.' I didn't want a parade of them. I wanted to set it up myself to avoid suspicion – and because, I'll admit, I was more fizzingly annoyed than ever – but for now, at least, it would look as if we were huddling to discuss the Basher-BigMan-Saleema scandal.

In the gloom of the back tunnel entrance the two men lifted the soiled mattress and turned it according to my instructions on to her bed. I had no other sheets: the ones I'd washed weren't dry and I had to strip the sheets from my own bed to clothe hers; a move that might seem foolish, given that she'd wet her covers almost every day of the past week. But I wanted her to feel that everything was normal.

'D'you want me to help?' Wide Boy asked.

Peej grabbed the flying edges of the sheet as I aired it into place. He tucked it in as if he'd done it all his life. 'Right,' he said, his head bent into the middle. 'Talk.'

'Talk what?'

'I tellt him, Yakkity.'

'Och, Wide Boy!' I scolded, so loudly I almost gave us away, though I should have known the others were oblivious to me shirricking Wide Boy. There's hardly a day on earth when I don't. 'I told you not to tell anyone.'

We tucked in in silence and I threw over the pillow.

'So, talk.'

'Give me that sheet.'

Peej threw it and I caught the ends and so it went with the blankets.

'How much do you know?'

He straightened and glanced behind him at the company, off in the other end, half a dozen lanterns showing them wrapped up for warmth in their outer clothes since Brain clearly hadn't felt any obligation to return to generating electricity. 'I know you think somebody's been trying it on wi' her.'

I nodded. Felt my diaphragm rise.

'Well, it's obvious there's something.' Peej bobbed his head at the bed we were making. 'Kid her age'll not keep doing this out the blue fur nothing.'

I let go of the covers and held my fingers over my mouth. It took me a minute to pull them away. 'The night before last I woke up with a man at the bottom of my bed.'

The wall of the two men moved closer. 'Who?'

I shook my head. 'I'm not saying.'

'Aw, fuck, Yakkity!' Wide Boy snarled, furious with me.

'No, I'm not. I want to get evidence.' I looked from one to the other. 'Or else he'll just say I dreamt it!'

Wide Boy growled, 'Was it The Gaffer?'

'Shut it!' Peej said. 'Lassie's right.' He threw over the duvet. 'How d'ye know ye weren't dreaming it?'

I sighed, but Wide Boy stepped in.

'Something's bothering her, Peejie. Ye said it yerself.'

'I'm not dreaming it,' I said. I moved round Robyn's bed, past Robina's and reached in under my own. The company was still occupied. I slid my holdall out. The incunabulum was wrapped in two layers of plastic bags at the bottom of it; on top, in more plastic, was the unwashed sheet.

'Smell this,' I said, holding it open under Wide Boy's nose in the darkness.

He drew back. 'That's bowfin.'

I held it to Peej.

302

'I'll take yer word fur it.'

'No, smell it. I took it off Robyn's bed the other morning and I've been worrying about it ever since.'

He bent his head till it was a couple of inches above the open holdall. I pulled a handful of white linen out and he gave a reluctant sniff. He sniffed it again and fixed his eyes on mine.

'Right, ye can put it away. Keep it safe.'

'What is it?' Wide Boy asked, looking puzzled.

Peej scowled. 'Use yer imagination.' He turned to me. 'He tellt me ye'd a plan.'

'You have to promise neither of you comes anywhere near.' Crouching, I pulled the other package out from under my bed and opened it on the ground. A coil of wire I'd secreted jangled against the bed frame. 'Remember that hedge we tried to get through in North Connell? I'm going to string up a tripwire.'

Peej stared at the loops I was holding. 'Well, so much for blaming Chis.' He held Wide Boy away and leaned in so close I could feel his breath on my ear. 'Is it who I think it is?' He pulled back so our eyes could meet. He mouthed the name.

I nodded.

His breath was at my ear again. I smelled his cigarette smoke and mustiness. 'Leave it wi' me. I know the kind of trap that bastard needs.'

Chapter Fifty-nine

I lay rigid, listening to the others' supple breathing while I stayed on alert.

We'd gone back to the living area, Wide Boy wrestling with his instincts since he couldn't get to grips with flesh and blood. I watched him try, judge and condemn the other men, his eyes squeezed into slits as if his skin was an executioner's hood. He sat beside Brain, a saturnine pair. Presumably they felt deprived of potential partners. I could understand that. There could only be about five years between Wide Boy and Robyn and he'd always been fond of her. I thought of him chasing her round the camp.

Robyn herself was holding a book to her face without turning any pages. Now and then she and Wide Boy's eyes met; once, Wide Boy broke off from gnawing his fingertips to up-nod, 'You alright?'

Peej went over to sit beside her and put his arm round her shoulders, shoogling her gently. 'Course she's alright. Aren't ye, hen? Ye're wi' me.'

Her smile made me want to cry. Once again her eyes sought out Wide Boy.

I was sitting beside Bill and Grace. 'It must be spring, Gracie,' I said, blowing my nose. 'Love is in the air.'

'Is that right?' She chuckled and patted Bill's knee. It could have been August on Palm Beach for all Grace understood.

I noticed that Basher wouldn't look at me. Nor would The Gaffer. Maybe that wasn't surprising. What a glum, pre-occupied, heavyweight gathering we were. We almost couldn't wait for the evening to pass.

*

After the young ones had their supper I followed Robyn and Robina to the back tunnel. 'I've done it, Yak,' Robyn whined, but for once I wasn't interested in her bladder.

'Shh,' I said, looking behind me and pushing the two girls further into the dark so that only the faint gloss of their cheeks was visible. 'I've got something to talk to you about.'

'What?' Robyn said. She shivered in the cold.

I didn't know where to start. 'In a minute or two when you're in your beds I'm going to pretend to get Peej over to catch a spider.'

'Oh, aye?' Robina said. I didn't like the implication. They were too young to suspect anything like that. Or at least they should be. I wondered which pile of my books they'd been reading. Then I remembered Robyn.

'Be serious.' I looked specifically at Robina. 'I don't know if you know what's been happening to your sister.'

Robyn's hand jumped to her mouth.

'What? Wettin' her bed?' Robina sneered but Robyn didn't notice.

'A bit more serious. Though it might be related.'

A cat meow of agitation came from Robyn's throat. 'It's nothin'.' she said. 'I've not done nothin'.'

I pulled her close.

She wriggled. 'How d'ye fun oot?' [NB: 'find out']

'Fun oot what?' Robina said.

Robyn squeezed tight round my waist. 'Don't tell her, Yak!'

I checked no one was watching. 'It's alright, Robyn.' She'd grown over the last months. Her hair was tickling my nose.

'He'll catch me; he'll beat me up. Or he'll do it to Robina. He said he would. If I tellt anybody.'

'Who would? Do what to me? Who tellt ye?'

'Shh!' My other arm had to get a grip round Robina now. 'You can't go shouting. We're going to get it sorted.' I squeezed the pair of them tight together. 'We'll get finished with this. Tonight. But we've got to be clever about it. Right?'

Robina nodded.

'Okay Robyn? Nobody's going to hurt you. Or Robina. Not

as long as I can help it.'

I kissed her cheek. It was wet and when I let her go she wiped it.

'Who's been hurtin' ye?' Robina asked her but her twin just shrugged.

I stepped back to the brink of the back tunnel entrance to check that no-one suspected anything. Junkie was sitting up in bed. She stared at me. I nodded to her. I'd probably end up having to explain it to her but I hadn't finished with the girls for now.

'This is what we're going to do,' I said.

Chapter Sixty

I lay in the dark, waiting for the first movement.

Beside me, across the three foot divide, Robyn had finally fallen asleep; I could tell from her breathing. Across from us, the end of her bed between ours, Robina too had drifted off. Convinced of the need to appear normal, she'd taken a book to bed and had pretended to read. I knew she was determined to stay awake but the fresh air and the calories we burn to stay warm soon put an end to any attempts the kids made at all-nighters. Even Junkie, who'd been shocked that something like that could be happening two metres from her bed, was breathing sludgily.

The whole pit was still. With no sheets my mattress felt cold and wet and I had to keep telling myself it wasn't. Beneath my pillow I kept a torch. I slid my hand under and brought it below the covers. 1.31a.m. What if tonight he didn't come? I switched the torch off again and pushed it back under the pillow then rolled on to my other side, facing the men.

As soon as our suspect had gone to take care of his ablutions I'd squealed *A spider! Under the bed! As big as a hamster!* and Peej made a dash for it, bringing the trap. We'd be the leading lights in any Dykend Amateur Dramatics company.

It only took him seconds to fix it and put a dark jumper over it. I felt his hand on my bed down near my calf. 'That'll do it. Keep yer feet in.' When he stood he ground the imaginary spider under his shoe as our suspect's head was appearing down the entry tunnel. 'That's what we do to big beasties,' he said and I loved him with every molecule in my body.

I couldn't sleep for waiting. One by one the others' lights went out and bit by bit our long home became black as thick as the thickest night without a moon; a black so total your eyes strive in their sockets for any thread of light; any pin point. I fell to sleep but not a deep one. I woke on my back hearing someone's mattress creak and I lay awake for the snap, my sense of dread a torsion, tight round my chest. But then it eased as Junkie moaned and turned over and then I was asleep again in a place where people surged in gaudy summer colours, lilac, nasturtium, down a placid green slope. And then Grace's cabinet clinked and I was wide awake. I couldn't lie flat: I rolled on to my side facing Robyn. I pulled the covers clear of my ears and muffled my mouth. My heart was stoonding: my covers would be pulsing. I heard him breathe. I lay as still as I could.

The breathing paused at the foot of my bed. I bit the blanket. Another step.

Another one.

Snap.

A jagged suck then a god-forsaken howl.

Chapter Sixty-one

Robyn leaped from her bed into my arms. Her high-pitched scream injected ice into my ear and I had to yell at her to stop, our voices reverberating through the cavern. Beams of torch light zigzagged from the other end as Wide Boy and Peej vaulted the beds, filling the spaces with their roars. Eric writhed, kicking out against my bed. In the shafts of light I saw agony in his eyes and blood on his fingers when they switched from tugging at the teeth to grasping towards us.

'Leave them!' Wide Boy arrived first and got his feet to him. Dull thuds kicked air out. Jagged cries. Eric sprawled further between our beds.

'Haud on. Haud on!' Peej pulled the Boy off. 'Has he not got enough to contend wi'?'

'Bastard!'

Basher arrived; The Gaffer. Brain stood on Bill's bed so he could see.

'What did ye do that for?' Eric was sobbing. 'I didn't do anythin'.'

'Like fuck!' Wide Boy swung his leg again but Peej shoved him onto Robina's bed before it could contact.

'Get a grip!'

She was sitting on her pillow; now she leapt over to Junkie.

'Yous alright?' Peej swung the torch round us, Junkie and Robina, little Robyn and me. Robyn was shuddering. The Gaffer wrapped somebody's duvet round us and I acknowledged it dutifully, still prickly from before.

Peej wedged himself between the beds, barricading the Boy out. He directed his light between Eric's face and leg. They threw back the light with a sleek lustre.

'I didn't do anythin'.' Eric's howls had changed to sobs but they were harder on the ears. 'Oh, Jesus,' he repeated. With one hand he tugged at the metal teeth, wiping his other hand over his face. In the glare of the torch and the greyscale of the pit his face was pallid, his chin charcoaled. Only the blood was vivid, an eye-feast of scarlet, crimson, vermilion, on his fingers, painted on his face and daubed on the winter-white cover on my bed.

I thought I'd pass out with revulsion. I used to be vegetarian.

'Let's see yer leg,' Peej said. He crouched to examine it.

'Get that trap off him,' The Gaffer said. 'Brain – away and get bandages.'

I thought about lockjaw; tetanus jags; whether the wound would be fatal. Last night it hadn't occurred to me. What had happened to my conscience? To fifty-odd years of civilisation?

'I didn't do anythin'.' Eric was still moaning as Peej and Basher hunkered between the beds to pull the teeth apart.

'Then what were you doing up here among the girls?' Clearly The Gaffer's brain was working.

Eric's eyes appealed to me. 'I was up to see Yakkity. Alice? Tell them. Tell them about us.'

I didn't answer. I turned my head from him, my arms shuddering, holding Robyn.

Peej passed The Gaffer the torch to shine on his wound. Robyn looked and gasped and I held her face away. The trap had bitten into the flesh; skin, hair and meat were seized in its teeth.

'My god,' I heard one of the women mumble.

Peej released whatever lever he'd to release and braced a hand against Eric's knee. He pulled one side of the clamp clear of the leg with a sucking sound. Eric fainted against the side of Robyn's bed and she wailed then, a lost, repeating wail that said something about her own pain and something about his, about it being her fault, when her only fault was to be his victim.

The Gaffer smoothed his hand on her head. 'Hey.' She wouldn't lift her face up, crying into my neck.

I shook my head to him. He bobbed his to Eric on the ground

310

between the beds and then Robyn and asked me the question without words. I nodded and he frowned and shook his head and that was how the judgement was made.

Chapter Sixty-two

I didn't need the sheet I'd stowed in my holdall; didn't need the clear record of events I'd memorised during the previous night. I was right – it was enough to catch him about to commit the act. I wondered if the trip wire would have been enough.

It took all of us long enough to get back to sleep that night. I lay, cuddling Robyn, sure I could hear Eric's whimper all the way from the other end of the pit where the men were taking it in turns to guard him. I'd never been comfortable with him, but I'd grown used to him over the two years since the strange circumstances when I'd first met him. Sara and me hiding from him in the sports shop; the CS spray in his eyes and the weird mental blank I had that night we spent in the room above the pub when he claimed to have sheltered us from the bikers. Me, cold and hungover on his couch and Sara, by contrast, flushed and warm in her double duvet.

A thought crossed my mind and I took my arm away from Robyn and turned on my back. Maybe we had misjudged Chis over what had happened to Sara. No. Surely it wouldn't have been Eric?

The more I thought about it, the more I fretted that it was Eric who'd been the one to make Sara pregnant. That night in his flat, when I'd been completely unconscious. I thought about those pills I'd found in the bathroom cabinet and how he'd taken my glass into the kitchen for my second refill. Could he have drugged me?

The flush on Sara's face. The iPod he'd given her. Yet that was March, not June. I turned over in the bed, the wooden slats beneath me creaking. Well, somebody had got her pregnant. Could he have carried on a relationship? Behind my back? I thought about our time in the library. How absorbed I was in ancient history, transcribing those fusty old court cases. How sorry for myself I was when I thought about The Boss. How drunk I let myself get, neglecting to keep track of her.

And then I thought about her locket.

I reached my hand under the pillow for my torch and slid out of bed on to my knees. Junkie had pushed a package with a few things of Sara's under my bed, at the back of my rucksack and I'd never gone near it. Too painful. I crept out of bed, switched my torch on and dragged it out, now.

Her hessian carrier bag – Sara's hessian shopping bag. My hands shook as I held it to me, the smell so familiar – Sara's strawberry bubble bath smell that permeated everything she touched, she used so much of it. Inside, there was very little: the sun hat and glasses from our shopping trip with Eric, her green hoodie still with its anarchy badge in place. I rested the torch on my bed and held the hoodie up in the light and as I did so a patterned paper bag dropped out of it and landed by my knees.

'Alice?' It was Junkie's voice. 'What are ye doing? It's the middle of the night.'

I looked over to her and shook my head but she probably wasn't able to see that. I could hardly make her out in the black of the pit but I heard her turn over and lie down again and then I waited so I knew she'd gone back to sleep. By now I was trembling with the cold and my hands were numb as I carefully uncurled the crimped top of the paper bag and let its contents slide out. A gold chain, like liquid flowing into my palm, then the weight of her locket.

Sara's locket! Sara's treasured locket that Eric had given her. Why had I never looked in it? Too drunk; too distraught; too caught up in my own grief to have any desire to become a detective. Well, I was no dick now but I was damned sure I was a detective. I bent my head to it and held the tiny locket close to my eyes in the torch light so I could make out the catch. Popped it and opened it. And there it was. Black hairs. Black hairs like wires! I snapped, then. I squeezed it shut, tightened my fists and swelled up in a fury, not caring who I woke and then I homed in on Eric at the other end of the long pit like a guided missile.

'You bastard!' I yelled. 'You nasty, evil, fucking bastard! How could you do it to her?'

Lights came on, voices were raised but by now I'd reached Eric and I shone my torch beam in his face. 'How could you? How could you?' I roared, quaking in my nightie.

'What's going on, Yak?' Peej said but I hurled the locket at Eric then I picked up a stool and hit him over the head with it till it was gripped, as I raised it again, by The Gaffer, who threw it down and wrapped his arms tightly around me, pinning me stiff.

'What's come over you, Alice?' he said. 'Calm down!'

I twisted round and sobbed into his neck, slumped and felt his arm muscles loosening. By now some of the others had come up to the living area and the locket had been found. 'Eric made Sara pregnant. Not Chis,' I said, pushing myself away from The Gaffer's heat.

Someone shone a torch on Eric's face. 'Eric?' The Gaffer said.

His voice was dead. 'She loved me,' he said. 'And I loved her back.'

Chapter Sixty-three

So many people, keeping so many secrets. All of it went round
my head that night. I think it was the saddest night I'd ever
spent.

We didn't even have a trial. We hung about our beds, eyes
drawn to the living area as it grew grey with the glimmer of
daylight, spotted with yellow when The Gaffer lit two lamps.
No one had the energy to go out and set up tents. Instead, The
Gaffer let us boil the kettles on the camping gas stove and we
ate what was left of yesterday's bread with tea and powdered
milk, hardly talking out loud, waiting for what was bound to
happen.

They kept Eric in the corner. Limpet passed Basher tea and
bread for him. Wide Boy tried to spit in it; the bubbling gob of
his white spit slopped off the side of the mug on to the ground.

The Gaffer cleared his throat. 'Just so everybody knows
what's happening.' He broke off, his eyes lingering on Robyn
before breaking away. 'I never for a minute thought the day
would come when we'd be charging somebody with this. And
then we find out about Sara. As if the trouble over Robyn wasn't
bad enough.' He shook his head and looked into his tea. Put it
down. 'Eric. Have you no self control? I don't understand how
you could do it.'

Eric kept his back to us.

'If there's anybody that doesn't know – Eric's been found
guilty of child abuse.'

Eric turned sharply, 'I've not been found guilty.'

'You have.' The Gaffer spoke louder and if it hadn't been for
what had happened over Saleema I think I might have felt quite
proud of him.

'I loved Sara. And as for Robyn: you just caught me over there. That doesn't mean I was guilty of anything. It's not a crime to be over there, is it?'

Wide Boy had been sitting with his knees apart, staring at his cup on the ground between his feet. He picked it up and drained it then slammed it through the air before anyone could react. It thunked Eric on the side of his head and shattered on the ground.

'Enough!'

'Fuck off!' Wide Boy was stiff with anger. He lunged at Eric but Brain grabbed him by the waistband and thumped him in his seat.

'I'll sit wi' him.' Robyn slipped her hand out of my arm and transferred into the small space beside Wide Boy, taking his elbow and leaning against his shoulder. I watched his chest swell and release a shaky breath as if he was the one who had been wounded. Across from me, his shoulder blades hooking the back of a chair and one foot outstretched on another, Peej caught my eye and winked.

'Have you got a grip now?' The Gaffer asked.

Wee Grace said, 'Och, that's terrible,' and Bill shooshed her.

When there was silence The Gaffer continued in a low voice directed at Eric. 'We've other evidence so there's no point challenging it.'

The quiet was thick enough to swallow the gulps Grace made upending her cup and the glooping of the elderberry wine. Leaning out of his mother's arms Salami squealed round a yellow and green rattle too big for his mouth.

'What can we do? There's no jail to keep you off the streets.'

'Give him to me an' I'll deal wi' him,' Peej said but The Gaffer cut him off with 'So we're sending you into exile.'

There was rumbling as Basher spoke to Peej. I caught the words 'lead them to us' before Eric's voice, falsetto, made him stop.

Straining round to see The Gaffer, Eric pleaded, 'You can't send me anywhere like this!' His leg was bandaged but blood had seeped through. 'I can't put any weight on it!'

316

'Your problem,' Peej mumbled.

The Gaffer looked towards Brain. 'We can give him some bandages? Antiseptic?'

Brain nodded.

'And you can take food and blankets. Then you're on your own.' The Gaffer stood up. Seeing him centre stage and having been in his arms the night before I thought maybe I'd misjudged him, too. He did have leadership qualities. He'd also grown leaner, and had a good square chin now the dewlap had been worked off. But he was still too old for Saleema.

'When am I leaving?'

'Not soon enough,' Wide Boy said.

The Gaffer checked his watch. 'Twenty minutes.'

I helped Limpet pack a holdall with a supply of food and water for him. Our hands trembled as we packed. Brain stripped the linen from his bed, rolled it into a bundle with some plastic sheeting and secured it with string.

'That's a sin fur that boy,' Grace said. 'What did he do?'

'Oh, he's been a naughty boy, Gracie,' Peej said. He rocked on the back legs of his chair, staring at Wide Boy and Robyn. 'A very naughty boy. But there's The Gaffer taken care ay it.'

Junkie and Robina chewed gum; the silence was punctuated by little cracks.

'See the kind a crap he's got under this bed?' Brain shoved it back when he saw Saleema looking over.

'Never mind that – just get him the basics. The rest can go on the fire.'

Basher and Brain shinned up the rope. They would lift him in the cradle because he said he couldn't walk. Bent at the tunnel, I watched him ready to go.

'Can I get a gun?' he asked.

There was a moment of indecision. Eventually Peej said, 'Give him yer knife.'

The Gaffer put his hand on his knife but changed his mind. 'Up top.'

I followed them to the bottom of the shaft. A thin light found its way in. Eric's face was grey as if the pit had got into him.

'Yoh!' The Gaffer called and Basher and Brain pulled on the cables.

When the cradle came back down the other men monkeyed up the rope and I scrambled up after them. I watched Eric hirple off over the tussocky ground, dwarfed by the pack on his back. Or maybe I should say, looking like a child under the burden he had to carry.

Later, the men lit a bonfire. I didn't see any of them gloating over what they'd found under his bed but I know that when I washed Eric's blood from my bed linen, and for a week or two afterwards when I thought about him, ours seemed like a very empty victory.

Chapter Sixty-four

More than two years had passed since the illness. I straightened up at the mouth of the shaft each morning and tried to feel a sense of forward motion. I could see that the sun's arc was inching higher each day in the sky, sizzling off the damp and relieving the chronic inflammation that constricted my bones and joints during the winter. More importantly, the limp green shoots I thought frosts must surely have crushed were beginning to erect sturdy stalks and spread leaves along our strips of cultivated earth. Within weeks we were enjoying spring greens – not yearning too badly for a knob of butter and not inspecting too closely if we bit anything chewy curled in the innermost leaves.

There'd been no repercussions after we'd banished Eric. Instead, a mood of relief followed on from those first few days of despair, and a desire to work together to engage with this new spring after what had been such a difficult winter. It was sad about Chis but there was nothing we could do about that. It was even sadder about Robyn, but now that Eric had gone – and now that the other men in the camp had found out what he'd put her through, and could treat her tenderly – she was calmer and happier than I'd seen her in months. She was closer to the child who'd arrived in our camp with her identical sister.

Anyway, the hunting was better, and the men were away from camp more often, engaged in stalking of a different sort, or working with the sheep and cattle, while we women weeded the fields to prevent the buttercups garrotting our crops. It was a shame they weren't edible. We made full use of the dandelions – our crunchy, albeit bitter, ubiquitous native crop – that we were learning could also be dried and roasted as a passable substitute for coffee. As for the marriage Basher had wanted to arrange – none of my veiled questions could draw any information out about that. And whenever I looked towards The Gaffer, he turned away or simply avoided me.

With spring coming we didn't have the same time for school, but I persevered. In fact, I insisted. Not through any lack of will to get my hands dirty, though I have to say fingernails crammed with dirt never was my idea of a fulfilled life, but because I was becoming more and more aware of how our standards were in decline. Our behaviour was regressing. It was obvious in our treatment of Eric. Despite his sins, that trap was little short of barbaric. And I wasn't free of condemnation: look how I'd reacted when I'd realised he was the one who'd abused Sara. Even the language we were using was letting us down. Peej's version reminded me of those buttercups: runners of words and phrases insinuated themselves through our daily conversations and new plantlets were strangling the way we used to speak. I listened in to conversations increasingly, noting the subtle changes and remembering that page 21 stamp on the books in the library: the little differences that added up till eventually two different systems emerged. It looked like our language was going to be the same. I fretted about it. I didn't know whether or not to give in to it.

The weather wasn't quite so cold and as we left April we cast off some of our skins. Peej had put aside his leather jacket and the dark grey fleece that had sculpted itself to his body. He was favouring an open necked polo shirt instead, which was quite jaunty, the short sleeves exposing just a little of the base of the flying eagle on his upper arm. The smoke from his cigarette rose like the spray from a reversed waterfall past the L-O-V-E – H-A-T-E relationship on the hairy bits of his fingers. He leaned forward to the fire and I caught a glimpse of his 'I love you' necklaces spangling.

He, The Gaffer and Basher were going over their farming plans for the full season and I tuned in and out of their conversation while I tried to work out my lesson plans for the spring. Saadi was grizzling, trapped by his father's constraining arms but Basher and the men only raised their voices above him to make themselves heard. I couldn't concentrate. Besides, the sky was harebell blue and calling me away from decimal multiplication.

And actually, the more I squinted to see, the more I thought Peej was wearing only one of those necklaces. I closed my books and weighted them down with a stone then went over to take Saadi from his father. In doing so, I'd manage a closer look at Peej's neck.

They didn't even pause when I reached in and lifted Saadi. I stood for a minute with him on my hip expecting them to at least acknowledge me and draw me into the conversation, but it was as if I wasn't there. Worse, I couldn't even see Peej's throat because he put his hand up over it for a scratch. At length The Gaffer glanced up and said, 'Are you waiting for something, Yakkity?' but the whole time Peej kept his hand at his neck as if it was sore. Caught out, I shrugged and blushed. Here were the three of them, looking at me expectantly when I had nothing to say. So I went off with Salami and took him a walk through the field, cross with myself and for some reason nursing a grudge with them. I tickled Saadi with a long stalk of grass and he giggled so I felt better then we sat down and I tried to cuddle him, but he wasn't having any of it. He was nearly a year old by then: he didn't want to be treated like a baby. I tried to hold him, but he dug his heels in, made his back rigid and complained. I plucked a buttercup and held it under his chin to see if he liked butter, but he was wriggly and restless. All he could think to do was grab at my breast. Still being breast fed.

Just like a man, I was thinking. We walked a bit further to take his mind off it. I walked bent over, holding his hands while he tried out his feet. I decided to talk to him while we examined how our vegetables were doing. I'd read in a book at the library that you should let babies hear you speak in a good, clear voice. I hoped I could introduce him to some proper pronunciation before he got into my 'school system'. After all, what hope did the boy have with a mother and father who spoke broken English and the rest of the camp only speaking slang?

I was so engrossed in my campaign of teaching Saadi English and showing him the sights that I didn't see an extremely important sight till it ran away from me. 'Look, Saadi,' I was saying to him as we settled on the grass in a sheltered spot and I pulled him on to my lap. 'Do you see how beautiful the sky is to-day? Look at the baby green onion shoots for dinner.' He grabbed my lips in his fist and his ragged nails scratched me. 'Ouch!' I said, getting really irritated at him, and shoved his fist away. He'd the cheek to laugh! I could feel the rage rising in me, and then he wrapped his fingers round my glasses and pulled them half off my face, taking a couple of head hairs with them.

I heard the sound of long grass swishing and a curious jingling. I finally released Saadi's hands from my glasses and got them back on my nose in time to see what looked like a man in black leather springing from the bushes and darting down the hill-side, running away from me.

Chapter Sixty-five

I blinked and blinked. My lenses were smeared from the baby's grubby fingers. It was a man, wasn't it? I couldn't be imagining things. Befuddled and in shock, I launched myself and the baby heavily off the ground and flew back to raise the alarm. Saadi's head was rattling; his hale – whole – body bounced as I ran, clutching him to me.

'Oh Jesus,' I was saying. 'Oh Jesus Christ, Salami!'

He was too young to understand and laughed out loud.

'Shh!' I whispered. I daren't shout. If I shouted the man would know there was somebody I was shouting to. I didn't know whether he knew we were there or whether he was just taking a leak or whether he was spying on me or anything.

It was weird, shouting without my vocal cords. 'Peej!' I mouthed, hurrying back into the camp again.

Basher assumed the worst about his baby. He grabbed him away from me and inspected him closely while I continued to try to get through to Peej.

Out of breath with my exertions and indignant that once again he was ignoring me, I yelled, 'Peej Jamieson. Why do you never pay any attention to me?'

'What?' he said, half rising. 'How? Whit did ye say?'

I leaned on his shoulder, trying to catch my breath. 'There's a guy in the field.'

'What?'

'You heard me.'

'In the field?'

I nodded, face to the ground, a pain in my lungs from too much deep breathing. 'Wearing black leather.'

'Are ye sure, Yakkity?' Still in disbelief. If a man had said it, he'd have believed it.

'Down the field!' I said. 'Down by the crop strips. Running.'

'The Gaffer! Brain!' he shouted. 'Oot here!'

He strapped on the chib he'd been sharpening. Basher handed me Saadi. Trusted childminder again, now, but that was beside the point.

'Man in the field,' Peej shouted. 'You two that way. Guy in black leather. Get him!'

I couldn't catch my breath again. I swallowed hard, forcing myself to think. I kissed Saadi's cheek and moved over towards the other women as fast as my lack of oxygen would allow me. Adrenaline must have helped.

Our pack drill in an emergency was for the women to huddle in a group with the children. Eric was one of the men detailed to look after us – ha! – but with him gone there was only old Bill and he wasn't Zorro. I passed Salami back to his mum then kept watch around our camp. The women and children and Bill were gathered in the open at the fire, all in one place and with no one talking. All I could hear was the hiss of the camping gas and the pot of scummy bones blubbering to the boil. I moved position to look down the field in one direction then another. There was no sign of anyone. I couldn't think where he had come from. I walked back and forth through the lank grass, still unable to bring my breathing under control. I guessed they called it the fight or flight reaction and – unlike in the library – this time I was ready. I recognised in myself that I had hardened. We'd experienced too many losses. There'd been too much deception.

There was a hiss when the stock frothed over. Limpet turned down the gas and the liquid plooped like a volcano, cooling to an eventual shimmer. Still the men didn't come back. My ears strained for their voices; for war shouts – the kind of street fighting roars that have decent people quaking behind their curtains trying to work out the denouement of the plot. I heard only the squawk of gulls and the flitter of an ancient carrier bag frazzled in a tree.

I knew, now, what these men were capable of – bikers and Dykenders. I knew they could come back with dribbling mouths

324

on cheeks and foreheads; bloodied slits in the flesh of their limbs or with their fingers pursing ruby lips in the hollow below their ribs.

I also knew what I could be capable of. I had my own knife. I'd originally packed one before I set out from my flat those two and more years ago but Peej had told me it would be too messy. I'd got rid of it but one day after my incident with the bikers I helped myself to a hook billed, zig-zag edged thing sheathed in leather. I'd tried it out on the body of a sheep when no one else was looking and I'd no qualms, now, about using it on a biker. If they came back. Not many qualms.

Peej surprised me by coming over the hill above us. He was unhurt: my eyes examined his polo shirt for neat incisions but there were none. And no red streaks on his arms or face either.

'No sign ay him.'

He lifted a bottle of water from the bag by the camp fire. I watched his throat work as he drank. He twisted the bottle lid and put it back, surveyed downhill then cast his eyes over us: me standing, the women and children crouched.

'Yous alright?'

'Aye.'

Basher and the others drifted in one after the other.

'I'm knacked.' Wide Boy threw himself on his back on the mat beside the twins. 'Ye sure ye didn't imagine him, Yakkity?'

Brain squatted to tie his lace. He snorted as if he thought the same thing.

'I did not,' I said. I knew what I'd seen. Well, I thought I did. 'It was a guy in black leathers and he flew down the hill when he realised I'd seen him.'

'Black bin bag,' Wide Boy said and Robina laughed.

I squeezed the hilt of my dagger. How dared they ridicule me?

'Nah, the bushes wis crushed,' Peej said. 'Somebody'd been there.'

'See!' I let my knife go and folded my arms.

'Eric?' The Gaffer suggested.

'Not running like that.' Peej's tic ticked. 'But I wouldnae be surprised if he wis at the back ay it.'

Chapter Sixty-six

That night instead of going hunting the men took it in turns to stay on guard. At first light, Peej and Wide Boy set off on foot to reconnoitre. They came back while we were having breakfast, heavy eyed with lack of sleep and too much walking. We sent them down to bed and they slept till lunch.

For days we stayed on alert but saw no other sign. Even I was beginning to wonder if I imagined him. The days were warmer now we'd left April; the gorse bushes were vivid with yellow. From that height the flowering cherries in the estate gardens were so many candy floss cones. The buzzard was hunting, motionless in the blue air with his blunt tail and the white tide mark on the underside of his trembling dun wings. My eyes were always drawn to him, wondering what he saw from up there. But it was Junkie, lumbering out to us at the crop strips with fresh nan and water, who noticed the smoke.

We all stood, staring. It must be two houses, three. The orange flames licked and chewed at the masonry, biting off some of the roof as we were watching. Of course, we wondered who'd set it. A gas explosion? The sun? But it sounded as if the roof collapse was followed by shouting.

At night, with the fire still wild, Peej and Basher headed out.

We waited, anxious, our men taking it in turns to stay up top on guard. I shinned up the rope once or twice – my old fear of being shut in resurrected now – and huddled beside Brain or Wide Boy or The Gaffer as they sat on the narrow wooden decking around the top of the shaft, watching the incandescent glow. With the naked eye it was just a spot: just a fidgeting splash of orange where the streetlights used to be a glittering sodium sea.

'Are you still seeing Saleema?' I asked Brain. The darkness leant itself to exploring secrets. It was well over two months since Basher's announcement, but I hadn't been aware of any kind of follow-up.

Brain snuggled his chin into the collar of his sheepskin jacket, the rifle ready across his thighs. Briefly, before he answered, he took his eyes away from the fire to consider me and shook back his blond curls. 'It's a stalemate,' he said. 'Nothing's happened.' His eyes went back to the fire. 'First Eric, then this.' He sniffed. 'It's not such a good time for a wedding.'

'Good,' I said, and patted his thigh. Couldn't help it. I supposed his mother might have done the same. I'd even started calling him 'son'. Now I'd admitted my age I thought I might as well act like it. Some of the time. Brain was a decent man and was the best-looking catch in the camp. As I told him. 'Basher would be mad to pass up on you. Especially for The Gaffer.'

When Wide Boy was watching I couldn't resist the temptation to climb the rope again.

'Hiya,' he said, shifting quickly and stuffing a magazine inside his jacket. He cleared his throat. 'Football.'

'Uhuh?' He shrugged his shoulders, seeing me still looking at him. 'D'you mind if I keep you company?'

'Naw, on ye go. Pull up a boulder.' He spat out his gum and I stifled the urge to reproach him. We sat in silence.

'How's Robyn?' I eventually asked for something to talk about.

'Good!' He scratched the back of his neck. 'A bit brighter.'

'Good.'

'Aye.'

I looked out of the side of my eyes at him.

'What?' he said. 'Ye keep lookin' at me.'

'Do I? Sorry.' I think I make him nervous when it's just him and me. After two and a bit years he's still a jittery teenager.

'What age are you, Widey?'

'Eh, nineteen.'

'Really?'

'Come October.'

328

Robyn was about thirteen. I hoped he'd give her a few years before he tried anything. You heard about girls getting pregnant at that age. But that was mostly in primitive societies.

I stood up, ready to climb back down. 'You'll take care of Robyn, won't you?'

'Who, me?' A grin. 'Aye, Yak.'

Down the pit was cosy without the generated light. My eyes had grown used to the lantern glow or the candles. Limpet was story-telling the baby to sleep. Grace, Junkie, Saleema and the twins were crocheting – squares for a blanket that they could all work on, since Grace had already done a shawl. I picked up a hook and worked lines of shell patterns in alternating pink, blue and white. When it was safe, I'd go to Glasgow's library HQ and find a book about spinning and dyeing so we could make use of the sheep's wool since it would be so much warmer.

The Gaffer took the final shift. By now it was late, and I was worried that Peej wasn't back. I couldn't sit still to crochet. Besides, the bones inside my right hand were growing stiff. The women's eyes followed me as I left the group.

'Off to see The Gaffer?' Limpet asked me and, beside her, Junkie and Robina smirked.

'Shh!' Robyn said and tilted her head to indicate Saleema.

'Certainly not,' I said. 'I just want to see if there's any sign of Basher and Peej.' Despite that, I could feel my cheeks heat. At the base of the shaft I paused. I was tired, now. But I was fired up by curiosity and indignation at what the girls had implied. I shinned up the rope, my arms straining, my feet slipping from the knots, but I made it.

'Hi,' I said.

For two months he'd been frosty towards me. I hate a man who bears a grudge.

'It's a cold wind, isn't it?'

'You should just have stayed in the pit, then,' he said and smoothed his hair down.

'And miss those stars?' I'd long since cleaned my glasses, but I gave them another quick rub. Without the city's lights the sky was no longer kept in the background; the black space was just that – space – and the stars sparkled round our shoulders, like plankton in a sea, or diamonds in suspension.

'It's about the only benefit,' he said.

'Peej not back?'

'No.'

I sniffed. We sat without speaking. I put up the hood of my coat.

'Are you cold?' he asked, not risking much more than a glance at me.

'A bit. I just wish they'd come back.'

He pulled off his gloves and passed them to me.

'Are you sure you're alright without them?'

'I'd have trouble firing this rifle if I was wearing them.'

Inside they were fleecy and impregnated with his warmth. I studied him as he studied the view down the hill. He'd always tried to keep his hair neat, but it was curling where it touched the top of his ear and collar. He'd kept a good head of hair for a man of his years. Small wonder he was always smoothing it.

'Are you going to marry Saleema?' I blurted.

He screwed up his face and shifted position on his stone. 'Well, isn't that the sixty-four-thousand-dollar question?'

Only he and I and Bill and Grace were old enough to know the relevance of that. I didn't get anything else out of him because we heard Peej's whistle. The Gaffer whistled back. We didn't see Peej and Basher till they were three or four metres away from us, our eyes trained to the orange glow or the tiny sparkles of the stars.

'Whit are you doin' up here?' Peej said, hard voiced, the minute he saw me.

'I just wanted to see what was happening.'

He tutted – I heard him in the dark and imagined him scowling. Then he squatted at the top of the shaft to be at the same eye level as The Gaffer. 'Eric's wi' them,' he said. 'That's how they know where we are.'

Chapter Sixty-seven

Eric was with them. It could be the worst possible news, or the best kind. If Eric was with them, they would have insight into everything about our campsite. Assuming he told them. Would he? I couldn't say. The three faces round me bore the expression I could feel on my own face.

We decided, up there at the mouth of the shaft in the dark, that none of us would let out a single hint of this to anyone. This was our secret. 'I mean it, Yakkity,' Peej said, singling me out as if I was most likely to tell everybody. As if I couldn't keep a secret.

'Yeah!' I said, angry with him. 'Nobody but the four of us is to know.'

Later that night I lay on my bed. Along at my end of the pit it was already quiet. Robyn and Robina were early to bed most nights (Robyn only occasionally now having an accident); heartburn was interfering with Junkie's sleeping patterns but she was weary in the evenings. It looked as if she was unconscious, cuddling round her unborn baby under the covers. Bill and Grace were sitting up reading which I should have done to keep my mind occupied. But I didn't: I just kept hoping sleep would come and drug all thought. I tossed and turned. Bill and Grace put their lights out, their mattress creaking as they settled.

I imagined Eric going to the bikers. Willingly, according to what Peej and Basher had said. They'd sneaked up under the shield of darkness till they were on the perimeter of the house-warming-party. Sure enough, it looked as if the bikers had lit it deliberately. A terraced row of six had gone up in the blaze. They could only guess at how they'd started it, but watching it the bikers liberally doused their throats with alcohol. And Eric was there, if not in the middle of them, at the very least in one of the groups on the fringes, drinking and laughing.

'Is he still limping?' I'd asked Peej.

'He'll be limpin' fur the rest ay his days, doll.'

No doubt he's holding that against us. Me, probably. Not for the first time I wondered if he really had loved Sara and I felt myself softening. But that didn't mean I'd forgive him for Robyn. Would Eric give our location away for revenge? If he'd wanted to join their club, it might have been the price of the membership.

Peej and Basher had been tired but they decided to take a car and drive to the army base even though it was nearly midnight. I'd stood up and kissed Peej's bristles when they were heading off.

'Take care,' I said.

'Who me?' He squeezed my waist and made me flinch away. 'You get down to yer bed.'

I'd kissed Basher too. He caught my hands and tried to keep me at arm's length.

'Let her have her snog, man,' Peej said. 'Then let's get away.'

Basher relaxed his grip on my wrists and I leaned in. His cheeks were fuller than Peej's.

'Bye,' I said.

'Cheers. Come here, The Gaffer.'

The Gaffer and the others had stepped aside to have a final word. When I asked him what it was about he said he'd just to stay on guard till Peej and Basher came back. I wasn't going to get any more and that's when I went to my bed.

After more than an hour of sleeplessness I heard their voices and something metal clunking the walls of the shaft as it was lowered in ropes. I sat up and switched on my torch. It was just a weeny one. Just a little dot of light that soon gave up when it tried to reach the other end of the shaft so I couldn't see what it was they'd brought. They saw my light though.

'It's alright, Yakkity,' Peej said. 'That's us back. Brain's goin' up on guard. You get back to sleep.'

And I did. I felt safe then, knowing Peej and Basher were

back. I wasn't too curious about the metal they'd brought: what good would it do me? They were men and we'd gone back to living in a men's world. Assuming we ever left.

*

I woke from a deep dream with a fright, hearing the ornaments jingle in Grace's display cabinet. I knew it must be Eric coming after me. My diaphragm rose in my chest but my voice wasn't with it. I stared wide-eyed at Robyn's bed, struggling in the dim light. He hadn't reached it yet. He hadn't put his hand on the rail at the foot of my bed either. I tried to remember where I'd put my knife. I pinched the covers from my ear to listen for his breathing. My heart was stoonding like before but I thought I heard him whispering. Maybe he had it in for me. Maybe he was standing behind me right now with a silenced gun. Or a knife. A serrated one. A silk stocking garrotte. Like a doe in long grass my eyes strained sideways but couldn't see the hunter.

Then I heard him.

'O-o-'

My other senses compensating.

'Open up fur Peejie.'

I flattened myself on my front and buried my face in the pillow. The bastard! The sheep-shagging evil cunt of a bastard!

A sleepy female voice murmured.

It wasn't Eric! It wasn't Robyn. It was Peejie, a metre from my bed with that little whore Junkie. And the bikers doing their war-dance up above us, ready to murder us.

Peejie.

And there I was positively palpitating for him. I cried real tears into my pillow. I cried sore tears as I heard Junkie's bed be nudge nudge nudged to that special rhythm.

I hated Junkie. How I hated her then. I was old and she was beautiful. I was past it and she was pregnant. She was probably even pregnant with Peejie's baby. And I was a stupid old woman, fooling myself about him all these months. He wasn't interested in me; never was and never would be and he wouldn't ever give me his baby because I was old and I was shrivelled up and I was ugly.

333

Chapter Sixty-eight

I let them all go out before me. Told them I didn't feel well. Why should I go up and make breakfast for them? Draw them water and warm it so it wouldn't be too cold to wash their delicate little faces? Scrub the nocturnal emissions from their sheets with my withering hands?

Peej wasn't in Junkie's bed when I woke up. That meant he probably made a habit of it. As for her, I wondered who else she got to do her servicing. The slut. The slapper. The hoore. Tart, slag, prostitute, harlot. And I wondered what she demanded from them instead of money.

I hardly slept a wink that night, listening to them. When it was time for waking up, who was the sleepy one?

'Are y'alright, Yakkity?' wee Robyn asked when she saw my head still burrowed into the pillow and my covers up over my ears.

'Leave me alone,' I said, not even looking at her properly.

'Aw – okay.'

Her voice sounded hurt. I sat up and apologised. 'I just don't feel well,' I said, which was, in a way, almost true. I checked for Peej at the end of the pit. In that quick look he was acting normal. Wiping the barrel of some big new super gun.

She perched on my bed and touched my hair. 'Well. Jist you have a long lie. D'ye want me to bring ye yer breakfast?'

I clasped her hand and put it to my cheek. 'No, it's alright, pet. Thanks. I'll get up in a minute.'

Off she went with the others. Including Junkie. I hadn't even spoken to her – pretended to be asleep when she bade her good mornings. *Cow* – I'd forgotten that one. She waddled like a fat *cow* up the passage between the beds. She'd put on weight at her fat backside this time. I watched her from under my covers. She was last and that so-and-so Peej was at the front tunnel end waiting for her but all they did was give each other a tiny smile. Bastards. Deceitful bastards. Doing that and not telling anyone.

'Y'alright, Yakkity?' he called to me.

'I'm fine,' I roared.

'Aye, well, don't lie there all day,' he said. 'Might need to get organised, remember.'

He put his hand on her back and helped her bend through the tunnel, following up the passage behind her.

When I heard the commotion that accompanied Junkie being hauled up in the cradle and I interpreted the subsequent quiet as meaning that Peej had climbed the rope, I relaxed my grip on my covers and sat up again. They'd left me the lanterns on, down at the living end. It was still quite gloomy here but despite a memory of Sara that I quashed quickly that was alright. I got out of my bed and crossed over to Junkie's. She'd spread it but I bet it was still warm. She'd a silky quilted mat, Junkie, in rose pink. Said it was the very nicest thing she'd ever owned. I ran my hand over it. I thought for about twenty seconds of taking my hunting knife and ripping it. Cutting *cow* or *harlot* on it. In fact I went as far as going over to my bed and looking under my pillow for it but I'd left it in my belt. There was only my torch under my pillow. I took that anyway. Took it and pulled back Junkie's covers so I could inspect for crispy semen stains. As I thought, there was more than one of them. I glanced at the tunnel entrance; couldn't resist sniffing them. Short little animal sniffs. Piss and come and fart concoction.

I was still in my jammies and it was chilly. That was why I slipped in and pulled her covers over me. Sashayed myself down into the position I'd seen her in during the night before Peej got in, wrapping her body around the baby in her womb. It made me think of when I'd been pregnant. I got back out and searched in my rucksack under my bed. Took out that long-preserved Cotes du Bourg and glanced down to The Gaffer's end where the wine opener would be but the need to see my baby was even stronger.

I took out all my photographs and went back into Junkie's bed, covers up at my ears, in peace and quiet to look at them.

I was right – it was still warm. It was still warm and it smelled – womanly, with womanly body odours and a fruity perfumy scent embedded in her cherry-patterned pillow. I pulled out a lavender sachet and a used handkerchief from under it along with her neatly folded cotton nightie. I stuffed it back in and looked at my pictures. I looked at my mum and my brother; one of my dad and my gran. Most of all I looked at the ones of me with my baby. My seventies photos when I was wearing my short skirt and my high boots with the platforms, the shawl my mother had knitted spread over my lap and my dainty little baby's face beside her brown teddy.

'Junkie?'

I jumped out of the bed, scattering my photos. The Gaffer was in the living area. I tugged at her covers. He stepped closer towards me. I raced for excuses.

'Alice?'

'Em – hi. I thought I saw a mouse in it,' I said, pointing to the bed. 'Or, well, a rat, really.' We were worried about the rats. We'd a shoot on sight policy if ever we saw them. So far they hadn't made it down our pit shaft, but we were waiting.

He kept walking towards me. 'What were you doing in Lee-Ann's bed?'

Fuck, this was going to look awful. I hung my head in mortification. 'Please, Frank, don't tell her. It's a long story. It's not what you think.' He'd think I was a lesbian. 'I just – I just.' How could I tell him?

He stepped right up to me and picked up some of my photographs. 'Are these yours?'

I pushed my hair off my face. Tried to hide my silly feet under the bed so he wouldn't see them. 'Yes,' I said. 'They're all mine. I wasn't touching anything of Lee-Ann's – honest.' Apart from her bed of course.

He studied the one of my mother during the war. 'Are you sure?' he said and turned it over to check the back. 'It kind of looks like her.'

I took it off him. 'It's mine,' I said. 'It's my mother.' I looked at her. It was a black and white portrait photo. A studio photo. How could a respectable 1940s woman with finger pressed waves look anything like a bleach-blonde Junkie?

He glanced through some of the others while I stood in shame-faced misery then he handed them back to me. It was like being reprieved for shop-lifting. I think. 'Don't do it again,' he said.

'I won't. You can rely on me.'

'I mean it. We need to respect our privacy.'

'Absolutely.'

He looked me up and down in my Betty Boo pyjamas. I hoped they weren't stained with anything. 'You should get dressed and get upstairs. Things are happening.'

Chapter Sixty-nine

The Gaffer had come down to have some rest. Up top, there were still only a few of us who knew the full situation. Peej had of necessity had to inform Brain and Wide Boy. Presumably pillow talk had passed the info on to Junkie and Limpet but I couldn't assume so. For all I knew everybody could have been pillow hopping while I slept but I had to assume that the danger of our situation was to remain a secret from Limpet, Junkie, Bill and Grace, Saleema and Salaam, Robina and Robyn. But how could you keep it a secret? We weren't permitted to leave camp; the weeds in the fields were to be allowed to unfurl tenacious tendrils; we had to return to the dishwater-dull-diet of dandelions and tinned tuna, so they knew something was happening. I crept back downstairs to check our stock pile and bring up something we could eat for lunch. Someone had messed up my arrangement: far from the orderly classification of meat, veg, soup, pud and the rota system of short dates to the front, longer to the back, it seemed some irresponsible person had ransacked them and restacked them willy nilly. And we certainly seemed to have eaten a lot, in comparison with the last time I looked at this pile.

Anyway, I found half a dozen ravioli tins that were only a month or two past their sell-by dates and threw them in a bag. It clanged against the new gun toy as I swung it over my shoulder. I froze and looked at The Gaffer. He snorted but stayed asleep. He was lying on his back, arms behind his head. I stayed well away from him and scurried back up the rope with the tins in the pack on my back.

'What's going on?' Junkie asked me as I was stirring and ladling.

338

'What d'you mean?'

'You know what I mean. What did the men fun oot? Last night? What's that big gun fur? And where did they get it? All Peej'll tell me is he got it from the army and he's testin' it.'

I kept my eyes on my pot. 'Yes, that's what he told me.'

'So, what did they see last night?'

I could keep her in ignorance. I could enjoy the power of knowing. But then again, I could enjoy inflicting the fear on her, of being an eight month pregnant young woman who was raped by the bikers and lost her last baby. And now they were coming back for second helpings. Imagine the damage the stress would do to her. 'You'll have to ask Basher.'

Imagine how she would run and fall and worry she'd ruptured her womb or something.

'Basher?'

'Or Peej. Or The Gaffer.'

Was that her waters she could feel, dribbling between her legs? And the barbarians chasing her. Or blood?

'How? Did they no' tell you?'

I spooned in two ladlefuls for her and passed her the plate. 'Who am I that they'd tell me?'

'I suppose so,' she said and went to sit down with her meal.

*

The men kept busy all afternoon. They took it in turns to patrol the grounds. 'What makes you think they're going to come after us?' I asked Wide Boy when it was only him and me sitting on the mat. 'It's been well over a year.'

'Yeah, but we cuffed them last time. Remember? An' it took them long enough to get themsels thegither.' He was dismantling and reassembling his gun. He lowered his voice. 'And if they've got Eric, they'll know everything aboot us.'

I sipped my rosehip and elderberry tea. The real stuff. 'Well, Peej told me they were covered in gold and jewels, so they must know we've nothing they'd want.'

He shook his head. 'Nah.' He checked to make sure Peej wasn't listening. 'They've no' got kids or women.'

Sex slaves of the rich and infamous. That was about the

339

worst thing I could imagine. That was the one comment that set my heart pounding. One image more than I needed.

Chapter Seventy

By evening I think I'd walked six miles in little circles. I'd play Yahtzee with the kids for a bit then be overcome by the jitters and walk round the circuit, up over the hill – never out of sight – then down towards the crop strips and round to the bottom field end and back. Then I'd come back to the camp and eat a handful of liquorice. Repeat the method then suck at a perfect peppermint. I couldn't risk having any whisky, even if The Gaffer could be persuaded to let me.

The children were becoming irritable. The men were strained and hardly talking. Grace started *Bluebirds over the white cliffs of* and Brain – Brain – said, 'Oh fuck's sake Bill can you not shut her up?' You could almost hear the collective in-breath.

'What did the boy say?' Grace said, but nobody repeated it.

Bill's eyes brimmed. He stalked off with her, hirpily, walking her down to the bottom field edge.

'Nice one,' Peej scolded him. Brain.

Brain didn't reply.

I had to get away, so I walked up the hill again. I felt close to Sara, here, near her grave and the tiny plot where Peej had buried Junkie's baby, but more and more I was drawn to the buzzard. It was there as always, performing slow figures of eight with the ragged tips of its wings barely wavering. The ground up here was rough and it took all my effort to lift my feet clear of the tussocks topped by long grass. Anyone could be hiding in the neuks. I scanned the field but there was only nature's tranquillity. Tranquil to me: a peewit was calling; the field mice would be standing frozen or scurrying. I remembered reading that buzzards hunted their prey by following the UV signature of their urine trail. Sometimes, I supposed, there were forces working against us using powers we couldn't predict.

My nostrils were filled with the scent of May flowers and I sneezed. The buzzard flew further off across the field. I turned to watch it and saw the whole valley, yellow lit in the late afternoon light. Then, like the Romans, I saw a light reflecting. Just a little light, like the sun on a car wing mirror. Or the chrome of a motorbike. I took out my opera glasses and swam my vision up through the yellows and whites of wild flowers in the grass, past the crop strips and beyond.

'Jesus Christ!' I yelled and started to run. There must have been more than a dozen of them.

'Peej! Peej! Peej!' I yelled like the peewit on high alert. 'Down the valley! Look!' My voice climbed higher and higher. 'Dozens of them!'

The Dykenders wouldn't move fast enough. I was at top speed; despite my crazy feet I leapt over the uneven ground making hardly any contact with it. In the time it took me to run fifty metres Robyn and Robina, Salaam and Saleema had only dropped their jaws.

'Down the rope!' I shouted.

Basher moved like a vinyl record played at the slowest speed. He pushed the kids towards the rope; they were big enough to shimmy down themselves now. Limpet and Salami followed; Junkie needed the cradle.

'Junkie! Junkie!' I shouted, angry for having strayed. She was over by the washing barrow, folding clothes.

Brain and Wide Boy had gone for a sleep; Peej ran with his gun in his hand to the crop strips and the direction I'd pointed. The Gaffer followed him.

Then we heard them.

Ululating.

I voided my ravioli.

Basher picked up speed as I came closer to the camp but he still ran through the air as if it was viscous.

I heard a zing as a shot whipped out. Junkie dropped.

'Junkie!'

When I reached the camp, Brain and Wide Boy were

342

surfacing with the cradle.

'Help her!' I screamed.

Basher had slung his rifle over his back and was crouched beside her. Peej and The Gaffer had thrown themselves to the ground, ready to shoot when the bikers breasted the hill. Peej saw Junkie drop and scrambled to his knees but more shots thwicked into the ground and he turned back and fired.

Now they'd caught up with my speed. Basher raised Junkie who was still clinging to her washing. He ran with her, half bent over and with his body shielding her, half way to where Brain, Wide Boy and I could help her then he ran to support Peej and The Gaffer.

'Shit!' Wide Boy said as the air destabilised with streaks of bullets.

My ears rebelled against the racket: men yelling and the explosions of gunfire. It made me even faster.

'Get her to the cradle,' I said, as if they needed someone to tell them.

'Get down, Yakkity.'

I grabbed the rope and launched myself into the hole.

'Bill and Grace!'

Wide Boy looked behind him. Bill and Grace were still at the field end. 'Can you two get her doon?'

I nodded and scrambled back up the rope to help Brain take Junkie's weight in the cradle, praying I wasn't more of a hindrance. 'Hold the rope, Junkie!' I shouted.

Her lips were colourless and her sweat top was grass stained as I watched her descending. She didn't seem to be bleeding. I prayed she'd just fallen and the washing had protected her baby.

'I'll never forgive myself if anything happens to her,' I said to Brain.

He was straining to take the weight, digging his heels in against the decking. 'You didn't do anything to her,' he said. But he didn't know what I'd been thinking.

When the rope went slack Brain told me to go down after her but I wanted to stay with them.

'Don't be fuckin' stupid. You're a woman,' he said. 'Get

down!'

I pretended to begin descending. When his back was turned I stopped to watch them.

There was an army of bikers coming. When Brain reached Peej, Peej broke away and ran towards me at the pit mouth.

'Get out ma way,' he shouted and I climbed up again.

'Are you going to check on Junkie?'

'What?'

'Are you getting out of it?'

He looked at me as if I was stupid. Maybe I am stupid.

'I'm goin' fur the gun.' He threw his leg over the edge then thought about it and took off his rifle. 'Take ma gun,' he said.

'Me? What'll I do with it?'

'P-p-p – Point an' fuckin' shoot!' Then he disappeared.

I heard a cry that wasn't an ululation. Bill's shirt was red with blood. Wide Boy was trying to support him but he was too stiff and heavy. Grace was howling.

The shots were still coming.

Wide Boy pushed them to the ground and shouted something, crouching low then threw himself to the grass between The Gaffer and Basher and started firing.

They would run out of bullets. I knew it. For now they were holding back the bikers, but what about when they used up all the ammunition?

I heard a noise and looked up over the hill, afraid they'd attack from another flank, but it was only Peej climbing back up the rope.

He checked the others then grabbed my upper arm.

'Are ye strong, Alice?'

I nodded.

'Can ye give me a haun haulin' the gun up?'

'I'll try.'

'Right, doll.' He glanced round again. The Gaffer's gun had stopped. 'Give us that.' He took his gun from me and ran with it towards The Gaffer, throwing it the last few metres. Then he was back beside me.

I was trembling.

344

His hands were quick and firm on the ropes. 'Grip that. Wind it roon' yer wrist. Now, pull! Pull!'

It was coming up unevenly. I thought it was going to tangle. Then I thought it was going to pull me into the shaft. I'd to let go: searing my hands.

Peej's heels smeared up the ground but he braced against the decking and caught it.

'Sorry!'

'It's alright – BASHER! Get ower here!'

Basher was behind me. He took over the ropes and they brought the big gun to the surface and swung it into position. I blew on my palms to try to cool them.

By now the bikers were beginning to run forward. Brain and Wide Boy backed away, edging closer to the pit mouth while Peej and Basher sought to align the barrel.

'To fuck wi' pinpoint accuracy. Blast them!'

The bikers roared towards us. A bullet whacked into the tree behind me.

'Get doon that shaft, Alice!' Peej yelled but I was frightened. I didn't want to be shut in the darkness.

'All ay ye, doon!' he shouted as Wide Boy and Brain reached us.

The staccato of his sudden burst of machine gun fire obliterated everything. I couldn't hear myself when I shouted, 'Bill and Grace! We can't go down without Bill and Grace.'

The gun was holding the bikers off. Their front line had dropped, defensively or because Peej had shot them. Under cover, Basher, Wide Boy and Brain ran towards the field edge to Bill and Grace and brought them over. Bill was bloodied. Grace's face was streaked with red; she had red on the palms of both hands and wouldn't leave Bill alone, not even to go down in the cradle. I was sure they would break it. Wide Boy scrambled in after them to help them at the bottom. Brain helped Peej with the ammunition.

There was a lull in the firing. In the silence my ears felt light. Then from the crop strips I heard wounded men moaning and Brain braced his foot against a stout low branch to give himself height.

'They're running! Away!'

'Get it up yez!' Peej's fist cut into the air.

Our men whooped but I couldn't help staring. Men were lying motionless in the grass and wildflowers where I'd gone on my walk with Salami. Closer to us, our sunlit camp was broken. Our camping gas stove had been clipped but hadn't exploded. The aluminium pan had a hole in it and the displaced metal twisted like a jagged tin foil flower. Over on my right my tent looked as if it had been streaked through with bullets. Further beyond, the grass between us and the fence post was colour-washed with Bill's blood.

'What a mess!' I said, unable to stop myself from shaking.

Brain had a marbled look to his eyes. 'We trounced them, Yakkity. They deserved it.' He worked frenziedly, ejecting used cartridges from guns.

Robbed of finesse I sat down clumsily. 'How could anyone deserve this?'

He spat. 'Maybe they should never have started it.'

Basher put his hand on my shoulder and told me to go down the rope.

I looked up past his brown tweed jacket to his brown face and into his eyes. 'I don't want to go down in the dark, Basher,' I whimpered. 'I don't want them to shut me in: I'm frightened.'

Peejie twisted from where he was crouched, adjusting the gun. 'I'll no' let them shut ye in, Alice,' he said. 'These guys are gonnie be back, but this time, once an' fur all, we'll get the bastards.'

Basher's massive hand tilted my chin. 'Alice,' he said. His voice was smooth and steady. 'You're a good woman. Go an' look after the children.'

Then Peej said, 'Aye, Alice. Go an' take care of Lee-Ann.'

346

Chapter Seventy-one

By dusk the bikers hadn't come back. Our men stayed on alert as before, only this time, two by two. Peej and Wide Boy took first watch, crouching back to back at the shaft top, half-expecting them to come from another direction. In the pit, despite the keening from Grace, Basher and Brain tried to sleep.

When Bill and Grace had been lowered into the pit, Wide Boy and The Gaffer had carried Bill and lain him on his bed. By the time I went down the lantern was lit beside him. Grace was leaning over him, fluttering her hands over his face and chest like a descent of moths. She was bloody from her elbows to her nails and impeding Limpet from peeling off his shirt. Limpet crooned to Grace while Saleema attempted to ease her away.

Salaam was helping The Gaffer sort through boxes of ammunition that seemed miraculously to have appeared and down at the far end, in the gloom, Robyn and Robina were playing with Salami on their beds. Salami was the only one who was neither subdued nor fraught.

I looked for Junkie. From the mound I deduced she'd taken to her bed and I hoped she didn't smell that I'd been in it.

'Alice!' Limpet called me to Bill and Grace. 'Saleema, get more towels.'

I slipped my arm round Grace's elbow and pulled but she was a heavy woman – a lot heavier than my six or seven stone – and didn't want to come away.

'Gracie, come on.' There was such a lot of blood. 'Let me clean you up.'

She wailed something incoherent. She wouldn't let Bill go. His face on the pillow was a slack beige, patterned with the bloody prints of Grace's fingers. His thin lips were indistinct.

His brows were unruly and white, though even those were tinged with crimson curd.

Despite Grace's interference, Limpet managed to undo his shirt. I saw the hollow at his throat, the white hair on his chest and dark blood oozing from the rawness at his stomach.

'Oh Bill!' I mouthed and sought Limpet's eyes.

Grace cried out loud when she saw his wound then her resistance broke. She stood, arms limp, not really seeing anything after.

Limpet asked, 'Are the rest alright?'

I nodded.

Saleema arrived with towels. We ripped them into squares and used them to staunch Bill's blood. Four of us round his bed was a crush: it really only needed Saleema and her mum. And a doctor, but we didn't have one of those.

I took a piece of towel and rubbed at Grace's arms, but the blood had dried. 'Let Limpet look after him,' I whispered to her. 'Limpet and Saleema'll take care of him.' She let me lead her to the living area. I had to watch where she put her feet. The ground was arrayed with packages and cartridges and wires that The Gaffer was hauling out of boxes, selecting some for Salaam to take to the cradle. There was no space for us and I still hadn't taken care of Junkie.

I took a bottle of water and led Grace away from the living area, back past Bill, whose hesitant breathing almost stopped us, up to the back where I sat her on my bed, facing Robyn.

Robyn gave Grace a frail smile. I poured water on the towel and squatted between the beds, took her hand and turned it over. Robina groaned. Junkie wasn't moving. I rubbed the blood with the towel: Bill's life was ingrained in the lines of Grace's palm. A damp towel wouldn't scrub it out but I cleaned her as well as I could then poured her a tumbler of water and got the twins to sit with her while I went over to Junkie.

The cherries on her pillow case were wet. So were her eyes.

'Hi,' I said.

She sniffed but stayed where she was.

I crouched beside her; rested my hand on her shoulder, on

348

the silky mat. 'Are you alright?'

She hid her face in the covers. I resisted my stupid instinct to stroke her hair. She sniffed, pushed down her covers and rubbed her eyes hard. 'What we gonnie do, Alice?'

'Peej sent me down to take care of you.'

'Peejie?'

I swallowed. 'Yeah, Peejie.'

She couldn't fight that one: she sobbed, open mouthed and panting. Neither could I. I clapped her hair: it was soft. I bent and kissed her temple.

*

We ate sardines out of tins and washed them down with water. I munched on dried-up brazil nuts and sultanas till their weight lay in my stomach like a lump of wood. We needed Bill and Grace to start a sing song to relieve the tension. Or Chis. But we had lost him too. The trouble was we'd made too many enemies. Escalated to war instead of negotiating peace.

I worried about everything and the time was slow to pass. Bill wouldn't stop bleeding. When Limpet and Saleema tried to wind a bandage round him, more blood oozed each time they slid a hand under his waist. In the end, they gave up trying. His breathing was more and more halting. I knew the worry on Limpet's face was the image of my own. Abandoned for too long, Salami started to girn and wouldn't go to anyone except his mum. Robina scolded Robyn for not taking care of him.

'Brain's had an idea about something,' Saleema said, out of nowhere, and rather shyly. 'He's been working on a new kind of connection.' She went to his bed with what I thought was just a bit too obvious familiarity, only restricting her movements when she realised how close to her sleeping father she was, and came back with some sort of heavy device. The Gaffer had finished sorting through the ammunition. I noticed the pensive look on his face when she was telling us about Brain. He moved his feet without saying anything so she could attach the gadget to the cycling generator and clear enough space for us to sit. 'It's for playing the DVDs,' she said and lifted a flap that turned out to be a TV screen. She put on an animation. Immediately the children were drawn to it and their mood lightened but Salaam kept forgetting it would cut out if he stopped pedalling. The wail of the soundtrack slowing and restarting was more irritating than Grace's singing. I didn't know how the men could sleep through it, yet they did. And the sound drowned out Bill's intermittent breathing. I met The Gaffer's eyes: the kids were laughing but there was a kind of sorrow in him.

I took Grace up to the living area and Junkie came and sat beside her, linking arms and asking if she was alright, but her eyes glazed over before Grace replied. Now and then I noticed her hand pick at the grass stain down the side of her sweat shirt. 'Are you sure you're alright?' I asked in a low voice.

The mistiness cleared. 'Aye.'

'Have you felt the baby?'

She smiled to me, a worry-free smile, and wound an escaped strand of hair back into a clasp. 'Aye.'

I wished I could be worry free. I jerked every time I heard a sound from the entrance tunnel. When I heard shouting it took all my resolve not to run to the opposite end.

'The Gaffer! Ye got the rest ay that ammo ready?'

It was Wide Boy's disembodied voice. The Gaffer scrambled to his feet and grabbed his gun, ungainly despite the weight he'd lost over the last two years. He paused by me, catching my eyes for a moment. 'Wish me luck,' he said and I realised he might be frightened.

'Take care,' I said. 'See you in a minute.'

He cleared his throat and dipped to go into the tunnel. Moments later we heard sounds in the shaft as if someone was coming down.

I rose and stood beside the entrance tunnel.

'Who is it?'

Whoever it was didn't reply. I looked to Basher and Brain's beds but the men were still sound. I touched the handle of my knife.

'Who is it?'

The footsteps stopped. It was too dark, lit only by the lantern beside Bill and the DVD to see. Salami stopped pedalling.

'Who's there?' I squealed.

'Waaa!'

Wide Boy burst out of the entrance tunnel with his arms in the air.

The children giggled but I slapped him hard a dozen times in a perversion of Grace's hands fluttering over Bill. I was close to crying.

'It's me!' he said. 'No' the fuckin' enemy.'

I turned away from him, fists clenched, remembering Sara's ned men. 'Don't you know we're frightened?'

He'd come to wake up Brain and Basher. When they went up Peej and The Gaffer came down. They ate and went to bed. Soon we all did, the DVD left for more settled times. I let Grace have my bed and I stayed up beside Bill, watching his chest rise and fall in his sporadic efforts at breathing.

I dozed in the chair beside him, the lantern still on and its yellow light gleaming on the china figurines in Grace's display cabinet, little Hummel children with ruddy cheeks; robins playing tug of war over a worm; slender fairies paler than Bill with their gossamer wings stilled. Her standing lamp didn't work but looked homely with its mahogany pole turned on a lathe and its shade trimmed with a fringe of dusty golden brocade.

Peej and Junkie touched fingertips before they went to bed. Down at their sides so no one would see. I saw. I saw the way each held the other's eyes. And now they were at opposite ends of this long pit, Junkie curled round her baby and Peej round his gun, sleeping with half an ear listening.

Chapter Seventy-two

'Alice.'

I woke with my neck stiff. The Gaffer's face was very close to me and his eyes were brown. I wiped a saliva trail from my cheek and straightened in my seat.

'What is it?' The rest of the pit was in darkness. Only Bill was lit. Somewhere I was aware of a distant sound of thunder.

'I wanted to give you this.' He put a black leather box on my lap.

'What is it?'

'I've to go up top again.'

I heard the quiver in his voice and forced myself to wake up more. Bill was breathing. The box was heavy on my thighs.

'In case I don't come back – this is something I want our settlement to have.' He paused to let me register that. 'Open it.'

My thumb trembled as I tried to unfasten the gold clasp. The hinge creaked slightly as it opened. Inside, on a bed of purple velvet, was our Provost's heavy golden chain of office. 'Where did you get it?'

He sniffed and looked around. 'I stole it.'

'You what?'

'I stole it. I didn't want just anybody to have it.'

I smiled and ran my fingertip over the enamelled medallions that represented our town's coats of arms through successive boundary expansions. 'It's beautiful. Does Peej know you've got it?'

'That rogue? He'd have pawned it by now.'

We smiled, frostiness temporarily forgotten.

'I want you to keep it. Safe. In case I don't come back.'

'Don't talk like that, Frank,' I said. 'We're going to be

alright.'

My eyes followed his to Bill.

'Not all of us, probably,' he said then he took my hand and lifted it to his mouth.

I always thought he had flabby lips. I forgot he'd lost a lot of blubber. His lips performed a gentle suction on my skin that wasn't unpleasant.

He winked at me and for once I didn't feel a sense of revulsion. It was just the way he was. He'd never expected his life to turn out like this and he was afraid. I watched him go.

'Go fur it, pet.' Bill's voice was broken.

I closed the box lid and put it on the bed. 'How are you feeling? Would you like some water?'

I poured some fresh and helped him lift his head off the pillow to sip but it made him groan. His wrinkly hand juddered as he brought it to his wound. A fresh wave of blood seeped into the bandage.

'In wan end an' oot the other,' he said. 'Where's Grace?'

I put the cup down and stroked his hair and cheeks. I was getting quite adept at this. 'Safe. In my bed.'

He closed his eyes and went back to sleep. When I was sure he was deep I edged my way to the backpack under my bed and put the box in beside the incunabulum and my photographs. None of them would help me survive, but if I had to run, these were my essentials. I thought back to the library, when I prepared to leave alone, or alone with Sara.

The twins, Grace and Junkie were breathing quietly. I crouched between the beds, still clutching my rucksack and let the regular sound steady me. I left that Cotes du Bourg under the bed. I didn't need it. Those days were gone. How much better, this home, with these people, than my sanitised flat?

Some part of me realised I couldn't hear the men. I tucked my bag away again and stood. It was too dark to see beyond Bill's lantern. If The Gaffer had gone up, had Peej and Wide Boy gone up too, swapping places with Brain and Basher? I fumbled my way back towards Bill's lantern then looked beyond it. Limpet was sleeping alone. I passed through the next partition to where the men slept, but Brain and Wide Boy, The Gaffer and Peej's beds were empty. They'd all gone up and left us.

The thunder rumbled again and I knew it wasn't thunder.

Chapter Seventy-three

It was the sound of guns. My stomach bit on that dense lump of wood I'd swallowed and I panicked. I ran to the tunnel entrance, hesitated, ran back and stood in the middle of the men's beds. What was I doing there? I turned back to the tunnel entrance and went through it.

At the base of the mine-shaft the noise was even louder. My whole body quaked in another blast. I looked up to see the rough-hewn walls clad in silver. Black shapes distorted the circle at the top. Our men were feet down, firing. I felt for the rope but it wasn't there.

'Peej!' I squealed.

I heard the zip of a low jet then a boom.

'Peej!'

In the next flash I saw them duck their heads. They were balanced four feet down, on the wooden ledge, firing from the protection of the shaft.

My hands found a hold and I climbed about a metre, bracing my feet against the stones. 'Peej!' I called again.

When the blast came, the shaft rang with it and my ears whistled like a kettle. The light was the sorest: I couldn't take my hands away from the walls to cover my eyes. Fumbling blind, I found the lowest of the posts Wide Boy had hammered in and kept on climbing. Soon my head was a metre below the men's feet. Close enough to smell them, I couldn't go further. They'd strung up the net.

'Peej!' I shouted.

He heard me. Twisted to look down. 'Yakkity? What the fuck are you daein'?' he shouted. 'Get intae the tunnel!'

Another blast and his spiky head had a halo. The hawthorn

that concealed our shaft was in cameo against the white sky. Then black again. I smelled acrid smoke.

'I can help!'

He climbed down and put his face close to the net. 'Ye cannae help, Yak: it's a man's job. Away an' keep the kids calm.' He cringed in response to another blast. There were flames this time; to the right the sky flickered red and orange.

'What *is* that?' I asked.

He gripped the thick net. 'It's the big one. A fucking rocket launcher. Eric knows where we are.'

'Eric?' I shook my head. 'Could Eric do that to us?'

His hand slipped through the net and I stretched up and fitted my face in it, grasping his wrist.

'Peej!' The Gaffer shouted.

He kept his attention on me. 'Tell Limpet and Junkie to get ready.'

I released his hand but clung to its scent. Cigarettes and ammunition. 'Don't let them shut us in!' I pleaded but he'd straightened up already out of my reach.

Nervous sweat made my hands slither, quiver back down the curtain hooks. A blast and I jumped the last metre. I folded myself at the bottom, my head tucked between knees and arms, a mouse in a hole with a cat paw reaching down for me. A rabbit trapped underground. Something solid rained on me. I pulled earth from my hair and flicked it from my shoulders. We'd be shut in. Eric knew everything. He knew my greatest fear and would wreak his revenge with that. Another shower of earth fell and I stood.

Wait a minute. If they wanted to bury us, wouldn't they just lob in a hand grenade? What was it Wide Boy said Peej heard them talk about? They didn't have any women. They could have anything they wanted – rob any amount of jeweller's shops, banks and building societies, drink any amount of booze they wanted – but they didn't have women. We were what was valuable. Women and the ordinary social bonds they represented. I remembered the fishermen in North Connell. The way they looked at Peej and didn't address their eyes to me. We were the most precious commodity. Saleema, Robyn, Robina, Limpet and even Junkie. My own usefulness was borderline. But I'd be safe if I just stayed with them.

There was another blast and this time one of our men cried and lost his footing. I saw him fall into the net, backlit, then clutch his leg, but I couldn't see which man or separate whose voice against the raucous backdrop.

'Alice! Are ye still there?' Peej's voice stood out from the others.

'Yes!'

'We're gonnie lower Wide Boy tae ye.' Wide Boy. 'He's blacked out. Can ye catch him?'

They strapped him up and unhooked the net then let the rope slip, pulley fashion, till Wide Boy reached my arms. Christ, he was heavy. I sank to the ground under his weight. My hands shook as I unstrapped him.

'Wide Boy!' I said, leaning my back against the shaft wall so I could nurse him. His weight compressed my chest and crushed my leg folded under him. 'Wide Boy.' His strong sweat, the earthy shaft and the sweetness from the men's urine bucket amalgamated with the fireworks smell.

I felt down his leg for injury. Felt the greasiness of his denim and railed at myself for not taking better care of him. What would his mother think? My hand touched something wet. 'Oh, Wide Boy. Don't be as bad as Bill,' I told him.

There was another shower of earth from above. They were becoming more accurate. I knew I'd have to get Wide Boy through the tunnel. I'd still to waken Limpet and the others. I thought hard about where I was and eased him to the side so I could rest his shoulder and head against the shaft wall; found the tarpaulin cradle. There wasn't much space. I managed to spread some of it out and drag his hips on to it, even though it kept wrinkling. I put my foot on it to keep it flat and dragged him, holding him under the arms. His hair smelled of smoke; the curve of his ear was hot against my lips.

I lay his shoulders and then his head down then crawled into the tunnel ahead of him. My fingers kept slipping on the taut tarpaulin but I managed to drag him in stages up the uneven incline into our living space. Caught my breath leaning on the tins of food and the scatter of ammunition. I couldn't move him another inch, but he was beginning to come round.

'Ahya,' he moaned and started breathing through his teeth. 'Ma leg.'

'Big baby,' I said to him. I kissed his forehead and he gripped my jumper.

'It's dead sair, Yakkity.'

I cuddled him round his chest; squeezed his skinny ribcage. 'I'll get help.'

I unhooked his fingers and dragged him a little bit over from the entrance then I went to waken Limpet. She woke like a switch and started dressing. I caressed Grace's head. Woke Robyn and Robina with a kiss.

'Junkie,' I said, shaking her shoulder. She was utterly sound. 'Junkie?' I looked around. Robyn and Robina were beginning to stir. Grace was still asleep. 'Lee-Ann,' I said, stroking my hand in long sweeps up and down her spine. 'Lee-Ann, you need to wake up now.' Her eyes flickered. The cradle was down. I didn't know how we'd get her out. The men would have to carry her. I toyed with her hair. 'We're going to escape.' She opened her eyes and looked at me and neither one of us said anything more.

I went down to the living space and lit the other lamp. Went to see Wide Boy. By now, Limpet had roused her children. Saleema had heard him moaning and was crouched beside him. I gave him some pills. They were only for headaches but it was the best I could do. I shone the lantern at his leg: the wound was near the top, but it was at the outside. 'How did it happen?' I asked him. I knew he'd been shielded by the shaft.

'That Irish bastard,' he said, glancing at Saleema. 'Rick O'Shea.'

I used my knife to cut his jeans.

By this time Robyn had realised he'd been hurt. She flapped her hands like Grace had and burst into tears, dripping on his chest.

Saleema and I peered up close at his wound; tried to work

358

out the angle. It looked as though it wouldn't have reached the bone. 'It's only a flesh wound,' I told him.

'Only?' he said and gasped. 'This is "only"? Fuck me.' He raised himself on one hand and slid over to the supplies. Helped himself to a long swallow from a bottle of Scotch.

Robina's hand touched my shoulder. 'Yakkity, where are all the men?

'Up top,' I said, dragging my thoughts from the bottle. I took stock. 'Get everybody to the living area.'

I went to wake Grace up. Sat her up and wrapped a blanket round her.

'Listen ti that weather,' she said.

I didn't answer, just walked her over beside Bill. 'Sit here,' I said. 'I'll be back in a minute.'

The others were all gathering in the living area. My voice started shaking as I told them. I told them it wasn't thunder. The gang had come back and our men were fighting. 'We can try to escape while it's still dark,' I said. 'We'll climb up and slip out one after the other and run down the hill before they can see us.'

There was a few minutes silence. I could see people looking to either side of them. 'Go and pack some bags with the very basics. Not food; not water. Just the things that are personal. Not even clothes. Travel light: just special jewellery, something that proves your identity; photos.' I steeled myself. 'Some kind of weapon.'

'Can A take ma See You Jimmy hat, Yakkity?' Salaam asked.

It was the tartan tammy with the ginger wig Peej and I had given him. 'If it's the thing that matters most.'

'Can A take ma iPod?'

'What about Bill and Grace?' Limpet said. Then, quieter, 'And what about Junkie?'

We all looked at her. She was enormously pregnant.

' Don't worry aboot me,' she said. 'It's Bill and Grace A'm worried aboot.'

I hadn't told her about the rope being down. But she must have been able to see Wide Boy on the cradle. Even with the rope, how would we get through the shelling? I rubbed my forehead. 'Everybody go and get ready.'

'Whit aboot you?' Wide Boy said when the others had moved off. 'What are you takin'?'

I shook my head. But I knew exactly what I was taking. I had it ready. I sat in silence, trying to make out from the guns what was going on.

'We'll never be able to get everybody oot here. Not that wey.'

I looked at him. Didn't have time to ask what he meant. There was a racket in the pit shaft. Men coming down fast: men jumping the last couple of metres. I recognised the sound of their feet slapping the rock.

Brain burst from the tunnel. 'Up the back,' he said. 'Everybody up the back. They're comin'. Come on – everybody!' He looked at Wide Boy as The Gaffer came through. 'Can you shoot from there?'

'Jist give me a gun,' he said, struggled to his feet and limped over to the screen that separated the area from the men's beds.

Brain and The Gaffer were dividing up the rest of the ammunition. 'Catch,' Brain said and tossed Wide Boy a stubby automatic. 'Get back, Alice,' he said, seeing me hovering.

Basher then Peej came out of the tunnel. 'That's the spikes out. There's nothin' else fur it.'

They'd pulled out the curtain hooks on their way down and turned the points upwards. Wide Boy's barbaric protection system. I ran to the back, crouched down between Junkie and Robina's bed with my arms round the twins' shoulders and prayed it would work.

Peej looked around us. 'No time for speeches. We know what we're doin. We'll pick them aff if they come through.'

I think his eyes lingered on Junkie but it might have been Bill and Grace. Then he squatted with his gun trained directly on the tunnel entrance.

Basher stood up. 'Have yez all got a torch? Keep them handy but don't put them on. We're gonnie put the lights oot.'

They put them all off and I felt a surge of panic. Only Bill and Grace's remained lit. There were sounds in the tunnel. Brain stretched to turn out their lantern as a glinting lump of metal described a low arc through our living area. There was a pause – not even a second – before our black mine went negative. I oscillated with the scream. My ears ruptured. I swore I'd gone blind. Then a geyser of light flashed out of Peej's gun and our home reverberated with the drill of automatic fire.

Chapter Seventy-four

The ground under my knees bucked and struggled. I've never been in an earth quake. It was coal black. My whole body, not just my ears or my head, was roaring.

Robyn and Robina screamed in each ear. I squeezed my fingers in their clothing, drawing them under, tucking them in. Ten metres of rock were going to fall on us.

We coughed in the coal dross. Other people were coughing. I heard it because the noise stopped: the rumbling and the firing. I opened my eyes but was still devoid of vision. All I knew was the twins were alive because they were screaming: screaming yelped between coughing and I wasn't letting go of them.

Louder than all I could hear someone wailing. Basher shouted, 'Cover yer eyes: A'm lightin a torch.'

I took my hand away from my eyes. A fog glowed at the far end. Yellow. Wherever I looked the image was the same, burned on my retina. I blinked to clear it but it didn't go. I heard relief in people's voices but dull, as if my ears were stuffed with asbestos.

Another wail turned my stomach rancid. Other torches clicked on. Soon we'd enough light to see. I cleaned my glasses. The pit was hazy: windowless black with dust morphing into distorted shapes.

Peej stood up, the back of his leather jacket soot-dusted. He carried his gun in his hand. Basher followed. They stepped over a fallen chair and some debris.

'Wait here,' I said to the twins and got up half crouched to follow the men. My lips were dry; there was too much dust for my tongue to lick off. My eyelids were stiffened by it. Under my feet the path was gritted.

The men had moved to the living area. Dirt streaked their faces. Brain was looking at me.

'What is it?'

Peej stepped back, his tongue bright pink and I saw that the tunnel had disappeared. Our shoring had given in. I clutched my stomach. But it was worse than that. Eric was caught in the tunnel collapse. The rocks lay on him at right angles. He was pinioned by the hips and legs.

'Eric!'

He moaned, face in the dirt.

'What are you doing here?'

'He's the wan that did it,' Peej said. 'He threw the fuckin grenade.'

I went down on hands and knees beside him, twisting to see his face. 'Why?' I asked him.

A jagged schist of rock was spiking his back. I tried to ease my fingers under it to see if I could pad it, but the rocks were too heavy. Ten metres of rock above us. There was blood and dirt in his hair and at his nose. I ran my hand over his greasy cheek, over his wiry black hair; the rubber necklace of skin at the back of his neck when he tried to look up at me.

'Only a stun grenade,' he whispered.

'It's alright,' I said.

'Don't give him any sympathy!'

'Shut up!' I shouted. 'He was one of us. And he's hurt.'

'A'll pit him oot his misery.' Peej clicked his gun's firing mechanism. 'Should've done it before. This wouldnae have happened.'

'No!'

'Yak –'

'Let me ask him something. Somebody get him a drink a water.'

'We need to find a way out here,' Basher said.

Brain passed me a bottle; I damped the sleeve of my coat and wiped his eyes.

'Why did you do it, Eric?'

He clutched my fingers when I held the bottle to his mouth.

'Because he's a fuckin pervert, that's how,' Wide Boy said.

The ceiling creaked.

Eric moaned. Blood trickled down his forehead. I moved closer to his mouth. 'Why, Eric?'

'I couldn't take bein on my own.'

'Yakkity.'

'...They were there for me at the beginning, when I didn't have anybody.'

I stared at him. 'At the Horsebrasses Bar?'

'I couldn't take being on my own.'

'Alice.'

I looked up at Peej.

'Come here a minute.'

I put the bottle down and stood up, wiping the dust from my clothes. 'He didn't want to be alone.' I looked at them all. 'You can understand that?'

Peej nodded, pointed and said, 'Stand ower there a minute, doll. Ower by the wall.'

'The wall?'

'See that book ower there, doll? Aye. Get it fur me.'

I looked at the other men. Their faces gave me no clues. I walked to get the book Peej wanted.

A single bullet cracked. Something sprayed the back of my trousers.

'No!' I spun and stared at Eric then moved my eyes to Peej. 'No!' I whipped the book at him.

There was a creaking noise from our ceiling. The crack extended, brittle as egg shell, a crooked finger pointing to the back of the pit.

'Look what ye've done! We're gonnie get shut in!' I went down on my hands and knees, oblivious to the gore round Eric's body. I scraped the debris with my fingers. Looked over my shoulder at Peej and Basher and the others just standing; the children crying behind them. 'It's not all down,' I said. 'It's just the beginning. Together we'll be able to move it.'

Dust drifted on to me from the ceiling.

'That's gonnie go,' The Gaffer said.

364

'Everybody back. Right back! Back as far as ye can go.' Peej tugged me by the arm. 'You as well.'

I shrugged myself free. 'You,' I said. My legs, stomach and arm were shuddering. 'How are your guns gonnie get us out of this?'

'Up the back!' he snarled in my face, his blackened skin stretching tight round his red mouth. The Gaffer put his hand on his shoulder but Peej tossed it off. I shrank back; sure he would hit me.

'Alice!' Limpet shouted and I dodged out of the way.

'Fightin among ourselves willnae help,' Wide Boy said. 'That crack's gettin bigger.'

The Gaffer tried the weight of the men's partition. It was an MDF display panel. 'We could try shoring it up,' he said.

Ten metres of boulders.

'That's nae fuckin use,' Peej said. His scar was twitching. I heard the children crying; looked over and made out Robyn and Robina clutching each other.

Dirt and a patch of cloud crumbled from the crack above the men's heads and settled on their hair. Basher shook it off then went up to the back to Limpet. The baby was struggling against being held; his round eyes were scarlet with rage and terror and tears were streaking clean tracks down his cheeks. Basher tucked him under his arm; he wiped the tears from Salaam's face with his thumb; the eleven-year old's arms were glued round his mother's waist.

'We'll need to try the back way,' Wide Boy said.

We all looked at him. He stood up, holding his wounded leg stiffly.

'What back way?' The Gaffer asked him.

'Ask Brain. It's his knockin shop.' Wide Boy looked at Brain. 'Sorry, pal.'

Brain glowered. 'Thanks, man.' He turned and looked up through the gloom to the back then rubbed behind his neck as if he was facing execution. 'It wis hardly a knockin shop.'

Basher stepped into the passage and moved towards us with the baby under his arm. Brain's lips were compressed but his focus was further behind Basher.

'Dad!' Saleema said and I knew where he and Saleema'd disappeared to.

'It's just a passage; it goes on quite far,' Brain said, clawing at his ear.

'How faur?' Peej asked, putting his arm out across Basher's chest to stop him.

'Fifty metres?'

'Fifty metres is nae good. Is there a wey oot?'

Brain was rubbing up through the back of his hair now. 'I'm not really sure.' His eyes darted on and off Basher. 'I've never went that far.' Basher glowered but Brain brightened. 'Ask the twins; they keep spare food there.'

Peej took a fistful of Basher's jacket and turned him. Basher's head was slow to turn from Brain, but he moved when Peej prodded him, to the back of the pit.

Peej shone his torch into the narrowing hole then onto the twins. 'How faur d'ye go?' he asked them.

They shaded their eyes. 'No faur, Peej.'

I found energy to climb the beds and reach them before the rest of the men. 'Ye're not getting a row, girls. Ye've not done anything wrong.'

Babes in the woods, their arms interlocked round each other.

'Twinty steps? Thirty?' Peej asked.

There was a loud creak and a fifteen-centimetre gap appeared in the ceiling over the living area.

'Shite!' Wide Boy hirpled from where he'd been sitting, heading towards the back.

'Are yez all away?' Grace had been sitting quietly. Wide Boy paused at her display cabinet. I swung over Junkie's bed and back towards her. I'd forgotten about Grace.

'Bill's no' talkin,' she said.

I stared at Bill's chest: it wasn't moving.

'He's deed,' Wide Boy whispered to me.

I patted his arm for him to move on. 'Grace. Ye'll need to come with us.'

'Yous? Where are yez goin?'

The ceiling bulge was dipping into the pit. I could hardly talk, I was so frightened. 'We're goin fur a walk, out the back there. Everybody.'

Basher passed me softly and picked up his family's holdalls. Peej and the other men packed quickly.

'Is everybody goin?'

'Aye. Are ye comin?'

'Even Bill?'

Junkie forced her way past me up the side of the bed and took Grace's arm. She linked fingers, the backs of her hands smooth, her purple tipped thumbs caressing the shrivelled skin on Grace's hands. 'Bill's deed, Gracie. Come on, babe. Ye need to come away wi us noo.'

Grace rose, confused. 'A havnae got ma purse. Are we goin in a taxi?' She touched her hair. 'A havnae got ma hat.'

'Ye'll no need yer hat.'

I looked up at the ceiling. It was the same shape as Junkie's belly.

'Hen, A cannae leave without Bill. A've spent twenty-five year wi the bugger. That's us had wur silver weddin.' She sat back in her chair.

'Come on, Grace!' Junkie said. As she tugged at her a pendant swung out from the neck of her sweatshirt. It glinted in the light and I recognised one half of Peej's I Love You.

I had a strange sick feeling and my ears popped. When I looked up the walls were bowing. 'Grace!' I shouted. I heard it ripping. 'Leave her, Junkie!' I wrenched Junkie's arm, trying to tug her awkward shape through the gap between bed and display cabinet.

Then Peej was there: he shoved the cabinet and all the ornaments shattered. He scooped Junkie up and ran to the back of the tunnel with her. 'Move it, Alice!' he shouted.

The ceiling tore. I sprang after him, swinging between Robyn's and my bed. 'My backpack!'

'Leave it!'

The bulge burst like an inverted volcano. Earth and rubble fell on our living area, the men's area, on top of Grace with her

367

head and arms on Bill's chest, heading for me.

'The incunabulum! My pictures!'

Someone's arm scrunched round my waist and hauled me into unrelieved blackness.

Chapter Seventy-five

Dropped on my feet I lunged forward blind through the tunnel, one hand above me and one to the side. Dust in my mouth. I tried to filter the air through the rough tweed of the coat I was wearing. The dampness from my breath pasted the fibres to my lips; the moist heat tattooed my skin. Behind me the rumble of the cave-in was diminishing. Only coughing gave me direction and told me I wasn't alone. Somewhere ahead, Salami was crying: the only one young enough to let it out.

'Watch yer feet.' Peej's distant instructions found a pin-hole in the darkness. I still tripped. A hand found my arm and hauled me up. It encircled me above the elbow.

'Ye're with me.'

I nodded, unable to see The Gaffer's face.

'It narrows up here – mind yer heeds,' Peej called. Then after a few minutes, 'It's awright fur you kids. Ah knew Peter Pan had the right idea.'

'Who's in the lead?' I shouted.

Nobody answered.

'Everybody stop.'

I bumped into Wide Boy. I knew it was him because I recognised his smell from when I'd cuddled him.

'A'm gonnie put on a torch,' Basher said. 'Cover yer eyes: it'll be bright.'

He shielded it inside his jacket. It was just enough to begin with, to make out where we were and the look of terror on our faces. Everyone was stooped; lit like the moon. Peej was in the lead, his hand holding firmly to Junkie's. Next came Robyn and Robina as if they were their children. Then Brain. Then Basher and his family. Then a small gap before Wide Boy and The

Gaffer. I was at the back. Poor Eric. Poor Bill, poor Grace, I was thinking. They should be behind me. Poor us, I was thinking. Poor me.

'Has anybody else got a torch?'

Two others were lit. We were a blackened and sorry lot.

The tunnel was narrow and crooked. Seven feet tall at one side, it sloped down to three feet at the other. Its walls were pock marked with weeping sores and striped in bands of brown and black which glinted like glitter as Basher swept over them with his torch.

Peej tapped Robina's shoulder. 'D'ye think that's gold?'

Fool's gold maybe. Even at this distance, his face was more lifeless than I've ever seen.

'Who's been as faur as this?' he asked but nobody answered. 'Aw, come on. Naebody?'

I caught Robina's eyes, hoping she was covering up, but she shook her head and I knew she was telling the truth.

'What're we gonnie do, Peej?' she asked him.

'What we gonnie do?' Peej said. He looked to the back where I was but more out of wildness than for inspiration. 'We're gonnie keep two torches on, that's what we're gonnie do. An keep the other as a spare. An we're gonnie keep goin, right? An every now an then we'll switch the torches aff ti see if there's any sign a light.' He sought the go-ahead from The Gaffer. 'Is that right?'

'Peejie?' Robyn put her hand on Peej's sleeve.

'Whit, darlin?'

'How long's it gonnie take us ti get oot?'

He looked at Junkie, who was leaning the small of her back against the rock. 'Jig time, hen. We'll be oot a here in jig time.'

*

My watch said 5.35. My watch said 3.83. It was the last time I was going to choose digital.

We didn't have a sense of direction.

We halted when Junkie or Wide Boy needed a breather; we put the lights out and searched with every rod and cone of our eyes for the faintest glimmer.

370

We had false hope when the path took the ascent. Then a steep drop that meant slithering heel-squatted down an escalator of grit betrayed it.

Salami was passed from adult to adult; when my turn came his face was sticky with mucus: opalescent strands from his nose to his hand glistened in the torch light. He wrinkled his nose against my shoulder before I could find a tissue. He girned in my ear and smelled as though he'd filled his nappy but I had no energy to make him smile and no nappy bag with its lotions and wipes to make him clean. Ahead of me, Limpet was dragging on Basher's arm.

I stubbed my foot and fell awkwardly to protect the baby.

'Alright?' The Gaffer asked, helping me up.

Up at the front Junkie bowed with both hands on her stomach. 'Oh fuck,' she groaned. Wide eyed, she searched for Limpet and me.

'Whit is it, doll?' Peej asked, as if we couldn't guess. 'Bastard!' he hissed into the empty tunnel. 'Fuckin bastard!' As if that was going to help anybody.

'Let's have a breather,' The Gaffer said.

'We cannae stop now,' Peej argued but she clutched his arm and squatted, and we all followed suit. My watch said 3.21. Or maybe it said 8.51. I didn't know. I started counting to see if her contractions were close together. They didn't last long, but she was tired: I could see it in her face even at this distance and in this light or maybe I knew it without having to see. I knew how I was feeling, and I wasn't pregnant.

I leaned on my backpack against the wall with Salami between my knees. My shoulders ached from the weight of the rucksack, my arms from restraining Salami. He was girning for his mum and I felt so much lighter when Limpet called him over, holding out a toy. He clambered over The Gaffer's knees, was lifted over Wide Boy's and struggled on.

'He's a trooper,' The Gaffer said to me.

I couldn't give a fuck about Salami.

Peej, at the other end of the line, was looking at Junkie. I should be glad they'd found each other. I turned my face the other way and stared back into the darkness. Once again, I'd lost everything. Everyone I ever loved was taken away from me. Maybe I could just lie down here and get it over with. Do a Grace, an Eric, a Bill. A Mum, a Dad, a Bobby. A Boss. A Sara. A Heather stroke Margaret Mary. But unlike my dad I didn't have the bottle – or the black bottle. Or the cyanide capsule in a cavity in a tooth. I wished I had the Cotes du Bourg. I wondered how much air there was and if it was lack of air that would kill us. My life was in ruins and I'd no enthusiasm to rebuild it. I lay down.

'Are you alright?' The Gaffer said.

What kind of stupid question was that?

He leaned up on one hip and fiddled in his back pocket.

I raised my head. 'What the hell are you doing?'

'Would you like a sherbet bon-bon?' he said, bringing out a white paper bag from his trousers. 'They're still quite good.'

I scoffed and put my head down again. I couldn't give a damn about his bon-bons. I had too many metaphysical concerns on my mind, trying to crowd out the physical ones. Like how it was I had come to this. I was a scheme girl, the daughter of a clapped out alcoholic. I had made a mess of my life and I had no right to dream of a better one. I was tortured by the weight of my own philosophising, but the bursting intensity of the sherbet and the luminescence of its probable colour insinuated itself till I couldn't resist it. I leaned up again.

'A strawberry or a lemon one?'

Even in the gloom, even with him moving the lump of toffee around his mouth, I could see his eyes grinning. He held the packet out. 'Guess.'

The paper was still warm from his pocket. I put my fingers in and separated one of the powdery pebbles.

'Close your eyes, mind. No cheating.'

I closed my eyes, even though it was almost pitch dark, and put the sweet in my mouth. It was just the way I'd anticipated it. I rolled it round my mouth – strawberry or lemon? Oh, it was absolutely clear. The colour flooded my head: winter sunshine filling my room. I smiled as I began to speak, and the excruciating sourness crackled in the hinges of my jaws.

'Lemon,' I said, rubbing my cheeks. 'So sour!'

He nudged me with his elbow and nearly knocked me down again. 'Good, eh?'

'Yakkity!' It was the alarm in Peej's voice, rather than my name, that made me stand up. I narrowly missed jarring my forehead against the projecting side of the tunnel's walls.

'What is it?'

'A need ye.'

I stepped over legs, plunging through shade and light, a sillier sausage than Salami as I answered Peej's call.

'What is it?' I asked him, trying not to let my eyes reveal what a fool I was.

Junkie was still squatting. The light glinted off the fine skin of sweat on her upper lip that had washed out the coal dust from her pores.

'A've had three contractions since we sat doon, Alice,' she said. 'What am A gonnie do?'

It hadn't been as long as that. I tucked the toffee to the side of my mouth and looked at my watch. It was 8.54, or maybe a digital curvy 9.34. I didn't know what time it was. I couldn't even remember the time I'd thought it was the last time I looked. I sat on the ground beside her.

'We'll count how long they last – and how much time in between them.'

She licked her lips. 'They're wan on tap a the other. This is it – A'm huvin it. It's jist like the last time.'

I pressed her hand and kept my eyes on the second counter of my watch – funny how that sort of thing comes back to you. The next wave gripped her for 52 seconds. When it abated, I waved my hand over her face to create a draught while we waited for the next. There was hardly time for two minute digits to change before it came and she was off, squeezing my hand and Peej's and not letting slip a sound.

'Oh Jesus,' she moaned when it was gone. 'A hope it isnae comin here!'

The meandering Salami's foot wavered, trying to find a flat

surface on Junkie's body.

'Get him aff!'

'He wants to tickle you with the feathers on his toy.' Saleema had moved into the space vacated by a squeamish Brain. She dragged her brother away.

'It's not, is it?' Peej said to me in a low voice. 'Tell me it's not.'

I was the best read non-mother in the universe. I recognised the irrational irritation of the transition phase. I couldn't avoid Peej's eyes now – I skipped over them, skipped away and nodded.

'Aw f-f-fuck!'

His shoe scored the sandy earth as he swivelled on it and stood up.

'Where the hell are you goin?' she yelled. 'Don't you think you can fuck off out of it!'

He spun, hands high up on the narrowing walls. 'Where the hell could A go?'

Brain moved down closer to Basher. Limpet swapped places with Saleema. Together we tried to make Junkie comfortable. But how could we? How can you make a woman comfortable when she's giving birth in a tunnel? But I wouldn't let her be like Sara.

She endured another contraction and Peej stood exactly where he was. Limpet and I took her hands. I kept an eye on my watch. A full minute. It wouldn't be long.

The pain subsided. 'Aw, that's a gorgeous wee breeze,' she said, lying with her eyes shut. But none of us had moved.

'Can you still feel it?' I asked her.

'Jist keep daein it,' she said.

I looked at Peej, wondering if he'd heard her.

'Naebody's fannin ye, doll.'

Junkie opened her eyes and looked straight into mine. 'Naebody?'

Limpet and I shook our heads.

'Or blowin on me?'

No. Maybe she was imagining it. Peej came over and squatted right up close to me; close enough to feel the warmth

374

from his arm and leg.

'Close yer eyes.'

'Wait a minute.' And she was seized in the fist of another contraction.

When it finished and she'd got her breath back we held ours and she shut her eyes.

'Naw – A can still feel it. A'm tellin ye,' she said.

I pulled my sleeve up and held my bare inner arm above her face. Everyone else stayed rigidly still, holding their breath.

'Put out the torches,' I said.

We put them off. I fought against the panic of being buried in the dark; controlled my breath. We waited, knowing it would take our eyes time to adjust. But even after another contraction in the dark – Salami whining, Junkie's faint whimper at the peak of the spasm – my eyes, bulging like someone with goitre, couldn't pick out any light.

'Imaginin it.' Peej switched the torch on, holding its face to the ground so that just the red rim roused our eyes.

'A'm no imaginin it!'

Hand on her shoulder. 'Look, doll, there's nothin.'

Salami's boot waved again as he tried to reach us. Junkie's face contorted in frustration and annoyance and Limpet trilled a litany of her own language at Basher and Salaam for not keeping a hold of him and Salami wailed as he was howked out and away again.

'He just wants to tickle you with his feather,' Limpet explained.

I had a lightbulb moment. 'Put the torches on. Saleema – pass him over again.'

'What?' Junkie panted.

'Tell him to bring his feather.'

I held him in my left arm, far away as I could from Junkie, considering the tight space. I let him tickle me the way I'd tickled his chin with the buttercup, his big eyes black in their massive den of lashes.

'Can I borrow your feather?' I asked him, tugging it firmly out of his grasp.

Junkie was suffering, but when the pain passed I held the home made tickling stick in front of her face and told everyone to hold their breath.

Peej moved the torch so it was shining down directly on it; we waited for any air current he might have caused to subside and we stayed still. I reckoned we'd about thirty seconds before Junkie's next pain started.

Salami wriggled. I squeezed my grip round his waist then bent my head to him, tickling his cheek with a butterfly kiss from my eyelashes. I couldn't see the wood pigeon feathers. Salami leaned his head back to give me better access to his plump brown cheek; the laughter gurgled in his throat. I felt the coarse skin on Peej's hand take the feather stick out of mine; recognised from my view of his leg and feet that he was slowly standing up.

Junkie moaned and Salami whipped upright, giggling out loud now, digging his boots into my leg and reaching for my lashes. I wiped his hand away so I could watch Peej. Like some fairy godmother he was holding the tickling stick out at arm's length, trying not to breathe on it and clearly following in the tracks of some faint breeze – some definite breeze that wasn't coming from any of us but was finding its way to us, ruffling the feathers.

'Boys!' Peej said and I fitted myself and Salami into the contours of the rock as the men's legs stepped one by one over and between us.

'A need ti push,' Junkie said.

'Wait fur me,' Wide Boy said. 'Ye're no' leavin me with this lot.'

Basher called for Salaam and the men went on, leaving us one torch to pick out Junkie, Limpet, Saleema, Robyn and Robina, little Saadi and myself. Junkie bore down again and I knew it wouldn't be long.

Chapter Seventy-six

My eyes gave up the ghost of the men's light but my ears clung to the echoes of their feet and the mumble of their voices. Junkie was pushing.

'It's comin,' she said.

I was sure it would be quick. Her first had been quick, while I'd been at school. The second was always faster – wasn't it – the road having already been travelled.

Limpet passed Salami to Robyn and Robina with a handful of biscuits from her pack. She and I tried to pad the rock under Junkie's hips and back; Saleema was ordered to find something warm to wrap the baby.

I tugged Junkie's tracksuit trousers off her and her pants, moving her to have the delivery end facing away from the girls. I took my coat off to cover her in case any of the men came back, but she was distraught with the pains and had lost any self-consciousness, possessed by the force that splits a woman, amoeba fashion, from single cell into mother and child. She dug her nails into my skin, gripping my arms.

'It's comin, Alice.'

I glanced at Limpet who was holding her other hand and shielding her from the children. It was taking too long. There was no sign yet of the men coming back. We badly needed good news.

Junkie was tiring: her groans were louder, protracted, moaned out each time her diaphragm convulsed to make her bear down and ghosting through the tunnel in both directions.

'Is she gonnie be awright, Alice?'

I heard the fear in Robyn's voice. Robyn, who, if she'd been a year or two older, that bastard Eric – poor Eric – might have made suffer this.

'She's going to be fine, darlin,' I said, squeezing faked optimism through a tight windpipe. 'And the men'll be back any minute, tellin us they've found us a paradise by followin that breeze.'

Again I met Limpet's eyes.

'Any sign?' she mouthed.

The gloom showed only the V of Junkie's smooth thighs and a wet gloss in the dark base. 'Pass me the torch.'

Her vulva was ruddy. Blood and mucus dribbled from it. The labiae were parted. I shook my head to Limpet but then another contraction came and Limpet raised Junkie to a sitting position and braced against her.

'Wait!' I said, seeing something white. Like cling-filmed heroin or cocaine. Oh shite. I growled at myself. How could I still feel this way about her? Purple-white. Would it be purple-white if it was a head?

It was a foot. Clear as could be it was a foot. My God, I couldn't speak to tell Limpet what I'd seen but she knew I'd seen something. I covered my mouth with my hand.

'Whit's wrang? Whit is it?' Junkie said.

I shook my head but she knew it was a lie.

'Has it got nae heed?' She tried to sit forward. 'Has it got nae heed?'

Limpet bobbed her head to look. 'It's fine – it's fine!' she said. 'Alice's sickly at the wetness.'

I checked for any sign of the men coming back but there was no light.

A foot. A foot and only one foot. My fingers touched my knife. I'd have to cut it out; I'd have to do a Caesar, or an episiotomy and all I'd had was a half day training in First Aid.

'Feel for the other one,' Limpet said.

'The other whit? Whit's wrang wi it noo?' Junkie, panicked, had to be told.

'It's being born feet first,' I told her.

'A'm deed.'

I sat back on my heels. I couldn't do this. I was a librarian;

I could only read about things. I wasn't meant to be crouched in the dark under some mountain with a tart giving birth to the yob I loved's baby.

Another contraction. A minute and a half of repressed agony. The foot slipped out, white with greasy vernix, red streaked with mother's blood. Pointed heel; perfect little toes.

And then I counted them.

I counted them and the pit around me convulsed with the shock I felt.

I pushed my fingers into her vagina: I felt I could reach right into her womb. I found what I hoped to be the other foot and pulled. My fingers slipped away empty. I rubbed the grease on my trousers and tried again. It was the foot: I could make out the indentations of the toes. I eased it further down the birth canal. It appeared, white, so bluey-white. I prayed this wasn't taking too long; prayed the baby wasn't going to be born too young.

'Here it comes again.'

I gripped Junkie's upper arm and fixed my eyes on hers. 'You can do this,' I said, repeating it, over and over, fusing through our eyes till the contraction passed.

And slithering out came the little bottom, the narrow back.

'It's a girl!' I said, before I even saw her face.

'A lassie!' our girls repeated.

And then the shoulders and arms and a full head of spiked hair.

'Is she awright?' Junkie asked.

'Wipe out her nose and mouth,' Limpet said.

'Has she got everythin?'

'She's perfect,' I said and held her, hiding her feet in my hands, until the mucus dribbled out of her lungs and she cried her first breath. I checked her feet without drawing attention to them then kissed her hot forehead, filling my nostrils with her coconut sweet smell and gave her up to lie on her mother's chest to be quilted by her mother's hands.

The afterbirth came soon after and I found a proper use at last for my hunting knife. A woman's use.

Chapter Seventy-seven

Junkie was tidied by the time the men came back. Their voices reached us first, then the misty sweep of their light on the walls of the tunnel. Peej knelt straight away beside his baby. He didn't see me but I had other things on my mind.

We stopped and started for a mile and a half along the tunnel, strung out, the men taking it in turn to carry Lee-Ann. She let me carry her baby. I carried her all the way and she was never heavy. My arms were shaking by the time we made it to the streamers of light.

'It's jist round this corner,' Salaam said and he broke into a run.

There was a wider bit. I stepped against the wall to let the children through. I wanted to be last. It was too much for me to take in – what we'd come through this last – how many hours. I couldn't see my watch with Junkie's baby in my arms. In the lateral shafts of light I made out her features. Her head was rounded, not compressed, because she'd been a breech baby. Her head was perfect. Her eyes were closed and her mouth was red and sweet as a wild rose hip.

'You alright?' The Gaffer asked me.

'Fine.' I looked everywhere except at him. I wanted to be on my own with this baby.

He put his hand on my arm as if to shepherd me but I shrugged it off.

'I'll come in a minute.'

'I'll be outside.'

He walked off and I waited between the light and the darkness. Six toes, she had. Six toes. I pulled back the jumper she was wrapped in. Her legs were pulled up and knitted. I

unfolded one little leg and kissed the toes. It was unmistakeable.
How could I explain it?

'Are ye comin, Alice?' Junkie called from Peej's arms with
the light streaming round them.

'Watch ye don't drap her,' Peej said.

I moved towards them; they turned and we walked to the
entrance. I could see colours again. I had to shield my eyes
against the sunlight, tucking the baby in to my breast to protect
her eyes. I filled my lungs as full as they could go with clear
blue air.

We were half way up a rough green hill at what seemed to
be a natural cave opening. Maybe it was the original entrance
to the mine. Below us the hill was grassy and rubble strewn
down to a small brown burn. A row of red tinged trunks of Scots
Pine, topped with their coxcomb of blue green needles, crested
the hill while the paper white bark of silver birch trees stalked
intermittently up towards them shaking their drizzle of leaves.

Peej set Junkie down on some soft grass and she turned to
me to take her baby. It was colder when I gave her away; The
Gaffer must have seen me shiver because he came over and put
my coat round my shoulders, even though it was almost summer
and I should have been warm.

The children were running wild as deer over the hillside.

'That's where we're headin,' Peej said.

Across the burn and in a loop of land skirted by water was
a square medieval keep, crenulated at the top.

'It's Dykend Tower,' I said, looking round. 'How did we
get here?' We'd cut across country, underground. 'The bikers'll
never think to look here.'

'Ye can forget the bikers,' Peej said. 'They'll either be
crushed in oor tunnel or they'll think we were.' He put his arm
round Junkie and their baby. 'But we'll stay ower there onywey.'
He winked at me. 'Drap bilin oil on their heeds if they come
anywhere near us.'

The men went to check it out, leaving us on the hill. I knew
where I was now. The nearest town was a mile or so to our
left; the moor stretched out in the direction of the sea over to

our right. The fields in the valley looked lush. I walked back to Junkie. She was sitting on Peej's jacket, on a boulder, with Limpet and the girls surrounding her.

'What're ye gonnie call her?' Robyn asked, her finger clutched in the baby's ruby fist.

'A don't know, babe. Whit d'ye think?'

Aleesha, Stacey, Bethany, Bernadette, Chantelle, Becky, Elise, Amanda, Rochelle.

'Naw, it has ti be a good name. A special name, know whit A mean?'

I saw my moment. 'What did you say your mother was called?'

Junkie wrinkled her nose. 'Naw, A'm no callin her efter ma mother.'

Sheryl, Andreena, Erin, Ainsley, Chloe.

'What about Heather?' I said and waited a moment. 'Or Margaret?'

'They're dead old fashioned,' Robina said.

'What about Margaret Mary?'

I think Junkie fleetingly looked at me, but Robyn spoke.

'Can A see her wee feet?'

My heart flipped. Junkie reached up into the jumper and unfolded her baby's foot.

'Aw, it's dead cute.'

I watched the frown crease Junkie's eyebrows. She tugged the foot away from Robyn, closer to her eyes to inspect it. Let it go and pulled out the other one.

'She's got six toes!' She looked at me, stung with the relived horror of the first deformity. 'She's got six toes!'

'Calm down,' Limpet said, taking the white topped foot in her brown hand. 'So she has.' She turned to me. 'Have you ever seen that? She's got six toes!'

I didn't answer. I stood, fixed in place and white as the birch.

'Has she got six fingers?' Limpet checked the baby's hands. 'No, they're fine.'

'That's freaky,' Robina said, and I could have thumped her.

A couple of tears dropped from Junkie's eyes, but she was brought up a tough one. Her lips pressed in a line. 'She's a freak!' Junkie said. 'That's me got another wan!'

'Nobody'll notice it,' I said, my voice growing stronger. 'It's nothing to be ashamed of and nothing to worry about. It's just a throw-back. Not a deformity. It's just a natural evolution. And anyway, nobody needs to see it.'

Nobody else spoke.

'A cannae believe that,' Junkie said. 'Jist cannae believe it.'

'Look at her,' Limpet said. She pulled the jumper back. 'She's perfect!' She turned the baby over onto her own arms so Junkie could see the baby's back. 'Not another thing wrong with her.' She rearranged the baby in Junkie's arms and squeezed Junkie's shoulder. 'It isn't important.'

A'm goin fur a sleep,' Junkie said, looking over towards the keep where the men had gone. 'A'm dead tired. Youz lassies keep thinkin aboot a name an see if yez can come up wi a special wan.' She eased herself on to the grass again with the baby in the crook of her arm then lay there, her lips against the baby's forehead.

We were empty, emotionally and physically. I set the girls to gathering dandelions while Limpet and Salami picked the white umbrella flower-heads of ground elder and I set a fire.

When the men came back our camps were divided. They were jubilant and we were despondent. None of us told them the reason. Peej went over to see Junkie and the baby: they were both sleeping but he touched their faces lightly.

Junkie woke when she heard the men talk about the tower with its walls covered in tapestries and deer heads with antlers, and its armoury complete with metal suits and crossbows. Out of the corner of my eye I watched her sit up, check her baby and come to join us.

Brain was describing how thick the castle walls were and how the door was set six feet above the ground.

'A couldnae make it inside,' Wide Boy said, 'because they bastards wouldnae carry me in the fuckin door. An then A thought, "A'm starvin. Whit the fuck time is it anyway?" So A had a swatch at the river. Went ower ti it an A sees aw these wee fishes so A tries slashin at them but they swam away, so A rolls up my sleeves an tickles them. Naw, serious! Ma grandda used ti dae it an he tellt me how. So A gits ma erms in the watter – pure cauld, mind – an wiggles ma fingers an afore too lang A gets this slimy feelin an A grabs it. Bingo! Wide Boy, Trout Tickler Extraordinaire!'

I enjoyed the men's gusty laughter.

'Wide Boy,' The Gaffer said, slapping his back, 'Ye finally found yer vocation.'

'Aye, jist as well,' Peej said. 'Or we'd be usin ye as bait.'

The laughter went on, the fish sizzled in the fire, kebabed in chunks with the vegetables. We ate; the sun stained the clouds trout-flesh coloured; white moths flitted from plant to plant in the grass and a heady floral scent vied with the fish cooking in the flames.

'We'll get ower there efter this,' Peej said, licking the tips of thumb and finger before taking two twig kebabs from the fire and passing them to the girls. 'What have youz been up ti while we were away?'

'We were helpin Junkie look efter the wean,' Robyn said.

'Aye – '

I knew what was coming.

' – guess what?' Robina said.

Everyone looked at her. I struggled with the bones in my mouth.

'What?' Wide Boy said.

'The wean's git six toes!'

Peej froze with the fish kebab upright in his hand.

'Robina!' Limpet said, sadly.

'Well, she has!' She looked around, enjoying her limelight. 'What? Somebdy had ti tell him.'

Robyn frowned. 'Aye, an it had ti be you.'

Salami at my side was bouncing at the table of his mother's legs. He made yum-yum-yum noises as she fed him another mouthful. No-one else spoke.

Peej passed me his kebab and stood up. 'Sh - show me.'

Junkie sniffed. She kept her eyes down. Pulled up the jumper and held the wee foot up for inspection.

It was just the tiniest of feet: it was just the tiniest of toes.

'That's weird,' Peej said.

My own curled in my shoes.

Salaam was sitting next to Junkie and under Peej's hooked shape. He looked at the tiny white and ruby-red foot. 'Och, aye,' he said. 'Jist the same as Yakkity's.'

Chapter Seventy-eight

I woke up lying at a strange angle in daylight and under a vaulted ceiling and for a moment I was confused by the light and space and then I remembered. I turned over and Robyn turned with me; she put her arm over my waist and I put mine over Robina's. The daylight highlighted the bends of auburn through her unruly sandy hair.

Peej and Junkie had been allocated the caretaker's quarters with their new baby. The men had already disposed of his body. The single men were downstairs; Basher and Limpet and their family were in what I took to be the great hall. Much to my dismay we were forced to take some of the medieval tapestries off the walls to keep us warm but today we'll go on a shopping spree to get everything we need then put them back.

The walls at the base of this tower are eight feet thick. It's stood for six hundred years and was built to stand for six hundred more. And my family will be living in it till then. There are fields for our sheep, Basher says we've found an asset in the horses, and we know how to make things grow. I feel much more confident about the future than I think I ever have.

I can see it all before me. Peej is going to marry Junkie; Wide Boy in a few years will marry Robyn; Salaam will be forced to settle for Robina – she's only a couple of years older than him and he doesn't seem to mind the way she blurts things out. Basher, I'm sure, will be persuaded that Brain's a good match for Saleema. Especially after Wide Boy let slip that they'd trysted in the tunnel while he taught our men his Middle Eastern dancing.

The Gaffer and I will develop our new role as community elders. We're replacing Bill and Grace. The repositories of

386

knowledge, experience and convention. I can see myself in that role. I think I've matured into it.

Peej made me show everyone my photos. It was getting late: we were still at the camp. My fingers trembled as I slid the toggle on my bag. I showed them the studio portrait of my mother first. They made Junkie pull her hair off her face and oohed at her. I showed them the photos of my father and brother but they passed them on without comment. I handed them the photo of Margaret Mary outside the house in North Connell, dressed for her first day at school and Junkie held it a long time in her hand before our eyes met.

'She wis an alkie, ma mother. Mind A tellt yez? The night we tellt wur stories.'

I nodded. Another inherited trait.

'She kept sayin A could come an live wi her but then she'd get slapped aboot or start drinkin wi some other man. Give us a fag, Peej.' She held out a quivering hand, the other balancing the baby on her lap.

'You're no supposed ti be smokin.'

'Give us a fuckin fag!'

He took one out and lit it for her, sucking in the first draw. I watched the bright tip crinkle before he passed it over.

'A wis better aff in the hame. But they pit me oot at sixteen. Tried ti set me up in a flat but A knew nothin aboot peyin bills.' She took a little bit of tobacco or paper from her tongue and flicked it at the fire. 'Ended up gittin thrown oot. A wis sleepin on some guy's flair efter a party in Blantyre an when A woke up they were aw deed. A wis out ma heid on junk when Peej an Widey fun me. Mind?'

'Some heroes, eh?' Wide Boy said.

'Some heroes,' I repeated.

'Aye, that's ma ma,' Junkie said, studying the five year old up close. 'Ye can see it across the eyes. An ma ma had that wee mole on her cheek.' She looked up at me across the flames. 'She never had six toes, but.'

'Skipped a generation,' Brain chipped in.

I passed her the one of me on the cream coloured PVC couch,

in my platform boots and my mini-skirt; the lace of the crocheted shawl over my lap and my little baby in it, whose heat and weight I could still feel; the brown teddy tucked in beside her. Junkie looked at it; she must have recognised the teddy as her own and pinched her eyes, the smoke curdling up her hair.

'I called your mother Heather,' I said. 'It was Mrs MacNeill that insisted on Margaret Mary.'

'Heather? That's nice,' Junkie said. 'What aboot Grace Heather?' She looked at the baby and then at Peej. 'Naw, wait. A think A prefer Grace Alice.'

'Aw Grace Alice Jamieson,' Wide Boy announced. 'G-A-J!' He got up, limped over to the baby and tickled her plump cheeks. 'Gajie-Gajie-goo!'

'How d'ye know her surname's no gonnie be MacNeill?' Junkie said.

Peej thought about it. 'Well, whatever she is, she's a wee darlin.'

Beside me, little Saadi was leaning against Limpet's knees, trying to work out how to put on his brother's tartan hat. 'What about you, Limpet?' I said. 'I can't keep calling you after a shellfish forever.'

She smiled. 'Then call me Letifa,' she said, fixing the hat on the baby. 'And I'll call you Alice.'

'In the old days my dad used to call me Pet.' God, I felt loved then, before my world ended the first time. I swallowed, tried to conceal the extent of my emotion. 'What about Basher?'

She grinned at her husband. 'Basher suits him.' She shook her head and pulled up the fine blue veil to cover her hair again. 'It's not much different.'

'And what about you, boys?' I asked across the fire.

'Brian,' Brain said, and we looked expectantly at Wide Boy.

'Naw, A'm fine wi Widey.' He scratched down inside the back of his jacket with the kebab twig.

'Go on,' Robyn said, sitting close to him and linking arms. 'Whit is it?'

'Aw, ye'll pure laugh,' he said. But she smiled up at him till he gave in. 'Och, it's Wattie,' he said and tossed the kebab

twig at a mocking Robina. He nodded over to Letifa and me.
'Walter.'

Chapter Seventy-nine

I could see for miles from the ramparts. I could see the hill with the cave in it, formed by the mine workings. I could see where the land rose into moorland heading for the sea and I could see the town, complete with its stocked up shopping centres, cars and petrol stations, though I hoped we'd not need to rely on those if the farming was good.

Peej came up behind me. I was just aware of his presence, recognised the sound of his feet, standing behind me.

'All's well that ends well then Alice?'

I'd been thinking about Junkie and how I could see myself in her. That self-destruct button. I turned round to look at him. To look in his eyes; at the gingerish fuzz on his skin, taut on his cheeks and chin; the tufts of hair. I curbed my instinct to touch them. Maybe he never realised how much I felt for him. But there was no hiding from it. I was fifty-odds. No. No. Let's get this out there. I was over sixty and he was in his late thirties. I might have been fitter than I've ever felt in my life but he was a man in his prime and I was in desiccating, post-menopausal old-womanhood. I'd have to banish the constant thought-bubble of my physical fantasies and treat him like the grandson-in-law who was giving me great-grandchildren, no matter how weird that thought.

'It's good,' I said, 'but I feel there might be some kind of loose ends.'

He rested his bony fingers on the coarse edge of the sandstone parapet. 'What kind?'

'I don't know,' I said.

Below us, Wide Boy was teaching Salaam the art of trout tickling. Limp – Letifa had found a way to wash and spread out clothes to dry and Brain and The Gaffer were trying to rig something up with a car battery and a cooking stove.

'Somethin ti do wi you an The Gaffer?'

I stared at him. What made him think I wanted anything to do with The Gaffer? I'd detested him since the day he'd tried to impress me by waving his fat foot around over the pit shaft entrance. Or even before then. Hadn't I?

'Guy's had the hots fur you from day one.'

Nonsense. I could feel myself blushing. But, if that was the case, why would he have made the arrangement over Saleema? I stared down at him, then back to Peej. 'What are you talking about?'

'Yous two are made for each other. Anyway,' Peej raised the usual eyebrow, 'who the fuck d'ye think it wis that saved ye?'

In the cave-in, when I dashed to grab my backpack. Not Peej after all.

'Hey, The Gaffer!' Peej shouted, while I was still reeling. 'Up here. Yakkity says she's git some kind a loose end that needs tidyin.'

Below me, The Gaffer looked uncomfortable. He dropped the wires he was holding and rubbed his hands on his hips then looked back up at me. Wide Boy jeered at him good-naturedly and I think his cheeks began to colour.

My hands started shaking when I thought about him coming up the stairs to see me. He knew everything about me; knew the seriously bad as well as the good. Could he really like me? I thought about our conversations – our closeness – in the last days in the pit. The way he'd dealt with Eric and Chis.

Maybe he wasn't so very much like The Boss after all. Maybe I'd been deluding myself about him, the way I deluded myself about so many things, dreaming up stories. He had saved me, after I had used him like some kind of scapegoat for all that went wrong in my life.

I met him at the top of the narrow spiral stairwell. He moved to my left at the same time as I did. We both moved to my right.

'I was going to find your chain of office,' I stuttered, looking down at him.

'Right,' he said, short of breath. 'We can put it in the safe together.'

'Safe?'

'Wide Boy found one last night in the armoury, behind a crossbow on a plaque.'

I put my book in it too. We both did. After we showed them to everyone over dinner. They wanted me to read it, but it was in Latin. I told them the gist of it, turning the glorious illuminated pages.

'It was written in 1519,' I told them. 'You'd think it was a manuscript, but it's an early printed book. An incunabulum.' I waited for them to take that in, but only The Gaffer understood me. 'What makes it remarkable is that it's actually printed. See? And it's so richly decorated.' I held it down so the children could get a good look, then straightened up and swept the hair away from my neck, aware that The Gaffer kept watching me. 'See how delicately painted it is? They used a woodcut to print a border of flowers and leaf scrolls. On a gold ground.'

'Real gold?' Salaam asked.

I smiled. 'Riches, eh?'

'What's the story about?' The Gaffer asked. My heart fluttered when he focused on me. I licked my lips and concentrated on the pictures.

'It's a chronicle,' I said. 'A kind of journal about a group of people over a period of time who suffer terrible trials and tribulations. They endured a huge storm – a tempest. See the waves swamping the decks of the boat? And the shipwreck? But they overcome that. They overcome all the ordeals.' I looked up at their faces, Junkie with the baby at her breast. 'They overcome all the obstacles and go on all the stronger.'

Basher nodded. 'Good,' he said. 'Good. We understand that.' He looked at Letifa and their children. Then there was a pause. 'What did you say the book was called? Anincu-.'

'Incunabulum,' A repeated. 'Incunabulum.' He was so keen to master his English. 'It's Latin. It means swaddling bands, from the Latin *cuna* for cradle. It means these books are from the cradle of printing: the birth of technology. It's about a society in its infancy, ready to grow.'

'Bit why's it in Latin?' Robina asked. 'Was it written by Latalians?'

When the laughter and her blushes faded I told her about Latin being the lingua franca, before it was supplanted by English.

'Bit we're Dykenders,' Salaam said, his face brown below the ginger wig of his tartan tammy. 'We speak Dykender.'

'That's right,' A said, an put the book down.

Acknowledgements

Incunabulum had a long gestation, and my thanks go to everyone who helped it on its way from conception to the cradle. Where to start? Keith McKay, of course, always and forever. Liane McKay, whose close reading and intuition demonstrate her novelist's skills, her unassuming talent and potential. My other beta-readers – Sheila O'Donnell, Jacqueline Smith, Leela Soma – all encouraged me with their insights and positivity.

The opening sequence of *Incunabulum* reached the final fifty in the Daily Telegraph's Novel in a Year Competition, away back in 2007. Around the same time, I attended a 'Work-in-progress' retreat at Moniack Mhor writers' centre near Inverness. Here, author Jane Rogers read the final 10,000 words and gave me invaluable, supportive feedback on it (and the quote on the cover). To all – thank you!

My family. I've already mentioned Keith and Liane. Thanks, too, to Ruth, Alison, Mairi, Susan, Simon, and all their partners and children. You bring the joy to my life. Thanks, too, to my sister Isabel and brother Allan.

Finally, there are all those who've formally and informally mentored and sustained me through the ups and downs of being a working class, female, older writer. Thank you!